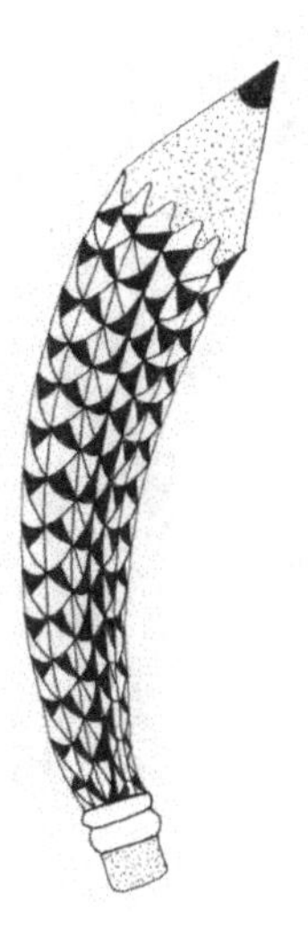

Mythorealism
Speculative Fiction
Surreal Spiritual Fiction
Metaphysical Adventure

OneMansDance.com

He saw all these forms and faces in a thousand

relationships . . . become newly born.

Each was mortal, a passionate, painful example

of all that is transitory.

Yet none of them died, they only changed,

were always reborn,

continually had a new face:

only time stood between one face and another.

HERMANN HESSE

All paths are paths to God because, ultimately,

there is no other place for the soul to go.

PARAMAHANSA YOGANANDA

PUBLISHER

OneMansDance.com

Beacon, New York

Editor: Melissa Moore
Book Design: Sally Stetson [SallyStetson.com]
Cover Photo: Steven Ainsworth [steven-ainsworth.pixels.com]
Cover Illustration (3-eye glasses) Bob Conge [BobConge.com]
Logo Design: Sally Stetson [SallyStetson.com], Bob Conge [BobConge.com]
Author Photo: Jamey Stillings [JameyStillings.com]
Audio Book: Chris Demars [DemarsMedia.com]
Page Layout: Abrah Griggs [in-my-nature.com]

Manufactured in the United States of America

10 9 8 7 6 5 4 3 2 1

The Library of Congress has catalogued the first trade paper edition as follows:
Roberts, Stephen X
Mirror man, a novel / Stephen X Roberts
Summary: A metaphysical adventure in the spirit of the universe--playful, loving, deep.

ISBN 979-8-9858670-0-8 (hardcover)
ISBN 979-8-9858670-1-5 (paperback)
ISBN 979-8-9858670-2-2 (ebook)
ISBN 979-8-9858670-3-9 (audio book)

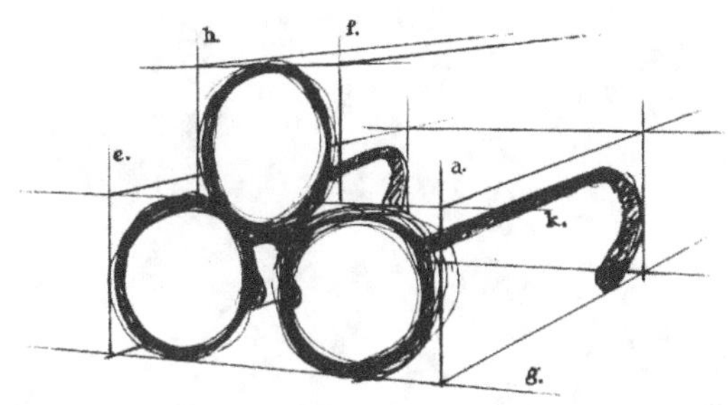

Mirror Man

A metaphysical adventure
in the spirit of the universe:
playful • loving • deep

by Stephen X Roberts

Dedicated to the spirit of
Paramahansa Yogananda (1893-1952)

And to Dear and Lissa,
beloved voices of the muse

In this lifetime, the universe has made sure that,
needing all the help I can get,
I've been a hermit, the disciple of an avatar,
and a person with many largehearted acquaintances.

Someday, just for fun,
I will enumerate everyone I can think of who has illuminated my life,
if only by rolling their eyes when they see me coming.
Each has contributed to the celebration that is Mirror Man.

In this space,
one lovely soul must stand in for them all:
my friend David Stember.

TABLE OF CONTENTS

The plot can't thicken without troublemakers.

—RAMAKRISHNA

Main Characters and Previous Lives

Hyman O'Malley
|
Jamula
Abraham

Pearl
|
Bella-Viola
Sylvie Marks *(possibly)*
Kashi
Brother Moon *(possibly)*

Charlie Fox
|
Angelo Angelino
Claira Lewandowsky

Carmella Puella
|
Bishnu

Puer Puella
|
Domenico Priami
Badger McTaggart *(possibly)*

Benny Apple
|
Tambo

There's a reason they call it fiction

Certain readers will not be surprised to learn that the
fictional Swami in Mirror Man is based on Paramahansa Yogananda
(1893-1952), whose spirit animates my life. That said, any reader
who takes literally anything the Swami says or does as an expression
of Yogananda is confusing my imagination (unencumbered by facts)
with the reality of Yogananda's presence in the world.
For an authoritative understanding of that, please turn to the
organization he founded: Self-Realization Fellowship.

1

On Your Knees, Blindfolded

The Iroquois and the Chamber of Commerce said that God created New York's Finger Lakes by placing one of His hands on the Earth, the resulting imprint giving birth to eleven lakes side-by-side, their size anywhere from six to forty miles in length, one of them shaped like the letter Y. Funny, Hyman mused, how you can spend your life getting to know somebody and never notice they've got a quirk in their anatomy.

When it came to knowing God, Hyman was nobody special. Like everyone else, he had spent innumerable lives brutalizing all sorts of people, himself especially, in the name of just about anything you can imagine—goodness, virtue, honor, and the hairstyles of others being among the more commonplace, big as they are on the list of things about which we humans have yet to develop much of a sense of humor.

But then, as we all do sooner or later they say, somewhere around the millionth time he'd swatted the fleas in his hair with an ice pick, or struck a "strike anywhere" match on the tonsils of a crocodile, or saved the world by killing everyone who didn't look like him hoping that, golly, maybe this time the outcome would be different—Hyman cried uncle.

In response, as always happens, every particle of creation put on a party hat and cheered.

Soon Hyman's existence, life after life, became an active practice of freeing whatever pain and fear arose within him, and of forgiving himself for any harmful choice he had made in any incarnation, past or present.

And the more fear and pain washed through him and each unloving choice was embraced and forgiven, the space created in its wake trembled increasingly with compassion. Such is the mathematical precision of the universe––the journey of souls over countless lifetimes to their inevitable and conscious union with the One: the Infinite Spirit beyond creation; the cosmic sphere of light, joy and love in which worlds and universes are floating like bubbles; the beginning, middle and end of every story . . . which is to say Samadhi, Nirvana, the Whole Enchilada.

To be sure, Hyman was still learning to behold all permutations as mere wavelets appearing and disappearing on the changeless *Ocean of Infinity*. He was no avatar, no Christ or Buddha. But his consciousness had evolved to where there were times Hyman couldn't look at a blade of grass or a tuna melt without hearing the Divine whispering in his ear: *Hello playmate, I am here.*

Then there was that other thing. In his presence, every once in a while and out of the blue, someone would experience a view of themselves that was much larger than what their ordinary, everyday perceptions told them. Hyman was no more responsible for these awakenings than a telephone, or a drum, or a paintbrush is responsible for the wisdom it transmits. He was simply the delivery boy. Who was given this blessing, or why, he didn't know . . . at least not ahead of time. Some recipients seemed ready for it. Others seemed simply to need it, ready or not.

It was as though a few select souls were being given a glimpse of the future, say a few thousand years down the evolutionary highway, when humankind would be more open to the notion that each moment is a mirror, showing us ourselves. And as a mirror, the gift of any moment is its revelation of what is calling to be embraced so that we may become more of who we truly are: beings with an infinite capacity to love.

On the day our story begins, the seldom-traveled country lane Hyman was hiking, part of an afternoon wander, ran near the top of a hillside that overlooked several miles of water given a place to rest by that most anomalous of the divine fingers. Vineyards banked most of the road, and hallelujah!, this was the season when every cluster was pregnant to near bursting with the year's crop, making your nose give thanks it was naked. Hyman had never been this way before. He had found it, like he found most things, not exactly by accident, but serendipitously, following the guidance of his inner compass.

Without breaking stride, he took his bandana from a back pocket and wiped his face, then tied the blue print cloth loosely around his neck. Weather permitting, T-shirt, chinos and hiking boots was Hyman's everyday wardrobe. This afternoon's shirt was white, the word *Yess!* silk-screened small in dark blue letters centered heart-high. His other T-shirts, in a variety of pastels, said other things in the same indigo type. Hyman had a slew of T-shirts, each one different. Every day, often more than once, he would shut his eyes, reach into his suitcase, feel around, and discover the message of the moment.

Some people threw the *I Ching*. Hyman picked T-shirts.

The home Hyman was drawing near on the right, sitting halfway up a long hill, had been built originally sometime during the 20 years prior to the Civil War, Hyman recalled. Hyman had been a slave in that life, a man. He'd never learned a whole lot about that incarnation except that he and his master's son, a female impersonator (which is a whole other story we'll get to a little later), were lovers and lived in New York City, where one of their neighbors was an architect. Maybe this was how Hyman acquired the cellular memory that told him that this particular house and the stables behind it had been authentically restored. It was a good story anyway.

A Kentucky Derby winner in full gallop would still take at least half a minute to cover the immense lawn that flowed down from house to road. A number of tall, mature oaks stood randomly among a few smaller offspring, creating a park-like feeling. Not far from the road, the land had been leveled off to fashion a family baseball diamond, and on the mound that afternoon a young woman, six-one or two, college age, dressed in black riding pants, a purple T-shirt and baseball spikes with short-cropped yellow socks, was pitching a neon-orange softball like a rocket to a man squatting behind the plate in a white paint-spattered jumpsuit.

Hyman didn't need any internal guidance telling him that the man was the girl's father, since the man considered the girl in a way that occurs when you believe that the only thing keeping your kid from walking on water is that it hadn't yet dawned on her to try.

Each pitch seemed faster, or somehow more powerful, than the one before. No sooner did the dad toss back the ball then the girl would whirl through her windmill windup, limbs ablur and seemingly out of control until the ball left her hand and, miraculously, smacked into the center of the catcher's mitt where the father had positioned it. And the instant that Whap! cracked, the girl's own gloved hand was up and open waiting for the ball to be returned to her, as though her very life depended on breaking the Guinness record for the number of strikes thrown in a certain period, or on mashing her father's alcoholic nose all over his baby-face jowls should he lose his concentration for a split-second.

So this is why I've walked this way, Hyman thought.

Hyman noticed a woman sitting not far from the road, her back against the trunk of a tree about as big around as a couple of sumo wrestlers. She, too, wore riding breeches, her's the color of a chocolate truffle, and a blue cotton work shirt, sleeves rolled to the elbow. Her feet were bare, her toenails painted American flag red. Next to her on the lawn was a cell phone, a small stack of plastic cups in primary colors, and an antique gallon jar sweating chilly with iced tea laced with wafers of lime and sprigs of mint. It was the girl's mother, both having the same lanky frame and ebony hair: the mom's cut hedgehog short with random straws of gray; the daughter's a long single braid dancing the length of her spine.

The mom gave a neighborly wave to the passing stranger.

Hyman returned the wave, adding a nod toward the mound, "Nice to see someone with a lot of passion," he said, stopping at the road's edge.

"She'd appreciate you saying so," the mom said. "Almost won the College World Series this year."

Hyman and the girl's mother stood and sat, respectively, watching the daughter and dad. Hyman felt the woman's response to his presence.

It surprised her. Having this stranger standing silent behind her—rather than be annoying—was oddly pleasant. The mom had this goofy fantasy of the stranger walking over to her and saying, "I'm sorry to disturb you, but I'm your twin brother, Bob, and we were separated at birth." She almost laughed out loud at the thought.

"Say," she asked, "care for some iced tea?"

"Why . . . how kind, sure. Thanks for asking."

"Well, come take a load off. I'm Shorty Fox."

"Hyman O'Malley."

"O'Malley. O'Malley. Are you by any wild chance related to Jackie O'Malley of California, the famous horse whisperer of my childhood?"

"Matter of fact, he's my pop."

"Good lord! I was just being silly. As a girl I read all his books. Again and again. Pardon me for not knowing, is your dad still alive?"

Within the hour, Hyman—kneeling on second base, wearing his blue bandanna as a blindfold—threw ten strikes in a row to Shorty's daughter, Pearl.

After strike ten, a curve that sailed around the moon before swooping to nip the inside corner of plate, Pearl jogged out to Hyman, pulled up his blindfold, handed him the ball and said, "Teach."

Hyman winked, "First, grasshopper, we must watch the sun rise over the lake."

Sunrise to Pearl, when school was out Hyman knew, was as familiar as licorice pizza. So he laughed when she, all business, took her ball back and said, "How about tomorrow, masked man?"

*T*here is a period at the end of night but before dawn when the earth holds her breath. Frogs stuff socks in their mouths. Owls zip it. Coyotes eat their chicken dinners in the dreamtime. Sparrows know that chattering now would be like gossiping in church. From the sacred peace of these few silent moments a new day is born in the east, the direction of awakening.

Should it have come to pass that, during this brief interlude, seven-foot green beings with pink stars for bellybuttons suddenly appeared and promised to free Earth of all pollution if only Pearl and the nice avuncular gent with her would teach the boys and girls of planet Chlorophyll how to cha-cha, the event would have been no more surprising to Pearl than what she actually was about to experience. But neither she nor Hyman, sitting together by the lake, had a glimmer of what was to unfold. Pearl because she couldn't see the future. And Hyman because he preferred not to look.

If he asked, his guides would show Hyman just about any future he wished to see. And someday, whether he asked or not, he was sure, second sight would simply be dumped in his lap, like it or not. That was fine. Hyman could read minds easily enough if he wished, which he almost never did. It was like listening in on random phone calls; the thrill wanes quickly. It was true that all sorts of extraneous information floated his way unbidden, some of it even about the future; still, he didn't pay much attention to it unless it became the equivalent of a tiger in a top hat offering free haircuts.

Hyman was uneasy when it came to clairvoyance—his own, anyway. In more than one former life he had been especially prescient and misused the gift, leaving a lot of blood on the highway, literal and metaphoric. While he had cleared much of the unforgiveness he carried from those choices, every once in a while an opportunity to serve by seeing the future would pop up, and his first reaction would be to shy away, afraid he might harm again. He was grateful whenever it was brought to the surface, however. Feeling it, freeing it, forgiving himself was always good. No question he was getting more sanguine about the prospect of foresight. He just didn't go out of his way looking for it.

Which was one reason he had no idea that, before the cock crowed the following day, his kidnapping would be ordered by the President of the United States, and executed.

2

Pearl's Mask

earl and Hyman were sitting next to one another on surprisingly comfortable seats that had been carved out of the stumps of two ancient elms. For more than a century, the trees had stood like twins facing east, soaking up the new day sun as well as the lake itself twenty yards ahead. They were now part of a tiny state park.

"Each time you take a breath," Hyman said, the soft rolling skyline two miles across the lake just barely evident, backlit by the first breath of dawn, "feel yourself being filled and nourished, from toe to head, by the earth—Big Mother I like to call her. Her love, her light, her fire and her acceptance know no bounds. Take her into you with each breath. And every time you exhale, let go of every bit of you. Die completely. Surrender your entire being to her.

Besides that, breathe through your feet and your bottom, those places in direct contact with her."

That was it. Not another word for two hours.

Hyman knew that Pearl was at a point of her unfolding where few words were necessary. She'd been meditating for many lives. She intuitively understood his meaning, the same intuitive understanding that led her, without hesitation, to accept his invitation the previous afternoon.

The predominant sounds besides the slow, gentle slapping of the water were the birds: sparrows, phoebes, mourning doves, an owl or two asking, "Who cooks for you?" and the occasional crow admonishing everyone to—above all—don't noodle. The odd outboard motor, always far in the distance, announced someone heading out to fish. And a time or two a duck quack-quack reminded all, even the crows, that there are few things worse than taking yourself seriously.

Pearl hadn't actually *watched* the sun come up. Her eyes had been closed. But she had experienced it like no other sunrise she could remember.

As the sun's nurturing bled into the earth, she had drawn that power, that warmth, that golden light, into her with each inhale. And as the sun rose higher, finally breaking the horizon then ascending into the morning sky, she drew ever more of its fire into her. The higher the sun rose, the higher in her body she felt its center, starting at her feet and working its way up to the top of her head. Two hours later she existed within a channel of light extending from earth to sky.

All from paying attention to my breath, she thought.

It amazed her how big her legs felt. Her hips, her feet, her stomach, her heart, her hands, her face—and her spine . . . .

Big, but light and loose, too.

I could sit like this forever.

But then Hyman's whisper broke the spell, his finger touching her hand. "What's say we toss a few?"

Under any other circumstance it would have been like being awakened from a deep sleep by some moron dropping a cat on you. Her eyes still closed, Pearl took a few more breaths before she said, "I gotta warm up first."

"I'm sorry. I don't mean for you to throw hard," Hyman said. "It's more an attitude, a state of mind, I'd like you to revisit."

Pearl stood and stretched. Then she loped up the lawn to Hyman's truck. She retrieved their gloves and ball from the front seat. Meanwhile,

Hyman took off the navy windbreaker he'd been wearing, revealing a pale pink T-shirt that said in small blue letters across the chest: *Everyone has the best seat in the house.* Pearl returned and handed him his glove, the ball in the pocket. Then she shoved her own glove between her knees, pulled off her sweatshirt, untucked her black T-shirt from her jeans, put on her glove, then flapped it at Hyman to toss the ball.

"I get into my attitude, as you call it, by warming up."

They played catch like two people underwater at first, lobbing the ball the five feet of distance between them. Every ten tosses or so, they'd each take a step backwards. The underwater effect would lessen as they threw just hard enough to cover the additional distance. When they reached roughly regulation pitching distance, Pearl began throwing marshmallows from a windup. By the time the marshmallows became golf balls, Pearl said, "Ready?"

Hyman squatted. "Just think of me as Roy Campanella," he said.

"You're not so esoteric as you think, mister; I actually know who that is."

"Ess-oh-terrick. Hey-hey. How many catchers get told they're not that?"

Pearl stuck out her tongue.

The time was 7:03. Before 7:04, Pearl's life changed forever.

When she leaned forward, as though to get the sign, all the serenity of the morning evaporated like spit on a skillet.

Pitching might be fun for some people, but for her it was life or death. You won or you died. Her hero was Bob Gibson, the great St. Louis Cardinal right-hander. He hated the hitters on his own team. It wasn't personal. He hated all hitters. Pearl refused to pitch batting practice at Stanford unless she could throw for real. Why the hell would she ever allow anyone, on purpose, to hit a ball she threw? Other than a kid. Hitters were the enemy. A hitter's sole purpose in life was to destroy you. And anyway, in the end, everything was up to you. You had the ball. Any hit, every hit, was your responsibility.

You were the samurai. It was an honor to have been chosen and trained for this duty, this moment. Protecting your village began with you.

Sometimes it would be the knife she threw, jamming you so tight that even if you swung and made contact, the resulting sting would make you prefer having a car door slammed on your fingers. An occasional riser up under the chin could whiplash you into the dirt. The samurai's objective, always, was to take something out of a batter with each pitch—a little confidence, a moment's focus, a small measure of skill—not unlike what the picador does to the bull before the matador enters for the dance and the kill. But don't get her started on matadors, those little pansies in their silk clam-diggers. They fight only wounded bulls. A samurai fights the greatest warriors on their best day. A samurai is willing to lay her life on the line to win this one game, this one inning, this one at-bat, this one pitch. She not only accepts, but expects, that her life will be like the cherry blossom's: beautiful, but brief.

As she began her windup two things happened simultaneously: a young Ali landed a solid left hook to Pearl's solar plexus as two white-hot coals, one on each temple, burned their way instantly to the center of her brain where they met and formed a single blue flame. It wasn't painful exactly, perhaps like the moment a soldier discovers his hand has been blown off. She saw nothing, heard nothing, wasn't really sure she was breathing. Yet she was conscious. Had she snapped a nerve? Had she been hit by lightning? She didn't think so because somehow she knew that whatever this was it had to do with Hyman, and that whoever he was, she knew in that place beyond deduction, this was the reason she had come with him this morning, and regardless of what was happening, she was safe. Even, strangely enough, if she were about to die.

And then, the samurai, her mind's invention, her ego's addiction ever since grammar school—sprang to life, literally.

It would have been completely unbelievable if Pearl weren't actually experiencing it. Pearl actually *was* the samurai, his body a good twice the size of her own, a body with stinks and aches and even a splinter of clove stuck between two lower front teeth and unresponsive to the probing of his tongue, her tongue. One thing not different, however, was his essence. After all, she had created it.

This man, whose gaze alone could burn a hole through armor. This man, with muscles of a mastodon, who, one-handed, could throw five knives at a time over his shoulder and kill all five warriors in pursuit. This man whose two horses were trained to gallop side-by-side so that he could ride standing with one foot on the back of each, holding the reins in his teeth, a sword in each hand, harvesting enemy heads left and right. This man whose bark could turn a rain of arrows into a shower of gold dust. This man who, blindfolded, could walk a tightrope secured between two ships tossing in a typhoon. This man whose hand threw molten balls of iron, straight out of the furnace, so fast and far that they passed right through anyone within a mile who stood in their path . . . .

And as real as all this was—and this was no dream, or no longer a dream—Pearl also knew that it wasn't all of her. That it was, in truth, a mask of some kind.

Pearl as samurai protected her from something.

And that something, under the mask, was a very special fear. One with many names. A fear that she wasn't worthy. A fear that she might never atone for some harm she had done. And the fear that others might discover this fundamental flaw in her being. Then there was the fear of being banished, of being vulnerable, of being completely without any familiar. And who knew? Maybe under that there were even more fears.

As this realization came to her in a crush of light, Pearl felt herself as samurai being transformed into yet again another person in another time.

Pearl's first sensation of this new being was the smell of horse and sea breeze. The first image she saw was the blur of white clouds seen through a window swept with rain. Only there was no window, and she was looking straight up at the sky because she was lying on her back, on the earth. There was something wrong with her eyes.

Cataracts.

Whoever she was, Pearl realized, her body was melting with age and starvation—and from the withering that occurs, within and without, when one's skin has not felt the touch of love, from another to be sure, but mainly from oneself, for many, many decades.

She was lying on a piece of earth that, tomorrow, would be upturned to make way for her own sarcophagus in which she would lie, embalmed like an Egyptian, her only adornment a bullwhip wrapped around one shoulder. On her right was the grave of her true love, who had died at her hand. On her left were the graves of her two lifelong servants. Only the four of them would ever inhabit this burial ground, overlooking the Mediterranean, on the island that was hers alone.

The rest of the woman's family was long dead, including four brothers and a father: all but one of them destroyed by her, deliberately, their bones scattered nowhere near her. Soon she too would be gone. "By sunset, please," she whispered. Hers, she knew, would be that special kind of death, the kind when one passes into whatever next world there was, completely unworthy of forgiveness.

For seventy years she had been living with the pain that being the wealthiest and most powerful woman in the Province could not procure a single thing to soothe her heart.

3

Hyman's Journal:
The Abduction

♥ When I was four, my mother and father took me with them to this gigantic event in New York City's Central Park: a Tibetan celebration from sunrise to sunset on the day of maximum light—summer solstice—a day beautiful in every way imaginable until I was abducted.

Since home was a ranch east of Los Angeles, our nearest neighbor the better part of a mile away, the gathering was the first time that I experienced so many people so close. It was unbelievably thrilling. But most thrilling of all was seeing so many familiar faces. Well, not faces exactly; familiar beings more like. One woman, who easily might have been mistaken for a child playing dress-up, was seated on a nearby blanket with some friends, all of whom were probably college students. Her face's youth was belied by a demeanor that, I've learned since, held the kind of fearless patience that comes to some people who are intimate with terminal illness. Unlike her friends, this woman knew she wasn't indestructible. (Lady Death is the name I've given her.) Whatever illness it was, an ebony cane lay at her side and, looking through her skin (one of the talents I had as a youngster that went the way of milk teeth), I could see her heart pumping much faster than my own. I recalled that she had loved strawberries. So I took a strawberry from the picnic the hotel had packed for us, walked over and offered it to her. I was surprised she didn't remember me. We had known each other as children, boys, in a former life where we had eaten a pile of strawberries together by a stream and then jumped naked into the water. It had been one of those unforgettable moments in that life. I don't know where this was, but our skin was rather dark. In Central Park that day, I was still learning that not everyone has glimpses of their previous incarnations. Not everyone senses how connected we all are.

It's not that I remembered everything about a person (nor do I today). Usually, it was just a flash of a moment we had shared, like the strawberries.

Lady Death said to me, "Ooooh, aren't you sweet? Thank you." To her friends, she said, "My favorite fruit in all the world." (Cravings carry over from one life to the next, the Swami once told me. If we die with the jones for curry, we may find ourselves reborn in India.)

Throughout the day, Lady Death looked at me from time to time, and I could tell she felt something, but didn't know what it was. There were no flashes at all for her. As I say, I came to understand that that's how most people respond to the world around them. They occasionally have some vague sense of connection, but for all sorts of reasons don't honor it, don't open to it, don't feel that it means enough to pursue.

The heat of the day had begun to wane and I was standing on the grass a few feet from my parents. They were lying on the gold blanket they'd borrowed from the hotel, eyes closed, listening to the Tibetan Tantric Choir perform live their "throat singing" amplified through huge speakers so that a hundred thousand people could hear them. My mother's head rested on my dad's slim belly, her auburn curls offset by his blue checked shirt with the pearl buttons. I have no photos to prove it, but it's a safe bet I was wearing jeans, T-shirt and cowboy boots. I was trying to get the hang of that rubber ball tied to a paddle with a rubber string thing when suddenly I'm lifted up from behind and carried away by a woman, not so tall but very strong, who smelled worse than a dead deer with its back end ripped open by coyotes, to that point in my life the most revolting odor I'd encountered.

I had never really been afraid before, surprising as that sounds. It wasn't the fear of some external danger exactly, as much as it was the fear of being separated from my parents, an event without precedent. If I'm not mistaken I'd never had a babysitter.

Yet, I was too shocked to cry out, and in the woman's grip I was essentially paralyzed. She held me so tightly that, to this day, I have a star-shaped scar at the base of my skull. My head must have pressed against a metal button or pin she was wearing. It looks like I've been branded on my medulla, which, curiously, is the principle point where life force enters the body.

The woman, her putrid breath slow and steady as a respirator, walked fast with me for what seemed a long while, then, without stopping, put me down—and before I thought to turn and look, disappeared into the crowd. She never said a word. I never actually saw her. All I remember of her is her smell, which I would recognize even today, more than 70 years later. I did eventually learn who she was, but that's not relevant here.

I was alone for the first time. Not alone the way most people think of it. Rather, it was the kind of alone I've since experienced in the hearts of some children who never meet their biological mother. Or whose father is jealous of them from birth. Or whose parents have no familiarity with the geography of emotions. It is an emptiness that is, to this day, impossible to put into words.

I have no memory of crying, but I'm sure I must have. No one came to my aid, in any event. In fact, all I do remember about those first moments alone pales in significance to my one feeling. Terror. There was not a person I recognized. There was no one whose skin I could see under. I felt no connection of inner hearts. It was as though I had been taken to another world. And although the people looked like me in a general sense, in reality they were all strangers. I didn't know it at the time, but I was seeing the world as most people do.

I've walked the 800-plus acres of Central Park a few times as an adult, and my best guess is that I must have been at least a half-mile from my parents, which, of course, for a four-year-old, is Mars.

I sat under a tree. Waiting to be found, I suppose.

After a while, I got up and started to walk. I had no plan, no destination. I was four. I just walked. And as I walked, I started to hear who I call my guides talking to me.

Guides have been part of my life since birth, but at first they didn't say anything. They were just there, loving me. Everyone has them, I've come to learn. I just happened to feel mine. The very first actual message (that I remember) came one morning when I was still in a high chair. The message was that this life was a dream, and that when it was over I would awaken where guides would be all I saw. At the time, the message had no special impact on me; it was just a message. After that, until that day in Central Park, I received messages only when I would ask a question. (I once asked why the spirit of my best friend, Freddy Kleehammer, woke me up one night, and I was told that he was leaving his body. Freddy's spirit had been crying. Next morning my mother told me that Freddy and his mom had been killed when a train hit their car at a railroad crossing. This was about six months before my Central Park experience. Years later, my guides showed me that Freddy's mom had planned their meeting with the train.) The point here is, if I didn't ask a question, and I seldom did, my guides didn't "speak." They were just there.

However, walking in Central Park that day, with what seemed to be the entire population of the world around me, my guides started actively directing me.

The first message was to follow the limping woman in the black dress who was walking next to the lake. I ended up following her to a large round pond. In the middle of the pond was a tall fountain with an angel on top. I gawked at the angel so long that when I finally looked around, Black Dress Woman was gone. But then I was told to follow a shirtless man covered in tattoos and carrying an infant in a sling across his chest. When Tattoo Man stopped for an ice cream, I was told to stand next to the ice cream man. All in white—pants, shirt and baseball cap—Ice Cream Man, a crowd around him, seemed to make his treats appear from out of nowhere, like a magician, presenting them to his customers as if he were offering them gold. He spoke in a Spanish accent that was probably Puerto Rican, though I didn't know it at the time. All I knew was that he wasn't Mexican, the only Spanish I was familiar with. His "store" was a white pickup truck with white tires. In the truck's bed was a large white freezer with four small doors on the back side. Painted on the side of the freezer was the picture of a lion swinging on a swing while licking an ice cream cone. I stood next to Ice Cream Man for quite a while until he noticed me.

"Ah, Marco Polo," he said, whereupon he opened one of his freezer doors and brought out an orange Popsicle, my favorite, presenting it to me with considerable flourish. He never asked for money.

"Ahora, busca tu mama," he said, patting my head.

To many, this story sounds fantastic, which is why, unless I'm guided to, I don't share much of my inner life. It asks too much of most people. I get into enough trouble as it is.

It wasn't like there was a running commentary in my head—there were no words. It was more like I was being physically guided. As I walked by a man on a bench, he called, "Hey, sonny," and all of a sudden I started to run as if I were being pushed from behind by a giant hand.

One of the Tibetan lamas was sitting on a platform under a big red and gold canopy talking to lots and lots of people who were seated on the grass in front of him. With his maroon robes and shaved head, he was different from anyone I had ever seen, yet somehow he was familiar. He had the kindest, gentlest smile, crooked teeth and very big ears. I was told to go up and sit on his lap. The audience may have been surprised, but he didn't seem to be. In fact, it was funny. He put our foreheads together, and I heard him speak, not from his mouth, but right from his head into mine. "Hello, brother. It's good to see you again." He gave me a piece of crystallized ginger candy. Then he stood me up and patted me on the fanny, and I ran out of the tent hearing his laugh and the laughter of the audience behind me.

A hand caught my arm. A blonde teenage girl in a blue dress with yellow stars asked if I knew where my parents were. I was told to point in a certain direction. She said, "Hop in," nodding to a kid's red wagon she was pulling. As we went along, she kept turning to me. "Now where?" and I kept pointing where I was told to.

I wish I could say that my parents were still napping when I returned, and that I realized that virtually no time had passed from when Dead Deer Woman took me to when Wagon Girl brought me back. That sort of stuff would happen later in life. The truth itself, however, was pretty amazing. My father, the famous horse whisperer, taught both children of New York City's Police Commissioner. His kids came to our ranch for a couple of weeks in the summer. My dad had all the Commissioner's personal phone numbers. Every cop in the city had a description of me and Dead Deer Woman. Roadblocks had been set up. K-9 teams had sniffed the jacket I'd worn that morning and were in pursuit. The miracle was that I had made it back to my mother's arms before anybody spotted me. She was alone, sitting on the gold blanket, my dad out searching.

Mother screamed my name.

I threw myself at her and held on with every ounce of strength I had. We rolled around on the blanket, she patting me all over, kissing me, laughing, crying. At that point in my life, my mother was still breast feeding me on occasion, and now that I had her arms around me, her comfort was what I craved more than anything in the world.

"Where did you find him?" Mom asked Wagon Girl, holding me in her lap, combing my hair with her fingers, occasional tears dropping onto my face as I nursed.

"Way up on the other end of the park," Wagon Girl said. "I asked him if he knew where his parents were, and I just followed wherever he pointed. It's obvious he comes here a lot. He knew exactly how to find you."

When I was older my mother told me, "At that moment I realized that I was simply your caretaker. Your real mom was Divine Mother, the mother of us all."

Even at four, I knew that that day was the start of my life in the world: listening and following.

4

Pearl 500 Years Earlier

he being who was Pearl had been, some 500 years earlier, a young woman with the face and bottomless black eyes of a Madonna. She had been christened Bella-Viola in honor of her Mama and her Nana—her mother and her father's mother.

As auspicious as her name was at the time of her birth, it became even more so when Bella-Viola was seven years old. It was then that the lives of her mother and grandmother ended together, arm-in-arm, when the *Dolce Vita*, the family sloop on which they were sailing, sank in ten quick minutes after a bomb exploded amidships, the work of enemies attempting to kill Bella-Viola's father, who, because it wasn't his time to die, was not on board.

Indeed, by a twist of fate that caused people to bless themselves whenever they heard the story, at the very moment the *Dolce Vita* erupted in horror, setting into motion events that would cause others to call her mother and grandmother saints because they had sacrificed themselves so that two family servants (husband and wife, Poq and Arlandarose Mulando) might escape in the ship's only usable life boat, her father was himself assassinating a man.

Given her father's business, this was not unusual.

What was unusual was a single fact about the man whose cause of death was having been boiled slowly like a cannibal's Christmas dinner. Her father and the man he cooked had been doing business together for many years—first cooperatively and then, unknown to her father until recently, competitively, hence the need for what her father termed "an adjustment." The single fact that her father did not know about his former associate was that, over fresh orange juice, sweet buns and espresso that very morning, the man had ordered the sinking of the *Dolce Vita*.

Her father's contemplations on the metaphysical were weighted by a perspective that has been commonplace since who knows when, and is certainly as ordinary as dirt in the 21st century—one that placed him at the center of all things. Amply is this phenomenon demonstrated by the frequency with which we humans become anything from mildly irritated to apoplectically outraged when life does not transpire as we have decided it should.

Bella-Viola's father believed, for example, that "Coincidence is nonsense." The universe, he was sure, operated in a very orderly way, "an impeccable quid pro quo," he would say. But it never would have occurred to him that, just possibly, as a result of that perfect order, his intention to murder another might have drawn to himself instant rebuttal. Instead, her father's assessment of events was that God, foreseeing the evil intent that led to the martyrdom of Bella-Viola's Mama and Nana, had used him, Domenico Priami, as an instrument of divine justice. Any qualms Papa Priami might have had about boiling his adversary, were he a man who had qualms in the first place, were instantly dispelled when he convinced himself of the solemn responsibility God had bestowed upon him to smite the murderer of the two Priami mothers at the exact same time their murder was taking place. As Domenico Priami said later to his daughter, "The divine symmetry is beautiful, my child, and I am merely a humble servant of the Lord."

And so, with the spirits of two sainted women overseeing the unfolding of her being under the devoted earthly eye of her father, she, Bella-Viola Maria

Priami, the first female offspring after four males, would be the treasure the Priami family would offer discretely and, of course, expensively to another powerful family, when the planets were rightly aligned, so that, bonded by marriage, both families would increase their wealth, power, and sphere of influence, but particularly the family of Domenico Priami, for her father was nothing if not the most calculating man who ever lived.

*P*apa Priami was different from most men of his time. He encouraged his daughter to develop skills far beyond those of traditional womanhood. In fact, he saw to it that she received a better education than any of her brothers, for he knew that she was the most gifted child of them all. He hired the best tutors so that she might learn numbers and writing and contracts. He brought her to the vineyards in every season, beginning as an infant, so that she would understand as much as he himself did about the science and art of wine making, for Priami wine was renown far beyond the Province. And what would have been most astonishing of all to anyone outside the family, had it ever been revealed, which of course, if it had, would have been punished by a death so cruel it was considered fit only for the rapist of the Blessed Virgin, was that Domenico Priami taught his daughter the fundamentals of the family business.

But anyone who thought that Domenico Priami was a progressive thinking man was either ignorant or in denial. Sadly, such a person might soon find himself among the compromised, the destitute, the indebted, the disabled, or even among the dead, which is to say among those who appreciated too late that Papa Priami had absolutely no values whatsoever except expedience: How to get what he wanted? And as far as his only daughter was concerned, what he wanted was an ally who, when she married into another family, could tell her father everything about that family's business, thus giving her Papa the leverage he needed to manipulate her groom's allegiances, should that ever become necessary . . . or desirable.

D omenico Priami was perhaps the easiest man to spot in the entire Province, even from a long distance. And not just because he was tall, razor-thin and carried himself with the alertness of a feral horse. At all times, whether he was indoors or out, curled around his shoulder was a bullwhip. He wore the whip more intimately than even his broad-brimmed white hat and hand-tooled boots, for at least he didn't wear those to bed (so far as anyone knew), whereas he'd been known to check on his nighttime sentinels dressed in only nightshirt and whip.

But it was more than the whip's mere presence that stimulated such intense speculation. Here he was, a man who was vastly imaginative in the ways he degraded his enemies, a man who had killed more men in duels than anyone could count, a man for whom an occasional assassination was good for the blood (his and society's, as far as he was concerned), yet he had never, so far as anyone knew, raised his bullwhip in anger against a soul.

No one seemed to be quite sure where the bullwhip came from or why Domenico Priami always wore it. Some whispered it had been the gift of the Devil, given to Master Priami when he was a child so that he could kill the uncle who had raped Domenico's sister. Supposedly, the curse that came with the whip was that, for the rest of Master Priami's life, the whip had to touch his body or else the arm he had used to kill his uncle would atrophy and fall off. Such was the nature of superstition. And yet, it was superstition that grew from a rumor so widespread that, in the minds of many, it was fact: that Domenico Priami didn't know how to use the whip. Almost every gentleman of privilege in the Province handled a bullwhip as though it grew right out of his hand. Not Domenico Priami. It was said that, every morning, his man servant, Poq Mulando, would line up thirteen bottles on a stone wall—always thirteen, for reasons known only to Domenico Priami himself—then Master Priami would attempt to knock the bottles off the wall, one at a time, with thirteen cracks of his whip. Other men did this as easily as fastening their fly. Not Domenico Priami. The rumor was that Domenico Priami suffered from the only condition that would prevent an otherwise healthy man from mastering the bullwhip: he was afraid of it. So far as anyone could tell, if it were true, it might be the only thing Domenico Priami was afraid of.

On Bella-Viola's wedding day, a celebration attended by every landowner in the Province, and one that contributed a purse of gold coins to every peasant family for one hundred leagues in every direction, Domenico Priami gave Bella-Viola's husband many extravagant gifts—first among them, the Stallion of Stallions, the black Arabian that was the fastest, most revered horse in all the world at that time.

In the Province, a stallion was a traditional gift to a bridegroom from his wife's father. It was also a sacred gift, since it represented the hope of progeny to perpetuate the husband's bloodline. And the rarer and more pure the stallion—which of course meant the more it cost in relation to the father's overall wealth—the more respect it showed for his daughter's new husband, the heritage of the husband's family, and the honor for the bride's father of contributing the blood of his daughter, and thus his own blood, to the continuation of that heritage.

When the Stallion of Stallions was trotted out at the wedding feast, a thousand mouths gasped, fell silent, and then cheered. What caused the momentary silence was the realization that, in comparison to every other marriage stallion that had ever changed hands, the gold needed to buy the Stallion of Stallions must have bordered on the outrageous. No bride had ever come with such a dowry.

Bella-Viola didn't even speculate why her father had given this particular horse to her husband, for she knew that virtually everything her father did was spurred by more than one ambition, and many of them were unknowable.

D omenico Priami had a perverse sense of humor that he kept entirely to himself. Even his intuitive, brilliant daughter (second in priority only to whatever piqued his insatiable need to feel powerful)—even she did not know of this door in his mind to which only he had a key.

To Domenico Priami, the Stallion of Stallions represented much more than a symbol of respect for his new son's family. It was a message to the boy. One that he, the boy, and everyone else, might never understand; in fact, should never understand, and that was the joke of it. It thrilled Domenico when, by a grand gesture, he could have the world thinking one thing about his motives (a perception which was accurate to a point) while he, unknown to the world, was at the same time communicating something entirely different. To his new son-in-law, the hidden message in the gift of the Stallion of Stallions was: *You will never be the man that I, Domenico Priami, am. In fact, you will never even be the man your own bride is. And since I own her, I own you, too."*

His only hesitation in acquiring the gift for his daughter's groom had been knowing that her betrothed was not a skilled horseman and, of course, that Bella-Viola was. She could handle the stallion—she was one of only two or three riders in the Province who could—but her husband could not, and so Domenico Priami had wondered whether others, who also knew the comparative riding skills of the couple, might suspect the subtle dagger of meaning underlying his extraordinary generosity. In the end, Papa Priami had made his decision based upon one of the simple truths that master thieves, pickpockets, assassins and magicians have used successfully since the dawn of time: *People see what they expect to see.* And while the Stallion of Stallions was perhaps the most dramatic and symbolic of the gifts Domenico Priami lavished upon his new son that day, it certainly wasn't the only gift that would take the crowd's breath away. The risk, therefore, was worth it. And so, on the day of his only daughter's marriage, Domenico Priami experienced, unknown to all others in attendance, the rapture of his own black chuckle.

Imagine, if you will, a scale used for weighing gold. In one pan, imagine all the gifts that Domenico Priami presented to his new son on his wedding day: the Stallion of Stallions; an island in the Mediterranean where the strongest workhorses in the world had been bred for more than two thousand years; a flying machine conceived by the great DaVinci himself; a first-edition of every book in existence considered worthy of reading by a gentleman; and, not least of all, enough gold that it took two wagons and six giants to deliver it.

Now, in the other pan, imagine the single gift that Domenico Priami gave his only daughter that day, a gift of one sentence whispered, a gift that had no physical weight whatsoever, yet one that, if the scales were capable of ascertaining value, would, as far as Domenico Priami was concerned, tilt the balance in his daughter's favor as though her side held a mountain of cannonballs and her husband's a straw hat filled with goose down.

In the giving of this gift, Papa Priami experienced once again the exquisite perversity of his hidden muse, for even his own daughter would not fully appreciate the gift's value until time allowed certain events to unfold. She was, after all, but fifteen, and while educated in many areas, including the intelligence Domenico Priami had gathered over the years about the family of her husband, she had been sheltered. Indeed, he had seen to it that she was schooled, but any sort of formal lyceum for women had been out of the question. Who knew what ideas might be caught like a disease, Domenico thought. No, her schooling came only from private tutors. When they could not come to her, she was permitted to travel to them, but of course only under the guardianship of Poq Mulando and his wife, Arlandarose, the most trusted servants in the Priami household. The two had arrived with Bella-Viola's mother, and both had adored Bella-Viola since her birth, Arlandarose having given the girl her first bath. With Poq and Arlandarose literally at her side, Bella-Viola had visited the great cities of the continent, with their libraries, museums, cathedrals and gardens. Papa Priami's rules were strict. She is to learn, not mingle. Now, as ever, she remained a quiet thing, industrious, respectful, at times almost invisible, riding every morning at dawn, tending to her studies, learning the family business, playing her cello in the cavernous warehouse that otherwise held only casks of aging wine. Unfortunately, no doubt the influence of her mother and grandmother, she was a bit too in awe of such things as the birth of foals or a spider web shimmering with morning dew. Ruthlessness does not come natural to her, Domenico Priami had observed to himself. But such is life. It will have to be taught. What Papa Priami said to his daughter that day was something that perhaps no other daughter in the Province had ever heard: "My child, any room you walk into, you should expect that you will be the most intelligent person there, man or woman, but to achieve all that the stars foretell and all that your gifts can acquire, you must never let anyone else even suspect the depth of your knowing . . . no one, not even your husband."

What Papa Priami couldn't know, because those who calculate can never develop the gift of second sight that allows the foretelling of the future, was that his advice to his daughter on her wedding day would eventually cost him his life, for Bella-Viola Maria Priami Angelino was nothing if not a voracious learner.

"What do you know about intercourse?" he asked. It was the first question directed at Bella-Viola by her husband when they were finally alone.

His name was Angelo. The marriage, like all marriages of the day among aristocrats, had been arranged, this one perhaps more carefully than most because the families involved were wealthy, powerful, and ambitious beyond imagination. The bride's virginity, the equivalent of her bloodline and thus the family's honor, meant that the prospective mates became acquainted prior to their wedding in only the most formal and superficial ways, which is to say they never really had a personal, un-chaperoned conversation until the doors of their candle-lit wedding chamber had been closed from the outside by a servant and locked from the inside by themselves. Even this privacy might have been wasted had not both of them been completely without guile. Indeed, before the sun rose the next day, the heavens would, by turns, celebrate and mourn. The celestial tears of happiness and sorrow sprang from the truth that many married couples live their whole lives together and never speak to one another as freely and honestly, and as intimately, as Bella-Viola and Angelo Angelino did on their wedding night, and would every day thereafter until death, inevitably, did them part before either reached the age of 20.

He was a tall version of his namesake, the youthful angel who accompanied the mother of Jesus as she ascended to heaven in marble above the entry to the basilica in Rome. Bella-Viola herself was taller than most other women in the Province, and as she and Angelo had danced for the first time earlier that day she had noted that her ear was even with his heart.

All his features were beautiful. His mouth smiled perpetually as though he had just tasted a delicious sweet. His brown eyes seemed to be amused by all they saw. And his skin. There was something about his skin. It was free of the ruddiness acquired by men who spent at least some portion of their day out of doors, which meant just about every man in the Province except an occasional monk or banker. And of the few things she knew about Angelo, she knew he was, even at seventeen, considered an exceptional agriculturalist. He grew trees that, it was rumored, survived in no other arbor in the Province but his. At the annual fair, when gardeners displayed the flowers, fruits and vegetables of their lands, Angelo's had become the standard by which all others were assessed. And yet, the back of his neck held no tan. Nor the cheekbone under his eye. She would understand it if it were just his hands. Many men wore gloves everywhere but to bed. But she spied not a freckle.

At least, not yet.

He fascinated her. She found herself smiling from every part of her body. It was amazing, really. The act of locking their bed chamber door had opened in her a feeling of absolute safety with this man, this boy. It was as if they had been waiting all their lives to be alone together. She wasn't apprehensive in the slightest. Quite the opposite. Surprise and delight filled her beyond anything she had ever experienced, and the feelings only intensified when, looking into Angelo's eyes, she could tell he felt the same way.

No, she didn't know much about intercourse except for watching animals mate, and she hoped that he wouldn't think that his family's top bull or stallion needed to be the measure of his own activities.

The sound of his laugh was like nothing she had ever heard before. It thrilled her, it was so full of pleasure. No one had looked at her in this way since she was seven years old—before the event that her father called "the martyrdom of Mama and Nana." Her mother had looked at her this way. In wonder. In gratitude.

She asked him what he wanted to do. They had been lying on the bed, fully clothed, staring at one another. And when he answered she knew, for as much absolute certainty as a 15-year-old can have, what it meant to be completely in love with another person. She also knew, for the first time, that she was much more than her father's daughter.

"I don't want to do anything," he began after a long pause. "Rather, I want each of us to be guided by our hearts. I have no desire to mate like a bull. But I have a very strong desire to love you in every touch, in every word, and in every thought. I'm not sure I even know what love is. I am hardly old enough to shave once a week. Who knows what I will call love a year from now, or five. But I do know that I feel such gratitude to God for having you appear in my life, and I don't even know why. I just feel it. So if I spend the rest of this night or the next month just looking at you, if that's what our hearts decide, that will be fine with me. But I must admit that my body is on fire and sometimes I can hardly breathe. I'm being crushed with feelings."

Tears began to flow from Angelo's eyes, and from Bella-Viola's eyes, and from the eyes of all the spirits who were present to bless their reunion, for a reunion it surely was, since all people who discover a soul partner have known that person in many, many previous lives.

Being essentially children, eventually that night they played a game. Each would ask the other a question, a question so personal that it was very unlikely that the person had ever been asked it before. Their answers to one another, they knew, would never be the answers of lawyers or diplomats, answers designed to evade or protect. Theirs would be answers of the heart. And while answering, the person would simultaneously remove a piece of their own clothing, whatever they might choose. What's more, they would play this game, for days if necessary, their meals sent in, until they each were completely naked.

Who scares you that no one knows?

What causes you the most pain in your heart?

Could you kill someone?

What have you done that if your father found out he would really be angry?

What part of your body are you most shy about?

What do you hate?

If you could change anything about yourself, what would it be?

What is your experience of God?

If you were to permit me to touch any part of you other than your hand or your face, where would it be?

Why there?

Would you like me to touch you there now?

During the course of the night, the sound that came from the bedroom of Bella-Viola and her Angelo was felt in vibration by everyone in the Province, not because it was loud, but because it was pure. It was not the sound of passion, though passion was certainly present. Theirs was a much more penetrating sound than that. Indeed, theirs was the purest sound in the world. The sound of joy.

*B*ecause their trust had been forged throughout many incarnations, the commitment made by Bella-Viola and Angelo, each to the other, was among the simplest, deepest, strongest promises one can make: *I will not hide from you.* There was nothing that either would keep from the other should circumstance, or even curiosity, bring it to the surface.

They traveled as far and wide as their whims would take them that first year, their anticipated honeymoon season. Quickly, however, because of their commitment, one year became not enough. As they gave themselves to one another, a cool awareness emerged from the ether, and with it a measure of apprehension, and thus, from time-to-time, the compulsion to tell each other everything. And from that telling came a need to plan—all of which would take as much honeymoon as they could inveigle without raising suspicion.

The lovers knew that if their confidences were ever disclosed beyond themselves, the relative peace they had enjoyed in childhood, and the bliss of their covenant, would be altered irrevocably. Death or exile were the two most likely responses to what would be perceived by both of their fathers as betrayal, for these two children of the heart were choosing to step outside of their families' priorities, and therefore potentially outside of their families' protection and good will, by placing their own love above all other considerations.

To their good fortune, the two discovered that they knew a great deal about the inner workings of their respective families, since each had been afforded a meticulous indoctrination. Plus, both of them were very observant. Also to their benefit, they recognized that it would take every ounce of their combined knowledge and (there was no other word for it) cunning to protect themselves, if their love were to ripen in whatever ways a long life and normal good health might permit.

In the end, they remained away and, by choice, virtually incommunicado from their families for two and a half years. By the time a locker of exotic gifts would arrive back in the Province, accompanied by a long, rambling missive full of the colorful anecdotes and trifles one might expect from newlyweds free to partake in the amusements of the world, Bella-Viola and Angelo were already en route to their next destination, unknown to all but themselves, making it next to impossible for their fathers to divert their intentions, should they have had the desire to do so. Their fathers, though possibly a bit put out, would, the couple knew, attribute their behavior to immaturity.

"My father will tease me that I'm thinking with my penis," Angelo said one day.

"I actually find that one of your most attractive qualities," Bella-Viola said. "Especially since it leads to your heart."

And so it was that Angelo Angelino learned that his wife knew as much as he did about his own family's affairs, a fact that his father, Agua Angelino, would consider a declaration of war by Domenico Priami. And the first, but not the only, casualty of that war would be Angelo's bride, her arms and legs amputated, her tongue removed, the mutilation of choice for the Angelinos' most despised enemies, and one that did not always end in death, much to the victim's horror and eventual insanity, the few times it had occurred. Agua Angelino might look like a monk, with his slight build, soft voice, quick smile, his short white hair and matching beard, his manicured fingers, but before the age of 20 he had killed with his own hands the entire families of six men who were responsible for him being convicted of a crime he did not commit.

And so it was that Bella-Viola learned that Angelo was the son of his father but not the son of his mother, a fact that her father would consider the ultimate in treachery, a betrayal that no amount of bloodletting might ever completely redress, though, as the Lord knew, Domenico Priami would certainly try. The fact that Angelo was the son of his mother's sister because his mother had become barren, and indeed had asked her sister, a young widow, to conceive her husband's fourth child, would mean nothing. Deception was deception.

Were Bella-Viola's mother alive, it would be only a slight exaggeration to say that, for Domenico Priami, it would have been preferable to be cuckolded by every gardener in his employ than to have his only daughter marry a bastard deliberately pawned off on the Priami family by the bastard's own father. Agua Angelino, in the eyes of Domenico Priami, would be seen as a Judas Twin. If his bastard son were not destroyed, "the marriage hoax," as Papa Priami would likely call it, would taint the honor of the Priamis forever. And if all Angelinos were not destroyed, every living generation of them, like an infected herd of cows put down and incinerated to prevent the spread of disease, the sanctity of the Province itself would be perpetually in jeopardy of Angelino duplicity of the foulest kind.

And then there was the much more salient fact that the destruction of either family increased the power of the other.

To the lovers, Domenico Priami was their biggest danger. Agua Angelino would probably never discover the knowledge and talent of his new daughter, nor the subversive intentions of her father, since the only people who knew them were Bella-Viola, her father, and now Angelo.

Of the three, the only one who might alter that equation was Domenico Priami himself, should he share his strategy with one or more of Bella-Viola's brothers. But this was most unlikely so long as Papa Priami considered Bella-Viola the heir of his heart and mind, if not the actual heir to his place at the head of the family dinner table. That place, as was custom, was reserved for the eldest male child, Amin. "A good, honest man," her father once remarked to her in confidence, though not as a compliment. Only she, her father felt, had all the tools to guide the Priami empire past the inevitable disputes that would arise among the four brothers. The foundation for such influence went beyond Bella-Viola's talents and education. Breaking with custom, Papa Priami had given his daughter title to some of the richest land he owned, land he had acquired as part of her mother's dowry, thus exempting it from the laws proscribing ownership of property by a married woman. He also established for her a bank account which, if used judiciously, would give her complete independence and a level of power equal to that of anyone else in the Province, which meant nearly equal to just about anyone else in the world this side of royalty.

Papa Priami's guardian angel might comment that for a man so reluctant to trust others, he sure liked to roll the dice with his daughter.

But Domenico Priami would respectfully demure, replying to his angel that women, especially daughters, were different from the normal run of men, even sons. There was a bond between a father and his daughter, especially an only daughter, that made deception impossible. And so there were really no dice to roll. This did not mean, of course, that Bella-Viola was without her weaknesses.

"You need to sharpen your teeth, my child," Domenico Priami often remarked. "But that will come."

Bella-Viola knew, better than anyone else, one other quality of her father that would inhibit him from revealing to anyone the arrangements he had so painstakingly conceived with her at their center. Domenico Priami loved secrecy. Perhaps nothing thrilled him more than orchestrating the lives of those around him while keeping each person ignorant of the bargains and instructions he had given to the others. Each person, that is, but Bella-Viola. Perhaps without even realizing it completely, Domenico Priami had given his daughter an understanding of his affairs so detailed that it would have been impossible for him to conceal a change of heart, no matter how calculating that heart might be.

Or so Bella-Viola had to bet her life, and the life of her Angelo.

Perhaps more of a problem was how to manage Papa Priami's expectation that he would receive from Bella-Viola valuable intelligence about the Angelino's commercial interests, political alignments and overall ambitions, as well as any personal peccadilloes that might be useful in negotiation.

There would be no question in the mind of Domenico Priami that Agua Angelino, or Bella-Viola's own husband, for that matter, would ever reveal such things to a woman, much less someone from outside their family. But Papa Priami also knew that his Bella-Viola could make meaningful inferences from everyday occurrences that wouldn't mean a thing to almost anyone else. Who visited, where they came from, who traveled, where they went, how many people were hired, for what jobs, who was healthy, who was not, who had a drug problem, who was skilled with a knife or a gun, who gambled beyond his means, who had a wife he couldn't control, who took his pleasure in boys, whose opinion was sharp but undervalued . . .? From questions like these the right person could draw a picture of the Angelino family that would be as accurate as if each member had been interrogated by the pope himself.

This, Bella-Viola knew, was a problem. No longer could she even consider relaying to her father, as much as she was loyal to him, as much as she loved him, any information about the family of her beloved Angelo that might compromise the Angelinos' well-being.

One day the newlyweds were floating alone, and silently, in a single-sail rig off the port of Oran in northwest Africa. The wind was all but calm, the sail free to flutter. They were in a small cove of an uninhabited island where they had been diving for oysters in water so clear that the sun's light exploded off the gold sea bottom giving the water the look and feel of champagne. The oysters, opened by Angelo with his ever-present throwing knife, had been eaten with the juice of the lemon that he had magically materialized out of thin air. They had made love in the water, Angelo holding onto the side of the boat, Bella-Viola holding on to him. Now they lay in the boat, naked, a large muslin umbrella shading them from the mid-day rays. From under the floppy straw hat covering Angelo's face, Angelo said, "My heart is speaking."

Bella-Viola said nothing, waiting. Angelo then removed his hat. His eyes were closed. He began to talk as if his words were being dictated by someone else.

"You must be in a position where there is nothing you could report to your father even if you wanted to. Furthermore, he must know that, and accept it—even if it makes him grind his teeth a little. Otherwise, you, and we, enter a life of actively deceiving your father, each day or each week a new lie, built upon an old lie. And that, my heart, will drain our souls slowly but surely. We are not liars."

Angelo held up his left hand so that they might both see the single piece of jewelry he now wore, the ring they had commissioned an artisan in Morocco to make for them. Bella-Viola had an identical ring on her left hand. These were their true wedding rings. The setting was gold, holding a ruby cut in the shape of a heart, and set into the ruby at the heart's center, a small diamond.

"Yet, it is true," Angelo said, "no matter what path we take, we must deceive both your father and mine, if we are to live."

Angelo lowered his hand and turned his head toward his wife.

"I can imagine someone wiser than we finding it amusing that, because we have made the choice not to hide from each other, we must now hide from our families at the pain of either death, or a life of running.

"And, my love, I am willing to become Bedouins, if necessary, and to make our home in the wilds of the great Sahara where few who look like us have ever been. But the resources of our families would mean, I fear, we would never be safe enough. As we both know, blood vendettas last a lifetime. It could be some young boy who hasn't even been born yet who claims the honor of killing us and carrying our heads and the heads of our children back to the Province in retribution for a transgression that he couldn't even name, it happened so long ago. No. Our action must be one that does not require us to continually lie, or to continually look over our shoulders."

Angelo closed his eyes again and turned his head to the sky, waiting for more words to flow through him.

"A simple solution would be to stage our deaths so that our bodies would never be found. We could easily be swept out to sea. I know that, between us, we could create an illusion that would never be questioned. But this solution asks too high a price, I feel. It punishes everyone at home who loves us. I cannot imagine that my mothers, both of them, would sleep another night without weeping if they believed I had perished in such a tragic way. It would be unbearable enough that I had died. But to them the real hell would be never having my body to wash or to kiss or to cover with blossoms and sing songs to in the family crypt. The thought of my eyes being plucked by fish, my bones lying in some unknown place in the chilly depths, would haunt them for the rest of their lives. Surely it would punish your father, as well, and your brothers. And cruelty, for that is really what it would be, devastating the lives of those who love us so that we can create new life for ourselves in some distant corner of the world, cruelty is contrary to our hearts."

Angelo now opened his eyes, pushed himself up on one elbow, turned and began to gently lick the breasts of his bride, the sweetness of her skin spiced by the ocean's salt.

"Especially," he eventually murmured in a voice quivering in response to her hands on him, "if we have another choice."

*H*ad Agua Angelino ever heard the proposition that his youngest child was preparing to make him, he would have been immobile with sadness, and equally proud. His son and his new wife would be living far from the Province for several years, maybe longer.

Of course they would come home for visits. And he and the boy's mothers would visit them. But these visits could be years apart. Basically, this change was a kind of death. Angelo's laugh, his carefree whistling, the sound of his bare feet heading for the night kitchen, the unexpected bouquets of his rare flowers, the click of his horse's hooves, and the jingle of the boy's spurs, as Angelo set out for the mountains always well before dawn, and the same click and jingle when he returned a few weeks later—countless moments, almost never to be known again.

Every other man in the house, which meant Agua Angelino himself and his other three sons, would hang his usually dusty work hat on the elk antler rack in the entry when he arrived home at the end of the day. Not Angelo. In what, in other patrician homes, or by any other man in the Angelino home, would be considered a gross breech of etiquette, Angelo brought his hat into the empty, spotless dining room where, from a distance of as much as ten feet, so as not to put bootprints on the Persian carpet, he would toss the hat with deadly accuracy so that it landed on the back of his father's chair. And there it would remain, dusty and untouched by anyone else, until Agua Angelino, dressed for the evening in fresh jodhpurs, immaculate riding boots and velvet vest over a white linen shirt, came to dine. With the rest of the family and any guests present, Agua Angelino, without saying a word, would carefully lift Angelo's hat from the back of his chair and, with a slight bow, give it to a waiting servant who would then remove it from the dining room and hang it on the antlers next to the work hats of the other Angelino men. This happened any day that Angelo was in residence.

Had Agua Angelino been in a position to experience his feelings about Angelo's plan, the old man's imagination would have seen himself tearing with joy when, on some far future evening, he would come to dine and, unexpectedly, find his son's dusty hat once again resting jauntily on the back of his chair, the boy, now a man of the world, probably hiding under the table and laughing with glee at his father's surprise.

That is how much Angelo's absence on every other day would have strained the heart of Agua Angelino.

And yet, his heart would have split with pride, as well.

He would have considered the boy's proposition brilliant, and frankly a bit surprising. Not surprising that it was brilliant, but surprising that it would take the boy away from his home and his mothers and brothers.

Agua Angelino might have wondered for a moment whether his son's new bride had influenced the boy's thinking, wanting for some reason a bit more freedom from the sway of her father, or of possibly the Angelinos themselves, though he couldn't imagine why. It was obvious that Domenico

Priami carried a special affection for his daughter. He, Agua Angelino, knew only enough about his son's bride to feel that, besides representing an attractive alliance with the Priami's, if Angelo was satisfied, and she certainly was pretty and competent and knew her place, then, well, he was satisfied, too.

But Agua Angelino would have quickly dismissed all that because the proposal itself was so in keeping with the Angelino's overall desires, discussed in confidence many times with his sons, to find a way to expand the family's opportunities beyond their present sphere of power.

This could not happen, he had contended, by setting up elsewhere the same sorts of interests they had in the Province. There were other families in those areas who already controlled those interests, and the Angelinos, as outsiders, with their primary base of power leagues away, would find it too expensive to displace the other families, building the same level of control and intelligence-gathering they enjoyed at home. In short, there would be too much blood. And Agua Angelino was a firm believer in the old adage that, except when honor was at stake, blood was bad for business.

What he wanted, but hadn't yet discovered, was a venture that was absolutely distinct, something that no one else was doing, or at least doing so poorly that the Angelinos could supplant it by the quality of their offering, rather than by muscle. Low risk, high reward. That's what they had not yet hit upon. The boy, Agua Angelino would have laughed, might just have solved their dilemma with a solution that was not only simple and efficient, always priorities for Agua Angelino, but also beautiful in its symmetry, a quality, the father would have noted with increasing admiration, that always seemed to be associated with the ideas of his youngest.

One of the great pleasures of Agua Angelino's life, and one of the things he would have missed most about his son's departure, was the time the two of them spent together training horses without the use of a whip or other forms of intimidation. It was a revolutionary technique that Angelo actually taught his father, having learned it completely on his own by spending months alone up in the mountains with wild herds. So unusual a technique was it in the Province at that time, a province renowned for its skilled riders and handlers, that Angelo never demonstrated it publicly, knowing that tradition would bring him much more ridicule than curiosity. In fact, he went out of his way to have people think of him as someone who wasn't a particularly gifted horseman at all. No one would ever think to turn to Angelo Angelino to gentle or train a horse.

The principle was an obvious one to Angelo. He'd seen it in operation all his life among the men who worked for his father. The most effective leaders were those who were followed by other men willingly, out of respect. So why did it make sense, the boy had asked himself, for horses to be dominated by a master? Wouldn't a more effective relationship be one where both rider and horse came together as willing partners? To find out, Angelo went to the mountains. And there wild horses taught him.

There was no more memorable day for Agua Angelino than the day he and his son were camping in the mountains, just the two of them at Angelo's invitation, and Angelo challenged his father to a race. Agua Angelino had known that his son was studying the behavior of wild horses, but that was about all he knew. He was astonished to learn that Angelo meant to race him on the bare back of the immense white stallion who led the untamed herd. And his astonishment only increased when Angelo walked out into a field and simply stood there with a hackamore in his hand and the stallion eventually walked up to him and placed his nose on Angelo's belly. When Agua Angelino was murdered, having never heard his son's proposition, what astonished him most about the experience was that his last thought was of Angelo's belly being nuzzled by the great white stallion.

They each raced a unique loop, though identical in length, that would take them more than an hour to complete, and required a level of leaping and turning and just flat-out speed, at times straight up hill, at other times straight down, that only a strong, agile, well-trained mount like Agua Angelino's could complete at a gallop. And yet when the father finally reined in his lathered, exhausted gelding at the finish, there in front of him, grazing, was the white stallion with Angelo lying on its bare back, his dusty black hat over his face, as if he were taking a nap.

From that moment on, Agua Angelino was in awe of his son, an emotion that was brand new in the long life of this proud, accomplished and occasionally ruthless man.

In fact, it was Angelo's plan to invite his father to spend a week in those very same mountains, just the two of them. And there, over many days, in the pleasure of their reunion, Angelo would lay out his proposition.

"Papa, we can create some of the best race horses in the world with training techniques that are far superior to most of those used anywhere else. This alone can make us a fortune in both winnings and in breeding. But that, really, is only the beginning.

"By being leaders in the rarified world of the horse, we will be able to establish relationships of respect and mutual benefit with influential people in many countries—politicians, royalty, military, bankers, intellectuals, clergy, yes, all those who can, and will, willingly assist us in fulfilling your desire to expand our family's favor. These contacts will give us not just access, but also a level of intelligence that will be invaluable. You will be able to select with the greatest possible confidence those investments and alliances that give us optimum reward, as you define it. Of course, this cannot happen overnight, but is there any plan that could? This might just be the strategy that can give the Angelinos the greatest leverage over the years for very little risk. No bloodshed. No direct link to present operations. And really, no financial drain to speak of, since in a relatively short period of time the horse business will pay for itself.

"Of course, Papa, I don't claim to be an expert on business affairs. You know that. I'm just offering a suggestion that might be worthy of examination.

"One thing I do know, however, Papa, is that the biggest cost, and I appreciate that it will be a large one, is that I must live elsewhere. We both know that my training techniques would be denounced as childish here in the Province until they were proven successful. That seems like an unnecessary burden to add to an already ambitious undertaking. What's more, you have said you want to establish a foothold outside of the Province. There are any number of ideal places for raising strong horses, and where we could create a training center that would attract no outside attention until we felt the time was right.

"Another cost, of course, Papa, is that Bella-Viola will not be living near her family, either. And this is something her father might not take kindly. But I wonder if you might speak with him. I wonder if he might not be made aware of our plan, and thus be able himself to benefit from it some day. As we strengthen our influence outside of the Province, should he not be able to strengthen his own influence, through us? You know best, Papa. But I wonder if Papa Priami might not feel that he is actually receiving much more than he bargained for when he approved the marriage of his daughter . . . and if that wouldn't be a good thing for all concerned."

Agua Angelino, most assuredly, would have had Angelo's proposition scrutinized by all his boys as though it were a blueprint for the world's future drawn up by Jesus Christ himself in his own handwriting. But of course, that would have been business as usual for Agua Angelino.

His initial response to any proposal was to instruct his sons to each, on their own, "Tear it apart. Determine its liabilities, and its strengths. Assess why it will work, and why it won't. And conclude the choice you would make if you were the head of this family. Then, come together as brothers and as men, discuss your individual views among yourselves, with respect, and agree on a recommendation you will make to me."

This was how Agua Angelino trained his heirs for a future without their father. Even though the eldest son would, naturally, assume the family mantle, Agua Angelino knew that a process for making wise decisions was as important as the person who sat at the family's head. One could not guarantee the wisdom of a leader, but men bonded by blood and guided by principle were, together, less likely to be led in foolish ways by an ignorant or arrogant elder.

If Agua Angelino had heard the proposition of his youngest progeny, at this point he might have speculated that perhaps it was *he* who was arrogant, since, without hearing the recommendations of his sons, he would have already made up his mind to approve it.

*T*he last port of call for Bella-Viola and Angelo, before the final leg of their return to the Province, was really not a port at all. It was the island, Sasi, their wedding gift from Papa Priami. They had saved it for last, a deliberate sign of respect to Domenico Priami for such an extravagant endowment. It was also where they intended to conceive their first child.

Six months earlier, included in their regular shipment of gifts back home was an invitation from Bella-Viola to her father to rendezvous with them at Sasi. It would be, she had told him, an opportunity to share with him all the wonderful adventures of their honeymoon before they arrived back in the Province and were besieged with social invitations and family responsibilities.

Of course, her father would know by that frivolous turn of phrase that she meant no such thing—for what invitations or responsibilities could take priority over personal time with her father? What she really meant was that she could give her father some important news that he would appreciate having before she and Angelo completed their honeymoon, which, to Papa Priami, could only mean that something was afoot among the Angelinos that he needed to know.

She was sure he would meet them on Sasi.

The first step of their strategy for managing Domenico Priami was for Bella-Viola to relay to him, in secret, the proposition that Angelo was about to make to his father. Any frustration that Domenico Priami might have felt about having been kept in the dark concerning the couple's whereabouts for the past many months would evaporate, Bella-Viola knew, in the light of learning the long-range desires of the Angelinos, the particulars of Angelo's impending proposal to his father, and the benefit that the ensuing plan could very likely have for Priamis, which her father would instantly infer without her having to provide any of the details.

Domenico Priami would also feel remarkably proud of his daughter, since he would be of the opinion that her husband, despite being a better horseman than Domenico ever gave him credit for, was incapable of such sophisticated thinking on his own. She wouldn't correct her father's interpretation that she had been responsible for extending their honeymoon so that she might manipulate the boy's reasoning in her favor. Such a conclusion would cause her father to reassess the one area of her skills that he had found wanting—calculation.

The sticking point, she was sure, would be her leaving the Province, not that there was much her father could do about it, but she and Angelo wanted more than his acquiescence, they wanted his support. And they felt that by her telling him first, in secret as it were, they would be giving him time to acclimate himself to the likely prospect of an essential change in his access to his daughter, and thus to the kind of information about the Angelinos he would receive from her in the future.

She and Angelo had also decided not to tell her father that Angelo planned to ask Agua Angelino to share the Angelino plan with Domenico Priami. For one thing, it was possible that Agua Angelino might decline to do so. Unlikely, but possible. Mostly, they wanted Papa Priami to be pleasantly surprised by the overture, not just the fact that Agua Angelino would sit down with him and lay out the Angelino master plan that would be taking Papa Priami's only daughter away from the Province, but also the specific inclusion in that plan of opening doors outside the Province for the Priamis. Of course her father would have already anticipated this benefit, but he would have been very pleased, and maybe a bit honored, to have it be explicitly put on the table by Agua Angelino himself. This event, Bella-Viola knew, would demonstrate to her father both the good will of Agua Angelino and the unexpected influence that his daughter already had in her new family. For Bella-Viola and her Angelo, this approach to Domenico Priami gave them, she felt, the highest likelihood that the two fathers would bless this venture.

*T*he island was about thirty square kilometers in size. It was shaped similarly to a slice of cake placed on its side, rising steadily from a long, white pebbly beach on the south, where boats anchored, to a massive bluff on the north, creating on the east and west coasts sheer cliffs, also white, of increasing size the further north from the beach one traveled. Over the centuries, the limestone content in the soil had created strong bones in the Sasi work horses, and the steep hills had no doubt aided the development of the horses' unmatched endurance. Roughly a third of the island was pasture, two-thirds pine forest with riding trails. A single estate, located on a plateau overlooking the harbor, was home to the dozen or so workers and their families who, like ten or more generations of their ancestors before them, managed the breeding, training and shipping of the famed Sasi steeds. For twenty years, until the marriage of Bella-Viola and Angelo, everything had been owned by Domenico Priami, acquired by him, so the story went, after chopping off the owner's foot then placing the foot on a desk in front of the man, along with a box of gold, a deed, and a pen.

They had been there a week, and Bella-Viola was a little surprised that her father had yet to arrive.

"Maybe he's giving us some of our own medicine," Angelo mused. "He knows we plan to be here a fortnight. And he knows that it won't take more than a day or so for you to tell him whatever it is he needs to know. So maybe, to show us who's boss, he'll show up just about the time we're ready to set sail again."

Angelo talked as though what he said made perfect sense, but Bella-Viola knew that her husband was just acting, trying to diffuse any prickles of worry she might have. She had thought her father might very well have been there to greet them. He would have missed her tremendously, as she missed him, and he would have been doubly eager to hear her news. But a week here or there was really no time at all.

Angelo, meanwhile, was in heaven. Shirtless, dressed only in jodhpurs, boots, and a white bandanna around his head, he walked for hours among the horses. He had already accomplished the impossible according to island legend—he'd ridden a young, untrained Sasi without a bridle or halter. Bella-Viola, one of the strongest riders in the Province, marveled at her husband's attunement, and knew she would never match it. So on the sixth afternoon of their honeymoon's last chapter, wearing black riding breeches and a red silk long sleeve shirt, hatless, her black hair in one long braid, she selected a well-trained Sasi and rode bareback and bridle up the island and through the wide pine needle trails of the forest to a remote overlook on the northern tip, the island's highest point.

She sat on a bench someone had hewn from a fallen tree. Five hundred feet below she could see the ocean surf repeatedly exploding against the rocky coast, yet at this height the sound of it was but a faint throbbing hiss. The wind, however, was raucous at this elevation, ripping over the top of the cliff, pushing back the tall grass, nipping at the tail and mane of her Sasi as its head bowed to graze. All of the seagulls Bella-Viola saw were below her, their wings outstretched, circling casually, gliding on the updraft. The ocean air was sweet at this elevation, not fishy. The horizon, she realized, was further away than perhaps any ocean horizon she had ever seen. She could not recall ever having felt the world from this point of view. She imagined a monk from a bygone age building a hut here and talking to God. She was at such peace that when Poq Mulando sat down beside her she was unsurprised.

"*H*ello Miss," Poq said.

It was the first time in Bella-Viola's life that she noticed that someone had gotten appreciably older since the last time she had seen them. She wondered if *she* looked that different to Poq. Poq Mulando had grown up in the mountains, a descendant of a long line of mountain guides. He was not a tall man; no taller than a jockey, really. But his thighs were bigger round than Bella-Viola's waist; indeed, Poq's neck was almost bigger round then her waist. She had seen Poq pick up a sick calf with one arm, heft the animal over his shoulder, and walk a mile through mud up to his knees. While Poq's head matched the rest of him in size (Bella-Viola had often wondered if a bigger brain were why Poq knew so many things), Poq's face was the face of a baby, and his hair was the short, almost invisible blonde peach fuzz of some infants.

And now, while the body was pretty much the same, Poq's face had the sag of a pumpkin recently turned beyond fresh.

"Oh, Poq!" Bella-Viola cried, hugging the man she loved in some ways as much as her father. "You've found me. You who could track a mosquito in a windstorm. I was hoping Papa would bring you with him. How are you? And how is my beloved Arlandarose? Did you see Angelo? I have so much to tell you . . . ."

She stopped suddenly because she saw something in Poq's face beyond unexpected age. There was no light in his eyes. Tenderness, yes, as always. Love for her, as always. But no smile. Only pain. No, something beyond pain.

"Poq?" she asked. "What is it?"

Arlandarose Mulando, because she was a woman, knew more about Bella-Viola than any other person alive, even more than Angelo at this young time in their love. Poq Mulando knew almost as much as his wife. He had taught Bella-Viola to ride, to paint a picture of a bird that looked like a bird, to care for animals, to tell jokes in Greek, to weed a garden, to measure the height of a standing tree, to track animals . . . all of which really meant that he had taught her the art of paying attention. It was really because of this training that Bella-Viola knew so much about her father's affairs. Bella-Viola never discussed with Poq nor Arlandarose the ambitions of her father and the role he had planned for her to play in them. Her relationship with the two servants didn't require such discussions. To Bella-Viola, they were the best possible servants: those who knew everything and said nothing, but if you asked, would always tell you the truth—and without being asked, would step between you and danger.

"I have news that you must hear," Poq said. He never spoke like this. Bella-Viola wondered for a second whether he were teasing her, but his pale blue eyes were in complete harmony with his words.

"Your father did not bring me here. I came alone. Only Arlandarose knows I am here. If your father knew, he would feel I had betrayed him. And in a way I have. I have come to tell you that the lives of you and your husband are in danger . . . ."

"Right this minute? Is Angelo's life in danger right this minute?" Bella-Viola asked so forcefully it was as if she were angry at Poq, yelling at him.

"No, Miss," Poq said quietly.

Bella-Viola bowed her head in apology. Her father would criticize her for such an emotional outburst. And Poq did not yet know of her bond with

Angelo. She looked up at her teacher and spoke precisely the two words her father always used in the face of bad news, "Tell me."

*P*oq sighed and wiped his mouth with the back of his hand. "There is an old woman, a servant, who works in the Angelino household. She sent your father a note. It said that your father had been duped by the Angelinos. That your marriage was not valid because Mister Angelo's mother is not Agua Angelino's wife. Your father sent for the woman. She told him that she was present at the birth of Mister Angelo, in France, and that it was Agua Angelino's wife's sister who gave birth to Angelo."

"I know the whole story, Poq," Bella-Viola interrupted. "I can even tell you this servant's name, Vitna Palmata. Did she also tell Papa that she came to him because, for nearly 20 years, she has wanted revenge on Agua Angelino because he did not choose her as the mother of Angelo? Not only that, but he wouldn't even lie with her so that she, a spinster, might have her own baby with no family ties at all to the Angelinos, if Agua Angelino wished? Did she tell Papa that? And did she tell him that on the day Angelo was born, Vitna Palmata exposed her breasts to Agua Angelino and there was milk running from them just as though she had been pregnant, even though she was a virgin. And did she tell Papa that she said to Agua Angelino that day, on the very day his Angelo was born, that someday he, Agua Angelino, would know the pain that she carried because he had denied her her life's purpose—to be the mother of a saint? She calls Angelo 'The Saint.' Did she tell Papa, also, that Angelo's father has never said an unkind word about her, either before that day or after, and that he has permitted her to remain in service to his family all these years, even though her mind is like a fruitcake soaked in rum, because Agua Angelino is an honorable man and her family has been with the Angelinos forever?—"

"Miss," Poq held up his hand. She had hardly taken a breath.

They sat quietly for a moment before Poq said, "Your father knows all that, Miss. Your father wrote a letter to Agua Angelino demanding an explanation. And Agua Angelino immediately responded that he would gladly honor your father's request. He invited your father to a meeting at the residence of the Bishop."

"Ah!" Bella-Viola said. "Bishop Chamundi?"

Poq nodded.

"Papa's old friend from childhood."

Then she laughed, "I know all about him, too.

"Did you know, Poq, that long before he was Bishop, Pater Chamundi counseled Agua and Patricemay Angelino that their desire to have another child with the participation of Patricemay's sister, Orlanta, as mother, would be blessed by God, because it would be a child conceived in love? And did you know that he counseled them explicitly that not a soul would ever need to be told differently. The biological parents coupled only for the purpose of conceiving this child. Pater Chamundi himself baptized Angelo. And it was Pater Chamundi who took up a pen and actually wrote the names of Agua Angelino and Patricemay Angelino on Angelo's birth certificate. Did you know that?"

"I only heard of it from your father after their meeting, Miss," Poq said.

"Oh, Poq. I'm so sorry. I'm not letting you speak. Forgive me. You're trying to tell me something, and I guess I'm afraid to hear it. Please, tell me everything."

Poq looked out to sea for a long moment before he continued.

"When your father met with the Bishop and Agua Angelino, and after he had heard their story, he told them how much it relieved his heart that the servant had not told the real truth. He knew that he had not been deceived. He said he understood, and agreed, that Angelo was a child of love, and that if he had been in either of their positions, the bishop's and

Papa Angelino's, he would no doubt have acted just as they had. He also told them how much he appreciated the honor they bestowed on him by being so completely honest."

"And then?" Bella-Viola asked, knowing that her father had been lying.

"And then Agua Angelino invited the Bishop and your father and your brothers to his home to dine. Your father said that his first available evening was one month hence, so that was the date selected. Also present at that dinner was Angelo's mother, her sister, and all of his brothers . . . ."

At this point Poq was so overwhelmed and could no longer speak. He stood and vigorously shook his head, attempting to clear his emotions enough to continue. Bella-Viola had never seen him so disturbed. He was ordinarily the calmest man she knew. And more than any other person, he had been privy to some of her father's most extreme acts. There was an odd arrangement between her father and Poq. A devil's agreement, Poq had once referred to it as. Years before, Poq refused to help plan or execute any violence on behalf of her father. Her father, surprisingly, accepted Poq's decision. But in return he demanded a single concession. Poq must listen to Domenico Priami whenever he needed to test his thoughts, or purge his demons, as he called it, by speaking out loud. Poq was not required to respond. He could remain completely mute. Then again, if he were so moved, he was welcome to offer whatever counsel he felt appropriate. Sometimes deliberately, but at other times not, Domenico Priami's thinking out loud would include plans so unnecessarily brutal that Poq felt obliged to point out the excesses. And whenever he did, Poq knew that Domenico Priami had imposed his will upon him. To her father, it was simply a matter of honesty. Everyone who worked in service of Domenico Priami participated in violence, one way or another. It was as natural a part of life as breathing, and Papa Priami would not have it denied.

Now Poq couldn't look at her. She sensed that he would have willingly jumped off the cliff if it might have made even the slightest difference. That's how much he hated what he was about to tell her.

"Poq, please!" she pleaded.

"Three masked men suddenly entered the home and held everyone at the sword," Poq began. "The Angelinos and the Priamis were all seated at the dining room table. A number of other men had already killed the Angelino sentinels and any servants they encountered. One of the intruders yelled 'Silence!' and with the echo of dinner conversation hanging in the air, he walked over to Agua Angelino and lanced him right up the ear canal with his dagger, pushing the blade cleanly through Agua Angelino's head. Of course he died instantly, though strangely, it was reported, with a smile on his face. Then the man said that if everyone else didn't wish to die also, they would do as they were instructed. Your father spoke up and said for everyone to be calm and to give the men whatever they wanted. The man who had just dispatched Agua Angelino, evidently the leader, immediately walked over to your brother, Mister Amin, and drove his dagger straight down into the top of Mister Amin's head, killing him also, then turned to your father and said, 'Shut your mouth, old man, or I will execute every one of the girls you call sons.' The intruders then bound everyone to their chair and pushed napkins into their mouths and tied their mouths shut. Then, with all the remaining Priamis and Angelinos, as well as the Bishop, sitting around the table, tied to their chairs, silent, able to move nothing but their eyes, the masked men, without saying another word, slit the throats of Angelo's three brothers, his mother, and his mother's sister. Then, without any explanation, they departed, sparing the three remaining Priami brothers, your father, and the Bishop."

*T*here was a long empty moment before Bella-Viola vomited. Then began the scream of the tortured. On and on and on it went. It subsided only in exhaustion, collapsed on the ground, moaning, vomiting, babbling. Poq sat on the ground next to her, his hand on her back behind her heart, weeping his own tears of anguish for this child he was giving his life for in the hope that she might, at least, live to know a moment's peace someday despite the horror she was entering.

The sun had moved west a half dozen hands by the time either of them spoke again. During this time, Poq had lifted Bella-Viola and carried her a short distance to the leeward side of a round stone altar. The altar was as tall as a horse and rider; laid across its top and pointing in the direction of true north was a four sided granite slab, a rod in length (roughly three Poqs laid end-to-end) and a yard in diameter. The overall effect was similar to balancing a square candle across the top of a water glass. By sitting with their backs against the southwest side of the altar, Bella-Viola and Poq were protected from the incessant wind, and thus felt the illusion of calm.

"How is my father?" Bella-Viola asked.

It took Poq a while to answer. "Your father, Miss, is very ill in his mind."

"I'm not surprised," Bella-Viola said softly.

"No Miss. It's not that. You see, Miss," and here Poq paused. "You see, Miss . . . it was your father who arranged for the assassinations of the Angelinos."

Bella-Viola moaned. This was too much. She simply could not respond. Was it possible that a person could die from too much truth? She began to let out every breath with an explosion of her lips. "Paah. Paah." Over and over and over. "Paah. Paah. Paah."

Many minutes later Poq said, "Miss, Amin's death was part of your father's plan. So was leaving the Bishop alive. He wanted the Bishop to witness your brother Amin's death because he knew the Bishop wasn't familiar with death, not that kind of death, and would never think that a father could have his own son killed just to create an alibi. And so the Bishop would tell the world how Domenico Priami mourns the murder of his eldest son as well as the murders of his daughter's new family . . . and that, in sorrow, the families are united stronger than ever. He also wanted his three younger boys to witness the murders, so they would be easy to send off on any mission of revenge."

"I must go to Angelo," Bella-Viola said immediately. Whatever was happening, she wanted to be with him.

"Before you do, Miss, there is something else you need to know," said Poq.

Bella-Viola had been standing. Now she dropped to her knees. "Tell me."

"Your father's motives, I am quite sure, had very little to do with Mister Angelo's birth. For quite some time, your father has wanted to take over the Angelino business. That's why your marriage was so important. You know this. You also know that your father is a very impetuous man. I think he decided on the spot at the meeting in the Bishop's office that, if he could convince the Bishop and Agua Angelino that his misgivings about the matter of Mister Angelo were completely put to rest and that the whole affair had only increased his respect for the Angelinos, he could then seize that moment, hire foreign assassins, and use the Bishop himself to cover his actions. Your father had no unbreakable commitments during the month he told Agua Angelino he was unavailable. He was just giving himself enough time to find the right professionals from outside the Province. You can be sure no one can find any of those men today, no matter what sort of bounty is placed on their heads. And even if they were found, the assassins themselves would never know who put out the contract that they fulfilled."

"Are you suggesting that my father intends to kill Angelo?" Bella-Viola asked without emotion.

"Yes, Miss. And you with him, if necessary."

"I don't understand. Why? What does he gain?"

"Fear never lacks for reasons," Poq replied.

"Your father is convinced that you will find out that he is responsible for the Angelino deaths. Not that he will tell you directly himself, or that anyone else will tell you. Some lies are just hard to keep. Sooner or later, he fears, you will learn the truth. But that's not what worries him the most."

Bella-Viola had once again sat and was now holding her wedding ring up to the setting sun in such a way that, to her eye, the top of the ruby heart glowed as if it were a hot coal.

Poq paused, but only a moment.

"He's afraid that you will be unable to keep such a secret from your husband. That it will require too much of you, that you are simply not . . . well, not man enough. You have just never had to keep a secret like this, and your father feels that your husband will sense something is the matter and start to speculate as to what it is. Or maybe that this lie between you and Mister Angelo will cause mistrust and eventually jeopardize your ability to control him. For your father, Mister Angelo is a loose end, and Domenico Priami is a tidy man."

Poq paused again, contemplating what he had to say next. Bella-Viola continued to examine her ring, squinting through one eye.

"And then there's the fact that if you and Mister Angelo die together, when your boat sinks on the open seas—and that is your father's plan—it will once again divert attention from him. Who would ever think that Papa Priami would kill his only daughter, the joy of his heart? And yet that is the sacrifice he is prepared to make in order to eliminate the last Angelino without anyone in the world ever even blinking a doubt in his direction."

If Poq had climbed onto the altar and then flew off into the sun she could not have been more stunned at how naive she was. She and Angelo had thought they were so clever, so creative, so inventive in their plan to get what they wanted from their fathers. God above, compared to her father, she knew nothing about getting what she wanted. She was . . . astonished. She was so . . . what? Simple minded? A child? This news was unbelievable, but she knew it was true, and not just because Poq had told her. How could she have been so stupid not to have known, somewhere inside her, that there was nothing, not even her, that Domenico Priami would not sell if the terms were right? Or had she known it but refused to admit it? Her father was one of those rare men who was willing to destroy what he loved, or whatever emotion it was that he called love. He had said she needed to sharpen her teeth, and he was right—if she and Angelo were to live.

She put her hands in her lap and leaned against Poq, both of them staring out to sea. The sun meeting the horizon looked like a lemon cookie, its lower edge being slowly dipped into a cup of tea.

"What's the plan?" Bella-Viola asked.

"Tomorrow, a boat will arrive with a message. Your father will give you a good reason why he cannot meet you here, and will ask you to arrive home in a week's time. From that he will be able to know when you will be on the open sea. He presumes you will set sail the day after tomorrow."

They sat again without speaking until the lemon cookie was half submerged.

When Bella-Viola spoke again, Poq knew that she might live beyond the next few days.

"There is something you have yet to tell me, isn't there?"

This was true. He had been testing her. He was gratified that she had spotted it. He hadn't told her everything because he hadn't been positive that she would be able to deal with what he had said so far. If she had been overwhelmed, she would be incapable of thinking clearly enough to protect herself, and she would be dead shortly—tomorrow, a few days, a week, a month, it wouldn't matter. No one could protect her. She had to be able, and willing, to protect herself. Some news isn't worth relating unless a person can use it.

"When my father wants to kill someone," Bella-Viola said, "his plan covers every possibility. Waiting for our ship to cross the open sea leaves too much to chance. We might be delayed, or take a different route. But more than that, killing me doesn't make any sense. If Angelo's family is dead, and then Angelo dies, I inherit the Angelino estate. Keeping me alive should be the thing he wants most. I'm his link to the Angelino fortune."

"I beg your pardon, Miss," Poq replied. "But it didn't seem fair to tell you some things until I was sure they might be useful to you."

"You mean until you were sure I wasn't so quivering with fear that I was an idiot."

Poq said nothing.

"Let me tell you something, Poq Mulando," Bella-Viola said, pushing herself away from Poq so that she could turn and look at him. "For the past two years, Angelo and I have stayed away from the Province, and out of communication with our fathers, because we were figuring out how to create a life for ourselves that would be completely beyond the influence of our families. Now most people, maybe you included, would say that this is an impossible goal. We could never get away from our families. Well, I would respectfully suggest to you, Poq, that if you do believe that, then it is you who are an idiot. Angelo and I, the so-called children, have developed a plan that will mean a mountain of gold for each family, a plan that will help each family grow far into the future, all while allowing Angelo and me to live as we wish. Of course our plan doesn't mean much now, since Papa has murdered Angelo's family and might end up killing us as well, but my point is this: if you ever underestimate me again, if you ever hide anything from me again—anything, goddammit—I will pick you up by your balls and throw you right off this goddamn cliff. I don't care how strong you are. Am I making myself heard?"

Poq could not help himself from smiling. She was the woman he had always known she could be, it just happened years earlier than he had ever thought possible.

"I will take your stupid grin as a yes," Bella-Viola said, a small smile crossing her lips.

"Now speak to me directly or get ready to fly, you son-of-a-bitch," Bella-Viola said, then laughed. She wasn't really angry at Poq. She was scared, scared nearly to death. And she was glad that he could tell the difference.

Poq was now his usual self: calm and direct. "Your father has convinced your brothers that Mister Angelo has held you hostage for at least the past year. And that it was he, Mister Angelo, who had his family assassinated. Or I should say, your father has convinced your brothers that no one other than Mister Angelo benefits from the death of his family. He inherits everything."

"And so the plan is what, exactly?" Bella-Viola asked.

"Your brothers are arriving tomorrow in place of your father to celebrate your return. It is they who will carry the message from him. Your father wants no violence to happen on Sasi. Your brothers' plan is to accompany you and Mister Angelo home. At least one of them—probably Tino, the baby, the one you love most—will propose that he sail back to the Province on your ship. And on the way, Mister Angelo will meet with some accident, perhaps stumble overboard in the night, or be accidentally speared with a harpoon— as you know, a ship at sea can be a dangerous place."

"Oh," Bella-Viola whispered, as though she finally understood all that Poq had been telling her.

"So my father intends for me to be a widow," Bella-Viola said.

"Yes, Miss," Poq said. "He presumes that you are loyal to him above all others, that any affection you have for Mister Angelo will fade quickly enough. Your father needs you. He knows the Priamis have no future unless you are running the family business. He's missed you terribly."

The lemon cookie was now so far into the tea that, any second, the person holding it would have to either let it go or get her fingertips wet.

Her eyes on the sinking sun, Bella-Viola said, "I must now ask you a favor, Poq. More than a favor."

"Miss?" Poq said.

"I must ask you not to kill yourself."

Poq had definitely not expected this request. He was touched that she knew him so well. He had brought the poison with him. He had little choice but to take his own life. He had betrayed Domenico Priami, his benefactor, a man to whom he had pledged his allegiance. Death by his own hand was the honorable path.

It didn't matter that, if Domenico Priami ever found out that Poq had come to Sasi and warned Bella-Viola, Papa Priami would kill Poq himself.

Bella-Viola continued: "This business is not a matter of your personal honor, Poq. Please excuse me for speaking to you in this way. You are far wiser than I. But we are also friends and right now I need to speak to you as a friend. I am concerned that your sense of honor will cloud your judgment. My father, by your own admission, is a sick man. Who in their right mind plans to kill their children? Who in their right mind has their son executed for no reason other than to create an alibi? My father is like a rabid dog. Would you consider it disloyal to your dog if you were to warn other people that the dog were rabid? I don't think so. I also doubt that you would consider it disloyal to the dog to end its life in a humane way—cracking its skull with a stone, say—rather than have it inflict pain and disease on others. So I ask you, please, don't destroy yourself."

Before Poq could respond, Bella-Viola said, "And Poq, I have another request, as well."

She put her hand in his. "I may be dead in a short time. But if I am not, I would consider it a great honor if you and Arlandarose would live with me. I don't think I have ever before appreciated how much I need the support of the two of you. I don't ask for a response at this time to either of these requests. You will do what your heart tells you, and I will know your answer in the course of time."

"Miss," Poq said, putting his second hand on top of hers. "If I did not tell you this here and now, it would bruise the heart of Arlandarose. We are both at your service."

"I am blessed, Poq. Thank you."

Poq reached inside the small leather pouch he carried on his waist and drew out a small vial. "I will give you the poison. As a token of my loyalty."

Bella-Viola put the poison in her pocket, kissed Poq's hand, then walked out in the field to gather in the Sasi.

"I shall meet you here at sun-up with a plan," she called as she cantered away.

She didn't return to the cottage. Instead, after unbridling the Sasi, she asked one of the servants to tell Angelo she wanted to walk the beach and would be home after dark.

Her thoughts were only of Angelo. She knew her brothers. Her father called them "My hammers." Their strength was obedience. Only her father admired their scruples. They respected their sister's brains and abilities, but they would never take her word, or anyone else's word, over their father's. If her father told them that Angelo was responsible for their brother's death, then Angelo's death was virtually assured. And as Angelo himself had once said, vendettas last a lifetime. Her brothers would follow them to the ends of the earth. Her father's sons were nothing if not relentless.

But if that were all there were—three dangerous brothers and a demented father—she and Angelo might still stand a chance. With Poq's help, they could kill all her brothers tomorrow night while they slept. Then they could sail back to the province and surprise her father with a stiletto in the heart. Then, she and Angelo would be free.

But free to do what? It would be freedom only in a very limited sense. They would be fugitives. Their wealth would afford them great advantage. Yet, because of their wealth, they would be the targets of all sorts of bounty hunters and blackmailers and sycophants.

Yet, even that—killing her family and spending their lives as nomads and criminals, living in shadows, bribing their freedom—wasn't the worst of it.

The worst of it was that some part of her, some taint of her blood, willingly destroyed the people her Angelo loved most in the world. She was possessed by some indelible evil.

How could he survive such news? How could he look at her in the same way? How could some part of him not hate her? How could he not have his heart ripped from his chest forever? How could he not lose his purity, his joy?

How could she not protect him from this?

How could they conceive a child that would have her blood?

She would personally kill her brothers and her father on her own and keep the news from Angelo all her life, breaking her vow never to hide from him, if it also meant that he would never have to bear the pain of his family's annihilation, and the pain of knowing that the mark of Cain responsible for that annihilation was carried within his wife and any children they might conceive.

She could hear Angelo's voice from the past—on that sailboat off the port of Oran, "My love, we are not liars." And she could hear his voice from the future—tonight or tomorrow, "My love, we are not murderers. We are not criminals. To live in this way would drain our souls."

But he was mistaken. She *was* a murderer. She would leap into hell and murder anyone who threatened his happiness. She would slit the throat of Jesus Himself and spit in His face while she did it if it would spare her Angelo the pain no soul of such beauty should endure. She *could* endure it. She was her father's daughter. She was unworthy, flawed, despoiled. But not Angelo. He made pets of wild horses using only love for enticement.

Suddenly, she stopped walking. She stared out to sea. Her course of action had become as clear and uncomplicated as the moon's light gliding over the water straight to her.

Refusing to listen to her heart, she left all her clothes and all her jewelry in a pile on the beach, walked into the surf and started to swim out on the path of moonlight to the edge of the world. And on each stroke, as she exhaled into the water, she let loose a sound that terrified every living being in every ocean on earth.

*S*eventy years later, lying on her back, seeing only vague shapes and muted colors through her cataracts, those screams were one of only two sounds that Bella-Viola had heard every day since that night, when she had poisoned her Angelo rather than allow him to die at the hands of her brothers, or from desolation.

She never heard the sound that her father had made, if he had made any at all, when, less than a year after Angelo's death, she informed Domenico Priami that she now held title to all his debts and all his assets, which meant that the chair in which he was sitting was hers and he would kindly stand up and never sit in a home of hers again for as long as he lived. "Unless, of course, you prefer to have your arms and legs and tongue removed, a custom that my family, the Angelinos, reserve for our most despised enemies."

It hadn't been difficult. Her intimate knowledge of his dealings, and her wealth, made it simple to arrange details that, earlier, would have been impossible to slip by this most calculating of men.

She had informed her father, "From this day forward, you may live only out of doors, in the mountains of the Province." She would provide him food, and that was all. She was having him transported there in a wagon that very day. Once there, he would travel only by foot. He would be watched at all times. Anyone who spoke to him would be executed. Escape was impossible. Because her brothers worked for their father and owned nothing in their own right, she essentially seized control of their lives when she appropriated Domenico Priami's holdings. And that was her intent. They would now work for her, or be paupers. And to commemorate the occasion, she gave each brother and her father a gold vial of poison, and said to them, "Anytime you wish to end our arrangement, here is your quickest and, believe me, easiest way out."

It was an option her father availed himself of before the wagon in which he was riding ever reached the mountains.

Bella-Viola refused to have her father buried in the family crypt. Her mother and grandmother would be the last Priamis to be interred in that sacred sepulcher. Instead, Bella-Viola had her father's body burned in one of the many fires that consumed all of his worldly possessions, including the vineyards, the winery, the homes, the barns, the ships and every other scrap of Domenico Priami's domain. The only personal effect of her father's that Bella-Viola did not burn was his bullwhip. This she placed on a hook over the fireplace in her sleeping chamber, Angelo's sleeping chamber on the Angelino estate, the blessed chamber where she and Angelo had spent their wedding night, and now a room whose walls would remain forever bare, save the whip.

In the harshness of the rules she imposed on her brothers, one of them followed their father's lead soon after his cremation.

Another disappeared until, a year later, a foreigner arrived at Bella-Viola's gate with what he claimed was her brother's head in a box. The foreigner said he wished to give the head to Bella-Viola for proper burial. According to the foreigner, her brother had been beheaded by pirates and the foreigner had been her brother's friend. The foreigner hoped that, in return for his kindness, Bella-Viola might see her way to giving him a small pouch of gold to cover the expense of his journey. Without even looking at the head, Bella-Viola laughed as though this man were a traveling jester, then she said, "You are to take yourself and the head out of the Province by nightfall or I shall have your eyes removed." The head could have been that of the Blessed Virgin and Bella-Viola wouldn't have cared.

Tino, the youngest, died in a duel, or so it seemed, which is precisely how Bella-Viola wanted it to appear. By the time of her fifth wedding anniversary, in her 21st year of life, the bride and widow of Angelo Angelino did not have a single living blood relative.

Angelo had, of course, died in her arms, his face covered in her tears. He had needed to taste barely a sip of the wine that was their nightly ritual before making love. She had lain next to him, their faces inches apart, as he struggled to breathe, her hand on his heart. "My love. My love," she repeated, weeping, until he stopped her with the other sound, the second sound that had haunted her every day since. Looking into her eyes, he whispered something he had never said to her before.

"Why . . . are you . . . hiding from me?"

Now she lay on ground that tomorrow, she prayed, would be her own grave, next to the graves of Angelo, Poq and Arlandarose, each body carefully prepared and entombed in the Egyptian tradition so that it might be preserved in case such preservation gave their spirits a better chance to meet in the afterlife. Their graves marked the four directions around the stone altar: Angelo in the east; Arlandarose in the south; Poq in the west; and tomorrow she, Bella-Viola, would be buried in the north, her only adornment her father's bullwhip coiled around her shoulder. Her wedding ring she had thrown into the sea after burying Angelo. She wasn't worthy of it.

No one but she, Poq and Arlandarose ever knew how Angelo had died. Now it would be just the four of them on the island, the four of them and dozens of wild Sasi horses.

Once again, as she did as a bride, as a girl full of love and dreams, she would give herself completely to Angelo.

It was too much to ask that he might ever again look upon her in wonder and gratitude, as he had every day of their lives together. But she prayed, as she had for seventy years, that he might at least forgive her. For seventy years, she had lived with that look of bewilderment on his beautiful face. If she could only just erase that look. "If he can forgive just that much." That was her heart's only hope.

For certainly, she could never forgive herself. A vial of the poison she kept on her person all these years as a reminder that she was undeserving of a quick and painless death. She had earned these 70 years of hell, not to mention the eternity of damnation that was sure to follow.

5

Death

As her essence dissolved into the One—the wave sinking back into the ocean from which it arose—Bella-Viola was overcome by a deep, quiet sense of absolute belonging. It was as if she were resting in the crook of her mother's arm, feeding at her mother's breast, bare minutes after birth, and everything that had occurred over the succeeding 90 years had been no more than a firefly spark.

Simultaneously, for she now existed in a kind of eternal present, a little like being in two places at once, well, more like one hundred and two, or one thousand and two, Bella-Viola felt a pain that surprised her. She could have opened the door to this boundless acceptance at any time. The key had been nothing more than forgiveness, forgiving herself for any choice, ever, made in fear. And if she had, when she had, as she had, utterly, completely, forgiven herself (no longer holding to her even the smallest vibration of recrimination), she would have entered this sacred space, this holy sound within her where spirit and nature danced together perpetually, ecstatically, blazing like a million suns.

Which was why, like just about everyone else when they die, there was a moment when Bella-Viola found herself shaking her head so to speak (given that she had no head), saying it's hard to believe that the only thing I have ever been afraid of is loving myself.

Leaving behind her little hut of bones and small self perceptions––which she had cherished so strongly and grasped so ferociously––she knew that everything about herself except this fire of her inner heart was nothing, really: the way a bloodthirsty dragon made of soap bubbles is nothing, really. She realized that, over lifetimes, she had created and perpetuated a mosaic of beliefs, habits, judgments and preferences for no reason other than fear, the fear of opening to the supreme truth at the center of her being: that the Cosmic Beloved, the Divine, the Mother Of All Mothers, the Friend Behind All Friends had become her. Everything that kept her from that knowing was simply a part of her that was afraid to surrender to the inevitable embrace of who she really was, unwilling to join the call animating her every breath, her every heartbeat: *Hold on to nothing / Hold on to nothing.* It wasn't that she was God. It was that God has fashioned Itself into all manner of identities she mistook for her, including a woman capable of betraying her one true love. She was no more that than she was a horse that pooped chocolate drops. She had been clay shaped into a goblet, or a statue, or a dog's bowl for that matter. Then, at the instigation of some strange alchemy, some divine trickery or test perhaps, she began to think of herself as a goblet, a statue, a dog's bowl—forgetting she was nothing but clay, ignoring the whisper of her inner heart: *No, no, my dear, you are much more than that.*

And so, as it does for everyone at death, her self-hatred dissolved in the presence of a love so encompassing that it obliterated anything that was not love, and as it did Bella-Viola knew, without any guilt or blame, how simply unaware she had been. Not evil, or damned, as she had believed, just unaware. Ignorant. She had been viewing all of her experiences, making all of her choices, through the eyes of fear. Now she saw them through the eyes of compassion—the eyes of the universe as a whole, the eyes of love. This didn't make the consequences of her choices go away. The pain they caused, to herself and to others, to the web of creation, was real. But now she knew the true nature of pain: that it was a call to awaken, a bridge to heal, an opening to ever-deeper forgiveness—as her being continued its journey in whatever lives of mind and body lay ahead. And, in the presence of this unalloyed acceptance, she felt something afresh, something she remembered from her previous returns to spirit at the completion of other lives.

She felt gratitude.

But this, all this, was nothing new. She had learned it before. Endless times before, even, each time her spirit dropped its most recent physical husk and returned to this astral consciousness unencumbered by the dualities of this and that, right and wrong, us and them, success and failure, praise and blame, on and on. The world as ordinarily perceived was no more real than a pencil sketch. Everything she believed about herself was no more real than a story that began, "*Once upon a time . . . .*" Only this, this all-consuming vibration of unconditional love was real. This was the essential substance of the universe. This was who she truly was.

Why, then, when she returned to earth for another round of worldly birth and death, did she forget?

Isn't it odd to think of myself as Pearl, or as Bella-Viola? I'm neither, really, am I? Reliving life as Bella-Viola is essentially the same as reliving a game I played last week, or an apple I ate this morning.

*E*xperiencing the death of herself as Bella-Viola, Pearl met her True Self.

Gone was her identity: woman, daughter, friend, athlete, student, samurai . . . .

Silent was the perpetual chatter of her mind: weighing, assessing, criticizing, cajoling, rebuking, comparing . . . .

Absent was the drive to *be* anything: responsible, kind, worthy, honorable, loyal, thin, beautiful, smart, persistent . . . .

Evaporated was the need to *do* anything: compete, achieve, acquire . . . .

And vanished was the quest for amassing knowledge.

Empty of every familiar born of fear, Pearl experienced what could only be called her heart's desire. Understanding. Not the mind's acquisitiveness, its grasping, its need to build, to know, to hoard, to leverage, but the soul's openness without aspiration, its attunement without conditions or preconceptions, and thus its recognition that every conceivable question has already been answered, has always been answered, and that life has nothing to do with creation and everything to do with discovery.

And what Pearl discovered, understood, knew, was that a butterfly's flutter in Africa can indeed contribute to an Oklahoma tornado. There is no incidental corner, or being, or feeling, or action, or thought. Separation is an illusion. Differences are an illusion. A smile of the heart in her backyard kissed babies who wouldn't be born for a million years. Every choice ever made reverberates throughout the web of creation for all time.

And no matter what sound she ever heard . . . or what image she ever saw . . . or what object or being she ever touched . . . or emotion she ever felt . . . or food she ever tasted . . . all she would ever be experiencing—truly— was the call of the universe to love. And it was a call expressed, among other ways, by the most powerful word in any language, more powerful even than the word love itself, for this word represented the choice that set into motion all of one's life that led to joy, a word that she could feel and hear and touch and taste in every atom of creation, for it was the word that her newfound heart exclaimed with passion.

"*Yess!*"

$$6$$

Freeing Bella-Viola

ritten somewhere is a story of a man who relates a remarkable and elaborate tale about his life. Only at the end of the story does the reader learn that the entire account, thousands of words, has been told in the time that it takes for a bullet to exit the barrel of a gun and smash into the storyteller's brain, for the man was standing in front of a firing squad. Which is to say, not much time at all.

Pearl's life, that morning, had been concentrated in a similar fashion. All that she experienced as she attempted to throw that first pitch to Hyman took but a few ticks of the world's clock. Yet, she emerged from a journey of years, lifetimes really, so deepened was her awareness of who she was.

Only one who believed that the world ended at the limits of reason would call this a miracle.

True enough, though, Pearl felt changes within her that she might never have words for, as if each of her cells were now fatter, bigger, more alive, able of absorbing more dimensions of existence, a greater spectrum of light, more frequencies of sound, more subtleties of touch, and so forth.

Like a hundred cups of paint, each paint a different color, tossed simultaneously into a hundred roaring fans, which then explode the paint against a single giant canvas: the resulting image might begin to suggest the emotions that coexisted within Pearl: Bella-Viola's despair, her fear, her hatred, her loss, her love of Angelo, Pearl's own rage at her father, her fear of her mother, her love of them both, her pain at the loss of innocence, her longing to love without reservation, her terror of not being enough—and all of that at one with the inherent benevolence of the universe, loving her without condition, without reservation, nurturing her.

The collective hurricane of sensation overwhelmed her body's wiring. She was on fire. Her teeth chattered. Her muscles collapsed in the way that a marathoner's might upon crossing the finish line. She wept. And laughed. And wept some more.

She was lying on wet grass, that she knew. She hadn't remembered falling. Her glove had been placed under her head. Her sense was that Hyman was beside her, sitting on his haunches, his right hand, palm down, in the air a couple of inches over her heart. Her stomach, her heart and her head felt acutely warm.

She opened her eyes for a moment, wet with perspiration and tears.

He was looking out over the lake to the east and smiling in a way that gave her comfort. Whatever it was that had just happened, she was alright, even though she couldn't have stopped the tears if she had wanted to, nor the million emotions that accompanied them.

He looked at her and said, "Stay within for now . . . ."

She had already closed her eyes. Her face was on fire. All of her was on fire. Her hair was soaked in sweat.

"The things you have experienced are not small," Hyman said. "You probably feel that even the cells of your body have been changed. And they have. So now is an especially good time to love yourself by becoming energetically as big as you possibly can."

Hyman paused, letting his words sink in.

"Feel yourself as a hose trying to contain a torrent of water," he continued. "Only this torrent is Niagara Falls. So you need to be a very big hose. That's why you want to breathe-in the unconditional love of the Earth Mother, making yourself as large as you can be. And when you exhale, let go of everything that comes up, everything you meet within: fear, pain, love, everything. Even gratitude. Let it go out your muscles, out your bones, out your skin—right down through your buttocks and down through your feet into the earth. Nothing serves us if we hold on to it."

Pearl felt Hyman put his other hand, palm down, a couple of inches over her stomach. The two hands, one over her heart, the other over her belly, helped to focus the energy that was flowing out of her.

On her in-breath, she felt the love of creation rush through every pore. It frightened her. This acceptance. So much love. Her first impulse was to run. But her connection to the ground steadied her, soothed her.

But then, when she exhaled, she felt naked, incredibly vulnerable. Fear alive with panic. She shook.

Still, she found that as she opened her body and grew bigger, she could guide the fear out of her quite easily with her breath.

A new awareness arose within her cells. Fear limits the amount of love we can take in. It was like physics. Two objects cannot occupy the same space at the same time. And as more fear now moved from her, the more pliant she felt, the more soft, spacious—ready to take in a deeper breath the next time, and the next, and the next. Her legs and pelvis felt large and supple.

Then another new sensation arose. Softness in her face. A mask was melting. An old her, a familiar her, was dying. The Samurai. Her life was slipping away. The fear of it caused her to shake.

Again, grow bigger, make room.

If you were big enough, it was possible to let go of anything.

Each inhale increased the intensity of the fires she now felt: below her belly-button, in her solar plexus, her heart, her throat, and in her forehead. And as she breathed out through her pores, she felt the fires form a river flowing down her spine and out of her body to the ground, washing her clean of any fear that she had been willing to let go of.

She was a fish: breathing in water, breathing out water; breathing in love, breathing out love. She was a thousand feet tall, draped over the countryside, being nursed by the earth, yet also giving all of herself to the earth.

"*P*earl," Hyman said after a while. "If you choose, you can perform a great service to your self as Bella-Viola."

Several breaths later he continued.

"You can serve her in a way she could not serve herself. You can free the unforgiveness she carried to her death, unforgiveness you yourself have been holding onto all your lifetimes from then to now.

"You know that Bella-Viola couldn't free herself. That she was too afraid. But you, Pearl, can do it for her. You can free that part of you. All you have to do is feel her fear and let it wash through you. Under it you will find the unforgiveness that dried the life right out of Bella-Viola. And you can let that go, too. You can allow the you that is Bella-Viola to forgive herself, and to find peace."

Bella-Viola's fear rose to Pearl's throat causing her to gasp. And as she allowed the fear to become present in her being, and as she felt the pain created by that fear, Pearl's heart split open.

Bella-Viola's choices, Pearl understood to her soul, had been made for only one reason: she had been afraid, and instead of freeing the fear, she held onto it year after year, lifetime after lifetime.

Her fear had led her to choose to murder the love of her life, her heart's true playmate, and the losses she had to live with from that one act alone were more painful than being burned alive: the loss of his touch, his laugh, their games in bed, his attunement to his heart and to the hearts of others, the loss of their children never to be, the loss of his way of looking at her, the loss of the life they had planned, the loss of watching him train a horse, or tend a garden, the loss of becoming friends with his mothers, his father, his brothers, the loss of perhaps even burying him as an old man, surrounded by their children and grandchildren . . . all these losses and countless others . . . all because she was, simply, utterly, afraid. And because she was afraid, Bella-Viola had made herself deaf to her heart as it begged her, implored her, pleaded with her to make another choice that night on Sasi. And the pain of denying that request had been unimaginable ever since.

Fear had also led her to choose to destroy her father and brothers. And what had she gained? Unforgiveness is no more than fear—the fear of loving something in another that we hate about ourselves. Bella-Viola was her father's daughter in that respect, for sure. As insane as her father was for killing the Angelinos and his own son, it was her fear, not his insanity, that had prevented her from loving him and her brothers. They had, all of them, been afraid—she, her father, her brothers—always, and that fear literally ate them alive.

For five hundred years and whatever number of incarnations, the agony of Bella-Viola's choices and her unwillingness to forgive herself for them had been a prison for the heart of the being now known as Pearl. By feeling the pain of this prison, and the fear that created it, and by forgiving herself for her choices, Pearl opened her being to greater love and compassion than she had ever known. And with that compassion came a kind of cellular, universal knowing of things. She, Pearl, now understood the fear that drove her father's addiction to alcohol and women and work, and her mother's addiction to power. She understood the fear of the many politicians, business bigwigs and various celebrities who passed through their home. And just as clearly she understood the fear that spurred her own need to achieve, to be the best at everything, to be perfect, to be beautiful, to be smart, to destroy anyone who came to bat while she was on the mound.

It was her True Self, her soul, she was speaking to as she whispered over and over, "I am so sorry." Again and again, her heart shuddered as she experienced and released the pain of denial—denying the call of her heart to love. Waves of fear and pain washed through her into the depthless Mother of All.

R e-entry was a kind of re-birth. So much was new in the world that had once, minutes before, seemed so familiar.

A dragonfly landed on a stem of wheat grass, and sat there swaying in the breeze, serene as a queen, delivering the message that it was now Pearl's time to begin seeing beyond the illusion of everyday experience.

An ant hiked over Pearl's outstretched arm. Patience, it counseled. What is yours will come to you, my dear. Trust in the universe to provide.

And what of Squirrel who stopped to check her out between trips around the neighborhood? Create a safe place for your treasures, but don't be fooled. The only safe place is an untroubled heart, and the only treasures are wisdom and caring.

Pearl recalled a radio interview she once heard with a famous avant-garde composer who, when asked what his favorite piece of music was, said the sound of the avenue outside his Manhattan apartment. It was always fresh, always an expression of the full range of life's possibilities, and most importantly, it was, in all its diversity, a celebration of the heart. Even the murder he had once heard, surprisingly enough. Now Pearl knew what he was talking about, not just in terms of sound, but also in terms of smells, light, shadows, shapes and movement—of birds and breeze, clouds, a dog's yip across the lake, the rise and fall of her own breath, the sun's hand on her forehead, the scent of burning brush from somewhere down the way, the skin on her face—all new, all new.

Again, tears. A heart breaking with reverence.

Gratitude. Such gratitude.

Then, after a tender, leisurely while, she and Hyman ate bananas.

7

Uncle Charlie

As the sun burned off the lake's early morning mist typical in late August, the only signs of human life had been a few solitary souls in rowboats with small outboard motors—trolling for trout. They sat like monks in prayer, these folk, one hand rising and falling repeatedly to and from their heart, though not in mea culpa. Line in hand, the gesture kept their lure tantalizing. Their engines putt-putted a nearly inaudible "*. . . om-om-om-om-om-om . . . .*" If there were ever a daybreak from April to October when a dozen or so trollers were not scattered up and down the lake as far as the eye could see, a person would know that the world had come to an end.

Now that the dawn was well into morning, most of the trollers had gone home; if lucky, to a breakfast of pan-fried fish and eggs, maybe a few onions, some hash-browns, a cold beer perhaps. That was Pearl's father's favorite.

It was one of those mornings when the water was glass. "Virgin water the water-boarders call it," Pearl had said.

They sat barefoot at the lake's edge, pants rolled, water just over their feet.

Even a blind woman would have said that Pearl was radiant. That's because a person's skin glows in direct relationship to how much their cells vibrate with love—and it is a glow that, like an evening bonfire, one feels as much as sees.

For some time the two of them had been sitting there all but wordless. Once you've experienced the universe at work, Pearl thought, what's to say?

After an hour or so in which the only sound either of them made was Pearl plopping an occasional pebble into the water just beyond her toes, Pearl snorted and put her hand over her mouth, attempting to contain an amusing thought.

It didn't work.

She exploded in gaiety as if witness to the silliest scene a person could ever behold. She whacked Hyman a playful slap on the shoulder then collapsed onto her back, shrieking in delight, on and on, unable to speak, barely able to breathe, her laughter soaring and diving, subsiding a little until she seemed to remember the scene afresh whereupon hilarity, once again, whirled her out of control. This continued for several minutes before Pearl was finally able to speak, squeaking out words quickly before she lost control: "I was just thinking of all the things I take so . . .," then, a quick gulp of air permitted her to pour forth in a pretend radio announcer's basso, ". . . so goddam seriously"—which set off another round of laughter, somewhere within which Pearl peeped: "Sam Are I."

Joy, it must be said, is highly contagious, if one is open to its infection, which Hyman O'Malley most assuredly was, the way a screen door is open to the breeze. So he joined in Pearl's mirth with a gusto seldom seen in those parts since the day God put His funny looking hand on the Earth and created all those lakes.

Only to someone like the passenger in the limousine now parked next to Hyman's truck would revulsion be the response to the scene below: A middle aged man and a college girl rolling around on the shore howling with laughter. And then, spurred by their rapture, tossing pebbles at each other, then splashing one other, first a little, then more frantically, until they were both soaked, and then, standing in water up to their knees, dripping with pleasure, they suddenly flopped backward into the lake, limbs flailing, mouths hooting, legs kicking—school children on the first day of summer vacation.

Finally, they helped one another up, clothes sloshed to their bodies, faces suns of delight and tenderness, each illuminating the other.

Had he known what had transpired between the two since daybreak, the man in the limo would have pursed his lips ever so slightly. It was an involuntary reflex that his closest associates recognized as the precursor to a strong opinion.

As it was, what the man saw next provoked that tremor of lips and jaw. Just before the man and the girl stepped onto the shore and looked up to where he was now standing in front of his bullet-proof Lincoln, they hugged.

"*I*t's Uncle Charlie!" Pearl sang, delighted and unsurprised.

Whoever Uncle Charlie was, Hyman thought, he traveled with a number of folks who dressed like the people you see in movies playing Secret Service agents.

Uncle Charlie, by contrast, dressed like the people you see in movies playing important men brunching at a posh yacht club on Sunday—white linen suit, aviator sunglasses, sky blue oxford shirt, and a striped bow-tie the colors of which reminded anyone in the know of where the neck it encircled had gone to prep school.

Uncle Charlie was probably even more important than that, just going by people you see in movies, because although he wore alligator loafers as soft as your grandmother's ear lobe, he was evidently confident enough of his place in the world to wear a gold sock on one foot and a blue sock on the other.

Besides that, whoever Uncle Charlie was, energetically he reminded Hyman at first glance of the cartoon character he sometimes faced on the mud flaps of eighteen-wheelers—Yosemite Sam—a short, fierce, bow-legged backwoodsman in a humongous handlebar mustache, cowboy boots and shapeless hat who sported a six-gun in each hand, and whose two-word message, imprinted boldly under his image, was *Back Off*. Not that anyone present but Hyman would ever make that association by simply looking at Uncle Charlie. His mask was that of a man in complete control of his world, a man who was seldom not the smartest person in the room, and if, on some rare occasion, he wasn't, well, he was surely the most influential. Tanned and manicured, thick salt and pepper hair brushed straight back, but a bit wild, like Beethoven, flares of white at the temples, teeth that long ago had been braced to uniformity, even the scar slicing his eyebrow and the nose which had obviously been broken a time or two added to his aura of worldly competence.

Yet what Hyman felt most for the guy was brotherly compassion. It arose, at least in part, from the recognition that what possessed Uncle Charlie was what had possessed Hyman in more than one previous life: a deep desire to serve, to love—imprisoned—as if wrapped in concertina wire, by the need for others to think he was larger than life.

Since she was soaking wet, rather than give Uncle Charlie a hug, Pearl bowed and said, "Hello, uncle dear. Meet my new friend, Hyman O'Malley. Hyman, it is my honor to introduce you to my favorite uncle, Mr. Charles Greenstreet Fox, my mother's baby brother."

Hyman held out his hand, "Mr. Fox, a pleasure to meet another member of the family. How do you do? I hope my hand isn't too wet for you."

This was Hyman's way of making it almost impossible for Uncle Charlie to avoid shaking hands, which, Hyman knew, had been Charlie Fox's intention—his way of conveying displeasure to this middle-aged stranger who was attempting who knew what with Fox's only and beloved niece.

Hyman couldn't tell why, but he knew that in the circles Uncle Charlie traveled, his conspicuous avoidance of shaking someone's hand carried with it an implied judgment that the person left standing with an empty palm found unsettling. But Hyman had long ago given up enabling such childishness, so he simply did Charlie Fox the favor of making it unrewarding for him, in that moment, to choose pettiness.

Fox hesitated. Then, because he was a master of cutting someone off at the knees and getting a thank you in reply, he took Hyman's outstretched hand and said with all the warmth of a Christmas Eve fireplace on television, "Not at all. How do you do, Mister O'Malley. I've enjoyed catching up on your life story."

To be sure, the purpose of Uncle Charlie's statement was intimidation, to demonstrate that he, President of the United States, could know everything there was to know about anyone, and furthermore that he enjoyed the discretion to use that information as he saw fit.

Hyman was oblivious. Without even trying he always knew a person's intentions; that was how he knew Fox's plan not to shake hands, and of course when Hyman felt like it he could read minds, but what he didn't read was the newspaper, or magazines, and certainly not electioneering propaganda, nor did he watch television, or listen to the radio. Unless of course directed to by his inner guidance, which happened seldom enough to keep Hyman in relative darkness about the ever-changing currents of so-called worldly affairs. So when it came to knowing the precise earthly identity of Uncle Charlie, at least before he shook the man's hand, Hyman knew only that Fox must be important, if only to himself and some number of others intoxicated by a certain kind of social achievement.

The handshake was something else again. To all others present—Pearl, the Secret Service detail, Miles (the President's lifelong chauffeur) plus Fox's aide, Vicky Ski—the handshake lasted no longer than what might be called normal. But to Fox and Hyman, it lasted five days. And on the other side of those days, Hyman knew several things about Uncle Charlie, the least important of which was that he was President of the United States.

More noteworthy was the fact that President Fox feared Hyman O'Malley more than he had ever feared any other person on earth, and thus would destroy O'Malley at the earliest possible moment. Uncle Charlie thought, *If I could have the Secret Service blow his brains out right here, I would.*

It wasn't that he might die at the hand of Charlie Fox that unsettled Hyman. Death, he knew, when it came, was full of grace.

Rather, it was the chilling and savage insanity of fear, the unwavering disregard for its consequences, its consuming delusion that revenge or retribution or annihilation of a despised "other" led to resolution or satisfaction rather than to ever-greater fear, darkness, self-hatred, harm and heartbreak—this was the insanity that Hyman knew had been set into motion through his handshake with Charlie Fox.

This was the black side of being the person his clairvoyant mother had nicknamed Mirror Man. Some people, like Pearl, flowered with what the Divine, using him as a playtoy, revealed to them about themselves. Others were indifferent, not ready to comprehend the gift, the way a stone-age man might ignore the utility of steel, or an illiterate man might not grasp the power of a fountain pen. Hyman never quite understood why the Divine gave people experiences they weren't ready to use, but that was God's problem. Hyman was merely an instrument. Who experienced what in his presence and for what reason was completely out of his hands. But in some people, in this case Charlie Fox, what was awakened included the willingness to destroy anything and anyone to preserve the illusion of control, to deny the void of unknowing and depthless vulnerability at the core of normal human consciousness, and in particular to prevent the world from learning secrets that would mean public humiliation, which, for Fox, meant the end of his presidency and the end of the life he had manufactured so scrupulously.

8

Charlie Fox, 20 Years Earlier

This was right up there with the first time he and his sister made love.

Imagine. Him, a Yale man, a Rhodes Scholar, some day with any luck President of the United States. What was the most outrageous thing you could ever conceive such a person doing?

An ingénue, a teenager most likely, pure as spring—tossed overboard in mid-ocean, his rose in her hand.

Whoever she was she'd be light in weight and gladly spending time with him in a quiet corner of the deck when just about everyone else was otherwise occupied. Late at night, possibly. They'd make up stories about the many glamorous passengers who've sailed the *Proteus* over the years. Or early morning, heads over the rail, straining their eyes for dolphins at first light.

A girl with a melancholy turn, someone who wrote poetry about the beauty of death, would be ridiculously ideal—since suicide was to be the natural inference. The savage god. The voluptuousness of oblivion. It happened, he had read: sometimes planned, other times the open arms of the ocean were just too seductive, the way scuba divers sometimes removed their mouthpieces to breathe as one with their true family at sea bottom.

The possible scenarios were endless, but none of them made any difference to him. His capped teeth, the crook in his Roman nose, the new moon scar slicing his right eyebrow reminded him every time he checked the mirror that he'd been a hockey All-American in college. He knew the principle of taking what your opponent gives you, going with the flow.

For these and other reasons, not the least of which was that this would be a one-time event—for, as Voltaire said in declining to participate in a second consecutive evening of orgy: "Once: a philosopher; twice: a pervert"—he, Charlie Fox, would not get caught.

The possibility never entered Fox's mind until, upon being awarded the Rhodes, he learned that, for Yalies, it came with complimentary first-class passage on any of the ocean liners owned by alumnus Theodoros "Teddy" Padopolous, himself an old Rhodie.

Fox had traveled by ship once before—the reward for winning an essay contest by detailing why the formation of an international body, similar to the United Nations only with teeth, would give the planet even a remote chance during his lifetime of preventing irreversible degradation of the oceans—so he knew that shipboard was an ideal venue for a clean, quick, virtually invisible murder: no blood, and no evident corpse. If you were smart about it. It really was efficiency at its best. His job was to also make it elegant.

The superior hunter feels the lioness long before she appears. So he would feel the moment approach. And when it did, he would, effortlessly as you please, introduce the topic of the foot.

Know what standing here reminds me of?
What?
A foot . . . . No, really, a person's foot.
Goodness. How?
The foot is symbolic of the human soul.
Umm . . . what's that mean, exactly?

Well, the foot supports man upright. If it weren't for our feet, we wouldn't be standing here, right now, experiencing all this . . . Neptune's magic.

Maybe she'd be Miss Curious. Maybe not. He was ready regardless. If she hadn't thought he was wonderful she wouldn't be there. If the world hadn't thought he was wonderful, he wouldn't be on his way to Oxford.

Soon there would be another moment, the one when he inquired, as if it had just struck him, whether she would like him to point out a couple of details about her own foot. *"You know, things we all take for granted?" he would say with a chuckle. "Our Achilles Heel, for instance, since this is, after all, a Greek ship."*

She would brighten.

However it unfolded, with him on one knee in front of her (*"playing Sir Galahad,"* he would say, shyly), she would willingly place her bare foot in his bare palm, the same palm that had once snared a hockey puck out of mid-air at 80 miles an hour. It had been another jewel in his good name, preventing the crushed face of his coach's newborn daughter sleeping in her mother's lap at practice one morning. He'd played out the season with a broken hand, which was nothing. Now he carried the pain of that choice, constant as his heartbeat. And, like his heartbeat, he felt the pain most acutely when he exerted the hand. But that, too, was nothing—would be nothing. Pain was the measure of all things, and he was destined to be its master.

He might ask her to close her eyes and rest her hands on his head for balance so that she might feel her foot more completely: a gesture of intimacy that could be the perfect punctuation to his betrayal. He would also ask her to exhale through her fingers and toes, emptying her body of all tension so that, again, she might deepen her sensitivity. This would, of course, also empty her lungs, limiting the sounds of surprise or, more problematic, terror, though the wind and the sea were excellent mufflers and he and the girl would be on the lowest deck, closest to the water, and the entire event would be over in not much more than the time it takes to sneeze. He would ask her to snuggle her foot even further into his hand so that he might discern its subtleties, and the instant she did, he, as though giving her a leg up on a horse, would thrust her into the air and over the railing, backwards, into the black. Her foot might kick out involuntarily in defense, but that would simply propel her faster, pushing as it would against the resistance of his rising hand. There would be no time to thank her for making his task that much easier and, truth be told, enjoyable.

Which is why he couldn't act in a way that was gutless. That didn't fit his standards. An older woman on her own, say, while perhaps easy, was cheap. Who cares about the disappearance of someone who has pretty much lived her life compared to the unexpected death of a teenager? That was his preference. More than a preference. He wasn't committed to murder. He was committed to the right kind of murder.

And as it had his entire life, Fate answered his desires, this time presenting a possibility so remarkable he felt anointed.

To sit with a family in warmest conviviality for a dozen meals and then, with them feeling blessed by the serendipity of you as their dining companion, crush their life's continuity by inflicting a tragedy of Shakespearian proportions—that was the level of darkness he was being offered. It was as if the universe were holding up the sign that hung in the men's locker room at Yale: *Go Big or Stay Home.*

Still, he mustn't be impetuous.

Surely the Markses were unbelievably tempting. Father Clyde, a bald, kindly old bulldog with tortoiseshell glasses and a gray fringe of hair that would pass inspection at Parris Island; a professor at the Wharton School in Philadelphia, on his way to a year's sabbatical in Malaysia to immerse himself in something incomprehensible to anyone but a handful of international monetary experts. Mother Queenan: all she lacked from being someone's favorite nana were the offspring of her son or daughter. She had just retired as Headmistress of an exclusive girl's academy on Philadelphia's Main Line.

She was a woman who had never bought even a hairpin that wasn't the very best. Son Arjay, age 28, budding art history professor at Princeton, built like a Number 2 pencil, eraserhead brown hair, black round glasses, never without a book, a clean shirt at every meal, possibly gay. He'd be flying back to the states as soon as they reached Singapore. And, the prize, daughter Sylvie, 13.

"We're a lucky family, Charlie," Queenan had said. "Our kids still enjoy traveling with the old folks. This is the fifth time we've spent a month on the water like this."

Yet, fixating on Sylvie, or on anyone too soon, might blind him to danger. He mustn't abandon his original strategy: cultivate the affections of three girls, then select the best as his trophy. The other two would become alibis, along with everyone else with whom he would strike up a conversation and swap addresses: proof of his sociability far beyond the sphere of his acquaintance with the deceased. All of them would, in fact, confirm his immaculate reputation.

Timing was tight. The *Proteus* would be at sea only four nights. The toss would take place either late the last night or early the following morning before they docked in Southampton, unless opportunity smiled on him before then. First, he had to identify three prospects, though that was by far the easiest part: watching from the sidelines came naturally to him. Then, each girl had to become appropriately infatuated. Not romantically infatuated. Or sexually, to be sure. But infatuated in the manner that a young person is around a rising star who takes special interest in her—exploring her aspirations, pointing out her talents, and perhaps most of all . . . listening. He was exceptional at all those things. That was what this whole venture was about: testing the fruits of his hard work in creating himself. A sort of valedictory.

The first of the two other girls was on her way home to Austria. She'd just spent her last year of high school in Manassas, Virginia as an exchange student. Her world was music. She didn't play any. She studied it. Her father was a cobbler. In the evening cool, she wore a royal blue wool cape trimmed in green filigree. Her red-haired, green-eyed purity reminded Fox of a young nun, though her god was Mozart. Crossing the ocean by ship had been the reason she'd signed up for the exchange program; she was thrilled to travel "last-class," as she put it: a berth with five other girls. Fox engaged her while tug boats were guiding the *Proteus* into Chesapeake Bay. Miss Mozart and he had found themselves elbow to elbow at the railing before the ship cast off: she waving to her Virginia family on the pier below; Fox's eyes riveted on his sister, Shorty. Shorty was looking up at him, her right hand on her heart signing, "I love you." Once they were beyond the harbor, Fox suggested to Miss Mozart that they take a walk and explore the ship, and when in their travels they encountered the baby grand piano sitting unused in the ballroom, Fox sat down at the keyboard and sealed the girl's admiration with a respectable Adagio and Fugue; or at least the first few minutes of it: the part he rehearsed regularly, just as he rehearsed bon mots in a variety of languages, for precisely such occasions. At sunrise the following day, they took tea on the fantail. If he didn't have enough cocktail knowledge about the world's greatest composer before meeting Miss Mozart, he certainly did after. Within a couple of days, at Fox's enticement, she wrote Amadeus a letter. When she read it aloud to Fox, he made particular note of one line: "Your sweet soul I shall never know 'til every string lifting this adoring puppet is snipped."

Then there was the captain of a high school cheerleading squad in Florida whose peroxide hair looked as though it were regularly nibbled by goats. Fox first saw her sitting on the deck, wrapped in a blanket, reading Emily Dickinson. How perfect is that, he thought. It turned out she knew next to nothing about the reclusive Belle of Amherst. The book had been her older sister's. And her sister had died of cancer in the Spring. The cheerleader kept the book with her all the time, along with a journal, her first, a gift from her minister. She was on her way to South Africa with her grandmother to visit family she'd never met before. For Fox, she wrote in her journal 10 things she wanted to say to her sister. They included questions about the sister's new life and the pain of her death, as well as an expression of the joy the cheerleader would feel when she and her sister reunited in heaven.

Sylvie, youngest of the three by several years, almost always wore a blue button-down shirt and a bow tie some variation of purple. This would be accompanied by men's tuxedo trousers abbreviated into shorts with cuffs. She usually wore suspenders, bright orange. Her shoes might be rubber flip-flops, or hand-painted Converse sneakers. She didn't own a pair of socks she told Fox. Her shoulder-length hair, most often casually twisted and pinned with a brass butterfly clip, was the color of dark maple syrup animated with manmade flecks of magenta, turquoise and gold. Sometime during the day she might wear a fake mustache. Without it, a person might wonder if she were a model, so classically beautiful was her face.

"Hello again, Mister Fox," was her opening remark when they were introduced at dinner that first evening.

There were to be six of them dining together for the Baltimore to Southampton leg of the *Proteus's* round-the-world voyage—the four Markses and Fox, plus a tall black kid from Chicago, Pittman Diggs, on his way to Paris where he was about to begin his third year of dance school despite looking barely fifteen.

"We've met before?" Fox inquired.

"Oh yes. Many times. We've been great friends. And enemies. What do you suppose will happen this time?"

She could have been speaking in tongues; all Fox could do was smile and allow the moment to pass.

Next morning, after breakfast, he was sitting by himself in a starboard deck chair staring at the southern sky, Bolitho's *Twelve Against the Gods* open on his lap. The last thing he'd read was, "*We, like the eagles, were born to be free. Yet we are obliged, in order to live at all, to make a cage of laws for ourselves and to stand on the perch.*" Suddenly there was Sylvie sitting next to him, red plastic sunglasses with heart-shaped frames, her hand on his solar plexus. He almost threw up, so strong was his aversion to being touched—anywhere, but Jesus, not there.

"Easy, Mister Fox," she said. "No need to be afraid of me. I'll leave you in peace. But when I get up, feel inside of you. There are two big horses in there, one pulling your heart open, the other pulling it closed. You want to be invulnerable. But you also want to love. That's why I'm here . . . to help you."

Then she stood and skipped down the deck toward Mike the Magician who was shaping long, skinny balloons into animals for children. Fox stumbled, walked, flew, as invisibly as he could, to his stateroom where he got into bed, fully clothed, and, within minutes, escaped into sleep for an hour. He'd trained himself.

He skipped lunch.

After dinner as they arose from the table, Fox touched Sylvie's arm, "Miss Marks, might I interest you in a game of some kind? Darts, ping-pong, Mahjong . . . whatever your pleasure?"

"Oh, Mister Fox," Sylvie said. "But you hate games. Why torture yourself? Soon, though, we shall take a walk, and it shall be a gift you will treasure forever. I'll tell you when."

She wouldn't have such a smart mouth gasping for breath in the midnight sea, watching the ship's lights flicker to nothing as they pulled away from her. That's what Fox thought. But what he said, as though he were Dimitri the Maitre d', was, "Miss Marks, I await your beck and call. Or even just your beck, or . . . maybe just your call."

Sylvie's mother was charmed.

Fox was enough of a bridge player to partner with Queenan for a rubber against her husband and a Mrs. Dow-Wells from Western Massachusetts. He was enough of a chess player to lose to the masterful Clyde while earning the man's respect. And since he had taken a dreadful, year-long art survey course for precisely this purpose, he kept Arjay talking for an hour one afternoon by simply asking him question after question.

Young dancer Diggs was a mouse. Around this table, he was the sort of person Fox was glad to meet. Bringing Mister Mouse out of his house was easy, given Fox's encyclopedic self-education: Savion Glover, Garth Fagan, Judith Jamison—Fox knew just enough about a dozen black dancers and choreographers to get Pitt Diggs talking about his own accomplishments and aspirations—thus demonstrating to one and all the charm, and power, of Charlie Fox.

Fox's talent as a pianist made him a welcome addition to any gathering he chose to entertain. People asked, as they often did, where he'd studied, he played so well, but the truth was he'd studied nowhere. He was born with this odd ability to play what he heard, and even some things he hadn't heard, as if he were telepathically wired to someone from another time.

"What's the name of that piece?"

"Oh, no name; I just made it up this minute."

"Really? You should record it. It's wonderful."

Nikos, their waiter, in his starched white tunic and wavy gray hair, looked more like the Greek ambassador than a 20 year veteran of shipboard service. He could hand you a salt shaker and make you feel like royalty. The third night, as he was circling their table, presenting each of them their dessert as though it were a dish of diamonds, Sylvie said to Fox, "Mister Fox, my guardians say it is time you took me for a promenade on the promenade. After supper, if you would be so kind."

Fox smiled warmly at Sylvie's mother and father, "As you wish, I'm sure."

Sylvie giggled, "Oh, not them, you silly man. My guardians are angels. You cannot see them, though you will before you die. But that won't be tonight." Then she laughed as though Fox's misperception had been deliberate, and that next he would be Charlie Chaplin mistaking a garden hose for a snake in the grass.

If he had been anyone else, the fury within him would have been evident, he was quite sure. *And her parents and brother . . . encouraging her antics.* Thank god he was Charlie Fox.

As soon as Nikos had completed his task, Fox stood so that all eyes were looking up at him. He reached out and freed a yellow rose from the table's centerpiece and presented it to Sylvie, who was seated two places to his left, her mother between them. "Miss Marks, it would be my honor if you would promenade on the promenade with me after supper, which is to say a saunter on the sidewalk, an airing on the arcade, a little exercise on the esplanade, a perambulation on the passageway. If you catch my invitation. Would you be so kind?"

Except for Arjay, everyone laughed, enjoying Fox's good humor in continuing the charade. Sylvie feigned a swoon, reached out and accepted the token. "Oh, Sir Galahad, I thank you for this rose," she said. "But, alas, I must decline your generous invitation. I have a previous engagement with a certain Mister Slyly Fox. You see, Mister Fox is in desperate need of my assistance. And while you, kind sir, have savoir-faire up the yin-yang, Mister Fox has something even more going for him . . . ."

She could have honked a fat loogie on his baklava and he wouldn't have felt more nauseated. *Sir Galahad*: just the name he was planning to use as he knelt before the foot he would seduce into his palm. It was as though Sylvie's hand was once again on his solar plexus, this time squeezing, as she had earlier in the meal squeezed a wedge of lemon on her snapper.

But Fox was quick. With a wink and a bow, he said, "Ah miss, as ever, I am helpless in the face of your beauty, wisdom and colorful turn of phrase." And then, as the others, led by Clyde the bulldog, softly tapped their glasses with their teaspoons, Fox lowered himself into his seat, smiling, nodding to acknowledge the approval, and burning inside.

When it was clear that Sylvie wasn't about to continue her explanation, her brother said, "Well, Syl?"

"Arf, arf," her father said.

"Darling," Queenan said, "we don't doubt it for a minute, but do tell: How does Charlie have more going for him than Sir Galahad?" Queenan turned to Fox, "Our Sylvie has a world all her own, Charlie. I'm sure you've noticed. We love to learn of it. And you're such a good sport."

Sylvie raised her milk glass and, smiling at Fox, said, "Mister Fox is ambitious. He intends to be President."

"Well, hear, hear," Clyde Marks said, raising his Ouzo. "To President Fox. We knew him when."

Now, five glasses were lifted in Fox's direction, and all Charlie Fox could do was hide behind his mask of aplomb. He felt humiliated, which wasn't Sylvie's intent, but those who have a compulsion to remain hidden often perceive being seen as humiliation.

But he . . . he was Charlie Fox.

So with the cool of a king among a flock of adoring school children, Fox raised his water glass, smiled warmly for the second time that evening, and acknowledged the toast.

She would be his.

"Mister Fox, could you imagine how an elephant might walk if he were on his way to the dentist?" Sylvie said after they had made one complete loop of the ship's deck in silence.

"I'm not quite sure I understand," Fox said.

Sylvie laughed in pure delight. "Sure you do, Mister Fox. Watch. This is you . . . on the inside, I mean."

She bent forward at the waist, letting her arms dangle in front of her like an elephant's trunk, then she contorted her face into a scowl, and shuffled down the deck as though each of her feet were wearing a bucket of cement.

"That's who you are behind your mask of Mister Wonderful. Life is so serious."

"Your imagination knows no bounds," Fox said.

"You wish it were so, don't you, Mister Fox? That would make it easy for you to dismiss me." For the briefest second she placed her palm on Fox's heart.

"Wouldn't it?"

"I don't know what you're talking about."

Sylvie laughed, "Oh, Mister Fox, you're turning yourself inside out trying to find a mask I can't see through. Don't bother. It will never work. I'm the most amazing girl you've ever met, you lucky man."

"What is your game?"

"No game, Mister Fox. Remember, I know you from way back."

"You're a child. You don't know me at all."

"Care to bet?"

"What kind of bet could you make?"

"The kind friends make. You'd lose too much if we bet serious."

"You are presumptuous, I'll give you that."

"Whatever that means, I'm sure you're right, Mister Fox. But who cares? The only thing about me that's important right now is that I am here to serve you."

"Serve me? You know nothing about me . . . ."

"How about the message you wrote on a piece of paper last fall, the one you threw into Long Island Sound?"

Fox stopped.

He'd never told anybody about that day, not even Shorty. He'd driven around, alone, no destination. He'd ended up at a beach outside New London. He'd walked by the water most of the afternoon, thinking, talking to himself. The last thing he did before driving back to campus was pick up a scrap of paper and write on it his life's intention . . . a sort of solemn promise. Then he tucked the paper inside a clam shell and threw it as far as he could out over the sound in the direction of a passing Coast Guard cutter.

"Let's stand by the railing, Mister Fox," Sylvie said, guiding him like a blind man. "And you might want to breathe a little, so you don't faint."

"What is this bullshit?" Fox finally said. "Who put you up to it? Is this Papadopolous's doing? Part of some Oxford hazing stunt?"

Sylvie laughed as though he were a talking frog. "I can assure you, Mister Fox, that I have nothing to do with Oxford. And I've never heard of—Papa-Dappa-Liss?" she giggled. "May I show you something?"

"I suppose."

Sylvie reached into her pocket and pulled out a crumpled piece of paper and handed it to Fox.

He didn't remember the paper. At the time it had been just a scrap of whatever was handy. But he recognized his own handwriting. And there was only one piece of paper on which he had ever printed the words: *I will become President of the United States or die trying*.

"I don't understand," he said, holding up the paper in the space between them. "So you and whoever you represent are able to retrieve some shred of a person's life? Big deal. What are you, the CIA? Trying to recruit me or something? What do you . . . ?"

He jumped when he realized the paper was on fire. He threw it into the air. It floated there, burning, not moving, until Sylvie reached out and took it with her fingers. Fox instinctively bent over and attempted to blow out the flames. But instead of extinguishing them, they exploded as though Sylvie had been soaked in lighter fluid. She was a statue of flame from the waist up, still holding the burning paper in her fingers, staring into his eyes. Her face was melting. Her hair ablaze.

Afterward, he realized that he must have ripped off his cashmere blazer and thrown it over her. But he had no memory of it. His only memory was wrapping his entire being around Sylvie, willing the flames to suffocate, to stop burning her.

And just about as quickly as they began, the flames disappeared.

From under him on the deck Sylvie laughed. "You may get off me now, Mister Fox. I am saved, I assure you."

Had he been slipped some drug? Was this acid? In school he'd seen tons of kids zooted on the shit. Why anybody would give up control of their mind was beyond him. He didn't even take aspirin, and drank only water.

She wasn't burned. Fox wished he could flip her overboard right then. Instead, he sat, immobile, his rage frozen, his head and neck twitching, Sylvie kneeling at his side.

She handed him the paper. Not even singed. His message as fresh as the moment he had written it.

"OK, OK, OK," he was almost yelling. "So you're able to do magic. So what? That was a pretty cheap trick. Does it give you a thrill to have somebody try to save your life so you can laugh at them? What . . . ."

Now Fox couldn't talk. His mouth was moving, forming words, but no sound followed.

"I'm sorry, Mister Fox, I just had to shut you up," Sylvie said.

"You're afraid. That's all it is," Sylvie took Fox's hand. "You want everything to fit into your world. And it's just not going to. Look in my eyes, Mister Fox. Listen carefully. Your life is never going to be the same after meeting me. Don't worry, I'm not going to hurt you. I actually think you're pretty neat. But there is not a thing you have ever learned in any classroom that will help you figure me out. You think I'm out to make you look foolish, but I'm not. I'm here to open your eyes, if only for a second or two, to something pretty wonderful. Right now, right here, this minute, Mister Fox, you have two choices. Be miserable. Or acknowledge that, for this tiny moment in time anyway, there are things you cannot explain—and enjoy the mystery. Isn't it wonderful, Mister Fox, that you get to choose how you respond to life?"

She stood and shook out his blazer—not a hint on it of having smothered a fire. She draped it around Fox's shoulders. "I must go to bed now, Mister Fox. Don't be alarmed, but you won't be able to get up for several minutes."

Fox then realized that he hadn't moved since she took his voice away. He could breathe, that was it. The rest of him was paralyzed.

"You know, Mister Fox, you have just done the most important thing a human being can ever do—you have acted spontaneously from your heart. You might want to enjoy it for a few moments. And while you're at it, ask yourself: Are you ever going to do it again?"

*S*he was right. He really couldn't move. Or talk.

Damn! he cringed, as out of the corner of his eye he saw two obviously intoxicated couples heading his way. Again he would be humiliated. They would see him sitting on the deck and ask if he was OK, or if he wanted to join them. He couldn't respond. He couldn't even smile.

But the four, while looking directly at him, passed as if he were invisible.

Which, oddly, made Charlie Fox only angrier.

*T*here was a note from Sylvie under his door when Fox awoke to workout before meeting Mozart for sunrise tea, then Emily Dickinson for a morning deck chair chat.

The note said:

In your Manhattan safe deposit box, there is a small spiral notebook. Only 10 of its pages have writing on them. From the time you were twelve until this year when you graduated from Yale, on every birthday you took a fresh page and wrote the same message over and over until you filled that page. You have now "retired" the notebook. It has served its purpose, you feel. My question to you is this: Are you willing to also "retire" the message itself? Your answer to this question will shape your destiny in this incarnation.

Your friend, Sylvie Marks.

The point wasn't why did somebody get access to his safe deposit box. Regardless of the reasons, it could happen. But there was no way in hell that anyone, not a living soul, no one, not even Shorty, could know that he had retired the notebook, and why.

Unless they could read his mind.

Charlie Fox put a pillow over his face and screamed.

Then he did the thing he feared most. He lost control. He shit his pants.

He got to the toilet quick enough to avoid complete disaster, but not quick enough to avoid filling his jockey shorts and staining the white linen suit he had laid out for the afternoon's excursion with Sylvie to St. Catherine-Sur-Mer.

Filth was the same as being covered with leeches. Possessed, he ripped off his underpants, rolled them up in the suit, swiped his dripping butt once with the entire bundle, then, as though it were a live hand grenade, flung the whole disgusting business out the porthole.

It was one of those rare moments in the life of Charlie Fox when he hadn't calculated ahead of time the impact of his behavior on the public. Passengers had lined the decks as the ship approached the harbor. Townspeople had filled the docks to greet the ship. Now, all were pointing, wondering: *How did a man's beautiful summer suit come to be floating on the water like a corpse? And my, was that a bloodstain on its back?*

Mirror Man | *Charlie Fox, 20 Years Earlier*

Or so Fox imagined in his paranoia. In reality, it was 4:15 a.m., and the only ones who noted Fox's derangement were dolphins playing in the ship's pre-dawn wake, and they knew exactly what had been tossed out of that little round window and, believe you me, they steered clear.

"AAAAAAAAHHHH," Charlie Fox screamed and slammed the porthole shut.

The dolphins, who of course heard him, continued jumping with their usual abandon.

You can never be too cautious.

As Sylvie had written, each year for 10 years he had filled an entire page in his notebook with that sentence. But now he had stopped. And the reason he stopped was the same reason he was going to kill somebody—Sylvie, if possible—and get away with it. He no longer required the external structure that had brought him to this point in his life.

He was caution itself.

When Fox was twelve, he read a story about the new Mister Universe, the king of bodybuilding. Mister Universe was eighteen. In the article, Mister Universe said that, from the time he had been twelve, he knew that he would become Mister Universe one day. It was more than just a visualization, he said. He knew it completely in every muscle of his body. And from that day until he won the title six years later, Mister Universe knew that all he had to do was the work—the title was already his.

Fox had always known that he would be somebody important, though at age 12, unlike Mister Universe, he didn't know exactly how. All he knew was that it was time to translate his knowing into a regimen of work.

For his birthday that year, his mother had given him a book titled Ancient Wisdom, quotes of famous people throughout history. With his eyes shut, young Fox flipped open to a random page and dropped a finger to the paper. If he had been older, or a different person, someone with a sense of humor, say, or at least a sense of perspective, he might have laughed at the irony of where his finger landed. *The cautious person seldom errs*, said the wisdom of Confucius. The irony Fox missed was that telling Charlie Fox to be cautious was like telling Mister Universe to lift weights. In later years there would be those who joked that Fox had probably looked both ways before popping out of his mother's womb. So naturally, as a 12 year old, he took Confucius's pithy remark as a sign of great portent. Caution became the number one discipline he imposed on himself.

But Fox, being Fox, was cautious about caution itself, which meant that he defined the term in his own way. Caution, for Fox, was being a master at shaping the world's opinion of him.

At this point in his plan—Yale behind him, Oxford ahead, Harvard Law after that, then a stint as a prosecutor before running for Congress—to be cautious could no longer be something he needed to think about, to remind himself of, to work on. That's why he retired the notebook. Caution had to be in his blood, as natural as breathing.

The sail to Europe was the perfect beta test of his self-education. In the hothouse of an ocean liner, his life's one and only consciously evil act would put to trial many of the things he had worked to develop over the past 10 years. His cool under pressure. His charm. His intellect. His ability to shape the perceptions of others to his ends. His gift for walking unscathed through the unknown, the dangerous. Surely these are qualities of a President. This was a powerful way to find out just how much of a Renaissance Man was he—at least, as he defined the term: a master of all the talents needed to play a leading role on the grand stage of human affairs.

*T*he only immediate chink in his plan, now, was Sylvie. Part of him hungered for her to be his prey. But there was a problem. She seemed to know things about him that no one else did. He had to find out who she was, what she knew, how she knew it.

Stuff like this just didn't happen.

And Christ, while we're being honest, he felt something absolutely unprecedented—a certain tenderness and, if the truth be told, affection for Sylvie. If she weren't thirteen, if she were closer to his own age, he might even entertain the possibility that he cared for her. He wasn't quite sure, since he'd never actually had a girlfriend before. Shorty, his sister, was hardly a girlfriend in the traditional sense. Well, maybe caring was a little excessive. But in Sylvie's bizarre and completely irrational way, she just might know him better than anyone else—better even than Shorty—and what was even more amazing, Sylvie seemed to accept him . . . as is.

Oh, the gods were really testing him. Was he going to have to kill someone he actually liked—or was at least fascinated by? Were the stakes being raised? Were other factors being introduced to make the situation not quite the walk in the park he had planned? Was he up for it?

Of course he was up for it. He welcomed it. How could he not and aspire to greatness? He wondered if Sylvie were aware of his other notebook, full of his personal reflections. It was in his suitcase. On one page he had written what was perhaps the defining belief of his life.

Nothing is too intense for me.

*T*hat afternoon, the ship docked for a few hours on the France side of the English Channel so that passengers might enjoy mussels, oysters and other saltwater delicacies in the village of St. Catherine-Sur-Mer. Charlie

Fox and Sylvie Marks were not among those who took advantage of this culinary opportunity. They, instead, went for a walk together, ending up at a cloistered convent. The abbey, named after the town, probably didn't look a whole lot different to Fox and Sylvie than it did to the abbess who, a century before Yale was founded, first opened its gates to young women in search of a life of contemplation, or perhaps merely a life free from the dictates of their fathers to marry some mule for money.

Fox was dressed in white deck pants, docksiders, and a navy polo shirt, a yellow cotton sweater tied around his shoulders in case the day turned as cool as was forecast. Sylvie wore her customary sky blue shirt, purple tie and tuxedo trousers, adding a fleece vest, lime green.

Quite by chance, or so it seemed to Fox at the time, Sylvie opened a small door in the outside wall of the cloister and they found themselves in a garden the size of a small city block, a garden that might do a national arboretum proud.

There was no one in sight.

"Do you suppose this is open to the public?" Fox said.

"If we're trespassing, I'm sure someone will tell us," Sylvie replied.

They explored until they noticed a bench on a side path nestled under lilac bushes and in front of a small pond. On the edge of the pond were lily pads. In its center, just at the surface, was a metal ring, two feet in diameter, that sprayed maybe a hundred pencil-thin arcs of water anywhere from two to four feet into the air. The result gave the impression of tall grass blowing in the breeze. There they sat, surrounded on three sides by lilacs whose blossoms had long passed, the pond and fountain to their front, and beyond that a display of color and symmetry they would remember as unique for as long as they lived.

"I want to apologize for speaking to you so harshly last night," Charlie Fox said, looking straight ahead. "It's just that I have been . . . I don't know . . . dumbfounded is the only word I can think of . . . by some of the things that have happened with you."

Sylvie had cocked her head and was looking at him. Her look told him that she had no intention of saying anything until he was finished, and that he should take all the time he wanted.

"As you pointed out, I've been trying to fit you into my way of seeing things. Maybe you fit there. Maybe you don't. I honestly don't know how to make head nor tails of who you are, and frankly what it all means. It's all so unfamiliar."

At Yale he had once heard an ambassador give a talk about his work as a career diplomat. The ambassador had said: "One reason honesty is the best policy is because it can be completely disarming."

"So I'm wondering," Fox posed, "will you tell me? Please?"

"Mister Fox, have you ever heard anyone say that honesty is the best policy because it can be completely disarming?"

Fox's breath popped as if he'd just been punched in the chest.

"A guy at Yale once," he said. "You're right. That's what I'm doing. Partly. But I really don't want to be fighting. Well, I don't mean you were fighting. I was. And I don't like it."

"I can't tell you," Sylvie said.

"I beg your pardon?"

"I can't tell you what you want to know."

"I don't understand. Why not?"

"Because I don't know, Mister Fox," Sylvie giggled.

"Who does?"

"You."

"Riddles! Can you say anything I can understand?"

"I am being told to tell you this," Sylvie said. "It may not help you much, but it is all I can do for now. You are like a person who has lived his whole life in a place like this—this garden. It's certainly beautiful, but to spend your every day here would give anyone a pretty limited view of life. I, on the other hand, have grown up with eagles who carry me on their backs wherever they fly."

"But you are only thirteen years old. How can you know and do . . . whatever all this is?" Fox said, mystified.

"Mister Fox, you are confusing the age of my house with the age of my being. My house, this body, is thirteen. I, however, am ageless. As are you. You just don't know it. And that's the difference between us."

"So you, or your dad or your brother, are not working for the government or anybody else? You just have this unusual ability to know things about people and perform, I don't know, miracles?"

Sylvie's laugh filled the air like a wind chime. "Is it so remarkable for an eagle to see things differently than a rabbit?"

"You're right," Fox said. "I don't understand this much. But I do see that you don't behave toward everyone the way you are with me."

"I'm always the same, I'm never the same," Sylvie said.

"What makes you behave one way with some people and not others?"

"You mean why am I bugging you so much?" Sylvie laughed. "Orders from headquarters."

"There you go again."

"Not really, Mister Fox," Sylvie said. "My world is completely different from yours. I live from my heart. I do what my heart tells me. I am here with you this afternoon because my heart has guided me to be here. I don't have any motives for being here other than that."

"Guardian angels?" Fox asked.

"If you wish."

"Forgive me, but it just seems that there has to be a way I can grasp what is going on here. Is there anything you can tell me? I mean, what the hell was last night all about? The fire and all. And your note this morning. I really want to understand what it means."

Sylvie laughed. She seemed to laugh every time he spoke.

"Mister Fox, you are so funny. You act as if life were this big important test that you have to pass. That's because you live in your mind. Maybe the only reason we met is to give you a chance to lighten up a bit. Life is anything but serious, Mister Fox. Life is a celebration. You are going to have a really tough time being President if you don't develop a sense of humor."

"Am I going to be President?"

"That's not for me to tell you."

"But you know. I mean, you can see it?"

"Yes."

"My god, girl. What can you tell me?"

"I can tell you this: Whether you become President or not will have no bearing on your happiness."

"Happiness? I don't even know what happiness is."

"That, Mister Fox, is the second time since I met you that you have done or said something that was completely honest."

"What?"

"Saying you didn't know what happiness is."

"I figure happiness is something that happens, or doesn't, when you look back at the end of your life."

"What if your life ended tonight?"

Fox looked at the fountain for several minutes. "Then I guess I would be happy," he said at last.

"Now you are playing make-believe, Mister Fox."

"What do you mean?"

"You just said what you wished you would feel, not what you would really feel," Sylvie said. "What you would really feel if you died tonight is pain and fear—pain that you have passed up so many opportunities to love, and fear that the universe will judge you as somehow deficient, because that's how you feel about yourself. You don't like yourself a whole lot."

"Believe me when I tell you there are a shitload of people who would love to be me."

"I'm sure that's true, Mister Fox, but please, don't be a fartbird. We haven't got time. The answer to your question is that I have died many, many times—as have you—and the difference between us is that I remember a great many of my deaths. So you might say I've been there. I know what you feel because I have felt it myself."

"Is that why you don't judge me?"

"Ooooh! Another honest moment, Mister Fox. Yes, that's true. I look at you and I see myself. And I've learned to love what I see. It's called compassion."

"And if you died tonight?" Charlie Fox pressed. "How would you feel?"

Sylvie sat with her eyes closed for some time before she spoke. "I would feel the pain of my family's loss," she said, turning to look at Fox's eyes. "I am the jewel of my family. Their lives would be shattered, but maybe in a good way; they depend on me too much for their happiness. But I would feel nothing but joy at the loss of this body."

"Nothing?"

"Well, almost," Sylvie smiled. "You see, Mister Fox, in order to live from my heart, I must die in every minute as it is. I must surrender everything to Spirit—my desires, my dreams, my body, everything. I have been doing this—practicing, you might say—for many, many lives. Just as you have been working to make yourself something in this life. So I might feel a flutter of fear if I were leaving my body right now, but I would also make room for it and let it fly away—like a great seagull."

Sylvie giggled. "You might find this hard to understand, but I love dying. It's the only way to be more and more alive."

"How would I know if I were living from my heart, as you put it?"

Sylvie laughed again. "Mister Fox, you already know it. You did it, last night, when you were saving my life."

"But you were playing games with me. You weren't in any danger."

"The only person in any danger in your life is you, Mister Fox. You were given an opportunity to respond completely spontaneously from your heart, and you did. Whether I was playing games, as you say, doesn't matter. Only your choices matter."

"You created that whole business just to test me?" Fox asked. "To see whether I would act to save your life? What was so special about that? Anyone would have done what I did."

"It wasn't a test, Mister Fox," Sylvie said. "It was an opportunity. For all you know, you could have died last night—or become the first president with no lips and eyebrows—and you were willing to risk that just to keep me from harm. You say anyone would have acted that way, but you know that's not true. You're just trying to diminish what you did so you don't have to actually feel what it means to act from your heart."

"*T*his is definitely getting strange," Charlie Fox said to himself in the mirror as he dressed for dinner that evening, his last as the guest of Teddy Papadopolous. Tomorrow at this time, either Mozart or Emily Dickinson would have disappeared and he'd be in London, about to begin a short pre-Oxford holiday by indulging his favorite hobby: museums—observing the lives of people who couldn't observe back.

In a way, Sylvie was like the V&A or the Tate: infinitely fascinating. He had always been suspicious of people who used terms like "forever" when they spoke of their relationships. He had Shorty, that was forever of course, but it was also completely different; she was blood, even more than blood; they were bonded by a common purpose: to share their lives and to have the greatest possible influence on the world. Now he had at least an inkling of what those "soul partner" people were trying to say. Whatever feeling it was he had about Sylvie Marks, he had never experienced it before.

The whole thing was absurd, really.

"Why Mister Fox," Charlie Fox said to the mirror in his best English accent as he gave his thick black hair fifty strokes straight back with his favorite Mason Pearson brush. "As a way of introducing yourself here at Oxford, perhaps you would tell us about the person you consider to have been your most important teacher . . . ahem . . . until now, of course."

"Well, boys and girls, I'll tell you," Fox replied, holding the brush as if it were a saber and he a Musketeer effortlessly dispatching innumerable foes while explaining, "It was this little thirteen year-old *chica* I met on the ship I took to get here from the States. (Slash.) Why, she can read my mind like it was Doonesbury. (Slash-Slash.) She can set herself on fire and walk away from it like nothing happened. (Slash-Slash-Slash.) Believe it or not, she knows whether I'm going to be President. And, if I'm lucky, she going to teach me how to live from my heart, whatever that means—and, oh by the way, be my wife. Every leader needs one."

Fox suddenly stopped the hairbrush duel, peered into the mirror, his eyes wide in surprise. "I'm sorry, you're all looking at me like I just French kissed the queen's butler."

He laughed and continued brushing.

Sylvie's acceptance of him, and her ability to see who he really was—were, by turns, frightening and a peculiar source of comfort. He had never known someone so absolutely sure of herself, and so honest with him. What was love, anyway? He had these flashes of him waiting for Sylvie until she finished high school. Imagine being President of the United States with her as his wife. It was incredible. Imagine anything with her as his wife. Or partner. Or at least his closest confidant right along with Shorty. For the first time in his life, Charlie Fox felt that he had actually made a friend, someone he knew for reasons other than leverage.

But wait a minute. Wouldn't Sylvie know he had thrown overboard one of the others? Was this a whole new level of challenge he would have to master—controlling his mind so Sylvie's radar wouldn't beep?

Was that even possible? No, it wasn't possible.

Of course she'd find out. And if she knew that, why wouldn't she know that she was the original intended trophy? How would he explain? Would she understand? Or would she change her mind about seeing herself in him, and loving what she saw? Would her so-called compassion dry up like Death Valley at the real him?

How could it not?

"I've brought you a going-away present," Sylvie said.

It was after dinner. Fox and Sylvie were in deck chairs on the fantail. The chairs, with fold-out leg-rests and reclining backs, were wood shellacked the color of bourbon, the same color as the deck. They were covered with blue and white striped canvas cushions, and neatly folded over the back of each was a beige fleece blanket embossed with the blue *Proteus* logo face-up. The air, as predicted, was cooling over the English Channel. The sun had retired, though the sky was still very much alive. Sixty-seven shades of red and gold were jockeying to be first over the earth's west edge. Against this backdrop, a squadron of white gulls played. Their collective flight patterns resembled a vaudeville team impersonating rush hour plane traffic over Heathrow shortly after all the air controllers started speaking Swahili. A guitar/violin duo, husband and wife, Tom and Julie, students from the Eastman School in Rochester, New York, were performing a piece of their own composition called *Bluegrass Beethoven*.

Sylvie had changed from her "dinner duds"; Fox had not. For the first time, Sylvie wore something different: all white—sweatshirt, sweatpants and Converse hightops. A white rose was tucked into the white band securing her ponytail. Fox wore charcoal flannel trousers, a black turtleneck and a gray herringbone wool vest. Over this ensemble was a black cashmere blazer. When he had arrived for dinner, Sylvie had already pinned a rose boutonnière on each of the other men, each rose a different color. The rose she had reserved for Fox was red. "Fire," she giggled, as she affixed it to his lapel, where it remained. A larger than usual number of other passengers were on the deck, as well, since this was the last night for everyone disembarking in Southampton and, if any extra enticement were needed, an amber moon, close to full, was already up in the east.

Sylvie reached into the patchwork cloth backpack she carried everywhere and brought out a box about the size of a hardback novel. Scotch-taped all over the box were cartoons she had cut out of a Gary Larson anthology. The one centered squarely on top, with Fox's name on it, was a scene of a half-dozen very odd-looking people sailing a ship. The caption read: *Mutants on the bounty*.

"I didn't have much to wrap this with," she said. "And then I realized, for you, Mister Fox, whatever might tickle you is a good thing."

She handed the box to Fox. "I am giving you this on one condition."

"Yes?"

"I want you to promise that you will wear what is in this box one full day every year for the rest of your life."

"You want me to promise without having any idea what it is?"

"Of course, Mister Fox. What's the fun without a little risk. You're certainly free not to accept my gift. Honest. I won't be offended."

"No, no, no, no," Charlie Fox said. "I promise. I will wear what is in this box for an entire day, one day each year, for the rest of my life . . . and I just hope that it's not a negligee."

"Mister Fox," Sylvie giggled. "Is that a sense of humor I hear peeping out of your mouth?"

Fox came as close to blushing as he ever would.

The box contained a pair of men's wool socks: one dark blue, one gold.

"One day a year, huh?" Fox said, reluctant to take them out of the box where they might be seen in public.

"Wear them with a white suit, Mister Fox, and you'll have the team colors of the universe."

"I will adorn myself with you in mind, Miss Marks."

Fox closed the box and tucked it under his deck chair.

"I have another gift for you, as well," Sylvie said in a tone that brought a searing ache to Fox's throat. He was afraid she was about to say something that would confirm the obvious, that she was going away from him. Once the ship continued on to Singapore he might never see her again.

"Yes, but first, my turn," said Fox. "May I ask you a question?"

"Oui."

He didn't actually have a question. He was buying time, stalling, groping, distracting, diverting, delaying, anything-ing . . . .

The words out of his mouth were as new to him and they were to her.

"This is all very confusing for me, Sylvie. I've never really had feelings for another person, a girl, like I have for you. You're thirteen, but you're not thirteen. I just need to ask, can we be friends? I mean after this boat ride? When you get to Singapore, may I write you? Maybe I could come see you."

From Sylvie's expression, you could have thought that Fox had just given her a dozen hand-painted silk bow-ties, each a different riot of purple.

"Oh, I would love that," she said. "But it depends."

"Depends?"

"On what you do with the gift I am about to give you, and whether I'm there."

"Damn, girl," Fox said. "Don't talk to me in riddles, please. What do you mean? What's the gift?"

Sylvie pulled her legs into the lotus posture then turned her body, sideways, in her chair so that she faced Fox more directly. Then she took the blanket from the back of the chair and put it across her lap.

"I intend to jump overboard," she said.

To Fox, the moment was the exact opposite of the fire the previous night. There, he'd reacted like lightning. Here, he was concrete.

His mind could have asked at least twenty questions. But every one of them would be like asking a girl what color nail polish she intended to wear during the surgery to remove her brain tumor.

It was another brand-new moment for Fox, a moment of absolute clarity that prevented the possibility of responding with shock or humor or indignation or anger or any of the other ways he might deny the reality. Instead, he just looked into her old, wise eyes and began to weep.

As though she had foreseen just this eventuality, Sylvie reached into her sweatshirt's front hand-warmer pocket, pulled out a white tissue and offered it to Fox.

"Don't worry, Mister Fox," Sylvie said, "I'm not doing this to kill myself. Just about everybody on this deck is going to see me go. They'll all have a chance to rescue me, just as you had the chance to rescue me last night. And I gotta assume the ship's crew is prepared for such, shall we say, emergencies."

Another person would call her, what?—insane? Another person would try to restrain her, or would at least attempt to persuade her that this was more than a little risky. Not Charlie Fox. Fox knew that Sylvie didn't live in the world where those sorts of issues mattered.

Worse, he knew she was acting for reasons that he might never really understand.

He could hardly get the words out, his breath was bucking so. "Wh-wh-why should I . . . c-consider this . . . a gift?" he finally stammered.

"Well, Mister Fox, one reason is so you don't have to pay the price of going through with your silly plan to throw somebody overboard."

Fox was beyond being shocked.

"Every choice has consequences, you know," Sylvie said. "And that would be a particularly misguided choice on your part. Maybe I can help you make another choice, maybe many other choices as your life unfolds."

Sylvie paused as Fox blew his nose. Tom and Julie were playing something they called *Charles Ives meets Charles Addams*. Sylvie put her hand out and, with her fingertips, touched the tears on the side of Fox's face closest to her.

"You see, Mister Fox, no matter what happens, whether I am saved or I die, you will have to choose what you do with this experience. And that is my gift to you. It will scare you. Big. The question is, will you change your habit of being careful, which is really just being afraid? Will you open your heart and feel your life—the pain and the joy of it? Or will you do what you usually do—pretend that all the things that have happened since we met were a fantasy, pretend that I'm a fantasy?"

"Who are you?" Charlie Fox groaned.

"Mister Fox!" Sylvie said. "All that matters is: Who are *you*?"

"Why can't you just tell me?"

"It's only your tricky old mind that wants to know," Sylvie said. "And your mind—everybody's mind pretty much—is mostly fear, Mister Fox. It can tell you the time of day, it can even build a ship that can sail a thousand people across the ocean in luxury, but you sure don't want it running your life."

Sylvie suddenly laughed and looked up at the moon.

"Let's see," she said, then looked back at Fox. "Maybe I'm the ghost of your dead father who left you as an infant to prospect for gold in South America where he died in prison, a swindler and a murderer—you know, your real father, Mister Fox, not the courageous explorer you tell people about. Or maybe I'm a messenger from one of the countless parallel worlds that exist right along with this one. Or maybe I'm just a kid whose brain is completely farked so I'm able to know things most folks don't. Or heck, maybe I'm just plain nuts.

"Don't you see, Mister Fox? No matter what I said, your mind would go crazy making up stories about why what you are feeling and experiencing is not real. Who am I? I'm just somebody who is reminding you to listen to your heart. What you need to decide, Mister Fox, is whether that's good advice. Who I am is beside the point."

"Why must you do this?" Charlie Fox said.

"You know the answer, Mister Fox."

"Orders from headquarters? Oh, come on."

"Alright," Sylvie said, letting a story appear in her mind. "Imagine a baby, Mister Fox, born with a heart defect, who dies before the age of one. Most people think of that as a tragedy. Yes?"

Fox nodded.

"But maybe that baby came on earth in that incarnation just for those few months in order to give its parents the opportunity to open their hearts to a depth of love that was far beyond anything they had ever experienced before. In other words, through this baby, the parents learned just how really big they were capable of loving. Is that a tragedy?"

"Not when you put it that way," Fox said.

"Well, perhaps every situation is just that—a gift given to us so that we might choose to open our hearts. Only, most of us don't think of the events of our lives as gifts. We see them as good or bad, or coincidence, or luck—or even punishment—"

"What are you saying?" Fox's agitation rising, "that there are people who come to earth just to play some small role in somebody else's life, and then—poof—they're gone?

"You think that baby is playing a small role?"

"I don't mean the baby. I'm talking about you. Do you feel you were born just to jump overboard so that I will learn something?"

"Why not? Do you know how the universe operates?"

"Well, no . . . ."

"No?!" Sylvie said, pretending surprise. "No?!" she squealed with laughter, as though Fox had admitted that he didn't know who Sting was, or Tina Turner, but was perfectly comfortable being the Yale Professor of Rock & Roll. "You are a riot, Mister Fox. You must spend a bundle in paper bags."

"Paper bags?"

Sylvie leaned closer so that she was all but whispering in Fox's ear.

"The bags you are forever sticking over your handsome head. You don't know how the universe operates, so you say, yet anytime you run into something that doesn't fit into the little world you have made up for yourself, you pretend it isn't there. You stay small, holding on to what's familiar, instead of opening to the unknown. You gotta trust yourself a little more, Mister Fox. Gosh, you're thinking about marrying me. You think I may be your first friend. You wonder if I'm going to stop loving you when I find out that, not one day ago, you were ready to murder me. And what about when I find out that you and your sister are lovers? What then? Come on, Mister Fox, give your brain a break, man. Haven't you gotten a hint in just the past twenty four hours that there is more to life than what your mind can grasp? Loosen up, Mister Fox. Your heart can soar like an eagle if you let it. But you are choosing to be a rabbit. And why? Because it's fa-mill-yar. Boy. Familiar? Familiar to what part of you? It's sure not familiar to your heart."

Sylvie sat back. Tears lit up her eyes, even though she was smiling. "Sufferin succotash, Misther Foxth," Sylvie said in a perfect impersonation of Sylvester the cat. "Isn't 'Because it's familiar' just about the silliest reason to do anything?"

"OK, OK, I'm a moron . . . ."

"Oh, Mister Fox, you're no moron," Sylvie said, taking another tissue from her sweatshirt and handing it to Fox. "You're a human being. You wish you weren't, but there you are. Like most humans, you live in fear. It's nothing to be ashamed of. Everybody does it. Sooner or later we learn to free our fear. What you don't know yet is that fear is the world's best teacher. It shows us what we need to pay attention to. The only way we love is to go through fear. But we must go through it, Mister Fox, not run from it. Mister President, look in the mirror, bud. Open to the possibility that the universe is knocking on your door, trying to tell you something."

"What? That my thirty seconds of conversation with Aristotle, the porter who brings me two apples and a bottle of water every morning, is some deliberate act on God's part, or somebody's part, to help me, Charlie Fox, open my heart?"

"Ooooh, Mister Fox, you have learned something," Sylvie squealed.

"Forgive me, it just seems so ridiculous. You're saying there are no accidents?"

"Whether there are any I wouldn't know," Sylvie said, "but I've never experienced one, and I remember lots of my former lives. But you'd be amazed at how many things people call accidents get prevented because some spirit intercedes without anyone knowing it."

"You mean the arsenic soup Nikos didn't serve me? The iceberg this ship didn't hit?"

"Very clever, Mister Fox. But how about a real live example: one of those girls you have been planning to murder in place of me? If my leaping overboard is enough of a shock to your system so that you change your plan, then a life will be saved. And the girl in question will probably never know how close she came to an unpleasant death."

Fox put his head in his hands. "You must hate me," he said.

Again, Sylvie leaned toward Fox so she spoke right into his ear.

"No, Mister Fox," she said, "I gave up hate a life or two ago. I realized we only hate ourselves. Hate is very habit-forming, though. Worse than drugs. You have a bad case of it. You might want to look at how it is killing you."

Now the corners of their foreheads were almost touching. Sylvie put her arm around Fox's shoulder.

"I love you, Sylvie," Fox said.

"I know you think you do," Sylvie said.

"*Think* I do? I've never felt anything like this. I am naked in front of you, Sylvie, and I'm still here. I'm not running away. Do you realize how significant that is? I am yours . . . completely."

Sylvie closed her eyes and rested the top of her forehead on Fox's temple, her arm still around his shoulder.

"I know, Mister Fox," she said, "but you don't need to be mine completely. You need to be yours completely. You know that old cliche. No one can really love another until they can love themselves. My gift to you, Charlie Fox, is an opportunity for you to make that choice . . . or at least know the price you're paying by not making it."

Sylvie stood, collected her blanket and began refolding it.

"Sylvie, please," Fox said.

Sylvie placed the folded blanket over the back of her deck chair, then picked up her patchwork bag from the deck and placed it on her seat. Squatting down next to Fox, her eyes, still full of tears, looking up at his, also full of tears, Sylvie took Fox's hand.

"Mister Fox, it won't be your job to save me," Sylvie said. "Starting right this second you won't be able to move until after I dive. But don't worry. No one is going to wonder why you didn't stop me. If anyone asks, tell them the truth. Say it all happened so fast, and was so unexpected, there was no time to react. Once I'm overboard, you'll be free to help rescue me, and I hope you do. I hope we're pals a good long time in this life."

Then Sylvie stood and arranged Fox's blanket around his feet before bending down and placing her mouth to his ear one final time, "Love yourself, Mister Fox, just as you are."

Tom and Julie were playing what they called *Moussorgsky's Pictures at an Exhibition of Stock Car Racing*.

Immediately behind the railing, dead center on the ship's stern, was a white flag pole, empty since sunset. Sylvie climbed up on the wooden top rail, four and a half feet off the deck and eight inches wide. She wrapped one hand around the pole, stood up on the rail, and turned her back to the sea.

Tom and Julie stopped in unison, mid-bar, mid-note. When others looked toward the musicians to see why they stopped so abruptly, what they saw were two bodies frozen in snapshot, instruments still in place, mouths slightly open, eyes unblinking, staring at something they obviously couldn't quite believe.

Holding the flagpole, silhouetted against dusk, all in white, Sylvie reminded Fox of Joan of Arc in a summer stock production he'd seen a few years earlier—not quite real.

Sylvie called out to the crowd, "Hey everyone. May I have your attention?" And when she had their absolute, riveted attention in complete silence—after several people gasped, a few shouted demands that she get down though no one dared approach her, and now the only sounds were the wind, the wake, and the ten piece orchestra just barely audible from inside the ballroom two decks up—Sylvie said loud enough for everyone to hear, "Please don't be alarmed. I'm about to dive. After I do, if you can rescue me, that would be great. But if you cannot, I'll understand. I love you all. May God bless you." And then, while Charlie Fox sat in his deck chair, a weeping statue wrapped in a blanket, Sylvie Marks, her arms straight out to her sides like an Olympic diver, executed a slow, graceful, perfect back flip accompanied by a chorus of screams from the crowd. She floated into the darkness through a gaggle of white gulls gathering in anticipation that her raised hands might contain food. The ship's alarm siren exploded before she was out of sight.

*W*hen Fox disembarked in Southampton the next morning, he was a different man, a man who had just discovered that he was more powerful than he had ever imagined possible, perhaps more powerful than just about anyone else on earth. The universe had given him what he had wanted. The details may not have worked out exactly as he had envisioned, but the essence, the end result, was what he had dreamed. Because of him, a young girl, the most perfect and beautiful he had ever known, had gone overboard and died. Her family was wounded in ways that would never heal. No one would ever connect her death to him. He was free.

He was some sort of god. And the price he paid for that was a feeling of utter loss beyond anything he had ever known or imagined. Plus, a need to plumb new depths of caution so that his love for Sylvie and his guilt about her death would never impel him in a moment of weakness to do anything that might jeopardize his intention to be protected by the cocoon of power and adulation that came with being a world leader.

9

An Open Safe from the Dead Sea

Fox was relieved that Pearl had declined his offer of a ride.

"I'm too wet for your car, Uncle Charlie," she had said. "Besides, there are a few things I'd like to discuss with Hyman here in case he's about to disappear. I'll meet you at home in time for mom's birthday party."

Gesturing to Fox's socks, she said, "I see you're dressed for the occasion."

As O'Malley and Pearl drove away, Fox turned to his aide, Vicky Ski, a woman so universally respected in Washington that even five-star generals sprang to attention when she entered a room. She looked and dressed like the organist at the Evangelical Church of Spinster Librarians: blue suit, white blouse buttoned at the neck, blue pumps, hair in a bun, no jewelry, and so little makeup it would take a forensic expert to find it. Rumor was that, at age 36, Vicki Ski was still waiting for her first date. Another rumor said that she had a beautiful smile, which prompted the publisher of *The Washington Post* to offer a bowling bag full of silver dollars to anyone whose camera could verify this outrageous allegation. Two years later, the bag still adorned the publisher's roll-top desk. One thing not rumor: While Shorty was the composer of Charlie Fox's life, Vicky Ski conducted the orchestra.

Put a zucchini in the ear of every left-handed cowboy west of the Mississippi by day's end? Consider it done.

"Just for fun, Vic," the President said, "find out everything you can about our Mister O'Malley. Make it a priority. Give me the first read, say, by three. Shorty thinks he's wonderful; let's just make sure."

Mary Victoria Szczesniakowski, Vicky Ski to everyone, even her mother, with whom Vicky Ski still lived, replied with the only word she had ever used to convey to her boss that only the Earth being sucked into the sun would hinder her meeting his request, and even then it would be only by ten minutes or so.

"Chief," she said.

"Miles," Fox said to his driver, a bald black torpedo of a man with a gray whiskbroom mustache, "since the beach is empty, I'm going for a walk."

Those responsible for the President's safety, as well those whose job it was to anticipate his every whim, all knew what Fox's remark was code for.

I need to be alone.

He could smell Sylvie.

At the time he hadn't noticed what she smelled like. Now, it was as though she had walked right up to him from out of nowhere, a beautiful woman, 33 years old, put her hand on his heart, her face against his cheek, and said, "Hello again, Mister Fox."

If people weren't watching, he would probably weep.

The ship's captain had said it was most likely that, upon impact, Sylvie had had the wind knocked out of her and immediately drowned. But Fox had always wondered if that wasn't just the captain's way of giving the family a story that would ease their uncertainty. He'd heard somewhere that people can get sucked into a ship's propeller. *The Cuisinart Effect*, went the joke.

Fox's only tangible proof that Sylvie had existed were her notes to him. All of them were now stored in his Manhattan safe deposit box, including the one she had tucked under the socks and he hadn't found until he unpacked his bag in Oxford: *Remember what you learned in the boys' locker room, Mr. Fox: "Go Big or Stay Home."*

Again, how could she possibly have known about that sign?

Was it any wonder that he never shared anything about her with anyone? What could he say? Even to her father and brother? Even to his own sister. What could he tell them about the Sylvie he knew?—at least, what could he say without also, inadvertently, revealing what Sylvie had known about him?

The socks.

He had kept his promise. For many years he would go off on his own, where no one knew him, usually to the outer banks of North Carolina, or Truro on Cape Cod, and walk the beach all day by himself, wearing her gift with a pair of white deck pants. When life began to make those solitary excursions too cumbersome, he came up with the brilliant idea of wearing the socks in honor of Shorty's birthday. Many thought of it as a rare display of playfulness by buttoned-up Charlie Fox. His public relations team was happy that such a visible and harmless personal eccentricity could be used to show that President Fox was a regular guy.

Pearl was his own. If she needed a heart transplant, he would give her his heart. He'd already planned the accident that would leave his organs healthy.

Shorty was his own, as well: as close to safety as he could ever imagine. He wore Sylvie's socks on this particular day to remind Shorty of his devotion to her, as well as to make up, in some way, for what he withheld from her: his plan to murder someone on the *Proteus*; that if Sylvie had lived, he probably would have written a note that said *I will marry Sylvie Marks, or die trying;*

and that, by his own curious reckoning, he considered himself a widower twice over: losing Sylvie to the sea, and Shorty to another man.

*I*f, earlier that morning, before meeting O'Malley, terrorists had kidnapped Pearl and threatened Fox that they would chop off her feet if he didn't reveal the truth of his shipboard voyage two decades earlier, Fox might not have been able to prevent his niece's mutilation.

Fox kept a large, ornate iron vault in the most inaccessible corner of his brain. Anyone but he might call that place the Dead Sea. In the vault were secrets so dangerous that he no longer acknowledged their existence. In fact, he didn't acknowledge the vault itself. One didn't get the top job in America without a very sophisticated capacity for selective denial. But now, in the time that it took to shake a stranger's hand, the vault had been delivered dripping wet and unlocked, placed bulls-eye on the priceless Persian carpet at the center of Fox's life. As the vault's door swung open, out floated, not necessarily *every* secret, but every last detail of that voyage 20 years earlier, all of it as real to each of Fox's senses as if it were occurring right then and there. Equally present, beyond the events themselves, were their implications.

And what about when I find out that you and your sister are lovers? What then?

Since their teens, he and Shorty had been in love. Even as young kids they talked about getting married someday. When Shorty first menstruated, she didn't run to her mother; she ran to Charlie. "Someday we'll have a baby, Charlie," she had said. And he said yes. They never outgrew their childhood comfort with one another's nakedness. But they talked about sex for more than a year before they actually came together. She was sixteen; he a year younger. They were no different than any other teenage sweethearts who had no doubt that they would be spending their lives together. It was a matter of trust. Fox trusted Shorty as he trusted no other. Who else could he be so vulnerable with? It went without saying that they were monogamous. In fact, Shorty was the only lover Charlie Fox would ever know, and he was her only lover until she married. They didn't keep their love a secret out of shame. It was secret for the simple reason that its revelation would destroy the life they had planned together. It was perfect how things evolved. They wanted a child of their own. It was Shorty who conceived the plan. She would marry and have one baby; Charlie the father. She would have her tubes tied after the delivery, thus eliminating the possibility of accidental pregnancy with her husband and the potential complications that would come with it: abortion, to which she was morally opposed; or comparisons between offspring, which could be disastrous. Shorty's preference was a husband who would be a good friend to her and a good father to what he presumed was his only child. Shorty had no desire to be a single parent. "Kids need the best home we can give them, and that means two parents, if you have a choice in the matter." It was a painful decision for Fox: sharing the woman he loved with another man, yet an even bigger sacrifice for Shorty, he knew. She was the one who would be married. She was the one who would have to share herself. Her courage awed Fox. Not that there was any real choice. They wanted a child, an expression of themselves. Over time, their collaboration on his career, always first priority, absorbed much of their physical passion for one another. But not all. There were many occasions when the two of them shared uninterrupted time alone in hotel suites. Shorty was, after all, his sister and chief confidant. There was a reason people called them the Siamese Twins. Find one, you find the other. No one thought a thing of it.

You wonder if I'm going to stop loving you when I find out that, not one day ago, you were ready to murder me.

He was willing to murder, considering it no more than a test of his ability to endure intensity. His desire had been to act in the most inexplicable manner possible and be impervious to the consequences.

And basically that's what had happened. Sylvie died. Her mother committed suicide, leaping into the sea not a month after Sylvie's own jump, just before the ship reached Singapore. Her father became a recluse: retired immediately, commissioned a one-man boat, and has spent his life sailing the world. Not too long before Fox became President he read in the paper that professor Arjay Marks of Princeton had committed suicide and was survived by his father, Clyde, renowned monetary expert, and Pittman Diggs, Arjay's longtime companion. So the Marks family that he had met was, in fact, no more, and certainly he, Charlie Fox, had played a role in its demise. But the real point was that, until today, until he met O'Malley, he actually had been impervious. He'd certainly walked off the ship without another soul being the wiser. He had wept with the Markses. Things had gone just as Sylvie said they would. No one ever accused him of not doing enough to stop Sylvie. Everyone agreed it all happened so fast.

The iron vault of Fox's past also presented him with Sylvie's words, also locked away until he shook O'Malley's wet hand: whether she lived or died, he would have to choose what to do with the experience.

Will you change your habit of being careful? Will you open your heart and feel the pain and the joy of your life? Or will you do what you usually do—deny your heart and pretend that all the things that have happened in the past few days were a fantasy?

Long before he was in the running to become the nation's second bachelor President (after James Buchanan in 1857), Fox had made it very clear to the American people that he would probably never get married, that he was married to the nation, and to the world. "My family is all of you," he said. And while it was an answer that many voters considered a bit extreme, they believed him when he also said that his choices were right for him.

In truth, for Charlie Fox, being married would have been the equivalent of being raped.

Fox become a master at turning his personal terrors into apparent strengths. The most conspicuous example of this was his ability to bring opposing sides of bitter conflicts to meaningful common ground. As a politician it set him apart, which was why he'd been tapped to represent his party as president at such a young age.

What anchored Fox's reputation was the time, as president, he followed Gandhi's example, if in a modified manner. No one knew until it was over that he had brought two adversaries to a secret location and refused to eat anything but water until they agreed to publicly pursue peace. He also had the room in which the two leaders met filled with cans of gasoline, boxes of matches, loaded pistols, knives, hand grenades, brass knuckles, whips, chains, swords, and two cat-o-nine-tails.

"I just wanted to remind them of the obvious: the stakes are high, choices have consequences, and I am prepared to give my life for peace," Fox later said to the world.

In truth, this was how Charlie Fox balanced both his compulsion to be perceived as an enlightened global leader, and his fear of risk.

He'd be the broker.

Fox almost never came down on any side of any issue, yet he was as explicit as a fanatic about where he stood: "My side is the middle," he said. "No issue, in itself, is more important than having people of honest purpose come together with respect for one another. To serve that cause is my life's work. There are enough people in the world taking hard stands on issues. And their voices are necessary; I respect them. But my interest, frankly, is beyond the simplicity of what's right and wrong. To me, the real moral issue of our time is how can we come together and move forward, step by step. Isolating people you don't like is not a very productive strategy, especially when they have the capacity to cause great harm anywhere on earth."

Fox said repeatedly: "I don't believe you make the world a more peaceful and healthy place to live by calling other people evil. Nor do I think that it is appropriate to say that the United States is the greatest nation on earth if what we really mean is that other nations are somehow less than we are—as though the citizens of those nations are less honorable and less worthy of God's grace than we are. As a wise man once said, the only reason to look down on others is to help them up. It seems to me, we're all on this planet together."

In response to allegations that he was soft on terrorism, Fox would reinforce his drum beat of common ground. "Of course we need to protect our nation from danger," he would say. "That goes without saying. But as citizens of Planet Earth, we no longer have the luxury of keeping our distance from people because we differ from them, because we don't like them, or because they have caused us harm. To understand and accept and work with differences is the quality that will define the health of our human family from this point onward. It's not neat and tidy, but it's real. If you can't deal with people you differ with, you haven't a prayer of making the world a better place."

Predictably, Fox's adversaries said he was so middle-of-the-road that he had a yellow stripe up his back. He was a man without principle, they charged, who would sell his soul to get the deal.

Voters, however, found Charlie Fox to be precisely the visionary leader the nation needed "in these perilous times"—which was why Fox won his second try for the White House by a landslide.

Yes, Fox had to admit, he did just what Sylvie said he might. He had pretended that what had happened with her was a fantasy.

Her last words to him, *"Love yourself, Mister Fox, just as you are,"* were today no more than a billboard left out in the sun for twenty years, decaying by the side of a country road long ago replaced by the interstate.

But god, what if people found out—the real truth, the whole story?

That was the question. That had always been the question. The first question. Everything else came after.

Maybe he wasn't the man he could have been, the man that Sylvie saw. He had sidestepped the choice of living from his heart, and he had avoided considering the price he paid for doing so.

And so what, really? If that were the price for being the most powerful man in the world, very possibly one of the most respected men in history, he was glad to pay it. He'd worry about living with an anguished heart in his dotage, long after he was sure O'Malley could not threaten him.

Fox had dealt with politicians who would barbecue their child on network television if it would expedite their agenda, and half of those people were right in his own party. He could deal with Hyman O'Malley.

The thing was, whoever Sylvie had been, this O'Malley guy was more so. Would he tell Pearl? Shorty? Who else? And what if the truth about Pearl came out, even as rumor? There would be the call for DNA testing. Sure, he could refuse . . . would refuse. But it was a complication. Possibly a serious one.

The key, as always, was—what did the man want? The answer Fox entertained chilled him. O'Malley had the feel of those do-gooders who live by principles so la-la there's no bargaining with them.

Had Fox really wasted the opportunity Sylvie had given him?

He could feel her saying, *"Mister Fox, you can always make another choice."*

Perhaps. But not today, not at the risk of letting O'Malley whisper to anyone what he knew about Charlie Fox.

10
Hyman's Journal:
The Swami

I had just turned eight when I met the Swami. For some reason the very first question I asked him was "How old are you?" He laughed and said, "You are asking the age of my house. My house is fifty-seven. But a house is nothing. What's important is the soul who lives there. And my soul is the same as yours. Ageless."

I had no idea what he meant.

Our ranch was near the Mojave Desert, east of Los Angeles. Turning eight, I was permitted to ride Lady, my Spanish Colonial, anywhere I wanted so long as I could still see our property, and the Swami's place, a mile away, was the furthest point I could go and still make out the stand of willows overlooking our pond. He was our closest neighbor, although he was seldom there.

"Feel free to get acquainted," my mom said. "I hear he's a very nice man."

The first time I rode to the Swami's, no one was home. The second time, he was outside with a couple of men who were building a stone wall around a garden. I later found out that these workmen were monks who had joined the religious community the Swami had started many years earlier when he arrived in the U.S. from India. I also came to learn that the Swami's fellowship had a big headquarters in L.A., a number of temples and other sorts of places, but that this particular spot was used as the Swami's personal retreat. Very few people were ever there with the Swami, just a handful of the monks and occasionally a few of the sisters, or nuns.

On the day I rode up, the Swami was watching one of the monks attempt to put a rattlesnake over the stone wall so that the rattler would be in the desert, not in the garden they were trying to enclose. I reined Lady, without saying a word, curled one leg around the saddle horn and sat looking down from her as the workman tried unsuccessfully several times to lift the curled snake with a long-handled shovel. I could tell the man was petrified, and the snake wasn't too pleased either.

I was what you might call a snake charmer. I don't know why, but I was born with an understanding of snakes. It was like I could read their minds. Really, I think it was that snakes could read my mind. They knew I wasn't a predator. I'd picked up many a rattler and played with it. So when I saw this workman afraid, as most people are, my first instinct was to help. I was just about to say, Mister, I can get that snake over for you, when the Swami looked up at me, smiled, and gave his head a little shake "No." The Swami had read my mind. No one had ever done that before. Just as surprising to me, I knew for certain that the Swami was also a snake charmer. He could have picked up the snake himself and not thought twice about it. He was the only other snake charmer I had ever met, and he was even better than I was because he could have communicated with that snake by some sort of mental telepathy and had the snake leave the garden of its own accord. But, I somehow understood, the Swami was teaching the man to have faith in the Swami's power to protect him. It was obvious that the man needed the Swami's protection, since the man was a long way from understanding the snake. I felt the Swami ask the snake to cooperate. The snake stretched out, a very un-snake-like thing to do when there's a man with a shovel and the man is afraid. The monk grabbed the snake's tail and whipped the rattler into the air and away from the garden as quickly as he could. Unfortunately for the monk, he didn't aim and the snake sailed right at me and sort of draped itself around my neck. All I could do was sit quietly and let the snake regain its equilibrium. Had Lady been almost any other horse, she would have bolted. Most horses hate snakes. But Lady had been trained by my dad, which is a whole other story. The monk was sure he'd killed me. Finally, I took off my hat and turned it upside down in my lap so the snake could slide down my chest and cozy himself inside the hat if he wished, which he did. I then dismounted and put my hat on the ground, and shortly the snake had had enough excitement for one day and slithered off for parts unknown. The monk looked like he'd seen a miracle, which, on his terms, I suppose he had. The Swami said to the men, "Why don't you boys get back to work now," and then gestured for me to join him on the veranda.

"So," the Swami said, handing me a glass of lemonade after I'd hitched Lady, "we meet again."

The greeting didn't surprise me. No flashes told me when or how, but my heart knew that the Swami and I had met before. But one thing did scare the heck out of me. And that was how deeply I felt that the Swami knew and loved me more than any other person on earth ever would.

Thus began the most important two and a half years of my life.

He wasn't a very tall man, the Swami, not much taller than that long-handled shovel the monk couldn't quite get to work. And he was plump, there's just no other word for it. By plump, I by no means imply that he was in the slightest unhealthy, lethargic, slow, or even old, for he was just as much the opposite of all those qualities as I was. I've always had the impression that he had to be a little roly-poly in order to carry around all the energy inside him; he would have burned up a skinny body. His hair was long, beyond his shoulders, slightly curly, and black without ever having known a strand of gray, I would bet. His skin was a color so much its own that it is impossible for me to put a single word on it. What I remember is the visual combination of milk chocolate and rose lit from beneath by a light so golden and bright that, if you were to cut the Swami with a knife, instead of drawing blood, you would reveal the sun. The skin of his face was soft; his beard almost non-existent; I'm sure he shaved every day, but not because his entire face required it. His face made me smile. There was always kindness in his expression, even when he would tell me stories of people betraying him, such as the man he loved very much who had stolen a large amount of money from him, or another man who had poisoned the Swami's dog. His eyes, however, could stop a train. They saw everything. It's hard to explain. When he looked at you, you knew he saw everything about you, and he loved every single bit of it, even the parts he suggested (and sometimes more than suggested) that you change. But then, when you looked into his eyes you also saw that his consciousness, while paying attention to you, also was elsewhere. Well, not just elsewhere: attuned to the entire universe. I came to discover that two or more people in completely different locations might report that they had seen him, in the flesh, and even talked with him, at exactly the same time.

Why the first words out of my mouth were "How old are you?" I may never know. Perhaps it was just one of those questions that helps to reestablish a sense of reality with somebody you know you know but can't quite remember. I was eight years old. I didn't live in the world of religious beliefs. We didn't go to church, didn't belong to any denomination. In my family, everything was sacred, even if we didn't understand it. When your life is horses and the desert, that's not a surprising view. What you don't respect can kill you. I did know that I felt the world in ways that many other people did not. And with the Swami that afternoon, I felt so much love pouring into me that I wondered whether I was about to turn into that shiny ball of light that my dad was always saying we all were. Which may be why my second question to the Swami was, "Are you God?"

He chuckled. "No more than you."

He wasn't God, but in years to come I would understand that his consciousness and God's consciousness were one, or as close to it as I'd ever known. He explained to me that he had been my guru for several lives. One reason he used this retreat, he said, was so that we would have the opportunity to meet again.

"It's not just in previous lives that we've known each other, you know," the Swami said one day. "Remember the woman who abducted you in Central Park?" He smiled at the surprise on my face. I hadn't yet told him that story. "What is it you call her, Dead Deer Woman?" he said. "Well, that was me. Awakening you to the call of your heart."

"Well, I'm glad you smell different today," I said.

He patted my arm. "I had to completely mask my identity to distract you from feeling the depth of my love for you."

"What about the star? That scar that's burned into my skull?"

"A kiss," he laughed, as if any further explanation was unnecessary.

The Swami spent most of his days at the retreat either in solitude or writing. And yet he invited me to be with him whenever I could, which was quite extraordinary I was to learn later; even the location of the retreat was kept secret from all but his closest disciples. Several days could pass without the phone ringing. His writing often meant dictating to a secretary or to a team of secretaries working in tandem, because he could speak for hours without interruption, stopping only for a sip of water. Yet when I would arrive and slip into the room as quietly as possible, the Swami, without breaking the flow of words, would bow to me, pour me a glass of lemonade and place some sweets or a piece of fruit by my chair.

Sometimes the Swami would stroll the room while he talked. Sometimes he would sit with his eyes shut. Sometimes he would lie down on the floor, on his back. Sometimes he would stand before the picture window and look out over the desert—all the while speaking the words that were being channeled through him by some divine force.

I loved it when he lay on the floor. You could just feel the tremendous fire within him melting into the ground, as though he and the molten lava inside the earth were one. And whenever possible I would lie down next to him, so that I could melt into the earth with him.

Occasionally, I needed a nap. I would curl up on his sofa and he would put a blanket over me, then rest his hand on my head. I'd be asleep before I knew it. And while I slept, I would hear different sounds. Sometimes it would be the sound of rushing water. Sometimes it would be chimes. Sometimes it would be the wind in the willows by our pond. And sometimes it would be a sound that the Swami told me was the heart of all creation—*Aum*, what the Swami called "the vibration of the Cosmic Motor." I didn't really understand him, but it sounded cool.

When I awoke, he might suddenly stop his dictation and say, "My prince arises. Let us take a walk." And then the two of us would tromp out into the desert.

Sometimes we wandered without saying a word. Other times we'd talk about anything that came up: cowboys, horses, pirates, some book I was reading, how the mountains were created. Whatever I was interested in, he was interested in. It sounds funny, but I felt like I was playing with my best friend—you know, a kid my own age—while also being with this wise old man who had known me forever, loved me even more than my parents did, and could teach me everything I would ever need or want to know.

I understood hardly a word the Swami spoke in his dictation sessions. I was eight, nine, ten. He was speaking the wisdom of the ages, explaining the meaning of timeless scriptures like the New Testament or the Bhagavad-Gita. Or he was speaking poetry. But while I didn't grasp the verbal concepts, what I felt always was the all-consuming love that the Swami felt for the Divine. That's all he was really doing, regardless of the words: expressing his boundless and passionate love for God. And that love showered me constantly, whether he was dictating or not.

There were times I was quite sure he fainted in the ecstasy of communion with Spirit. There were times when he would have a dialogue with Divine

Mother—his consciousness in some other world, his voice speaking both parts of the conversation. And there were times when he would sit in meditation so still and without a breath for so long that I began to wonder if he had died. One time, when he'd been a rock for a couple of hours, I actually pinched his nose shut to see if he would notice, since his mouth was already closed. Nothing happened. He just sat there. My hand got tired holding his nose, that's how long it went on. I got really scared, thinking maybe I should call somebody, when all of a sudden the Swami starts laughing.

"I did the same thing to my guru once," he says, patting my cheek. "What is your diagnosis? Is the patient alive or dead?"

No matter what he was doing, I was welcome to join him. (As I say, this was quite unusual, I later learned, since he knew he was approaching the end of his life and was in seclusion, trying to finish a few things.) I have come to understand that by allowing me to be in his presence no matter what he was doing—writing a letter, giving directions to those who served him, preparing a meal—he was teaching me that any activity has meaning only by the spirit of love that infuses it. And while I may not have known what his words meant when he was dictating, I certainly felt the power of his love; such power, in fact, that I could feel it inside me, changing my body, as if turning my blood into light.

It is true that in the time we spent together during those three years, the Swami showed me many things about myself. Through him I met some of the people I've been and courageous choices I've made in former lives. Fearful choices too. The Swami also showed me unforgivenesses I still held from some of the fearful choices, and told me I would meet others as I grew up. He revealed a bit of my future, telling me about some of the people I would meet, which included some of those I had harmed in previous lives. But he never made a big deal about it. It was like he was explaining how a toy worked.

He also taught me a form of yoga meditation that is remarkably effective in awakening us to the God within, but he didn't make a big deal about that either.

And there were always numerous, fascinating anecdotes about great masters he had met. At first, I wasn't sure if he had met them in this world or some other—until he started introducing me to them—and I realized that there is no such thing as "this world" and "some other." My mother later told me that the Swami had once said to her, "Just as songs passing through the ether may be tuned in when you have a radio, so it is possible to tune in with saints, who are just behind the etheric veil of space."

Most of the time we did only everyday things, the Swami and I. I taught him how to rope a steer. He was a surprisingly good rider for a man who had seldom been on a horse. He taught me how to make various Indian foods, especially desserts. He taught me how to fold paper into any number of fierce looking birds. He knew a lot about desert plants and animals—and the name of just about every star in the sky, it seemed to me.

Shortly after we met he invited my parents and me for dinner. He had the best time introducing us to his favorite Indian dishes, which he had made himself, explaining where they originated, and what all their ingredients were, and so forth. My mother was also a very good cook, and the Swami loved Mexican food, which was one of her specialties. So, to reciprocate, she invited him to our house and prepared a banquet of her favorites. This became a ritual. We'd go to the Swami's for Indian food and he'd come to our house for Mexican. We probably had six dinners together over a period of three years. Each occasion a celebration. The Swami and my mother both loved very spicy food. Whichever one of them was cooking would make one special dish that was the hottest of them all, to see if they could get the other to finally say "Uncle." At dinner, they'd each have tears streaming down their faces from the curry or cayenne or jalapeño, and yet each would say, "Oh, this is delicious," and then laugh and laugh and laugh.

During all these gatherings I don't recall that the Swami talked about God in any direct way except that, before supper and before we would part for the evening, he would say a prayer; and when he spoke, you knew he was talking to God as one speaks to a lover. And he initiated my parents to the yoga practice that he had taught me. The only other sort of "spiritual" thing that happened was that our wolf puppy, Amigo, whose parents had been shot and we were raising for a few months, ate a prairie chicken and shards of bone got stuck in his throat and he was nearly choking to death trying to get them dislodged. The Swami rolled Amigo onto his back and scratched his belly with one hand while gently putting his other hand on the wolf's throat. Amigo immediately stopped choking and started to yowl that little yowl that all dogs have that says, *You may scratch my belly for the rest of your natural life.* The Swami never said a word about what he had done, but I knew what had happened, and I think my folks did, too.

As I say, I came to learn that the Swami was always teaching. And I don't mean about nature or cooking. I mean that he was always teaching me about God. No matter what he was doing (and in my presence I once heard him sharply reprimand one of the monks for not paying attention to something—and in middle of scolding the monk, the Swami turned to me and winked) he was the same: a fountain of love. That was his teaching. Do whatever you do joined with the Divine within. He was so busy with his dictation and other duties, yet he would spend many hours over two or three days preparing dinner for my family, and you'd think he was doing the most important job of his life. (On his own he would hardly eat at all, and when he did it was pretty plain.) His example is what helped me to learn that no moment or activity is more important than another. They are all opportunities to love.

One day, he told me about his mother's sudden death. He had been eleven, a year older than I was at the time. He had brothers and sisters and a saintly father but his mother's love was a universe unto itself. He hadn't known how he would live without her. Over time he came to understand that the reason his mother had been taken from him was so that he would look for solace beyond his earthly mother, finding it instead in his real mother, Divine Mother, whose presence is not circumscribed by the boundaries of life and death.

It probably wasn't more than a week later that I re-lived for the first time being murdered. What triggered it was the death of my horse, Lady.

We were cantering home from the Swami's, the air thick with electricity and churning with pin-needle sand in the whirlwind of an approaching gullywasher we were attempting to outrun. Bandana up, Stetson down, head on my chest, I gave Lady her head. She knew the way as well as I. Nearly every free day for a year she and I had traveled the mile that separated our ranch from the Swami's retreat: over in the morning; home by supper. Even if I knew the Swami wouldn't be there. My father had picked Lady to be my first horse, a present on my fifth birthday. My babysitter dad called her. So I was only half-surprised when Lady suddenly stopped. But then she reared gently, the cue that I was to dismount, indeed fly off her instantly. Whereupon Lady began to trot a furious circle around me, snorting, whinnying, shuddering head-to-hindquarter as if trying to parry a swarm of hornets, reins jouncing free, stirrups knocking her ribs. Her one black eye visible to me demanded that I stand still. Her intent remained unfathomable until blue veins of electricity sprung from her body, worming over every inch of her with an opalescent aura: a silver mare glowing in the dusk. Lady shrieked and wheeled, galloping away from me when lightning exploded from her head, creating the flash of a squirming luminescent snake so long that it connected the point between Lady's ears to somewhere within the dark, low-slung clouds roiling overhead. Lady's spirit willed her already dead body to take two more full strides before slamming into the earth. I ran to her. She lay on her belly, head outstretched toward the coming storm, saddle straight, legs crumpled askew, a fetlock splintered, coat smoking, brain exposed, her head all but unrecognizable exuding the unforgettable stank of hair, flesh and fire, her body empty of even a twitch. I removed the saddle and lay face-down on Lady's steaming body as the storm engulfed the two of us. Lightning, rain, hail, thunder. Without looking, I reached out to pat Lady's forehead but instead touched the warm raw inside of her skull. I examined my hand, smelled it, put my tongue to it. In time, I repeatedly dipped my fingers and painted myself with Lady's essence. Don't hold back I remembered the Swami telling me. Speak to God your true feelings. "Mother-fucker," I sobbed, finding myself standing on Lady's back, hat in the mud, my face a mask of snot and tears and blood, my glare turned toward the cocksucking Almighty. "Limp-dick turd-burglar. Son-of-a-bitch. Paper-ass scumbag."

(Jimmy Washburn, who delivered feed to the ranch, had the foulest mouth of anyone I had ever heard. No matter what the subject, Jimmy peppered his sentences with terms like, "dung-puncher," or "broke-dick dog," or "pussy-wrangler." And when Jimmy got pissed, he could machine gun a hundred curses in a row, a feat I secretly admired despite seldom knowing what the words actually meant.)

I bared my teeth like a snared wolf lunging at its captor, then screamed and screamed and screamed at the sky every curse of Jimmy's I could remember, repeatedly, until my voice withered in exhaustion and futility to a series of rasps, there being no words, not even Jimmy's, the equal of my rage. It was then, mutely snarling, my entire being frantic for destruction, that I, age ten, was also suddenly, simultaneously, another person, an adult, in another time and place, looking into a face, hardly a hat brim from my own, close enough to smell the breath of utter detestation, the face of an unknown man whose hatred for whoever I was in that life mirrored exactly my hatred for whatever force had killed my Lady. The man's eyes were yellow with the bile of loathing. His random teeth, poking through bloody gums, seemed to have been deliberately chiseled into a weapon whose sole purpose was ripping flesh. His gullet bucked to suppress the vomit rising on waves of pure odium. In that life, this man lived to hate the being that was me. In this life, at ten, I had never known hatred directed at me specifically, personally. I couldn't imagine anyone hating me. Later I realized I was being taught. Hate isn't about the person being hated. Hate is only about the hater. At that moment, however, to be the object of unquenchable abomination was like being tossed in the air toward a gasoline bonfire, or worse, abandoned by my parents. All that bothered the man about killing me was that he could do it only once. The presence lasted just long enough for the man to quickly step back, whirl and with a roar from hell and a thwunk of his cutlass completely sever my head.

Instantly, from out of the storm, the Swami appeared and held me. The two of us soaked to the flesh, as I wept and sank into the endlessly numbing depth of lost love for the first time in this life.

A week later, the Swami and I built a cairn to mark the place where Lady fell, then shared an apple and a carrot in her honor. It was then the Swami told me that when he left the retreat the next morning he wouldn't be coming back. His time on earth was nearly over. He would be leaving his body within the next few days.

I was overcome with so many different emotions—about him, about Lady—that the only thing that made any sense was to hit him with all my might. Which I did, accompanied by a wail of pain. I gave him a shot Rocky Marciano would have been be proud of, on the arm, just below the shoulder. Ten or not, I was a strong kid, so it hurt, I know, but the Swami didn't flinch. I, on the other hand, burst into tears. He just looked at me with all the love in the world and said, "I know."

It was my mom who later pointed out that maybe there'd been a reason why the Swami told me the story of his mother when he did.

That afternoon, the Swami and I walked a long time in silence, holding hands. By this point in his life he didn't talk a whole lot. He was already leaving this world, I figured out later. Usually, when he was quiet I was quiet. I could tell when he was ready for me to ask him any of the many questions that were often on my mind. On this particular day, however, he was willing to talk, but I had no questions. I just wanted him. So I was rather surprised to suddenly hear myself ask him if I should join his monastic order when I grew up. As I look back on the moment today, I feel he planted the question in my mind because he knew that, eventually I would wonder, and for some reason he wanted to give me the answer himself while he was alive.

He smiled and said, "No. That's not the path for you."

And then he said, "Very soon, one of my dearest disciples will ask me how the work I have been part of here on earth will continue without my physical presence. And I will tell that disciple something that will become the cornerstone of my teachings. I will say that when I am no longer here, only love can take my place. But even as I say it I will know that it may take years, maybe even lifetimes, for even some of my most devoted followers to really know what 'only love' means.

"What I want you to understand, boy of my heart, is that we live in a time of tremendous ignorance on earth. You have been blessed by your devotion to Spirit in previous lives. Although you love me deeply, as I do you, we both know in our hearts that God is the only lover, and the only one loved. This Swami is no more significant in your life than a particle of dust on the moon. God is all. God is you. God is me. God is talking to God. God is listening to God.

"Most people, however, feel a need to be associated with a religion or a teacher. This is good, but only to a point. Sadly, it can be very difficult to be a member of a religious organization, or the disciple of a master, and know God. That sounds funny, doesn't it? But you see, in order to know God we must surrender everything to God, including even our attachment to our own guru and any organization associated with him. It's not enough to love a master, or even to follow a master. The goal is to become a master—a master of ourselves.

"I know this is hard for you to understand at this time. That is why, as I speak, I am also placing these words in your heart. As you get older you will be able to hear them whenever you wish and thus feel their meaning anew. I am giving you another gift as well. You will always be able to experience that the God in me and the God in you are the same."

The Swami put his hand on my chest. "No, my sweet snake charmer, in this life your ashram is the Earth Mother. Point yourself in any direction, you'll find everything you need right here," he said, tapping my heart.

"Don't worry," he said. "If you forget, I'll remind you. It's not like I'm going anywhere."

11

Sagacious Fanny

"Wow! What was *that* all about?" Pearl said first thing as they drove away.

Hyman's truck may have been a bit Willy Wonka on the outside—turquoise body, Mirror Man painted in silverdust on the doors, and behind the cab a giant geodesic dome made of varnished cherry in which Hyman stored his stash of antique mirrors, clothes and a cot for sleeping—but inside the cab, everything was cream: the faux leather bench seat, the padded dash, the carpet, the rubber floor mats, the interior roof. Only the steering wheel was different: spalted maple stained butterscotch.

Before setting off, Pearl had accepted Hyman's invitation to search the cherry dome for dry clothes. She had emerged in a pair of his sweat pants, yellow, paired with an apple green T-shirt that said: *Irish Alzheimer's: You forget everything but resentment.* Both a perfect fit since she was no more than an inch taller than Hyman.

"What that?" said Hyman, who himself had changed into another pair of chinos and a pale blue T-shirt that said, simply, *Breathe.*

"My uncle," Pearl said. "First he's standing there like a Roman centurion about to lop your head off for having fun with his beloved niece. And then, as soon as you two shake hands, he turns into a kid in short pants trying to hide behind the living room couch. He couldn't get away from you fast enough."

It surprised Pearl that she could feel so acutely Uncle Charlie's fear.

This must be the new me, she thought.

"I've never seen him so . . . I guess shocked," Pearl said. "Terrified in a way. Do you mind if I ask . . . did he have an experience like I did? I mean, well, you know: did something happen?"

"I can't say yes or no," Hyman said. "I'm sure you understand. Anything that you experience when we're together, for instance, will be up to you to share with someone else, if you wish."

"Why do I have the feeling you don't know who he is?"

Hyman looked at her with the wry smile that said I know that you know that I know that the real identity of everyone is the same.

"I didn't at first, actually," Hyman said. "I pieced it together. And just now as we were leaving I noticed the decal on the car."

"Incredible," Pearl laughed. "Here's the most powerful man in the world, and to you he was just some schmo in a limo."

It's often very amusing what we believe constitutes a powerful man, Hyman thought. He knew sadhus in loin cloths who could raise the dead or stop an avalanche.

"You might be surprised what I don't know," he said."

"You got something against the news?" she joked.

"Not a'tall. Just like I've got nothing against the weather. But neither rain nor sun play a very big role in the choices I make. Besides, news doesn't mean new. There's not a story in the world that hasn't occurred countless times before. But if my internal guidance directed me to pay attention to something, I surely would."

He glanced at Pearl. "Surprise you?" he asked.

"Mmm. Not really. It's just different, you know. My mother reads a mountain of newspapers every day. And there's a room in our home with a dozen monitors linked to satellites so somebody can watch news from all over the world. Is it ever a hindrance for you, not knowing current events, as they say?"

Hyman laughed. "I do have this one friend. He thinks I'm demented because I can't yack with him about the Yankees."

"Well, all right for your friend! Not knowing the President is one thing. But baseball. That is pretty retarded dontcha think?"

"Last year I happened to mention to him that the Yankees wouldn't make it to the World Series. On rare occasions, if somebody brings up a subject, I get spontaneous visions of things. Usually I just let them pass, or keep my mouth shut. But he's a good friend, and his father once played for the Yanks. Anyway, I let it slip. He wasn't surprised that I might know how the series would turn out. But he said, 'Man, I don't need somebody who can predict games. I need a buddy I can argue with. Quit with the hocus-pocus and start reading the sports page, will you?' Maybe you've heard of him, Puer Puella?"

Pearl looked at Hyman as if he had suddenly turned into a Golden Retriever, its paws on the steering wheel.

"You're kidding!"

"What do you mean?"

"Puer Puella? The Prince of Darkness? Mister New Age Gangster? The person whose life's goal is to destroy my uncle Charlie?"

"Really?"

Pearl laughed at the delightful insanity. "Man, you really don't get around."

"I don't get involved in the dramas of anyone's life, if that's what you mean," Hyman said. "Life on the surface is pretty much just a soap opera. Like all that stuff with you today. That doesn't mean anything to me. Everybody's got a million colorful stories throughout all their various incarnations. I'm only interested in what's going on underneath all those stories, the soul's journey, our growing awareness of who we really are, you might say."

They were quiet a while, then Pearl asked, "Is it ever dangerous being you?"

"I'm not sure what danger is, really. I don't feel un-safe, if that's what you mean. Everything is a manifestation of God, so far as I can tell."

"I mean has anybody ever freaked, you know, tried to hurt you?"

"I know what you meant," Hyman said. "I just didn't want you to use the word dangerous without appreciating that it's just an idea our mind makes up in fear, like necessary."

Hyman said it in the most nonchalant way, like it was the most natural thing in the world for every assumption Pearl had ever had to be no longer valid.

Pearl looked out over the lake to their right where a slalom skier, a girl, frosted blonde hair, sky blue wetsuit, was creating rooster tails left and right behind a small white inboard ski boat.

"I get that," Pearl said, still watching the skier. "The most difficult part of this morning has been feeling—or maybe it's accepting—the love within my own heart."

She turned her head toward Hyman. "It's like, part of me doesn't feel worthy of all this love. Does that make sense?"

"It's a common reaction."

"Why common?"

"This is a big change. For our ego. Making room for a tidal wave of love you might say. Anything that threatens its security sparks all sorts of violent reactions: anger, blame, unworthiness, you name it. And there isn't anything more threatening to the ego than when we choose to align our will with Spirit. That's tantamount to the ego's death—in the sense that it's no longer running the show."

But it wasn't so much the fear of giving up the familiar that Pearl felt, as it was the feeling that she could now see and hear and feel in ways that she would have called supernatural a day earlier. She didn't even need to look at the water skier, for instance, to know just what the girl was feeling.

"Can I learn to do what you do?" Pearl continued.

"Not a prayer."

"What not a prayer?" she said, feigning a swat with the back of her hand, "I thought that, sooner or later, everybody gets attuned to Spirit."

"True."

"Then why are you saying I can't?"

"You asked can you do what I do. Well, I don't *do* anything. Real life has nothing to do with doing. It's *being* something, not *doing* something, that matters."

"Being what?" She knew but needed to hear him say it.

"An instrument," he said.

"So . . . wait a minute. If you know Puer, does that mean you know his sister, Carmella?"

"Sure do."

"Tell me about her." Carmella Puella was one of the nation's most respected women, founder of the WOW Foundation –– Women of the World –– an advocate for the rights and welfare of the world's women and children. And someone who had a home down at the other end of this very lake, though Pearl had never been there, nor met Carmella.

The fact that Carmella had been a nun for many years before leaving the convent to start a foundation simply added to her celebrity. As did the fact that she was the sister of who some people called a notorious gangster. And it was the gangster's dough that bankrolled the foundation. Everybody knew this.

"Would you care to meet her, I mean, right now?" Hyman said. "We could swing over to her place, if you have time. I'm pretty sure she'll be there. It's where I'm bunking."

"The thing is," Pearl said, "I need to be home by late afternoon. And sometime today I have to go to the village and pick up my mother's birthday present."

"What we could do, if you wish," Hyman said, "is visit Carmella, then pick up your mom's present on our way back to your house."

"Speaking of which," said Pearl, "I forgot to mention, I've been asked to invite you to mom's birthday picnic tonight. A small, intimate gathering of 200, which in my mother's life really is an intimate gathering. She loves big, casual parties, the more the merrier kind of thing. You want to come? Or rather, *would* you come. I would really like it."

Hyman was silent for a moment, then said, "Happy to."

Carmella Puella's home on the lake was a farm that Hyman had teased Carmella could be its own country. The grounds included a mile of beach and nearly one thousand acres of actively managed woodlands, orchards, vineyards, pastures, ponds, and greenhouses. Its name was *The Island of Peace*, which was also the name of Carmella's best-selling first book. The title, she would write, refers to that place located within the heart of everyone where only the voice of Spirit is heard: *"When we come home to that place, we know who we truly are—beings with an infinite capacity to love . . . our earth, our fellows, ourselves. In fact, we know that there is no earth, or fellows, or selves . . . for when we are in our true home, the island of peace, we experience only the One."*

The driveway was at least a mile long and could be found only if someone knew where to look between a couple of huge hemlocks near the end of an even longer and deserted dead-end dirt road. Hyman turned in, down a lane between hemlocks, then over the gentle hills of an apple orchard, then a pasture with three chestnut Arabians, and finally through a small, manicured pine forest, at the far end of which, overlooking the lake, was the main house—a homey rambling Victorian with spacious porches and an attached flagstone portico under which was parked a lavender limousine.

"Tell me," Pearl wondered, as Hyman turned off the ignition, "how come Carmella is considered the next Mother Teresa and her brother is considered such a jerk?"

Hyman smiled.

"Have you ever heard, or maybe read in a fashion magazine, that sometimes there is more to somebody than the stories that are reported about them?"

"More than what my uncle says?"

"Anything's possible."

"Sagacious fanny," she said.

"I beg your pardon?"

"My mother frowns when I call people smart ass."

When Carmella Puella first saw Pearl, she reacted as any Lithuanian might who, when walking alone in the forest, turns to enjoy the view behind her only to find that her long dead brother is standing there, now fully alive, not ten feet away, and furthermore is wearing the ochre robes of a Hindu Swami.

Carmella gasped. Her hands instantly came together, as if in prayer, and covered her mouth. Tears filled her eyes.

"It's you . . . ," she said.

And then the two woman raced to each other. Anyone but Hyman O'Malley might have thought that Pearl was Carmella's daughter taken from her at birth. Such was their embrace.

Then, standing face-to-face, the two held each other and smiled into one another's eyes. For the longest time they just stood there, rooted, transfixed, beaming.

Pearl eventually lifted Carmella's hand to her mouth and touched the back of it ever so briefly with the tip of her tongue. "I lu you, Bee-nu," Pearl said, then giggled.

The hand that Pearl had kissed then reached out and wiggled the end of Pearl's nose.

"And I love you, my brother," Carmella said. "All that I have, and all that I am, is yours."

12

Brothers

hey were standing under the portico between Hyman's truck and Carmella's lavender limo in the Finger Lakes of New York on the continent of North America in the twenty-first century at eleven o'clock in the morning. They were also seated on the ground, along the banks of the Ganges in the city of Allahabad, on the continent of India, at a religious fair, a Kumbha Mela, with thousands of other pilgrims just like themselves, in the nineteenth century, at seven o'clock in the evening. It was a rare moment, particularly in India, since the being who would be called Carmella in a life 200 years later was leaving the body he had inhabited for three quarters of a century.

hey were both Swamis, members of India's most ancient monastic order. They wore ochre robes and each carried a bamboo staff and begging bowl. Their heads were shaved. Marking the point between their eyebrows, their third eye, the eye of omniscience, the doorway to the Infinite, was a single dot of rose-colored sandalwood paste. Each had been a monk for more than fifty years.

But they were more than fellow renunciants, sannyasis. They had been born brothers. Carmella, named Bishnu in that life, was the eldest of four children. Pearl, called Kashi, ten years younger, was the baby. In between them in age were a sister and another brother. Despite their age differences, Bishnu and Kashi had been inseparable for most of their lives.

Bishnu's room as a boy was the small attic, or fourth floor, located at the top of a steep skinny set of stairs in their large home. He had transformed a dusty garret of cobwebs into a shrine to Krishna. There, he spent his evenings in meditation. One night very late, upon completing his ritual, Bishnu found Kashi, not yet two years old, asleep on a nearby cushion. This meant that Kashi had climbed the stairs to the loft all by himself, and then had managed to open the large, heavy loft door, a potentially perilous undertaking for a toddler. Bishnu carried his brother downstairs to bed, tucked him in, and in the morning informed their mother of Kashi's nocturnal adventure.

"Mmmm," their mother clucked. "A budding seeker."

Being a woman who was both holy and practical, she then said, "Bishnu, perhaps if you create a small shrine in Kashi's room and also put a gate at the bottom of the stairs, we can satisfy your brother's yearnings in a way that won't risk his neck."

And then their mother explained to Kashi how dangerous it was for him to climb the attic stairs without someone there to watch him.

This solution worked well for one day. But on the second evening, again reviving from his meditation, Bishnu found Kashi curled up asleep on the nearby cushion. It was as perplexing as it was worrisome. How Kashi had been able to climb over the formidable gate was impossible to imagine. And since the gate's latch was located well above Kashi's head, it certainly seemed out of the question that he had opened the gate, walked through, then re-latched it.

Their mother gave Kashi a stern talking-to, all the while kissing and hugging him, and when she finished she gave him his favorite candy.

Bishnu, meanwhile, built a more elaborate gate, one that even he would have had a difficult time climbing over without the aid of a ladder. The gate's latch was much too complicated for a child of Kashi's age to unlock. And anyway, Kashi was too short to reach it.

But Bishnu didn't want Kashi to feel rejected when he found that his night wanderings would no longer lead him to Bishnu's loft. Therefore, on the first night of the new gate's operation, Bishnu hid behind a screen on the third floor landing in case Kashi needed comforting in the face of Gate Invincible.

Near midnight, Bishnu heard Kashi crawling up the stairs from the second floor, where Kashi's bedroom was located. When Kashi reached the new gate, he pulled himself up to his feet, then reached his little arms up to the sky and looked up at the ceiling for several minutes. Then he lay down on the floor in front of the gate and went to sleep. Bishnu decided that he would not pick up Kashi and return him to his bed. Perhaps if Kashi woke up on the hard floor with no blanket over him he would learn a little quicker that the new gate was insurmountable. Bishnu remained hidden, though, in case Kashi needed solace when he woke up. Shortly before dawn, Kashi awoke and, without a sign of distress, crawled back down the stairs to his own bed. Bishnu followed secretly behind to be sure he didn't miss a detail of the evening's drama.

The next night Bishnu opened his eyes at the end of meditation to once again find his baby brother asleep on the cushion beside him. The gate below remained as locked and as imposing as when Bishnu had secured it several hours earlier.

This was becoming unsettling.

The next evening, determined to unravel the mystery, Bishnu again hid behind the third-floor screen. Again, near midnight, Kashi crawled up the stairs. Again, he pulled himself to his feet in front of the gate. Again, he raised his little arms and looked up at the ceiling. And then it happened. Kashi lowered his hands and toddled right through the closed gate as if it weren't even there and began to crawl up the attic stairs. When he reached the top, he kept on crawling right through the closed door and into Bishnu's room.

Bishnu knew exactly what had happened.

Kashi's love of Krishna, kindled through previous lives, was so strong that Krishna himself had blessed Kashi by removing any obstacle to the baby's desire to be in Krishna's presence. Bishnu knew that Krishna had been testing Kashi on the first night by not allowing him to walk through the gate. But that was no disappointment to Kashi. If the gate were as close as he could get to Bishnu's garret, then that was where he would sleep. He would simply come back every night and let Krishna decide when to let him pass through the gate.

Bishnu also knew that this miracle was a message to him, from Krishna. Bishnu's own love of Krishna had drawn to him a brother who would be Bishnu's spiritual companion in this incarnation.

That night, the night Bishnu witnessed the limitations of Gate Invincible, instead of carrying Kashi back down to his bed, Bishnu held him and rocked him, chanting "Jai Krishna" over and over.

At dawn, as roosters were awakening the neighborhood, Kashi awoke, smiling at Bishnu.

Kashi said, "I lu you, Bee-nu."

Bishnu, his eyes sparkling with tears in the day's new light, reached out and wiggled the end of his baby brother's nose.

"And I love you, my brother," Bishnu said. "All that I have, and all that I am, is yours."

*B*ishnu was very studious. He spent whatever time was required each day to ensure that he received superior grades in school. Their father worked for the British Engineering Corp as an accountant, a very respectable position. He was acutely aware of the value of education and diligence in the world of the British Empire, and so was keen that his sons cultivate both. As the eldest son, it was Bishnu's obligation to set a good example. But Bishnu would have done well in school even without his father's expectations. He was a naturally curious and gifted child. His understanding of the physical world was so great that, even as a young teenager, everyone in their neighborhood turned to Bishnu whenever something needed fixing—from a leaky roof to a rose garden that wasn't producing to potential. When he was fifteen, Bishnu spent his summer holiday rebuilding a house for his grandparents. Kashi, age five, was his assistant. The project was so successful that word spread and Bishnu was showered with building opportunities. If business, instead of the Divine, had been Bishnu's passion, he could have quickly been making nearly as much money as his father, a fact that his father gladly advertised to friends and family as proof of Bishnu's exceptional potential. The dream of Bishnu's father was that his eldest son would earn a university degree in architecture and then would enjoy a career marked by the security and prestige of working, as he himself did, under the protection of the Crown. In his father's fantasy, Bishnu would leave his mark for generations by designing bridges, dams, railway stations, entire communities even, not to mention estates of the privileged. Given the call of Bishnu's heart, however, his father's aspirations for him never really had much of a chance—a fact that was amply demonstrated the day Kashi was kidnapped.

The note read: *You put a notice in the town square today. Say you will build no more homes. Or Kashi disappears. Notice appears. Kashi comes home.*

A street child had been paid a few rupees by a stranger to deliver the note to Bishnu. Even at fifteen, Bishnu was calm and knew that the note came from God. Not that God had kidnapped Kashi, per se, but that certain events had been set in motion that would test Bishnu's trust, as well as his ability to divine just what was right action. So the first thing Bishnu did was sit down and meditate.

Divine guidance didn't actually outline every step of what Bishnu's course of action should be, but it did reveal to him that Kashi was in no immediate danger and indeed was enjoying himself, and further, where he was—at the home of a neighbor, Roy G. Biv.

This last piece of news was gratifying but actually not at all surprising to Bishnu.

Biv Babu (Babu, meaning Mister, is commonly used after the person's name) was a carpenter who presented himself as a master homebuilder. He was also a man who, by reputation and public exhibition, had a drinking problem, making him unreliable and more than occasionally obnoxious. The gossip was that Biv Babu had once been a respected workman. Too many disappointed customers and too many displays of intoxicated lunacy made it impossible for most people to remember how good he had been. As a result, Biv Babu's family was very poor. Bishnu knew that drink and despair had prompted Biv Babu to take such a rash act as kidnapping. Kashi had been easily lured by Biv Babu because Kashi knew him as part of the neighborhood, and because Kashi liked Biv Babu's children, with whom Kashi was happily playing when Biv Babu had the ransom note delivered to Bishnu.

Mostly, Bishnu was relieved at his communiqué from the Creator. Kashi would be safe. Biv Babu might behave in a completely irrational manner—he had once begun to build a boat in his yard to save his family when the Himalayas melted; it sat there still, barely started, "Biv's Temple of Foolishness" some neighbors called it—but he had never abused anyone. Well, except perhaps with his tongue. Under the influence, Biv Babu had a scheme to rectify each of life's endless injustices, and was not reticent about articulating every one of them at high volume and in elaborate detail. Sober, one might mistake him for a statue.

Bishnu realized that his real challenge was handling the situation with love. It would be easy to report Biv Babu to the authorities. Probably something very severe would happen to him. Kidnapping a child, even when deranged by reason of drunkenness, is a serious offense. But what would this accomplish? Biv Babu's wife and children would be hurt as much as Biv Babu himself, if not more so. And what was Biv Babu's real transgression, anyway? Not being able to keep away from drink? Being afraid that some young fellow of fifteen was about to make it even more difficult for Biv Babu to earn a living? Feeling ashamed of his choices, including this one? Bishnu saw that Biv Babu's action, while potentially hurtful, was really a call for help. Biv Babu was like a small child himself. Surely that's how Krishna would see it, Bishnu felt.

Bishnu arrived at Biv Babu's door disguised as an anchorite. No one would know he was Bishnu. He wore a loincloth, nothing more. His body was covered with ashes literally from hair to toes, a custom to ward off heat and cold. The spiritual eye was vividly painted upon his forehead. He carried with him only a begging bowl. The anchorite asked Biv Babu for a cup of water. When the water was presented, the anchorite asked for the privilege of dancing for the children he heard playing in the home's inner courtyard. It was the kind of request that, among most Hindu families of that generation, was hard to turn down, coming as it did from someone who had renounced all for God and depended entirely on the generosity of others for even a drop of water. A request to give something in return, in this case a performance for children, though unusual, was not to be denied, since it was deemed a request from Brahma Himself.

Bishnu soon had the children squealing in ecstasy at this goofy booby who became several dancing animals right before their eyes and showered them with candies that appeared from out of nowhere.

It was clear that Kashi was safe. When the dance was over and the anchorite was about the leave, he asked Biv Babu if Biv Babu would bless him. It was another request that couldn't be refused. So Biv Babu walked the anchorite to the street, where, after Biv Babu's blessing, Bishnu said, "Biv Babu, look closely, I am Bishnu. I came to your home to make sure that my Kashi is in perfect health, and to tell you that I agree to your request that I build no more houses."

At this news, Biv Babu fell to the ground and touched Bishnu's bare feet. "Please forgive me, little sir," Biv Babu cried. "I am a wretch. I would never have hurt Kashi. You must believe me. I am so afraid. I drink to calm myself, but instead only lose my mind altogether . . . ."

Bishnu pulled Biv Babu to his feet. "I forgive you, Biv Babu. And to prove to you that I forgive you, I would like you to walk Kashi home. And when you get there, we will share mango juice and sweetmeats, and I will make you a proposition that you may find very attractive."

An hour later, when Bishnu proposed that he go to work for Biv Babu, the man nearly fainted.

"It's the only way," Bishnu exclaimed. "There are many people who want me to build something for them. If I say 'no,' they will be disappointed. There is no need for that, since I am willing to serve them. But I have given you my word that I will build no more houses. So what other alternative is there but for me to work for you? It is you they will be hiring. I will be your assistant, as will Kashi. Everyone benefits. You get paid. I am actually doing the work, which satisfies the customers. And you give me a small sum for my services. It needn't be much. My every need is provided for by my parents."

"You are no child, little sir," Biv Babu wept. "Only a man of wisdom, a man of God, thinks of such a plan."

"I can assure you Biv Babu that the plan is Krishna's," Bishnu said. "And he compels me to mention that, in order for the plan to succeed, you and I must work together at all times."

One year later, Biv Babu's reputation as an excellent builder had been refurbished. His skills, which had merely lay dormant under fear and self-hatred, gradually awakened in Bishnu's company.

Biv Babu actually had much to teach his assistant as a craftsman. All the while, the aura of Bishnu was so fertile that, by spending many hours in it each day, Biv Babu began to enjoy forms of intoxication that were far preferable to alcohol. One of them was having enough money to complete building the boat in his yard, creating a beautiful captivating playland for the neighborhood children. Much to the amusement of everyone who had seen the original monstrosity, Biv Babu christened his creation *The Temple of Foolishness*.

Meanwhile, Bishnu's choices did not go unnoticed by his father. The father knew it would be only a matter of time before his eldest son asked permission to take up the monastic life. And given the bond between Bishnu and Kashi, their father also knew that eventually he would be losing two sons to God, a fact which did not satisfy his mind's desire to live through his sons' worldly achievements, but did bring joy to his heart.

It wasn't until years later that Kashi learned that he had been kidnapped. His parents never knew.

*T*he moment before the Swami who had been born with the name Bishnu died as an old man at the Kumbha Mela in Allahabad, on the banks of the Ganges at seven o'clock in the evening, his brother, the Swami who had been born with the name Kashi, raised the dying Swami's right hand to his lips and tenderly touched the back of it with the tip of his tongue. As if in response, the elder Swami cried out, "Jai Krishna."

If the act had been recorded on film and subsequently analyzed by scholars for the remainder of eternity, only when their research techniques included communicating with Spirit might they have been able to glean the origin or meaning of what they witnessed—a trick the young Kashi had invented as a boy to awaken his brother from the slumber of delusion.

There were times when Bishnu would become so absorbed in his work with Biv Babu or his school studies that he was like a man who had been put in a trance.

"Bishnu, I am going to burn down the house now."

"Very good, Kashi, I love you."

"Bishnu, Krishna is standing behind you eating a wild elephant."

"Very good, Kashi, I love you."

This was not good, Kashi knew.

The goal of life was to become more present, and Bishnu was as good as asleep in these moments. But Bishnu's example of finding creative and loving ways to solve problems had made a big impression on Kashi. Besides, Kashi knew a secret about Bishnu. Bishnu had a small birthmark, in the shape of a heart, on the back of his right hand, between the thumb and first finger. This wasn't the secret. The secret was how sensitive the heart was. Kashi had watched the peace that came over Bishnu whenever he placed his left thumb on the heart and left it there for several breaths. So Kashi figured if he could touch the heart long enough when Bishnu was in one of his trances, Bishnu would wake up.

At first, Kashi simply stood next to Bishnu and casually put his hand over Bishnu's hand, or held Bishnu's hand, always so the heart was easy to touch for long periods. But for some reason this didn't work. Probably because he frequently touched Bishnu—hugging him, sitting on his lap, pulling his ears.

Once, Kashi poked the heart with the end of his finger. Bishnu jumped and yelled "Ow!" Obviously that was not the solution.

How could he touch the heart with love in a way that it had never been touched before? And once that question was conveniently placed in his mind by Krishna, Kashi knew just what he would do.

He picked up Bishnu's hand and licked it as a dog would. Bishnu jumped, but not in pain. He laughed, in fact.

"Nice puppy," he said to Kashi.

Well, this was progress, Kashi thought. But I don't think he will enjoy me licking him like that too many times. And that's when Kashi decided to try touching Bishnu's heart with the just tip of his tongue. On the very first attempt, Bishnu became immediately present and asked, "Kashi, what are you trying to tell me?"

Kashi didn't reply. He just put down his brother's hand, bowed to him, and left the room smiling.

His brother was wide awake.

*T*he most surprising part of meeting Carmella as Bishnu was how little it surprised Pearl. After the morning's inner travels, her definition of The Miraculous had slimmed down to not much. She had never even daydreamed that she might come to know and love someone in this life that she remembered knowing and loving in another. But now that it had happened, she felt: *Gee, why not? This must go on all the time. We just don't realize it.*

So many events throughout her life held deeper meaning now.

Pearl had always loved to meditate—sit quietly, feel not think, follow her breath . . . yet it wasn't something she'd learned anywhere; it just came to her. Her mother and daddy were born into Catholic families, but long before Pearl was born their "religion" had become some amalgam of horses, art and politics. Her dad went to church at least once a month, and Pearl usually accompanied him, but it was never the same church twice. When she asked him why, he said, "All religions are the same, Pea; it's just people trying to love. I'm fascinated by the different expressions, the way I'm fascinated by different forms of art." That might be true on one level, Pearl knew, but her dad hustled her out of a few sermons when the minister started calling certain people heathens whom God was going to roast for eternity in the fires of damnation because they believed, or didn't believe, this and that. Any church with a big choir was Pearl's favorite; she'd heard the Mormon

Tabernacle Choir in Salt Lake City, though the silence of a Quaker meeting was just as delicious. One of the reasons Pearl loved to travel with her dad was their shared enjoyment of experiencing the variety, yet sameness, of Spirit. From Sufis to Holy Rollers, each religion seemed to Pearl a tiny ornament of wonder hanging on the tree of creation.

Starting in first grade, Pearl was enrolled in the local parochial grammar school because her mother liked that the classes were small. But her connection to things Catholic changed abruptly in third grade the day Sister Marie-Clarice picked up Billy Boston by the ear so violently that Pearl had visions of the ear being ripped off Billy's head. Pearl ran out of the classroom, out of school, and would have walked the entire ten miles home if Mister Naukham, their farrier, hadn't spotted her roadside, turned his truck around and offered her a ride. Never, Pearl informed her mother, would she go anywhere where adults hurt children.

In the nearly ten years since Billy Boston's Ear, Pearl had come to feel that the lesson of Sister Marie-Clarice was: *Don't confuse Spirit with people who say they act in the name of Spirit.* But that didn't mean Pearl had stopped having fantasies of ripping off Sister M-C's own ear, and the ears or whatnot of anyone who misused their influence over kids. Now, however, after this morning, Pearl was presented with a deeper lesson. Her fantasies born of anger didn't actually stem from the actions of someone else, but rather from an unwillingness on her part to forgive herself for any time she expressed fear through violence.

My life is all about me, she thought.

Then there was her fascination with India. For years she had harbored a hunger to live there indefinitely as an adult. She'd had a big poster of Krishna in her bedroom since she was five. She saw the poster in a store and immediately became out-of-her-mind inconsolable until her mother bought it for her. Krishna was, simply, comfort. As were the few Indian dishes she had taught herself to cook. Samosas, bartha, gulab jamin.

*I*t could be 95-plus everywhere else on earth, but it would always be comfortable in the shaded womb of Carmella's veranda overlooking the lake. Its continual breeze had kissed sailors, danced with honeybees, and nibbled mint leaves on its journey to the *Island of Peace.*

They were eating chilled cucumber soup and tortellini salad. Champagne glasses held sparkling Catawba—the Rosé of grape juice. The food was set out on a stained-glass mandala coffee table between them.

Pearl and Carmella sat on one side of the table in a dark blue love seat. Hyman sat across from them, swinging gently, barefoot in a yellow canvas chair that hung from the ceiling. The surprise the universe had just pulled off caused him to think about the Swami. The Swami loved to give gifts so much that if you failed to rip open his present the absolute second he gave it to you, he'd start tearing off the wrapping for you. "That's how God feels," the Swami had said to Hyman. "He can't wait to have us dive right in to life."

"Pearl," Hyman said, "if you can, imagine for a moment that, when you met Carmella, your previous incarnation together wasn't revealed to you. How would you have felt about her?"

For at least the 10th time, Pearl stuck her index finger into her soup and popped it in her mouth. Then she took the same finger, put it in the soup again, but this time offered it to Carmella, who obliged, closing her eyes.

"Oh, I would have thought she was as wonderful as she is," Pearl said, her finger still in Carmella's mouth. "I still would have loved her instantly, I'm sure." Slowly retrieving her finger, this time she gently stuck it through the center of a tortellini and offered it to Carmella, who again closed her eyes and opened her mouth. "In fact, I believe I loved Carmella before I met her. Ever since I heard about her I've had this *thing* for her."

Carmella raised her champagne glass to her lips, smiling at Pearl. She sipped then said, "The only thing that would have been different, Hyman, was how long it would have been before we opened our hearts completely. I mean, people meet and fall in love in a day, but they still wait a while to get married. Here, we don't need to wait," she laughed a tiny chirp, "as it were." Putting down her glass, Carmella used her thumb and index finger (her unpainted nails tidy as a surgeon's) to pick up a tortellini. Feeding it to Pearl, she said, "We already know everything we need to about each other."

Pearl chewed slowly, staring into Carmella's eyes. Then, still looking at Carmella, she asked, "Hyman, when we meet new people, do you suppose we are always picking up where we left off?"

Hyman reached down with his bare foot and pushed against the floor, sending his chair into a slow half-spin.

"The mechanics of the universe are a mystery to me, Pearl, besides the big idea that love is the deal. But sometimes it must be as you suggest, I'm sure."

"Where did you and Uncle Charlie leave off, I wonder," said Pearl.

"Uncle Charlie?" asked Carmella.

"My uncle is Charlie Fox, the President? . . . you know, of the United States?" Pearl said, her tongue darting out of the corner of her mouth in Hyman's direction.

"Isn't that odd," Carmella said. "Your uncle has been trying to meet with me for a while now. Our schedules just haven't cooperated. He met Hyman today?"

"He's here for my mother's birthday party tonight. He tracked Hyman and me down over by the lake."

"And your Uncle Charlie had a reaction to . . . um . . . our boy here?" Carmella said, grinning, pouring everyone a measure more of juice.

"Yeah. At first I wondered if he thought Hyman was some sort of sexual predator or something—he had that kind of funky vibe. But then, as soon as I introduced them, Uncle Charlie acted like, I don't know . . . like he was afraid of Hyman. I was saying on the way over, he just couldn't get out of there fast enough."

Carmella laughed a soft hoot. "Well, my love," she said, "I can tell you one thing. You won't get the answer to this riddle out of Hyman. He reveals nothing about nobody."

"So I've discovered," Pearl started to laugh, but by the time the words actually escaped her mouth she was sobbing. Her head fell into Carmella's lap, convulsing in heartbreak as though she had just been informed that Carmella would be dead in a day.

Carmella stroked Pearl's face and hair.

"What is it, my sweet girl?"

Several minutes passed.

Pearl sat up. Under her wet face and trembling mouth was the searing reality of despair, the seed of utter loss from which, in time, acceptance may be born.

"My . . . life," she said. "My life . . . as I've known it . . . is over.

13

More Bad News For Mr. Fox

resident Fox once said to his staff, "Friends, if Abraham Lincoln himself wanders into the White House and asks what's playing at Ford's Theater, that's definitely a photo-op, but you can wait until I get out of the shower to tell me about it. But if Abe shows up and says he's going to campaign against me unless I agree to sing *Stairway to Heaven* with him on national television, that's news you bring me at the speed of light, even if I'm saving the world from an invasion of the body snatchers."

Everyone laughed.

They often did when Charlie Fox spoke. He could be very charming. But Vicky Ski had witnessed more than a few heads roll from the shoulders of those who neglected to comprehend the Chief's implicit warning: *Fail to bring me bad news immediately, and I'll fire you on the spot.*

Vicky Ski had no doubt that her sensible head would never be counted among the missing.

She prided herself on being able to swing with the peccadilloes of her boss. She held no illusions. Charlie Fox was funny but not amusing; people laughed but their eyes didn't smile. You might enjoy his fancy dress witticisms, but if you wanted to survive, you were attuned to the body of threats underneath them.

Vicky Ski didn't wait for three o'clock to tell her boss about Hyman O'Malley.

"He's a friend of Puer Puella—and his sister," Vicky Ski began.

*I*t was some five years before Charlie Fox was elected President that this frankly gorgeous young man with the oddball name of Puer Puella had appeared, suddenly, out of nowhere, on his own television network, calling himself a "New Age Gangster, a major underworld figure, if you will." In his late 20s with untold wealth of mysterious origin, Puer Puella had created a broadcast outlet named *Holy Cow* that televised, without commercial interruption or fund-raising solicitation, what critics claimed were some of the world's greatest achievements in "picture/sound communication"— beautiful, provocative, inspiring. Anything ever created might be aired— films, documentaries, cartoons, games, television programs, home movies, including the masterpieces of contemporary adolescents working out of their bedrooms with camera and computer. And while there may have been no commercial "interruptions" per se, there were definitely commercials, aired at no charge for the sponsor. Every evening while other networks ladled out the litany of predictable tidbits that has been called "up-to-the-minute news" since the dawn of time, *Holy Cow* broadcast a collection of advertisements whose only criterion was that they were outrageously funny or inspiring or both. Perhaps no single force in the history of Madison Avenue did more to improve the quality of advertising in such a short time.

And that wasn't all. The not-so-secret spice in *Holy Cow* was Puer Puella's weekly broadcasts as New Age Gangster. Dressed in what he called his hoodlum haberdashery finest—cashmere and silk topped with a Michael Corleone Homburg—Puer would stand before the camera, holding his unlit Cuban (or the occasional bubble-gum cigar), and hypnotize the nation with his exploits, one to ten minutes a morsel. Everyone who loved to see the fatuous eat humble pie, the "impossible" become possible, and ordinary citizens enjoy, if only for a moment, no more than they deserved, loved Puer Puella. Such as every person who needs a first-rate power wheelchair and is getting jerked around by their insurance company.

Of course, at first, the viewing public didn't know what to make of him. Was this guy for real, or was he part of some avant-garde ad campaign where we only later find out what the product is? Cigars maybe. Or expensive suits. But over time, Americans came to appreciate that, strange or not, gangster or not, this young man, charming Puer, seemed to be doing an awful lot of things that made the world a more congenial place. Which, Vicky Ski thought, was probably why Charlie Fox often pursed his lips upon hearing about the latest balloon Puer had stuck a pin in.

Vicky Ski's favorite Puer Puella spectacle was when he offered an exorbitant fee to any of New York City's slum landlords who agreed to allow the outsides of their buildings to be used as "canvases" for the city's most talented graffiti artists. The only stipulation was that the landlords use 50 percent of what Puer paid them to improve the living spaces within their buildings. Meanwhile, each building's exterior would be refurbished at Puer Puella's expense prior to giving the graffitists free rein to transform every inch of that outside surface into a work of art. It was called the Naked City Renaissance. Almost as soon as it began, crime in the affected neighborhoods started to decline while vitality in all its various expressions began to rise, just as experts had projected. What politicians couldn't achieve in a generation Puer Puella pulled off virtually overnight, so felt the general public. Puer's assessment was more generous . . . in his way: "Politicians are often obliged to sell out one constituent to satisfy another, which is how these slums were created in the first place. I don't have to sell out anyone. If the Empire State Building could be built in less than a year and come in under budget, there's no telling what lofty dreams and oodles of booty from a New Age Gangster can achieve." The entire process was documented of course. A popular program on *Holy Cow* ensued, as did worldwide exhibitions which ignited the careers of many talented kids. From key-chains to coloring books, predictably, the usual galaxy of ancillary products trailing any brilliant public spectacle helped to give it the widest possible international audience.

Editorials called the Naked City Renaissance an extraordinary combination of performance art and social conscience. Talking heads riffed that Puer Puella should consider running for Governor or something. Puer demurred. "I've got all I can handle just running for my life," he said.

Vicky Ski noted in hindsight that as this loopy zillionaire became a rising moon of favorability over the land, the emotions of her boss about Puer turned several shades beyond Charlie Fox's beloved cautious.

Nevertheless, the Richter Scale of Fox's sensibilities didn't tremble in earnest until right after his election when Puer, who by his own admission had never met the president-elect, intimated that he "owned" Fox. Total bushwa it may have been to everyone else, but to Charlie Fox the jibe seemed to be much more than a mosquito in the ear. For reasons Vicky Ski could never quite fathom, Fox suffered an uncharacteristic breakdown of self-control. Paranoia infected Fox's usually calculating brain. Shorty, surprisingly, didn't put a stop to it, or couldn't. Fox spinmeisters were ordered to twirl: *By Mister Puella's own admission, everything he does is paid for by his underworld activities. So there is only one reason he could be trying to tarnish the reputation of the President-elect. He knows that, come January, the Justice Department of President Fox is going to put Puer Puella where the gun don't shine.*

If only it had been a joke. A president who could laugh at himself was a rare and wonderful thing. Instead, the threat was as shrill as the pun it was spread on. There was bupkis to suggest that Puer Puella was guilty of anything more than having an imagination that exceeded even his wealth. The only 24 karat mystery was how did Puer get so much dough? And where was it?

To these questions there were no good answers. Not being an American, but enjoying dual citizenships of Lithuania and Argentina, Puer's financial status was a little hard to pin down. Not that too many people really cared to do much pinning. Conventional wisdom was that Puer Puella was more crackpot than crook. And since he was held in such high esteem by the public, most members of Congress and other influential shapers of polite society were disinclined to look an Argentine-Lithuanian gift horse in the mouth.

Then, five years later, in the Spring, a couple of months after Fox's inauguration, just like that, Puer announced his retirement. *Holy Cow* TV would remain, but Puer the public figure was bidding the world adieu.

The story went that Puer's older sister, Carmella, was the abbess of a small cloistered convent dedicated to poverty and prayer on an island in the Indian Ocean. She had lived there in complete seclusion since she was a teenager. For more than twenty years, Puer and Carmella had had no contact. Then, Puer was granted the rare privilege of visiting Carmella, and as a result of something that occurred during the visit declared that he was abandoning his underworld existence to begin a life of contemplation and prayer. And, perhaps most eyebrow-raising to the cynical, he begged his sister: Would she take his money and do good with it?

At that, Carmella had her own epiphany of sorts, so the story went. This must be a sign, she felt. Why, her fellow sisters could now buy a generator. And while that was true enough, Carmella soon learned that, with Puer's bounty, she could also buy Con-Ed.

The reported agreement she struck with Puer was that they continue to live separate lives. He might be her brother; she certainly loved him; but she was married to Jesus. Furthermore, if Puer was sincere, he could have no ties to his former wealth—which meant no ties to her, nor the Women of the World Foundation she would start with his money, nor with anyone with whom she might become professionally acquainted.

By the end of the year, Puer Puella disappeared.

In his way.

His money instantly made Carmella's brand new WOW Foundation among the wealthiest in the world. And when a portion of the fortune was delivered—in the form of gold bars, piled into large pyramids on the backs of six consecutive floats in the middle of Macy's Thanksgiving Day parade, right between the Branchport, New York Hay Baler Symphonia and Vermont's Bread and Puppet Theatre—Puer Puella was back on the front page for a day. One last rocket to the moon.

The tail of that rocket, it turned out, was Puer's final interview with the press before retiring. It occurred after the parade, while the gold was being unloaded into a squadron of Brinks trucks. He had just walked the entire length of the parade route, waving and shaking hands and handing out five million dollars' worth of gold coins. At first glance, the coins appeared to be small wafers of chocolate wrapped in gold foil. It wouldn't be until the recipients attempted to peel away the foil that the truth would emerge and the world, once again, would experience the New Age Gangster's playful largess. Meanwhile, Puer was asked by reporters for the umpteenth time how he felt about the administration's allegation that every so-called good thing Puer did was paid for by his underworld activities.

"Well, you know, we are all great teachers for one another," Puer said. "President Fox helps me every day. He will have to speak for himself about perhaps how I serve him. But I do know that he reacted with uncommon vigor when I suggested to some of you, just about a year ago now, that I had great influence over him. I believe I said, in so many words, that I owned President Fox. Now, it doesn't matter whether I was serious or not, which, as I'm sure you know, I was not. All that really matters is that Mister Fox reacted to my remark like his pants were on fire. So I guess, to a certain extent, I do own him. I yammer like the fool I am and he jumps. Given that definition, one might say that President Fox is my puppet. And isn't that a good thing to know about ourselves? I mean, aren't we all puppets? We're puppets to our beliefs. We're puppets to our habits, our hates, our judgments. And, we're certainly puppets to the consequences of our actions from who knows how many incarnations—until we learn to choose love, rather than fear, in our moments."

At that point, the reporters all but yawned. They had their story: *Puer Puella Donates Billions; Claims He Still Owns President; Calls Fox Puppet.* Saying that we are all puppets, and throwing reincarnation into the soup, while perhaps intriguing over an after-hours scotch, didn't glue viewers to their favorite media outlet.

When news accounts of Puer's remarks broke, Vicky Ski, in the privacy of her own home, with her mother tucked in for the night and the shades pulled down, did something she never did in public. She smiled. Then, for reasons never discovered by the local electric utility, fuses blew and circuit breakers popped in all the other homes on Vicky Ski's block, plunging into darkness the entire neighborhood, save the warm, ethereal glow emanating through the drawn shades in the home of the President's right hand.

"What do you mean, a friend?" Charlie Fox said sharply.

Vicky Ski had found the Chief where she expected to, in Big Stallion's pasture. His pedigree name was Ferocious Divine, a name that perfectly matched his unpredictable and often fiery personality. But since he was 18 hands high, and his son, also in residence, was considerably smaller, Big Stallion was what everyone called him. He was Shorty's horse, but even she, who would have been a world-class rider had she chosen not to manage her brother's career, didn't have the rapport with Big Stallion that Charlie Fox did. He was the only person around whom Big Stallion was invariably calm, and the thing was—the president had never ridden a horse. Yet, whenever Fox visited his sister's home, he would climb over the fence, walk out into the pasture and just stand there. Big Stallion would nicker and prance with pleasure, then walk right up to Fox and put his big black nose on Fox's belly. There they would stand, together, motionless, for many minutes. Then, Fox might walk around the pasture, Big Stallion, without any lead, at Fox's side, which is what they were doing when Vicki Ski arrived, Fox having removed his coat and tie; his loafers replaced by a pair of green Wellingtons. In all the years Vicky Ski had known Charlie Fox, this was the only place where she was sure the man was absolutely at peace. She had no idea why, and frankly she doubted whether he knew why. But she was grateful, and especially grateful at moments like this when she was the bearer of sensitive news.

She had stood outside the fence until Fox and Big Stallion walked over to her.

"O'Malley has been a guest at their homes many times, sometimes for as long as a month. In fact, he's staying at Carmella's retreat down the lake now."

"What's their business?" Fox pressed, his attention directed at combing Big Stallion's mane with his fingers.

"Doesn't seem to be any. Certainly nothing to suggest that O'Malley profits financially from these relationships. He's as poor as the proverbial church mouse. It's not clear when he met Puer, but it seems to have been before Carmella left the convent."

"Where does he live? I mean his permanent address."

"Strange. His legal address is Carmella's condo in New York City. When you call the number listed for him, you get Carmella herself saying if you want to leave a message for Hyman O'Malley, etcetera, etcetera."

"Odd," Fox said.

"And that's not all that's odd, sir. He travels the country buying and selling antique mirrors. Good stuff, really. He makes just enough money to keep going. Has one teeny bank account. No investments. No debt. One credit card, which he pays off religiously. No phone, other than the one at Carmella's. No health insurance. A passport, which shows that he makes occasional trips to India. His income tax returns are, as you would expect, immaculate. He contributes a few dollars to organizations that feed the needy, that's it. No police record. Never voted. No party affiliation. Never been admitted to a hospital, never taken a prescription drug . . . ."

"So you're saying he lives in his truck, except for visits to the Puellas and trips to India?"

"Well, he does spend a bit of time at a ranch in California where he grew up, and where his father still lives; his mother is deceased."

"His father's Jackie O'Malley."

"Yes, sir. You know him?"

"Shorty does. Well, I mean she had all his books growing up. He's a well-known horse trainer, riding instructor."

Fox had taken a carrot out of his back pocket and held one end of it between his teeth. Big Stallion chomped off a four inch section without touching Fox's face.

"Opinion, Mary Victoria?" Fox said in what sounded like a foreign language since the carrot was still launched in his mouth.

"No surprise, sir, this has the feeling of Puer Puella all over it. O'Malley's a little too mysterious for a fellow who is just about a nobody."

"Agreed," Fox said, holding out the remainder of the carrot in his palm for Big Stallion to take.

"At the same time, sir, despite his connection to Puer, I can't see how he represents a bother to us—there's no evidence of him having any strong views on anything, or being even tangentially related to a particular cause . . . "

"Recommendation?"

"Follow up on everyone he knows. Keep a tab. Continue to reassess." Vicky Ski knew that, for some reason, that was the recommendation Fox wanted.

"Make it so," Fox said.

"Speaking of which, Mister President, there is something else."

"Mmmm?" Fox was stroking the horse's nose.

"O'Malley's coming to Shorty's party tonight."

"I knew she'd invited him."

"What you may not know is that after Pearl and O'Malley drove away this morning, they ended up at Carmella Puella's retreat down the lake."

"Ha. Let me guess," Fox said. "Shorty's now invited Carmella, too."

"Yes, sir."

"That will be a distinct pleasure," Fox said, kissing Big Stallion's nose.

As soon as he dismissed Vic, Fox walked the perimeter of the pasture, Big Stallion at his side, Fox's hand resting on the horse's withers.

Only with a horse did he feel that he didn't have to be cautious, that he was free from running, free from wondering what might happen next and how to be ready for it. It was remarkable, considering how dangerous nearly a ton of unpredictability can be. Yet he'd never had a desire to ride. He just loved to muck stalls and groom and walk and feed and hang out. All he craved was the companionship. The calm of it was like a warm bath, but because it was so rare in his life—unique, you might say—it was also eerie.

When Fox and Big Stallion completed their lap around the pasture's perimeter, Fox fed the horse an apple that he'd sliced into eight pieces, then climbed over the fence. Only then did he remove the red phone from his pocket and punch a code that sent his call pinballing off an unknown number of satellites and other untraceable places before it finally rang on a sailboat tethered to a buoy not two miles from where Fox was standing.

"El Presidente," answered Benny Apple, Fox's friend since Oxford where the two of them were Rhodes Scholars fresh out of college.

"Ben, I've got a situation. I'd like you to be an invisible guest at Shorty's birthday party this evening. Gather the ducks and bring Adlai Stevenson. I have an acquaintance who's in need of a vacation."

"As you wish," said Benny.

"And Benny? This one time, not a word to Shorty."

14

Benny Apple and the Pope's Cookies

Factions within the Vatican had been debating whether to perform an exorcism on the pope's personal residence. There were many, the pope included, who had felt the spirit of the late Pope Pius XII inhabiting the rooms. This was the pontiff whose physical being became a mass of noxious, vomit-provoking flesh within minutes of his death, in contradistinction to many saints whose lifeless bodies exhibit no sign of decay for weeks, maybe months or years, after their passing. Cells that vibrate with the light of Spirit are very slow to decompose, it is said.

Pius XII was most notorious for his alleged silence about the treatment of Jews during the second World War—"The Führer's best imaginable ally" being perhaps the harshest characterization. Certain scholars have claimed that Pius never once explicitly spoke out in moral outrage, or even mild rebuke, despite his knowledge that millions of Jews throughout Europe were being exterminated. He knew of The Final Solution at least since the beginning of its wide-scale implementation in 1941. And when, two years later, the Jews of Rome itself were rounded up for deportation and certain death, Pius XII, the sole Italian authority in the city at that time, said nothing. In fact, there seems to have been no record of a single public prayer celebrated in solidarity with the Jews of Rome, either during their ordeal or after their deaths. By contrast, when Adolf Hitler committed suicide, priests in Germany were ordered to hold "a solemn Requiem in memory of the Führer."

According to some, Pius XII felt the Jews got no more than they deserved. They had killed Jesus, after all. Blinded by their dreams of material success, Jews brought down upon themselves their worldly and spiritual ruin. They were alien and therefore undeserving of respect and compassion.

Observers who believed that these were the sentiments of Pius were quick to infer that his instantly rancid flesh at death (at his lying-in-state, a guard fainted from the stench; later, the Pope's nose turned black and fell off) was a sign from God that the Pontiff's reign, and thus his heart, had failed to reflect the spirit of His Only Begotten Son, even if it did reflect the feelings of a long line of popes before him. Indeed, Pius XII himself canonized into sainthood Pius X, who had allowed the Catholic press to contend that Jews performed ritualized murder—an act on the order of baptizing a baby by slitting its throat.

Perhaps for many the telling depiction came from the American monk Thomas Merton, one of the most widely respected religious figures of the 20th century, who wrote: "Pius XII and the Jews . . . the whole thing is too sad and serious for bitterness."

To be sure, there was another view: that Pius XII had done all that a pope could in the midst of world chaos to protect the innocent, including Jews—at times, most notably Jews—while influencing the combatants to seek peace. Many Jews were publicly grateful for Pius's efforts to counteract the reality of the Holocaust. Plus, Pius had been a key figure in a plot by anti-Nazi German generals to depose Hitler. Also argued was that Pius XII, so charismatic and holy that many were known to weep uncontrollably in his presence, would surely be canonized in the due course of time, and that this would purge these unfounded accusations from the consciousness of all fair-minded Church scholars, the only people who really counted when it came to a pope's place in history.

Those in this camp naturally opposed exorcism. In fact, they said, if it were true that the spirit of Pius visited the existing pontiff's dwellings, it should be taken as a blessing, a miracle even, further proof that Pius deserved sainthood. Furthermore, perhaps it showed that, in God's judgment, the living pope had certain defects of character that benefited from such extraordinary divine intervention as the guidance of one of his predecessors.

The present pope, the former Father Michael O'Sullivan, had mixed feelings on the matter. There was no doubt in his mind that the spirit of Pius XII haunted his living space, and that his predecessor's vibration was not, to put it plainly, a happy one. But the pope would also point to a small silver picture frame on his desk that held a quote of the 18th century Jesuit, deCaussade:

> *God teaches the heart*
> *not by ideas,*
> *but by pains and contradictions.*

"I know that the presence of my brother Pius is a gift to me from our Heavenly Father," His Holiness told Benny Apple, the everyday name of Benjamin Franklin Appleton IV. "I welcome it. Or I should say, I have come to welcome it, which only means I have seen things in Pius that I have yet to accept about myself. The more I forgive my sins, and grow in loving Pius, the more I experience the love of Jesus. What greater teacher can there be, Mister Appleton? And when Pius and I meet in heaven, if it is God's will, I will kneel before him in gratitude. Historians will probably never know that among Pius's contributions to the Church has been his unsettled spirit peering over my shoulder all these years."

His Holiness chuckled: "Those who suggest that maybe Pius is haunting my chambers because I need all the help I can get, are correct, I'm sure."

And then the pope explained why he had asked to meet Benny for tea and cookies.

The pope wore his plain white linen cassock with the grace you would expect of a man who had been the Irish handball champion. As Mickey O'Sullivan's reputation as a cleric of wisdom and kindness rose through the corridors of influence within the Church, so did the legend of "Sully Hands," master of the wall. From the day of his ordination in Dublin some 30 years earlier, Father Sully made it known that, after mass on Saturday mornings, he would gladly hear the confession of anyone, so long as the person was willing to confess while playing handball. Becoming bishop, then cardinal, now pope, didn't alter the tradition one iota. Only now, Catholic handball players, and even a few courageous non-Catholic challengers, traveled to Rome from all over the world to participate in a confessional match with His Holiness on the pontiff's private court. The motivation behind these contests was the same as it had always been. As the pope put it, he wanted to offer the reminder that freeing your heart was not a solemn event, but rather a celebration of the highest order—and furthermore could, and should, happen anywhere, anytime. "Personally, I've had some of my most liberating spiritual experiences on the handball court," the pope was fond of saying. "Becoming friends with fear, for one—and of course learning that, in certain circumstances, only language that blisters paint can suitably convey one's emotions." Once he became pope, however, the handball confessions also held a more mercenary significance: "I'm getting old," the pontiff said, "I want all the edge I can get, and if spilling your guts to the pope takes your mind off your game a little, hey, that's your problem." The pope was a good sport about it though. Win or lose, he never handed out penance. Your willingness to play, he'd say, like life itself, was penance enough.

"A peach with midnight-blue eyes," was how Benny would describe the pope's head to Charlie Fox. The blue was the same color as the two glass cups into which His Holiness poured tea for himself and Benny. Next to the tea items on a small knee-high table between the two men was a platter made of the same blue glass. On the platter were seven gold cookies. Benny had never before seen cookies quite that color.

"Pius the twelfth has been here to serve me, I feel, Mister Appleton, but I also feel that it is not God's intention that Pius serve every pope until Resurrection. Pius's spirit deserves to be free. If God wants my successor to have a mentor like Pius, I'm sure the Heavenly Father will provide one. It's happened before. Pius is not the first spirit to walk these halls. But he is the first who seems to be stuck here. I feel he cannot leave on his own. He needs my help. Therefore, I wish the exorcism to take place, and I wish to do it myself—alone. I do not wish to open my decision to discussion. I want even my closest aides to be ignorant of my actions because, if they know, they, implicitly, will be deceiving some of their brothers and sisters. That can only cause disharmony. My problem, Mister Appleton, is how do I get my staff out of the way for an entire day, while I remain here undisturbed?"

A tiny grin did a soft-shoe across Benny's lips.

"So, um, you're saying you need to be in two places at once . . . a miracle, in other words . . . and you're not quite sure how to pull one off?"

This was a test. The pope passed: first with a belly laugh, then with a return of the needle. "What's your personal assessment of Jesus, mister Appleton?"

Benny's favorite people, even when they were cutthroats and swindlers, were those who had a sense of humor and were unafraid of truth. It was a combination rare among his bread-and-butter clientele of politicians and potentates. His Holiness seemed to possess at least the first half of the equation.

"I'm afraid I don't know a whole lot about Jesus, Your Holiness, beyond what I learned at Princeton—"

"Aren't you the same Benjamin Franklin Appleton the fourth who graduated summa cum laude in Theology?"

"The very reason, Your Holiness, why I wonder if knowing Jesus from the neck up isn't worse than not knowing him at all."

The pope's eyebrows rose and fell like a pair of dolphins.

Benny said, "My personal assessment, as you put it, is that I'm the sort of fellow Jesus would love but that most religions operating in his name would hate . . . if you'll pardon my candor."

"As Jesus himself was, many would say," the pope said. "Your candor is welcome here, I assure you. Your apparent lack of awe, as well."

Benny picked up his cup and saucer, but didn't drink. They were alone in the pope's private office, a space large enough to store an America's Cup yacht, but, except for the art on the wall, so simple you'd have bet the guy was an accountant, Benny thought. The yacht's mast would have had to have been lowered, since the ceiling was a mere thirty feet above the rosewood floor. French doors at one end of the office, the room's only source of outside light, opened onto the second floor balcony overlooking a garden courtyard maintained by someone who, in Benny's view, was sparing no expense to catch God's eye. Though open slightly, the doors' gossamer curtains made sure that light entered the room slowly, reverentially, on tiptoes. So it had been for a thousand years, Benny speculated, maybe more. Most of the room's light came from high-intensity lamps positioned directly over the many paintings in ornate frames that all but smothered the eggshell plaster walls. Here were the works of men so revered they went by only one name. Rafael and Michelangelo were among those in Benny's immediate line of sight.

A couple of these babies and every homeless person on earth is sleeping in a Rolls, Benny mused to himself.

"I helped smuggle lamas out of Tibet, Your Holiness," Benny said. "And my time with them made me think about becoming a monk myself. But I quickly realized that I was better suited to freeing a monk than being a monk. What I'm trying to say is, I am very much in awe of compassion. At the same time, I know the difference between a man, even a man of God, if you'll permit me to say so, and an icon. The job of your staff, as I understand it, is to serve you as God's representative on Earth. An icon, if you will. I, on the other hand, can help you only as a man."

"Can you help me?"

"I'll do my best, Your Holiness."

"No, no, Mister Appleton. Your best doesn't interest me. I need to be assured we can be successful. What I want from you is yes or no."

Benny smiled. "If I'm not mistaken, Catholics don't believe in reincarnation, correct, Your Holiness?"

"Not in a while. Not for the record. Why do you ask?"

"Just thinking of a few generals you might have been in a previous life."

"Ah," the pope chuckled. "A few despots as well, I shouldn't wonder."

"Your Holiness, I would like to say that my answer is of course we'll think of something . . . ."

"But you're not sure," said the pope.

"Oh, I'm sure of myself," Benny said. "I'm just not sure about you, nor, I would bet, are you sure about me. I'd say we don't know each other well enough yet. Success in odd situations like this is as much a matter of chemistry as talent. My best is all I can promise in this moment."

"Have you ever killed anyone, Mister Appleton?"

"Yes."

"Many people?"

"Yes."

"For hire?"

"Primarily."

"For personal reasons?"

Benny hesitated. "Well, when I was five, I was kidnapped by terrorists who hated my father's politics but loved his money. The law couldn't touch them."

"But you did, I mean when you were old enough."

"Yes."

"Have you killed for pleasure?"

"Pleasure's a little complicated, Your Holiness. But satisfaction, yes."

The pope leaned forward.

"Is satisfaction the same as revenge?"

Benny considered the question. Finally, he said, "Not anymore."

"Oh? Why is that?"

"I don't believe it's possible to get even."

"And what is it about your nature that made it necessary for you to take on this tremendous love affair with death and danger?"

Benny smiled, "You win the prize, Your Holiness—for asking a question no one has ever asked me before."

"Oh, I doubt that, Mister Appleton. I would imagine you've asked yourself."

Benny nodded touché. "I'm just a guy trying to figure out what it means to be a human being, Your Holiness. I just happen to be wired in a way that seems to learn best through intensity. The only God that means anything to me is the one I can find everywhere, and everywhere can get pretty weird, pretty ugly, wouldn't you say?"

"Amen," said the pope. "Thank you. Your answers are what I hoped they would be."

"Hoped?"

"Honest, without hesitation. I was already confident what the truth was, you appreciate—for the most part."

"I am not surprised, if that's what you mean, Your Holiness," Benny said. "In select circles, who I am is no mystery. But that's not why I told the truth. Somewhere, India I suspect, I heard that those who habitually speak the truth develop the power to actually materialize their words. Speak from the heart and mountains will move. That's the gist."

"But in your line of work, are you not a professional deceiver?" the pope asked.

"That's not exactly the phrase I would put on my business card, Your Holiness, but it is accurate, so far as it goes. I've been known to fool people. Sometimes more than that. But I don't lie to them."

The pope said with a twinkle, "Might not those be the words of a man expert in the art of rationalization?"

Benny snorted a barely-audible laugh, "I shouldn't be surprised to discover they were," he said, realizing he'd been holding his tea cup under his chin all this time. He took one long sip then replaced the cup, in the saucer, on the table.

"So many of us hate being fooled, Your Holiness, but we want to be lied to," Benny said. "Oh, we say we don't, but heck, we lie to ourselves as if we were Al Capone in front of a Grand Jury. We hate the crook who swipes our credit card, or the traitor who steals national secrets, or the so-called fanatic who straps a bomb to his belly and wipes out himself, ten strangers and our best friend's wife, but . . ." Benny took a breath and let it out, speaking softly, ". . . we'd run a mile barefoot over broken glass to avoid discussing the biography of the steer we happen to be savoring a slice of for dinner. Your Holiness, I've been paid a fortune to kill any number of people, but no one has ever asked me to commit murder."

Benny's solar plexus was tingling with the familiar hot stirrings of a rant. It was one thing to make the choice to kill, it was another to call it something benign, something that separated you from its reality. Benny's discharge from Special Forces came after he had slapped a Congressman for using the term "collateral damage" once too often. Only masters of denial thought that war was about patriotism, honor, duty, heroism and all that. Terrorism may have changed the face of war, the strategies and tactics of war, but not the essence of war. War was about death, period, and most of the people who died weren't even soldiers—and the soldiers who did die were themselves usually children. Benny wasn't against war, he was against glory. One of the reasons he was always available to President Fox, Benny's friend since graduate school, was to remind Fox, a man with no military service, that to call someone an enemy was short-sighted. "There are no enemies, Charlie, not really; there are only human beings. Kill them if you must, but don't be a sissy-boy and deny that when you bomb a city you are making a conscious choice to rip the arms and legs off children. If any military initiative that results in physical devastation doesn't make you want to puke, you don't deserve your job, Mister President." Perhaps no one but Benny talked to President Fox this way. Of course, all this had nothing to do with the pope, and certainly not this conversation. Besides, experience had taught Benny that his feelings on the matter were best howled to the wolves who circled his campfire in the Alaskan wilderness, maybe the only place Benny felt completely at home. He therefore employed the ancient spiritual technique he had learned from his friend the mullah who, under similar circumstances, once advised: "You can always shut your mouth, Benny Apple."

And since the universe rewards common sense, the pope extended a hand that held the blue plate of gold cookies. "Always in service of a higher cause, eh?" the pope said. "Well here's one. Tell me your truth about these, Mister Appleton."

Benny selected one, they were rather hefty, and immediately stuffed the entire cookie in his mouth. Every last crumb. It took up so much space he couldn't begin to chew until he'd added a sip of tea. But that was the way Benny Apple tasted just about everything. He was a William Blake man: *The road of excess leads to the palace of wisdom.*

"Mm-mm," Benny said a minute later. "Aren't you Catholics supposed to be against sin, Your Holiness?"

"Au contraire, Mister Appleton," the pope said, refilling Benny's tea cup. "Sin is not following your heart. These cookies were baked by one whose sole intention is the celebration of Divine Love that resides in every heart."

"Impressive," Benny said.

"They're one of God's little reminders, I like to think," said the pope. "If a simple cookie can be this full of love, imagine the splendor of living in attunement with Our Beloved Lord."

"Well, as a marketing program, it sure beats 'Wear this hair shirt or burn in hell,'" said Benny.

"Not everywhere, Mister Appleton . . . as you have probably noticed in your travels."

Benny picked up a second cookie, from which he took only a small bite before placing the remainder on the napkin next to his tea cup.

"Tell me, Your Holiness, why are you thinking about hiring a man who is paid to kill? Your problem isn't the most difficult in the world. I'm sure there are plenty of, shall we say, 'less morally ambiguous' people who can help you."

The pope angled his gaze to a large mural hanging above a desk in the corner. It was a preparatory study by Matisse of his Virgin and Child. *Rather hip for the Vatican*, Benny thought. After a moment, the pontiff, still keeping his attention on the image, said, "There are no doubt many answers to your question, Mister Appleton, but I will give you the one I know best. It's what Jesus would do, in my best judgment. And I try to make what He would do the only yardstick I use to guide my behavior. Maybe it's like your striving to speak the truth."

The Holy Father then turned his head so that he could see Benny. "Your profession as a killer, if I may put it bluntly, Mister Appleton, is not relevant to our negotiation, unless being a killer is all you are. But I doubt you are that small. Integrity, generosity of spirit, imagination, knowing your limitations, understanding mine, and a very particular set of skills are more to the point. And so far, on most counts, Mister Appleton, you seem to be who President Fox said you would be."

Benny's eyes widened. "And who was that, Your Holiness . . . if I may ask?"

"I told him I needed a magician, someone who could solve a special logistical problem without offending anyone, without being noticed; someone with the utmost discretion, someone unknown to everyone here in the Vatican, and someone who could deal directly with me, man-to-man."

"Well. What did he say to that?"

"He said he had a friend who was a ruthless saint." The pope spoke the last two words as if they were Nobel laureate.

"Did he?" Benny laughed. "And what did you say, Your Holiness?"

"I said the description fit Jesus himself, so how could I not at least meet you?"

*T*his is how the charade ended up going.

The pope got a call from the President of the United States, Charlie Fox, requesting an audience. Their meeting, President Fox said, needed to be absolutely confidential. The outside world could not, under any circumstances, be made aware of it. No one inside the Vatican, therefore, was to be informed of it, as well, except on the most restrictive need-to-know basis.

The pope drew into his confidence only his two closest aides. It was their idea to cordon off the Holy Father's residence for the entire day, preventing access even by themselves.

The President arrived before dawn, without escort, and was ushered by the pope's two aides through the Vatican's secret passageways into the pontiff's personal rooms. These two cardinals were so professional that they didn't even blink when the President stepped out of his unmarked limousine dressed as a priest. This so-called priest never spoke or looked up at them, but, as the aides delivered him to the pontiff's door, he patted each on the arm in thanks. A few hours later, when live television showed the U.S. President eating sugar cake in Tuscany, the two aides looked at one another in frozen, unbelieving amazement. Then, the truth, as they knew it must be, slowly melted their expressions into private, knowing smiles. That evening, the aides escorted the priest back through the Vatican's secret passageways.

Without ever once raising his eyes or saying a word, the man the aides were convinced was the real President Fox again patted the arm of each cardinal, then disappeared behind the black windows of his limousine.

The next day, when the aides were alone with the Holy Father, one of them said, "I hope your meeting with the President yesterday was satisfactory, Your Holiness."

The pope looked puzzled. "Yesterday?" he said. "President Fox was in Tuscany yesterday. This morning's newspaper ran a charming photo of him eating cake."

And so, the pope, who is infallible in matters of faith and on other occasions when it suits him, decreed without ever saying the words: *Yesterday never happened.*

"*T*he heart of a guerrilla," Benny told Fox.

"How's that?"

"Once the pope learned that I was pretty good at disguise, he asked if I could disguise myself as you disguised as a priest. I said 'You bet,' and he was off to the races. The basic plan was his. Scheduling it for the day you would be in Tuscany. Involving his aides. Even me tapping them on the arm. Emotional cement the pope called it. And the cherry on top: no one will ever know."

"What do you mean?" Fox said, "I know. You know. His aides know."

"Don't be too sure," Benny said. "For one thing, his aides think the real President was the fellow who showed up at the Vatican, and that the man in Tuscany was an impersonator, a decoy to distract the media. And believe me, his aides will happily take that secret to their graves. As far as you and I are concerned, who are we going to tell so long as His Holiness says he has no knowledge of it?"

"Pretty slick," Fox said.

"That day, Charlie, when he had completed the exorcism, which is a whole other story, the pope all of a sudden says to me, 'Kneel down, Mister Appleton,' which, I must admit, I did without even thinking about it. I'm looking up at the pope like a kid at first communion . . . disguised as you pretending to be a priest. The pope puts his left hand on my head, raises his right in blessing, and says the most incredible thing. He says, 'Beloved Lord, this is a good man. I beg of you, forgive his sins. His heart is a heart of peace. If you must punish him for any reason, punish me instead. Help his heart to grow ever more abundant in your love, and the love of Your Son . . .,' blah-blah-blah.

"Well, by this time I'm bawling like the babe who's just been crowned Miss America. It was the nicest thing anyone had ever said to me, by far the biggest moment of my very strange existence.

"And just as I'm saying to myself, 'Welcome to the summit of Mt. Weirdness,' the pope does an encore. He kneels down. We're face to face. We're belly to belly. He smiles the sweetest little smile and out of nowhere slaps my face with all his might—Once! Whap!—and let me tell you something, Charlie, something I never realized before that moment—no one has a more deadly open-handed slap than a handball champion.

"Next thing I know the pope is gathering me into his arms, and O God, Charlie, I melt and explode simultaneously. I feel everything that has ever happened to me—everything—all at once. It's the only way I know how to describe it. I just fall apart. Never in my life had I cried like that, even when I was kidnapped as a boy. The only thing that kept me upright was being wrapped in the papal bear hug. The rage. My folks refusing to pay the ransom. Well, you remember. Six weeks, every day, tattooing that mural on my back. The pope's this magnet. All the ghosts—the little girl in the park. Shame I didn't know existed is roaring out of me. And pain, Charlie. It was like the only person I had ever killed was me. I felt such deep sorrow, blubbering bits of stories that would cost me my life if they got out. The man is getting soaked. My mind is screaming, 'Have we all gone crazy?' But my heart, my heart is singing, 'Get back, Loretta!'

"I felt I might die, literally, honest to god, Charlie, right there in the pope's arms. And, you know—I couldn't have cared less. He wasn't pope. I wasn't Benny. It was just Spirit holding Spirit.

"Finally . . . I mean I'm cooked, man. I quiet down . . . I can't . . . the pope . . . he just rips my heart out . . . . 'Mister Appleton,' he says, 'I hope I can count on you to hold me someday, if you happen to be here when I have a heartbreak.'"

Benny wiped his eyes, first one then the other, with the heels of his hands.

"I tell you, Charlie, I don't know who the guy is as pope, but as a man, he is as good as they come."

"So why aren't you Saint Paul?" Fox said. "Seems you've been knocked on your ass by divine lightning. How come you're still killing people—and 'flickin snot,' as you call it?"

By the look on Benny's face one might have thought that Fox had just suggested they mud wrestle while continuing their conversation.

"Mister President, I may have had a moment in the sun, and I may carry that moment with me forever, but that doesn't change the reality that, in the world we inhabit, some people need, or deserve, killing."

They'd had this conversation before. At this stage of our evolution, Benny argued, we humans don't kill one another because we're so damned wise; we do it for just the opposite reason: we're dumb as a stone: "We're such bone-heads we can't figure out any better way to solve a problem," was one way Benny put it.

Now Benny was saying, "I put two bullets in your dear friend the Prime Minister who would have pulled off something far more sinister than nine-eleven had I not dissuaded him. Will you take a pass next time?"

"Of course not," said the president.

"So who do you want pulling the trigger, some super-patriot dildo with 'Nuke 'Em Till They Glow' across his baseball cap?"

Benny took a breath and let it out.

"I like to think there's a place for a guy who can grease a menace to society without actually hating the poor bastard. Every little bit of compassion helps, seems to me."

"Ah, Ben," Fox said, "you'll be Gandhi before you know it."

Benny's mouth twitched a pickerel smile. "If only I could give up feeling smug for just staying alive."

A small sound of amusement then hiccuped in Benny's throat.

"His Holiness, last thing he says to me, in that lovely brogue of his: 'Everyone's life is messy, Mister Appleton. The past, the future—they're really overrated. I prefer to think of them as two angels standing on either side of us, their only job to remind us to continually ask ourselves: *Where is my consciousness in this moment?*'"

Long after Benny Apple died, one of the fondest memories Charlie Fox held of his friend was what Benny had said next that day.

"Can't you just see it, Charlie? God and I meet up there in Pearly Gate Park. And by then I've learned how speak from my heart so well I can move mountains—well, I mean, you know," Benny laughed, "in my way. The Big Guy and I are reviewing my activities in this incarnation, and Ta-Dah!—I materialize a couple of the pope's finest. God nibbles. And hey, the guy's the Almighty, for Christsakes. He knows I'm showing off, employing mischief, what I do best, to lay on him the most loving gift I can think of. Gold cookies.

"Which is why, when He gets through licking His fingers, the G-Man looks at me and says, 'Mind if I call you Benny?'"

15

Hyman's Journal:
The Light

Since we choose our parents, I have always found it telling that I chose a father who was cremated wearing a dress and cowboy boots, and a mother who could make people nervous simply by asking them to set the dinner table.

I'd come home from school, open the hall closet to put my coat away and—surprise!—there Dad would be, standing with a big smile on his face, all dolled up: pink wig, a dress he'd bought at Goodwill for a buck, maybe an old pair of broken glasses upside down on his nose, cowboy boots of course, a cigarette stuck in each ear, lipstick, and an apron with the name Mrs. O'Flaherty embroidered across the chest. Mrs. O'Flaherty was Dad's alterego, the lady he became whenever he cleaned the house.

"Ah, me boy," Dad would say in his phony brogue, "Welcome home."

Dad had been a cowboy since before he learned to walk just about. He'd been enough of a rodeo star to sock away a nest egg. At 28 he met my mom on a Thursday and they married the following Tuesday. "Some decisions you don't have to wait on," was the way he put it. Mother's family were hand-to-mouth cattlemen, the sort of people who were just poor enough that they knew how to do anything. Mom and Dad spent their honeymoon buying a ranch. They went into horse training. Well, horses and anyone who worked with horses. Dad was what people today would call a horse whisperer.

"There's facts about horses, and then there's opinions," he loved to say, repeating the old saw. "If you want opinions, talk to a human; if you want the facts, talk to a horse."

Another was: "All a horse needs to learn from you is whether you can be trusted. But what you need to learn from the horse, if you really want to know a horse, is everything about yourself. And believe me, the horse can teach you that."

I remember Dad saying that all any horse ever does is show us our fears. More than once I heard him ask someone not to ride for a while, and this might be someone who'd been riding all their life.

"Right now, you hate fear," he'd say, "which means you hate everything that might cause fear, which means you hate everything—since every moment is full of the unknown and potential catastrophe. A person who hates fear can only harm a horse. No horse deserves that."

He didn't ask people to be unafraid, since everyone has fear. But his work began with helping people learn how to manage fear, developing inner skills so that fear became their friend—not just something they could tolerate, but something they loved. "Fear is always showing us where we need to surrender in order to be one with a horse," Dad would say, "which really means being one with our self."

Our ranch was named Egolightly. "The price for being a good horse handler is having to wear your ego lightly," Dad said. "Your strong beliefs, no matter what they are, are as tough on a horse as a saddle that doesn't fit."

It got to be very amusing. People who didn't know a horse from a water buffalo would call or write and ask if they could work with Dad—and these were people who had no intention of ever riding. They just wanted to work with the man who had had such an impact on some friend of theirs.

Just as Dad had his special ways of teaching, so did Mother.

She would go to auctions and antique shops and deliberately buy just one of something in a particular pattern. They were all very nice pieces, but as a collection they were just all different. Our kitchen was like a museum, only we used everything. It was how Mom reminded all of us, which included the never-ending stream of guests, that we're always making choices.

At our house, you made yourself a bowl of cereal, and not only did you get to choose the cereal, you had to choose the bowl and the spoon . . . or not choose it, at least consciously, as you preferred. You could just take whatever came naturally to your hand when you reached into the cupboard or drawer—discovering what gift the universe had for you in that moment.

Mom would almost always ask a guest to set the table for dinner. And of course the person would say, "Oh, I'd be happy to." But then, when they learned what they were really being asked to do, sometimes you'd sense this small "gulp."

And it wasn't just the silver and china and napkins and drinking glasses that you had to choose and arrange however you liked. You could add flowers from the garden and candles and anything else you could think of. Put a little poem on everybody's plate if you felt moved to do it. Have anyone sit in whatever seat you chose. That was often a tough one. People were always asking Mom, "Where does so-and-so sit?" and Mom would say, "Wherever you say, dear. The table is yours to create."

The only guiding principle besides "follow your heart" was that you were informed what we were having for dinner—Mom's way of teaching the importance of being aware of what this very moment is asking.

No matter how you set the table, there was always a big celebration about it.

When the Swami came to dinner, things got really wild. He insisted on setting the table. He was like a kid. One time he had us eating our soup while riding backward and bareback on a horse, a placemat laid over the horse's rump. And that wasn't all of it. Everything was always very orderly on the ranch. Things had their place. But before dinner the Swami engaged in a little mischievous rearranging. A rope, for example, that always hung on a certain hook, he took off the hook and laid it on the ground. That sort of thing. The game he made up was that we were to eat our soup without spilling any, and at the same time we were to spot how many items were not where they were supposed to be. It was actually rather difficult because no one could stop laughing.

Later, the Swami told us the story of an Indian king who trains a young prince by having him walk through the castle with a lamp that is full to the brim with oil. The prince's task is to notice everything he encounters but not spill a drop of the oil—so that he can answer any question about his journey the king might ask him.

During the time we knew the Swami my father had three birthdays. Each birthday the Swami gave my father the same present: a bushel of ordinary light bulbs. Dad used to say that under all the silly ways we humans behave we're all just shiny balls of light. We just don't know it.

The Swami's gift inspired Dad to start a tradition of his own. Whenever the spirit moved him, he would give someone—often a child—a beautifully wrapped box inside of which, cushioned in gold tissue, was one of the Swami's light bulbs.

Dad never explained that his gift had originally come from the Swami because sometimes, after receiving the bulbs, people's lives changed rather dramatically. An illness would suddenly disappear. A kid's parent would find a job. In one case, life-long depression went away. Dad preferred that people not make the connection between the light bulb and whatever blessing they received. That would have been a distraction. To Dad, all that mattered was the reminder of who we really are.

I was well over 60 when my father died. Pearl and her triplets were visiting. It was Dad's 100th birthday. For as long as I can recall, Dad told the story that when he was five, God told him to pick a number from 10 to 100.

For what reason, Dad didn't know, or at least never said. Anyway, Dad picked the number 100 because it was bigger than anything he could imagine, the closest thing to God himself. But then, as Dad's life went on, he came to learn that the numeral "1" actually represents God, the big One—and it also represents the sun, a big shiny ball of light.

None of us suspected Dad might die that day. It wasn't something he advertised. And he was certainly sparkly enough for a man of his years. As always, his birthday breakfast was chocolate cake. "Plan for the unexpected. Start the day with dessert," was one of his mottos. Then he said, as he often did, "I'm just going to take a little nap," and he simply never woke up.

At his memorial, when I got up to say a few words, the first thing I did was pull out of my pocket, and hold up for everyone to see, the light bulb Dad had given me for my eleventh birthday, my first birthday after the Swami died.

Then the most amazing thing happened. Just about everyone there reached into their pocket and pulled out the light bulb they had brought with them—and held it up. At that moment we all realized that this wasn't something anybody had planned. No notice had gone out: *Please bring your light bulb.* It just happened. Some of these people had traveled long distances, not having seen my dad in years. Many of them weren't even the original recipients of Dad's gift; they were the recipient's children.

Standing there in rather awed silence, our light bulbs raised like so many statues of liberty, we found ourselves weeping for reasons we might never be able to fully explain.

As I looked around the gathering, did I really see the better part of two bushels worth of light bulbs floating overhead, glowing ever so softly? It makes a nice story, but all I can say for sure is what I felt: the love I had first experienced well over a half-century earlier on that afternoon when the Swami said to me, "So, we meet again."

16

The Drive Home

"Why have I been given the privilege of meeting Carmella? I mean . . . well, you know what I mean. Our life together—Bishnu and Kashi?"

They were pulling out of the *Island of Peace*. They had two errands to run before Hyman dropped Pearl off home. After that, he'd come back to Carmella's, take a quick swim, put on fresh clothes, meditate, then escort Carmella to Shorty's birthday gala, though knowing Carmella they'd be riding in her limo, not in the truck.

"I honestly don't know," Hyman said.

"Well . . . what can you tell me? I've got questions, mister."

"No, no, dear girl, what you have is an itch."

Pearl tapped Hyman on the shoulder, and when he turned his head, she used the pinkie fingers of each hand to pull wide the corners of her mouth and stuck out her tongue in a way that, were it long enough, would have touched her belly button. On her tongue was a well-masticated mess, formerly an attractive stick of celery with almond butter and raisins in the groove, a snack she'd made in Carmella's kitchen for the ride home. She'd also pulled her Wayfarer sunglasses down to the tip of her nose so that Hyman could see her crossed eyes.

Hyman laughed. "Okay, okay, I give up. But how about if you let your breath do its magic for a few moments?"

The earth was handing out bonuses to those who rode their breath that day. The late August air, being warm, accentuated the aroma of grapes ready for harvest. It is a fragrance so intoxicating that newborn babies were known to float in air above their cribs. Grape growers occasionally awoke to find themselves driving their tractors naked through the vineyard in the moonlight.

To the left, among ancient shade trees at the far end of a sweeping pasture, a herd of forty or fifty bison were moving like a school of fish in slow motion.

"A few thousand years from now, Pearl, what you have experienced today will be much more commonplace. Human consciousness is evolving, after all. We'll be more aware that each moment is nothing but a mirror, showing us something about ourselves that we must basically make room for in order to love more fully."

Pearl was shaking off one of her sandals. "So," she said, placing her bare foot up on the cream dashboard, each of her toenails painted Nuclear Root Beer, each big toe accented with a gold star. "I meet Bella-Viola to free unforgivenesses about choices I made when I was her . . . and at other times, other lives . . . I get that. But I haven't sensed that I have any unforgiveness related to Kashi . . . ."

They eased around a tractor pulling a hay baler. "Mr. Boston," Pearl remarked the way one does when there is a whole other story that, if the moment were different, she might wish to relate. It would include Sister Marie-Clarice's transfer to a new job at the home for old nuns—a move precipitated by Pearl's mother who had phoned her friend, the Bishop, and said, "Let me tell you a story you don't ever want to see in the paper."

"There may not be any obvious answers, Pearl," Hyman said. "It would be merely a mind game to say maybe this, maybe that. Who knows why this entire day has occurred? The trick is not to get caught up in the questions, but to open to what is happening, welcome it, accept it, be present with it, play with it . . . but avoid feeling obliged to have it make sense. That's only fear. Only our ego needs to know things, to have things work out in the certain way. Your Spirit, your inner heart, knows everything is already perfect. You know this."

"So this is God being cute?"

"Eh?"

"Well, like winning the lottery, say. Suddenly you've got all this dough. Now the question is, is the money going to distract you from the real business of life? I mean, this whole thing today, as much as it's all a gift to me, it can also be a hindrance, I would think. My itch to understand, as you call it . . . ."

"That's why choice is such a big deal," Hyman said. He made a gesture as if he were picking an ornament off a Christmas tree. "We must choose to bring love to every breath. When we inhale," he said, bringing his open hand up to his chest, "such a simple act. What are we inhaling? Air? Or the infinite love of Divine Mother? And when we exhale," letting his hand drop to his lap, "what are we letting go of? Carbon dioxide? Or anything we hold in any cell that is not love?"

*T*hey were on the road that ran along the spine of the bluff that extended a dozen miles down the center of the lake, creating the lake's distinctive Y shape. On either side of them the land sloped down toward water, although they couldn't actually see the water from where they were. It was almost like being in a small airplane: patchwork hills—vineyards, wheat and corn fields, pastures, an occasional family cemetery as much as two centuries standing—rolled out to infinity left and right. Below most of those hills were other lakes, invisible to anyone not in an airplane.

Pearl was saying, "What is it with breath, anyway? . . . these meditation practices that say 'Follow your breath'?"

"Some say life's two biggest gifts are the power of breath and the power of choice," Hyman said. "Breath, according to a friend of mine, is the link between our mind and our body. Proper diet and exercise ensures physical health. Proper thinking and one-pointedness of mind, which we develop through meditation, ensures mental health. But without proper breathing we cannot really be connected to either our body or our mind."

"Is this some sort of Buddhist thing?"

"Many people think so," said Hyman, "but my sense is it's not about a particular path. As my friend puts it: When we learn to eat properly, exercise properly, think properly and breathe properly, we don't become a Buddhist or a Muslim or anybody . . . we become simply a healthy person."

"And we can't really breathe properly without learning to pay attention to our breath," said Pearl. "It's a skill, in other words. Like anything else."

"I find it so," Hyman said.

"So what's been the toughest thing you've ever had to learn?"

"Ever?"

"Mmmm."

"Jeepers," said Hyman before sitting in silence for a minute.

"Well," he finally said, "loving myself is the first thing that comes to mind. I can't tell you how many times—how many lives—I've worked hard to be a good person all because I believed I was a worthless slug. It's taken me a while to learn that you don't really start cooking on the spiritual path until you're up for being your own best friend."

"What else?"

"That no one action or activity is more important than another."

"Really?" Pearl exclaimed. "I mean, isn't, say, giving birth more important than peeling potatoes?"

"You'd think so, wouldn't you? But regardless of whether I am having a baby or making home fries, what my heart, my True Self, asks of me is exactly the same—bring all the love I have to this moment."

"Oh," Pearl said. "Of course."

Since that morning, she was discovering that she didn't always need to think about things. It was an odd, delicious sensation. She was hyper-awake. She didn't need to grasp. She didn't need to figure. She didn't need to probe. The more she just sat there, awake and ready, the more life presented itself. Answers were already there. She didn't need to find them. One didn't solve problems. One opened to solutions already present.

Then Hyman said, "But your question was what's the most difficult thing I've had to learn. Oddly, that's easy to answer because I think it's the toughest thing for any of us to learn."

"What's that?"

"That how we define our world creates our world."

"Say more," Pearl said.

"Other people and outside circumstances are not responsible for our feelings."

"What is?"

"How we define reality."

"Are you saying no one has ever made us happy or unhappy?" Pearl asked.

"Basically. Certainly not once we reach a certain point in our maturity, which sadly many of us never do, in this lifetime anyway. We die saying if it weren't for blah-blah-blah I'd be happy."

"We shouldn't be angry about . . . you know, whatever?" Pearl asked.

"Should or shouldn't is a whole other conversation," Hyman said. "What I'm saying is the cause of your anger is in you. Mine is in me. Something or someone may trigger it, but they don't cause it. The cause is always how we define reality, and how attached we are to that definition.

Our attachment to how we believe things should be, in other words. And when things aren't that way, and we're feeling unsafe, there's fear. The fear of pain for one. Unless we're skilled at managing that fear, it commonly sparks anger in one form or another—blame, unforgiveness, that sort of thing."

Pearl thought a moment, then asked, "That makes nothing unforgivable, right? There are just things we choose not to forgive?"

"Just as there are just things we choose not to accept," Hyman said. "Nothing's unacceptable in and of itself. I find it a useful working principle that all value judgments are self-created."

"So why do we make stuff outside us responsible for how we feel?" Pearl asked. "No, don't answer that. I think I know, from this morning." Pearl paused, then said, "We're not all that good at freeing fear and pain. We haven't learned how, or even know it's possible. So the best we can do is blame it on someone else, or some event."

Hyman jammed the brake, throwing his right arm out in front of Pearl to prevent her from being flung into the dash as—Bam!—a wild turkey in flight slammed into the windshield. The bird squawked its indignation and flew off minus a few feathers.

Hyman pulled over.

"You okay?" he asked.

"You mean did that jive turkey trigger fear?" Pearl laughed. "Let's see if it's okay."

The turkey, a big male, was back a ways sitting off the road in a wheat field that recently had been harvested. It didn't move when Hyman approached and squatted down next to it. After maybe a minute of staying absolutely still, Hyman slowly put his hand to within a few inches of the bird. Then, never actually touching the bird, he ran his hand over the bird's body, as though his hand were a metal detector. When this was completed, he put some kernels of leftover wheat in his palm and offered them to the turkey. The turkey eyed the hand, then gave it a few tentative pecks before actually snatching the wheat berries. As soon as the food was gone, the turkey bounded off a few steps then, flapping its wings, took to the air.

Pearl had been standing by the road watching.

"That was cool," she said, as they walked back to the truck.

"He was just stunned," Hyman said.

"Hey, look at this," Pearl said upon opening her door. A turkey feather, nearly a foot long, gray with white striping, had found its way onto the cream floor mat in front of Pearl's seat.

"Well, well," Hyman said.

"Well, well?" Pearl echoed, lowering her head and looking at Hyman over the top of her sunglasses.

"Turkey is the medicine of many saints and mystics," Hyman offered.

"Well, well," Pearl said again.

Hyman started the engine and waited for a rusty blue and white pickup to pass from the rear: two boys hauling a load of hay bales.

Pulling onto the highway, Hyman said, "Turkey is the medicine of helping others. By help I mean the kind that arises from the deep realization that all life is sacred."

Pearl had closed her eyes. She was finding that, when they were open, her consciousness was drawn outside of her, especially with all the words floating around.

"Turkey sacrifices itself so that we humans may live," Hyman said. "Turkey reminds us that we must be willing to give away everything to serve the One. And our biggest 'give away' is our fear, what we were talking about."

Pearl spoke as if she were reciting the title of a book, "We Love By Moving Through Fear, Letting Go of Pain."

Then she said, "I can feel it, what you're saying. It's our attachments we're afraid of surrendering, isn't it? Right, wrong, good, bad, all that . . . ."

"Believing we're our body," Hyman said.

"Which is why we're afraid of death," Pearl half exclaimed: another new awareness. "We want to feel safe. We want to be on the right side. To have control—" Her voice trailed off.

" . . . all that's gotta go," she said, opening her eyes.

"So imagine if we died right this minute," Hyman said. "We find ourselves on St. Peter's doorstep, where we see two signs, each pointing in a completely different direction. One sign reads: *God*. The other reads: *A Discussion About God.*"

Pearl laughed, "Yo! Tough choice."

"I have a friend," Hyman said, "I call him the Swami. He's long since left his body. I met him when I was a boy. One of the first things he told me was that it isn't accurate to say that we are God, but it is accurate to say that God has become us."

Pearl was running the end of the feather down her cheek.

"So you don't believe in hell or any of that," she asked.

Hyman's head started to bob ever so slightly back and forth as if he were listening to "Eeenie-Meenie-Miney-Moe."

"The real answer to your question," he said, "is I try not to have any beliefs at all. Nothing I'm very attached to, anyway."

Again, Pearl was surprised, but this surprise, she recognized, was only her mind restless in its desire to label, to contain, to confine.

"As you're feeling right now," Hyman said, "there's a big difference between living love and believing in God. This morning, when you experienced your True Self—were there any beliefs operating then?"

Pearl closed her eyes and after a moment said, "All I experienced was love."

"There you go," Hyman said. "Don't get me wrong. Beliefs have their purpose. They teach us things. But it's good to hold onto them lightly. God comes when the vessel is empty, some holy Joe once said."

A raven pecking at some road kill hopped aside to let the turquoise truck pass.

"You don't care about the doctrines of various religions saying they believe whatever whatever?"

Hyman took his time answering. "Well, sure . . . I care about them in that they reflect humankind's inherent desire for union. You know, for living in the One.

"But as a friend of mine says, identifying with a religion is one thing, practicing the spiritual principles set forth in that religion is something else entirely."

Hyman glanced at Pearl to see if she were following him.

"Those who follow a religious leader are sheep, my friend says—and he happens to be a religious leader people follow, which is kind of fitting—but he also says that those who embrace the teachings of the leader . . . say, the Bhagavad-Gita or the Bible or the Koran . . . and practice those teachings in their daily lives—these people are transformed from sheep to human beings."

Hyman down-shifted to fourth, then third. Two girls about 12, both in bathing suits—one green tie-dye, one brown—were walking with a young black lab. Hearing the truck, the girls glanced behind them and moved to the shoulder, calling the dog. The girl in green held the lab by the collar until the truck passed. Pearl and Hyman waved. The girl waved back; Miss Brown Suit did not; her look saying that waving to strangers was never a good idea.

"As I experience it," Hyman said, shifting back into the higher gears, "the purpose of existence is direct perception of God—you know, the experience of God, not the thought of God. A thought may serve our journey, but to mistake thought for experience is like mistaking a beautiful poem about blueberry pies with the actual experience of smooshing your face into one at the county pie eating contest."

"Monty Python!" Pearl exclaimed.

"Pardon?"

"You familiar with Monty Python?"

"Moi?" Hyman said in mock amazement, then sang with operatic fervor, "All-ways look on the b-rrrright sy-eyed of life—ba-doom, ba-doom-ba-doom-ba-doom...."

Pearl marveled at how much pleasure this man took in being silly.

"Well, in my house," she said, "when you want to change the subject, you say 'Monty Python,' as in 'And now, for something completely different....'"

"Marvelous," Hyman said. "Fire away."

"I want to live with Carmella."

Hyman nodded. "If you're trying to surprise me, you'll need to work harder."

"No, no. I mean live with her—l-i-v-e—permanently. Move in today," Pearl said.

"I know that's what you mean," Hyman said. "I'm glad you can say it."

"My parents are my parents. I love them. But Carmella . . . Carmella is . . . I don't know . . . my home. I belong with her. I don't know what else to say."

Pearl wiped her eyes on her green T-shirt. Hyman handed her his clean handkerchief. She blew her nose.

"And it's all your fault," she giggled.

Pearl's first errand took them down a dirt side road to a Mennonite farm stand, a shady, immaculate roadside lean-to where, if no one were there, you left your money in a quart canning jar. A brown-eyed mother and daughter, the girl maybe 10, each in a white bonnet, summer housedress, and an apron the color of a corn tassel, were unloading a small mountain of cabbages from a flatbed wagon. The wagon was hitched to a Morgan mare. A young boy, obviously the girl's older brother by a year or two, stood in front of the dark chocolate mare holding her halter, waiting for the women to complete their task. The boy wore a pale blue dress shirt, sleeves rolled up above the elbows, dark blue suspenders, dark blue trousers, brown work boots, and a man's traditional summer-weight hat, also blue. Even while chewing on one of his fingers, the boy kept his attention completely on the horse, as if the animal might, any second now, lift her head and begin to recite poetry.

Pearl bought the main ingredients for ginger peach corn pancakes, one of Uncle Charlie's favorite breakfasts, although whether he'd be staying overnight was never a sure thing.

When they were on the county highway again, each of them eating a peach, Pearl was surfing the wind with her free hand out the window. She had tucked the turkey feather into her hair just above her braid.

"We're like actors, aren't we?" she speculated.

"Actors?" Hyman replied while chewing.

"Yeah, you know, like in a repertoire company. Every lifetime is a new production. We play a different role. But the roles we play are not who we are. We are the soul."

Hyman raised his half-eaten peach in toast. "So a guy plays a pirate one night and a priest the next, is that what you mean? When he plays the priest, the man has a tough time loving his congregation because he's got urges to make some of them walk the plank."

"And when he plays the pirate," Pearl continued, "he feels bad about all the plundering and making people swing from the yardarms, whatever they are."

"Ooooh," Hyman chuckled. "Multiply that by a few thousand lives. It's no wonder we're a little wacky."

"So just like I have been carrying around Bella-Viola," Pearl said, "not forgiving myself for murdering my Angelo and my father and brothers, I'm also carrying around the effects of lots of other lives?"

It wasn't really a question.

"A lot fewer after today, I'm sure," Hyman said. "As you experienced, the practice of surrender is the practice of forgiveness. We don't need to meet all our past lives in order to let go of fear and pain. We need only meet the present with open arms."

Hyman had taken his foot off the accelerator and downshifted to a crawl. Now he threw the remainder of his peach out the window, as if he were anticipating something.

They were approaching a pale green farmhouse on their side of the road. A crude hand-painted black and white sign advertising rabbits was nailed to a fencepost standing alone at the near end of a semi-circular blacktop driveway. The driveway went up to the house then back out to the road a few dozen yards further on. Between the driveway's two ends, pine trees lined the front lawn next to the road, obscuring the driveway's far end until you were right on top of it. Hyman braked to a stop half-way down the line of pines just before, from behind the last tree, a blonde girl about eleven shot out in front of them on a skateboard. When the girl saw the truck, she lost her balance, spilling onto the asphalt. As she scrambled to grab her board and pick herself up, a barefoot man in a red golf shirt that hung loose over cut-off jeans appeared and screamed at the girl, "You stupid shit, you almost got yourself killed." His face was nearly the color of his shirt; his fists, held at his sides, were clenched so tightly they could have crushed stone.

The girl whirled and screamed at the man, "Go ahead! Hit me! Hit me! But if you ever hit my mother again, I'll kill you!"

They were another mile down the road in complete silence when Pearl said softly, "Fuck!"

Hyman glanced at Pearl. Her eyes were closed; her face wet with tears.

Then she said, "I'm going to get to know that kid."

From that point, they rode in the quiet healing of each other's company the remaining five miles to the village at the end of the lake. Through the truck's open windows, the Eau d' grape breeze swept the cab clean of all words. Clearing pain, Pearl and Hyman were doing on their own.

In the village was a gift shop. There, Pearl would pick up her mother's birthday present.

The "shop" was a very large and beautifully restored Victorian house, a Painted Lady in lavender, peach and plum with a cedar shingle roof, dedicated solely to the creations of New York State artisans. This meant, among other things, that each of the building's many rooms, of all sizes and character, each a unique color combination, held a new and different display of beauty. Pearl was there to pick up a mirror she had purchased for her mother the day before. The mirror would hang in Shorty's office bathroom, over an oval soapstone sink.

Across the top panel of the mirror's vertical rectangular frame was a wood sculpture: the head of a beagle, the beagle's nose and red tongue sticking out several inches over the mirror below. The beagle was wearing sunglasses. On the beagle's head was a beanie with a propeller. Extending from where the beagle's shoulders would be were angel wings, which formed the top right and left corners of the frame. Carved along both sides of the frame were some dog bones. And along the frame's bottom, under the actual mirror, was carved the refrain *Best Friend*.

"It's weird that I bought this yesterday morning, and met you in the afternoon," Pearl said.

From within her own skin she heard a voice she'd never heard before, *Hello playmate, I am here*. Though she was hardly surprised by it, the voice did give her goosebumps.

She glanced at Hyman, but he was absorbed in the mirror.

"I love my mom to pieces," Pearl said. "She's really a remarkable woman. But her whole life is Uncle Charlie. It's like, by making him who he is she'll prove to somebody out there that she's . . . something, I don't know . . . competent maybe . . . worthy, I guess."

Pearl took a step so that, in the mirror, she could see Hyman's face. She pulled up her sunglasses so they rested on the top of her head. "I've got more than a little of the same disease—not the Uncle Charlie part, but perform or die." Then gesturing to the mirror, she said, "I want this to be a gift that reminds her who she really is, all on her own."

"I cannot imagine how you could say it better," Hyman said.

"Let's browse. Y'mind?" Pearl said.

She guided them to the shop's backyard, a large fenced-in space shaded by several old butternut trees. Hyman whistled at the sight and sounds: brass fountains, chimes, bells, stone sculptures, including a large granite hippopotamus chair for two, colorful silk hammocks, green metal frogs as tall as your waist, a life size four-horse carousel for the toddler who has everything . . . .

Even a sales clerk on stilts.

The brick paths that wound through the displays were lined with flowers planted in every conceivable type of pot. Here a yellow rubber boot carved out of wood; there a Victorian umbrella stand.

They strolled, taking in the circus.

"I wanted to tell you. This morning?" Pearl said. "The details were different of course, but the underlying torment and longing of Bella-Viola. It is all too familiar to me."

"How so?" Hyman said.

Pearl gently nudged a set of large pipe chimes and made them gong.

"Sometimes I feel like a young queen whose life has been mapped out before birth, whose sheets and shit are examined daily by the royal doctor to monitor her health and habits. If I wanted to ride a camel across the Sahara before I went back to Stanford next week, my mother and uncle could arrange it. But they also have strong opinions about what's good for me. Y'ever play basketball?"

"I warmed the bench in three sports, hoops among them," Hyman said.

Right, Pearl's expression said, *Like after yesterday's pitching exhibition I'm going to believe that.*

"Let's sit a minute," she said, pulling Hyman to a maple rocking chair so big it easily accommodated the two of them with room to spare for a man named Fats to play a slide trombone if the opportunity arose.

"You know how a basketball player sometimes keeps her hand lightly on her opponent's hip—so she can feel at the first twitch the move her opponent is about to make? I feel like I have to pay attention to my mother that way, Uncle Charlie too, so I'm always aware of what they might desire for me."

"What about your dad?"

Pearl thought before answering.

"Daddy's a different story," she said. "You know he's an artist? Tommy McGonagle."

"Believe it or not, I think I've heard of your dad, but I couldn't say where."

"Daddy once floated an American flag a few hundred yards in the air across the entire width of the lake—can you imagine?—that's over a mile. The biggest flag ever made. Then he had the entire lake photographed from a satellite. The resulting image became that famous poster: "The Heart of America in the Heart of the Finger Lakes.""

"Oh yes, I've seen it," Hyman said.

"Daddy's got a great heart, and he just loves me. I could rob a bank, and he'd be there for me. He wouldn't think I was damaging his career. But daddy's got his demons. I'm not sure what an alcoholic is, but I wouldn't be surprised if he were one. He's not a liar exactly. Just unreliable. Incapable of doing what he says he'll do. Backing out of things at the last minute. Plus, he cheats on my mom. Or maybe that's not fair. He and my mother have a funny relationship. They like each other—maybe even love each other—but there's no passion. My mother and Uncle Charlie are more 'married' than my mother and daddy. I'm all passion, so it's hard for me to understand my parents. I don't think my mother has other relationships, but I know my dad does. He's a wonderful man when he's around. It's just hard to compete with art and booze."

"You resent it?" Hyman asked.

"Yes, no. I did a lot more before today."

"How do you feel now?"

Pearl scooched herself so that she sat on the edge of the rocker's seat; she put the heels of her hands on the seat's edge as well, which caused her shoulders to hunch slightly, then she let her head drop for several seconds before raising it as if to look at an early moon over the horizon. "I'm not sure. There's so much pain. I don't have a dad. He doesn't have a daughter. But right this minute I don't seem to be quite so angry. Today reminded me that the forces in my life are a lot bigger than my mom or dad. My folks aren't responsible for any unhappiness I feel . . . ."

She cocked her head so she could see Hyman out of the corner of her eye.

"You know what I mean?"

"I know what you mean."

She stood, offering Hyman her hand. He was barely upright when Pearl used her other hand to tap on Hyman's wrist. "See that man over there? The one just inside the door looking at the painting?"

"The guy in overalls?"

"Yeah. Maybe he'll turn again so you can see him. He reminds me so much of Carmella."

"That's because he is so much like Carmella, Pearl. That's her brother."

"The gangster!" Pearl all but shouted, then immediately put her hand over her mouth and whirled around, burying her head in Hyman's chest. "Eeeek," she whispered. "I am such a twit. Is he looking this way?"

Hyman laughed a whisper, "No dear, he didn't hear you. And it wouldn't matter if he did. Why don't you just take a breath and I will introduce you to him?"

As they walked toward Puer Puella, Carmella's younger brother looked up and smiled, though to Pearl it was unlike any smile she had ever seen. On the side of his face that been away from Pearl's view, Puer had a scar that extended from the corner of his mouth to his temple, as though someone had slid a dull kitchen knife between his lips and slashed. Puer's broad smile, therefore, caused one whole side of his face to distort like a man who was screaming in agony. The sight was strangely compounded by the black leather patch that covered Puer's eye on that side. Pearl found it almost impossible not to wince in sympathy. Yet, the contrast between the sight of Puer Puella's face and the sound of his voice was so dramatic that an apt comparison might be a chain saw that, when fired up, put forth the tones of a Stradivarius violin in the hands of a master.

The man's manner was something else altogether.

"Hey, Double M," Puer cooed. "Fancy meeting you here."

"P, may I present a friend, not only of mine, but also of Mel's as of today. Pearl McGonagle. Pearl, this is my friend and Carmella's brother, Puer Puella."

Puer Puella turned and stared his one good eye into Pearl's two. There was no question that he and Carmella were brother and sister. It could have been Carmella's eye. Puer was wearing a white bandana around his head. Under his dark blue designer overalls he wore a periwinkle long sleeve linen shirt. Over his shoulder was a small black leather purse. A tiny diamond stud set off his left ear. One of his front teeth had a gold edge on the bottom. The rest of his teeth were movie-star perfect. And on his feet were hiking boots. This man couldn't have been more unlike the Puer Puella her mother described if he were King Kong.

Now she knew why her mother and uncle detested Puer. She remembered something in a Tom Robbins novel, the difference between a criminal and an outlaw. A criminal breaks the law; an outlaw doesn't even consider it. Puer was an outlaw. Whether he was a criminal was another matter. But it was his outlaw self that would have condemned him in the eyes of Shorty and Charlie, that no rules pertained to him, or so he believed, or wanted you to. He hadn't even been to college her mother spat. He was *one of those* who had to buy respectability since his only claim to fame was too much money and a slick tongue. Puer's biggest sin of course was attacking Uncle Charlie, exactly how Pearl didn't recall; all she knew was how much it disturbed her uncle. Pearl had never seen Puer on TV. She probably hadn't watched five hours of television her entire life. As a kid, her parents, to protect her, put

TV in the same category as driving a car—something for later. A half-dozen televisions banked the wall of her mother's home office, another was in her parents' bedroom, and that was it. By the time Pearl was old enough to watch whatever she wished, she had no interest. TV had come to represent that part of her mother's world where so many of the so-called movers and shakers, despite any noble ambitions or how truly nice they were personally, spent so much of their public life blaming and complaining. They felt to Pearl like nut house inmates who are outraged that the mop won't stop talking. Maybe she'd feel differently about TV if her mother were June Cleaver, but she doubted it. Pearl couldn't imagine a television program more engrossing than Moby Dick, or Isherwood's biography of Ramakrishna, or a concert of Keith Jarrett, or a performance of Penn and Teller, or an afternoon of pitching under the quick eye of the current Cy Young winner—all of which she had experienced without leaving home, one of the perks of being the President's niece. Pretty much all she knew of Puer Puella, then, was what she had heard from others. The world in general said cool; her mother said shithead. And now she got why. He was everything her mother and Uncle Charlie disdained. Outrageous. Ostentatious. A deliberate mocker of social convention. So how bizarre to feel . . . what? It wasn't that she liked him exactly. It was how familiar he felt. Like her dad. Through all the pain, all the anger, there still was a tenderness, because she felt her father's own pain, his own anger, his own sorrow—even while he was killing himself. And without really knowing anything about this Puer guy, she also felt a similar kind of understanding. Like she knew him, underneath whatever he was, or thought he was, or whatever he had done— though man, let's be real here, Pearl thought, there is something about him that is just a little too . . . what was the word . . . staged?

Somebody needs to tell Puer that it is possible to be too cool.

Hyman could have told Pearl that the next time she met Puer, he might look, and act, quite a bit different, except for the scar. That was permanent, the result of a recent accident with a grappling hook aboard the boat of his business partner, Clyde Marks. In fact, if it hadn't been for Clyde's skill as an amateur surgeon, Puer might have bled to death. As it was, the result looked like something out of a horror flick. But Puer had nixed plastic surgery, quite a choice for a man who wasn't so much handsome as beautiful. "A new teacher," he had said about the scar. "Besides, I figure the universe is seconding my desire to be a lot less visible. And you gotta admit, since the world in general doesn't know I've had this little accident, traveling incognito is going to be a lot easier from now on."

"Pearl Pearl, the oyster's autobiography," Puer Puella said. "Pal-a -Mella, eh? Y'done good, girl. Ain't nobody cooler'n Mel."

"I'm pleased to meet you, Mister Puella. Any friend of Hyman's is someone I am glad to know."

"Hy-man the Pie Man," Puer sang. "Pearl Pearl, if you're buds with Mel and Double M here, the gods must tooting their kazoos when you walk down the street."

"Thank you," Pearl smiled. "What brings you to these parts? Will you be seeing Carmella?"

"Perish the thought," Puer said. "Why, some people, including myself, say I used to be a gangster . . .," Puer made a motion with his hands to suggest ships in the night. "And Mel's got her rep to think of, you know what I'm saying. Probably not a good idea for me to be this close to her as it is. It's just that I love this shop. People making beauty. Figure I can breeze in and out before anybody's wise to me."

Hyman put an arm around his friend and said, "They may not figure that out, pal, but it's a cinch no one's going to mistake you for Wally Wallflower."

Puer put one hand on his chest and leaned in to Pearl, saying in a conspiratorial tone, "My problem, Pearl, as Double M will tell you, is I got three heroes: God, Vito Corleone, and Salvador Dali. I'll leave stories about the Man and the Don for another time. But you know what Dali said," Puer paused for dramatic effect: "'I don't do drugs. I am drugs.'"

She'd heard the line before, but couldn't help laughing at him, with him. Unlike Carmella, he was such a doofus. Like Carmella, he was real. He might have been a jerk, but it was like he knew he was a jerk.

"Well, gotta run, kids," Puer said. "Pearl Pearl, a pleasure. Double M, as always, you have good taste in friends. You know, I was thinking on the way over here how much has changed since the day we met on the golf course and you introduced me to that rascal, Domenico Priami."

"*I*t's a good thing they can't arrest people for smirking," Pearl said the minute they left the shop.

"Ah, yes," Hyman sang. "Now that was a kiss. The universe says, 'Speculating on previous lives are we? Try this on, girlfriend.'"

The village was small, so it took only a couple of minutes for them to be in the country once again, on the final leg to Pearl's house. The highway rose above the lake enough so that they could see a good expanse of the water. Pearl suddenly knelt on the seat, stuck the top half of her body out the window, her face catching the wind.

She screamed, "I don't believe this day!" And then howled like a wolf.

Then she hooted and laughed, pulling herself back inside the cab.

She sat sideways, facing Hyman, her left arm resting on the top of the bench seat, her legs tucked under her. "Are you telling me," she said, astonished, "that Puer Puella was my father five hundred years ago—the father who I basically murdered?"

"I find the universe's way of revealing that to you unique, but yes, that is the case."

"And you knew this?"

"Of course. I learned it this morning, from you."

"What about Puer? Was he being funny back there? I mean, does he know I was Bella-Viola?"

"No, he does not. I ordinarily wouldn't do this, Pearl, but in this special situation I am being asked to tell you a couple of small facts."

"Thank you," Pearl said.

"The Domenico Priami that Puer met was a boy of ten. Some things happened to this boy. The boy made certain choices. These choices shaped the rest of that life . . . and have had a big impact on his lives since that time. Puer is not aware of how his life as Domenico Priami unfolded for him after age ten. He only knows that his choices, as ten year old Domenico, poisoned his heart in ways that continued to show up in this life . . . until, like you, he chose to forgive himself. That's about all I can say."

"Can you tell me what happened when he was ten?" Pearl said.

"No. Just as I wouldn't reveal anything about you to him. That's between the two of you. Keep in mind, it doesn't really matter."

"Yeah, but if I do find out—from him—and he were to find out—from me—about Bella-Viola, maybe it will help both of us in some way."

"Well," Hyman said, "God doesn't spill His milk."

"Pardon?"

"There are no accidents. If you weren't meant to discover your karmic link with Puer, then today wouldn't have happened in the way that it has. Now the question is, what do you do about it?"

They were riding in silence again.

Pearl was smiling to herself: A girl once saw me peeing in the woods behind school. She called out: "Honey, wherever you be let it flow free." Words to live by in ways she might never know.

Pearl cleared her throat. "Mister Double M, sir, your honor, I need to ask . . . well . . . more than a favor."

Hyman sang with Broadway gusto: "The answer is—Yeeeeeeeeeeeeeeeesssssss!"

"How do you know, smarty pants?"

"Ahhh! Well, you see, Pearl, I have this friend . . . ."

"Man!" Pearl sang. "Your address book must be a foot thick. My mother doesn't have as many friends as you, and she knows everybody on the planet."

"Yes," Hyman grinned, "but probably most of your mom's friends are living. The majority of mine gave up their bodies long ago."

Pearl wasn't prepared to explore that topic; she had other things on her mind.

"So you have this friend . . .," she said.

"And she says, whenever somebody asks you for something, if it serves Spirit and you have the power to do it, say yes, and make it snappy . . . because guess who's really doing the asking. So, no big deal, I'm just trying to follow a saint's advice."

"Good," said Pearl. "Now that you've given me the answer I was hoping for, let me tell you the question. Will you help me? I don't mean about Puer. You see . . . I want what you have. What I mean is, will you be my teacher? For real. Not just a friend."

Hyman didn't respond for so long that Pearl wondered if maybe she hadn't made herself understood. But when she looked closer, she saw in his eyes that this had been no small request.

"As you wish," he said finally. "So long as your parents agree."

"Really?" Pearl said. "What do they have to do with it?"

"Well," Hyman said, allowing the details to surface in his consciousness. "You're a minor. I'm old enough to be your grandfather. I drive a funny-looking truck. You have a very public family. Many people are frightened by the unfamiliar. Those are, what—four reasons?"

"Five."

"I'm happy to offer some more."

"No, I get you," said Pearl. "My mother will appreciate it."

"One other thing," Hyman said.

"Mmmm?"

"I will be very firm with you if you start getting attached to me. I will always be your friend, and if it pleases you to think of me as your teacher, I'm happy to serve. But I am not the point, as you know. Spirit is the point. God is the point. The One is the point. Your True Self is the point, and that resides only within you. At the moment, the universe uses me to be a sort of mirror. But it's not the mirror that is important. It's what you use the mirror for that's important."

"I know . . . I think," Pearl said, wiping her eyes with his handkerchief. It seemed that so much of their time together was spent either crying or laughing.

"Besides," Hyman said, "I am not your guru."

"I'm not sure I understand. What is a guru exactly?"

"Ah," said Hyman, beaming at a memory. "The guru is a being who is truly great, one who lives completely in the consciousness of Spirit, and someone whom the universe gives you in response to your deep soul craving for the One."

Hyman said no more for the moment, letting Pearl choose if she wanted further explanation.

"Wow," she eventually whispered.

Then she declared, "So is that it? That's all you're going to say? You lay this big guru bomb and shut up? You can't just leave it there, mister."

Hyman bowed slightly in her direction, keeping one eye on the road. "Okay," he said, "If the ego is a black hole from which no light can escape, the guru is the radiant sun . . . a sun that illuminates every dark niche in a disciple's character. The guru is your personal guide home to the Infinite."

"Soooo," Pearl said, "being a 'Tennis Guru' or a 'Mutual Funds Guru' is a slight misuse of the term?"

"O thou queen of the understatement," Hyman sang.

"You're not a guru?" Pearl asked.

"Oh goodness no, dear," Hyman said. "I'm a bug. There are lots of people with a few crumbs of understanding who mistakenly get called guru, but at best they're really only teachers. I guess I'm a teacher, since you just made me one. But everybody's our teacher when you think about it. And while your guru is definitely a teacher, your guru is much more than that. A guru is one who, when the moment is right, can introduce you to the One because, you see, the guru has walked one hundred percent of the path that leads to the Divine. When the guru speaks to you, it is the same as God speaking to you—there is no separation. That's who a guru is."

"What did I experience today, if not God?" Pearl said.

"You did experience God today, at least as much as your physical being could tolerate without being burnt to a crisp. Yes, you met your True Self, which is God. God in creation. But that experience took place in a nanosecond. In fact, all that you lived this morning with your Samurai mask, with Bella-Viola, and with your True Self took place in not much more than a few heartbeats. Imagine what it would be like to live consciously in your True Self all the time. When you can imagine that, you will have a sense of the consciousness the guru lives in."

"And where will I find this guru? I'm ready to go, Joe."

"Well . . . here's my story," Hyman said. "Your guru, I would bet, has been actively guiding you for a long time. You and I certainly didn't meet by accident. Maybe you've already met your guru in a former life. Someday, you will meet again on a conscious level. Maybe in this life. But you don't need to look. Your guru will find you.

"Meanwhile, you are learning one of the most valuable lessons a person can learn—a lesson, quite frankly, that many, many spiritual seekers have yet to really grasp. And that is that enlightenment doesn't come simply by being a disciple of a great master. Enlightenment comes from doing what the great masters did."

"So you're saying I don't really need a guru?"

"A master can help, no question," Hyman said. "Some say a relationship with a master is necessary to find God. And it makes sense. The wishes of a true guru are guided by divine wisdom, and if you tune in with their wishes you will become free, as they are free. But nobody can walk your spiritual path for you; nobody can surrender for you."

"So guru or no guru, the light of God comes from within," Pearl said. "The guru just turns up the juice, so to speak?"

"So to speak. The last words of the Buddha to his disciples were '*Be lamps unto yourselves.*'

"You familiar with Saint Catherine of Siena?"

"I don't believe so," Pearl said.

"Doesn't matter. The story is she was riding in a wagon one day. The wagon was crossing a stream. Something happened. Maybe a wheel fell off. It's the middle of winter. She is soaking wet. And basically she says, 'What's the deal, Lord? Is there some special reason I needed this?' And God says, 'Oh Catherine, this is how I treat my friends.' And Catherine mutters, 'It's no wonder you have so few of them.'"

Pearl snorted. "That's your kind of story."

"I do love it," Hyman said. "Her attitude is that God is the dearest, most intimate friend possible. He saturates every second of existence. Speak to Him accordingly, she's showing us. Get in His face. We're only talking to ourselves, anyway. But that's not why I mention her. Catherine's the one who said, at least I think it was her, 'All the way to heaven is heaven.' What she's saying is that every moment is our guru, guiding us home. If we open to it. Maybe someday our moments will include a unique, in-the-flesh, relationship with a being whose consciousness and God's are one. And won't that be wonderful. But Buddha sitting across the breakfast table, and our days guided by a host of angels doesn't change the reality that our spiritual journey is our responsibility—choosing love, breath by breath."

"My brother would like to speak to you, if you have a moment."

Shorty had appeared from the house when Pearl and Hyman drove up. Pearl had gotten out and walked around to the rear of the truck, where she had stored her mother's present and the groceries. Hyman was still sitting behind the wheel.

"Delighted," he said. "But right now, I must ask you to hop in and put your hands over your eyes, while Pearl carries a birthday secret into your home."

"Happy to oblige," Shorty said.

Shorty looked like the "See No Evil" monkey sitting next to Hyman. Today's riding breeches were black, as were her boots. The vest she wore over a short-sleeve white T-shirt was the same shade of gray as the gray in her hair. Her earrings, at least her left one, the one Hyman could see, was an onyx stud in a gold setting. Like yesterday, she wore no makeup, which gave her the look of a schoolgirl despite the faint web of lines spreading outward from her dark brown eyes.

"My girl looks radiant," Shorty said. "You two must have had quite a day."

"We have. She and Carmella hit it off like they'd known each other forever. It was really a pleasure to see."

"And your time this morning? How was that?"

"As you said yourself, she is radiant. But, you know, the sun is always there. Some days it just appears a little brighter because there are fewer clouds and the air is clean."

"Okay, mom. You can look now," Pearl called as she disappeared into the house behind her father who had carried in the mirror.

So that a caterer's van could pass, Hyman inched his truck just off the driveway onto the lawn.

When he stopped and shut off the engine, he said, "Shorty, Pearl has asked me to be her teacher. I said yes, pending the okay of you and Tom."

"In a week she'll be back at Stanford," Shorty said.

"She and I haven't talked about doing anything in particular," Hyman said. "I think what happened is that Pearl learned some things about herself today, and she wants to chat on occasion as she integrates this new awareness into her life."

"Just what did she learn?" Shorty said.

"I have to leave that up to her to tell you. I'm sure she'll want to share everything she can with you."

"Everything she can? What do you mean by that?"

"Sorry. I didn't mean to be mysterious," Hyman said. "You know how it is: our ability to explain something is trying to catch up to our actual experience of it? That's what Pearl is feeling right now, I suspect."

"Ah," said Shorty. It had happened to her just yesterday, trying to tell Tommy about her time with this very man. Tommy had left before the remarkable pitching demonstration.

Shorty, her hands in her lap, was looking straight out the windshield to the ball field below, to the road on the other side of the ball diamond, to the vineyard across the road, and to the lake a half-mile beyond where the vineyard disappeared over the hill in its steep descent to the beach. Without even glancing in Hyman's direction, Shorty said, "I'm sure you can appreciate that Pearl's life is different than that of most other young women. She is not only the niece of the President of the United States, she is a very visible person in the President's life."

"I understand completely," Hyman said.

In fact, Hyman's understanding was so complete that he knew what Shorty didn't say out loud, but her mind spoke clearly: *My brother says you're dangerous. I will help him keep you far away from this family. Bud, we've got resources you cannot even imagine. And if anything you do hurts my daughter, I am not above destroying you.*

Unknown to Shorty, her fear rebroadcast to Hyman the central part of the private conversation she and Charlie had had within the past hour.

"I don't know how he knew I was going to be here, Shorty, but he used Pearl—and you, I might add—to get to me. Pearl introduced us, and as soon as she was out of earshot, he says to me he has proof that I was responsible for a young girl's death. Twenty years ago. Remember? On my way to Oxford on the ship? She and her family and I shared a dining table? Strange kid. The last night, she jumps. Overboard. About a month later, her mother does the same. Despondent over her daughter's death. The whole thing was tragic."

"I guess I remember you mentioning it. So, what exactly was his threat?" Shorty said.

"The girl's family will go public with proof, unless I announce by Christmas that I'm not running for re-election. But that's not the point, Shorty. There is no proof. There's nothing. But the whole thing is being produced and directed by Puella. He's backing it."

"If true, he sure came back from the dead quick enough," Shorty said.

"Ahhh! If all that wasn't just a bunch of smoke, I'm George Washington," Fox said. "Sure, he gave his sister a fortune. But the guy used to make money like turning on a faucet. No reason to assume he's lost his touch. His dough floats all over the globe; it's too hard to pin down. My bet is he's just been biding his time for the right moment to jump back into the spotlight and attack me. He loves it too much. He's been out, what?—two years? 'Living a life of contemplation.' Please."

"You know," Shorty said, "I never really got it. For some reason, you were a favorite target of his. But he never actually made any concrete claims against you, just some silly innuendoes about you being under his thumb."

"Visibility," Fox said.

"Charlie, it's not like he needed it," Shorty said. "What I could never figure out is why he didn't come out and blast your positions."

She paused.

"Take that Naked City Renaissance business," she said. "He could have said he was protesting your approach to crime or poverty or drugs or gangs or whatever . . . ."

"Shorty, the event itself was a critique. Remember the editorials, the gum-bangers?"

"Yes, but he could have been much more obnoxious. He played it like an amateur. He could have rallied all sorts of big name people to join him, people who don't like you. It's like he was after you, but never had the smarts, or the guts, to pull the trigger, to really go for the jugular."

"What was it Vicky Ski called him?" Charlie Fox said. "The Bionic mosquito. Only a pest, but one you can never get rid of."

"Well, it seems he's a little bit more than a pest now," Shorty said, finishing her brother's thought, as she often did. "Which is why, if Puer is bankrolling a campaign to smear you, we can't do nothing. Have you any idea what kind of 'proof' they're talking about?"

"I want to meet with O'Malley, alone, as soon as he brings Pearl back. Draw him out a little bit. The whole thing this morning took about thirty seconds."

Then, remembering Shorty's question, Fox exclaimed, "Proof? Hell, Shorty, people can make other people think anything. We, of all people, know that."

It's simple why the man lied, Hyman thought *He can. It works.*

I might be the winner of an all expense-paid vacation to the Island of Nasty Snakes . . . if Uncle Charlie can't think of anything more unpleasant to do with me.

You're a good mirror, Charlie Fox. You too, Shorty. In how many lives have I let fear lead me around by the nose?

It's a bit like poison gas, unmanaged fear. Everybody gets hurt. Unless you have the equipment to breathe through it.

Well now, I wonder what my Beloved has in store for the President. For all of us.

*P*earl's bedroom was located on the second floor, above the library that Uncle Charlie used as an office when he visited. The library was where most private indoor meetings with visiting dignitaries took place. What no one knew was that Pearl, if she wished, could hear just about every word of any conversation.

A few years earlier, her bedroom had been renovated and, among other things, wall-to-wall carpeting had been installed in her walk-in closet, a room almost large enough to be a bedroom itself; large enough, anyway, so that she screened off a corner of it as a meditation space. That's why she wanted the carpet, for the quiet. When the closet door was closed it meant "Please don't disturb." When the house was built back in the early 19th century, air vents had been built into floors, as well as the ceilings below them, so that heat could rise and warm the upper rooms. When the library had been remodeled, its entire ceiling was covered with copper sheeting, and although the ceiling vent had been removed when the renovation began, the hole it left was never filled-in with insulation and covered with dry wall. Punched into the copper sheeting to form a lovely pattern of flowers were hundreds of tiny holes. Naturally, some of those holes were located over the empty space where the ceiling vent had been. In Pearl's closet, the corresponding floor vent had also been removed, prior to laying the carpet. Since aesthetics would not be an issue, a small piece of plywood had been nailed in the space where the vent had been. Pearl, simply curious, had watched the entire operation. Sometime later, her memory of the covered hole in her closet floor intersected with her wonder about the conversations taking place in the library below. She pried up enough of the carpet, figured out how to remove the plywood, and immediately gained access to a world that was, at least initially, beyond her wildest imagination.

She once heard Uncle Charlie telling the President of Colombia, through a translator, how sorry he was to have to report that the man's son had died of a drug overdose while skiing in Colorado, and then getting off the phone and remarking to Vicky Ski, "Isn't it fitting as hell that a guy whose country dumps the most cocaine up the noses of American citizens should have his son die of the stuff in the back seat of an Aspen taxi. Who says there is no justice in the world?"

She also heard Benny Apple tell her uncle the story of the pope.

She had actually recorded a few of the conversations when she thought she might want to listen to them more than once and learn.

And so, when she knew that Uncle Charlie and Hyman were about to have a conversation, she quickly changed into an old pair of black shorts and T-shirt, headed for her closet, closed the door behind her, pulled back the carpet, readied her recording system, filled a water bottle, lay down on the floor with a meditation cushion under her head, and waited.

17

Extravagant Humility

wo years earlier, Puer Puella met Hyman O'Malley the day Hyman got a job caddying on what was perhaps the only country club in New York State that forbid the use of golf carts. This most beautiful and secluded of courses, just nine exquisite holes, overlooking its own private lake in the Adirondacks, also forbid traditional golf attire. Instead, it provided players access to every sort of clown costuming the world had ever known—including wigs and hats and jackets and tights, noses and knickers and stupendous bowties . . . and of course all color of shoes, each the size of a watermelon—from which guests were invited to create the ensemble of their choice for the day's round. A round also included a nine course gourmet meal, one scrumptious dish served at the completion of each hole. Since it was not unknown for a golfer to faint in gastronomic ecstasy, downy chaise lounges dotted the fairways, a reminder that to enjoy playing *this* course one must rise above the tyranny of deadlines. Another idiosyncrasy: the prohibition of competition between players—as in, the player with the lowest score wins. By contrast, a player at the start of a round was obliged to predict what his or her score would be; success being measured by how close one actually came to meeting one's prediction. Atop each scorecard was the message: "How well do you know yourself?"

Who else but Puer Puella would own such a club; and who else but he would have named it, appropriately, *Extravagant Humility*?

Puer Puella was a terrible golfer. Not that he cared. It didn't bother him a bit that he wankeled most of his shots in every direction but straight ahead. Anyone who thought *Extravagant Humility* was about golf would think naked skydiving was about transportation. Nevertheless, on the day Hyman O'Malley caddied for him, Puer was immediately chagrinned when he sliced a shot so sharply that it bonked Hyman on the hairline. The ball, however, instead of ricocheting onto the ground, boinged straight up in the air like a pop fly. Hyman, dressed in a white jumpsuit, as all caddies were to distinguish them from the players in their clown duds, happened to be holding a two-wood in anticipation of Puer's next shot. Keeping his eye on the ball, Hyman sidled a step or two so that it would land in front of him. Then, a split-second before the ball touched planet earth, Hyman swiveled Puer's two-wood and cracked the pea right out of mid-air, sending it a good two-hundred yards down the center of the fairway where it suddenly hooked left, landed, and rolled to within a modest chip shot of the green.

On any other golf course, it would be highly irregular, purists would say outrageous, for a caddie to hit a shot for a player, regardless of the circumstances. But this was Puer Puella's course. Magic took precedence over convention any day.

"Are you OK?" Puer called, rushing over to Hyman, imagining that the knock on the head had possibly created an Idiot Savant of the Fairways—somebody who might not be able to hit a ball off a tee, but who could belt one out of the air and send it places even pros only dreamed about.

"Sure, no big deal," Hyman said. "I got lucky."

Well, he might have been lucky once, or gosh, maybe even twice, but when pretty much the same thing happened for the third time—three eggs on the noggin; three masterful whacks right out of the O_2—Puer said to his caddy, "Nobody's that lucky, pal. We gotta talk."

"Good," said Hyman. "Evidently, that's why I'm here."

*I*t was twilight. *Extravagant Humility* had been put to bed. All the guests had departed. A stranger surveying the empty manicured landscape through binoculars from the clubhouse might be startled to suddenly spy a clown sitting on a bench next to a fellow in a white jumpsuit, the day's last light in their faces, neither of them saying a word.

Indeed, Puer Puella and Hyman O'Malley were watching the western sky put on its evening fashion show with typical over-the-top flamboyance: *So, darling, how do you like the deep purple outfit with the gold clouds and the moon? How about the magenta and orange with a spray of white? And isn't the jet stream next to Venus just divine?*

Hyman and Puer Puella had been together for several hours. In that time, the Earth had begun to assume her rightful place in Puer's being . . . as she does, eventually, in all humans who choose to listen and respond to the yearning of their heart. The need of the heart, really, to be grounded in the Mother. Puer Puella's big clown feet were amusingly symbolic of the energetic connection their wearer enjoyed with the planet under him. Hyman had helped Puer use his breath to awaken his connection to the all-enveloping Mother Divine—as he would help Pearl do the same two years later.

And as it would be for Pearl when she wondered whether she had been struck by lightning, so it was for Puer Puella that evening. With no advanced warning, at the exact moment the last drop of color evaporated on the horizon, life as Puer Puella had known it from birth drained from him about as fast as water leaves an overturned glass. Before he could even think about crying out in astonishment, Puer had become someone else. But it wasn't a dream. And he wasn't dead. In fact, his "someone else" was more alive and thrilling than the most memorable event of Puer's life to that point: sitting behind first base in Yankee Stadium at age 12 when his father drove in the runs that won the World Series.

In Hyman's presence, Puer Puella had become a real, live, big-as-the-sky, angel.

But of course, not just any angel. This was Puer Puella, after all. This was Puer Super Angel.

This angel sang back-up for Gandhi when he recorded gospel tunes composed by Beethoven on the *Heaven Ain't for Weenies* label. This angel's territory included the wombs of certain pregnant Latino teenagers, where he introduced their unborn children to the rewards of having chosen, in this incarnation, a culture of the heart. This angel worked weekends weaving threads of hope into the nightmares of men who beat their wives. This angel even created the *Great Moment of Truth*, an ongoing afterlife gathering of those who have died in war—offering special comfort to incoming terrorists who are often disconsolate to discover that blowing yourself, and others, to smithereens does not buy eternal happiness.

While as real as Puer himself, this angel, Puer Puella knew, was also a mask—one that he had created to protect himself. Oh, his ego loved this mask. It was so cool. So powerful. So helpful. So (what else can you say?) extravagant!

But under the mask was someone else, one of the mask's creators, someone his ego feared, someone Puer had been, some choice he had made, in this or another life, that he had yet to embrace, a forgiveness he had yet to extend to himself, an experience of pain or shame he had yet to release and replace with love. That's how masks get created, after all. In this particular case for Puer Puella, the person he met under his mask of Puer Super Angel was the boy he had been more than 500 years earlier . . . a boy who, moments before, had methodically bullwhipped his uncle to death.

Incredibly, the boy was but ten years old.

His name was Domenico Priami.

$$18$$

Puer Puella Meets Himself
as Domenico Priami

omenico Priami's father, Lorenzito Priami, was among the most respected winemakers in the Province. His younger brother, Bocco, knew nothing about making wine. And around those two facts is the story that led Domenico to murder his uncle.

In brief, Lorenzito knew from the first moment he saw his son that this was the child who had inherited the family genius for making wine. Even as an infant, Domenico was brought to the vineyards daily during harvest by his mother, Felicia-Viola, so that he might nurse at her breast while she ate the freshest possible grapes.

By the age of five, Domenico had what Lorenzito called "The Nose." Set out ten glasses of wine on a table, and without moving from his chair Domenico could point to best of the lot. By the age of eight, Domenico had "The Touch." He produced the first bottles of his own recipe. Lorenzito couldn't have been more proud than if his son had been named king. By the time Domenico reached his ninth birthday, Lorenzito was dead of the plague. His mother, Felicia-Viola, was in a sanitarium recovering from the plague, a process that would ultimately take several years. Domenico, his sister Petra and brother Ottorino, both older than Domenico, became wards of their uncle Bocco, a man with a wife and no children.

It wasn't that Bocco Priami hated young Domenico. He didn't. In fact, in his own way, he rather admired him. But Bocco knew only one thing: how to buy and sell horses, and even that he didn't know all that well. So while he admired his young nephew, as one might admire a child with a beautiful singing voice, a nine year old winemaker under the roof of Bocco Priami was about as useful as a three-legged foal.

Bocco spent his days traveling the Province visiting breeders, trainers and owners—attempting, with no discernible success, to secure a reputation as the man who knew the most about the availability of horseflesh. No matter what you wanted to buy or sell or trade, if a deal could be struck in the Province, Bocco Priami could broker it, or so he wanted everyone to believe.

Bocco had long since given up training more than a few horses himself. He was away from home too much, he told anyone who asked. But the truth was that Bocco's training methods produced the most undesirable animals, valued only by those who could afford nothing better, or who knew little of horses in the first place. Bocco's approach was that if you broke a horse's spirit it would surrender to your will and do as you wished. Ignoring his results, Bocco figured the same technique would work with children, as it had for his wife, Kradle. Centuries later, the English playwright Somerset Maugham would pen a sentiment that aptly characterized the unfortunate wash of humanity that included Bocco Priami: *Like all weak men, he laid an exaggerated stress on not changing one's mind.*

Ottorino was sixteen, an age when many young men were masters of their own destinies. The first time Bocco raised his arm to him, Ottorino simply knocked Bocco out cold, walked out the door, took Bocco's best horse, one he had yet to train, and rode off down the road for good. Petra, three years younger than Ottorino at thirteen, being a girl, came under the supervision of Kradle, who was so enchanted with the joy of having a girl to care for that she made life for Petra as pleasant as Bocco would allow.

Bocco intended for ten year old Domenico to assume the meager barn management responsibilities, giving Bocco more time to make deals. Without question, Domenico's ignorance of horses stood out like a peg leg before he was at his uncle's farm an hour. So did his revulsion of his uncle's training methods, since a winemaker trains his vineyards by love, not violence. By the end of the first week, one day after Ottorino departed, Domenico received his first beating—with a riding crop that had been modified to sport barbs of sharpened flint. Bocco reserved this crop for his most willful horses. Since his older nephew had run off, Bocco was taking no chances with the younger one.

Even while the beating was taking place, and Domenico could feel the skin on his back and legs rip and burn and bleed, he was planning how and when he would learn to use the big bullwhip he'd noticed in the barn. He had never touched a bullwhip in his life. This one hung on a wall like a long sleeping viper curled upon itself. But Domenico knew that, to save his life and probably the life of his sister, he would need to master that whip.

What Domenico didn't know was that this was among the finest bullwhips in the Province, crafted by an old harness maker for anyone who could combine strength of body with strength of character, a person willing to invest heart and soul in learning the whip's subtle demands. To this person, the whip would obey any request. Bocco Priami knew nothing of the whip's spirit. All he knew was that the whip was impossible for him to use, and that he'd been a fool to accept it as part of a trade.

It took Domenico Priami a month and three more beatings before he could take the whip off the peg, uncoil it, recoil it, and place it back, without making a sound and without taking a breath. It took Domenico another three months and six more beatings before he could crack the whip somewhat regularly, swinging it with both hands. And it took another three months and three beatings after that before he could knock a bottle off a fence post at fifteen paces—ten times out of ten, without thinking.

Seven months, thirteen beatings. And toward the end, the screams of Petra in nights when Bocco was at home, and her whimpering during the day whether he was home or not: Kradle unable to protect a mouse.

One sunny morning Bocco opened the barn door and immediately lost one eye to the bullwhip. Naturally he cursed and slapped a hand over the eye, not actually realizing that it was gone, or what had actually struck him. Perhaps he had accidentally walked into the wrong end of a pitchfork. Before the pain of the first bite ebbed even a little, a second broke his nose, ripping a gash up one nostril and out across his cheek. Bocco now occupied both his hands while bending over at the waist and rocking in agony, cursing whoever was doing this to him. As yet, no one had spoken, and there were too many shadows to see the bastards. Then the ear on the side of his good eye was ripped off with a hiss and a crack. The explosion also broke the eardrum, which Bocco didn't know, but he did feel a pain like his brain had been stabbed with a spike, and sound that made him imagine that his head was inside a cannon being fired repeatedly. Bocco stood up straight now, one hand over his missing eye, the other over his missing ear. And as he peered into the shadows wondering who could be doing this, the whip smashed his other eye to mush, bringing total darkness to Bocco Priami's world. Now Bocco covered each useless eye with a hand. The whip snapped at his groin four times in succession no matter which way Bocco turned, and when Bocco finally brought his hands away from his bloody face and down to protect his crotch, where his trousers were torn open to the air, the whip went for his throat. Bocco Priami was dead after he'd been struck thirteen times.

Ten year old Domenico stepped from the shadows. He knew that this was the moment that would define his future. His father, Lorenzito, had betrayed him—first by dying, then by sending him into this hell. His brother, Ottorino, betrayed him by leaving him and Petra at the mercy of this devil. Even Petra had betrayed him by allowing herself to be destroyed by the monster, by forcing Domenico to fight alone for the both of them. Only his mother, the beloved Felicia-Viola, who had nursed him in the vineyards, was blameless.

If he lived for a thousand years, Domenico Priami decided in that moment, the only person he would ever trust was himself. Since this commitment betrayed the request of the whip—to balance strength of body with strength of character (fighting for your life, and the life of your sister, was one thing, but a commitment to trust no one was something else altogether)—in an instant, all Domenico Priami's skill with the whip drained from his body. He didn't know this at the time. All he felt was an intense desire to keep the whip with him, next to him, touching him, forever, as though it were his beloved mother. Indeed, 10 year old Domenico was as sure as he could be that, if he did not make the whip part of him, he would die. And so he curled it, bloody, around his shoulder where it would remain, constantly, for the rest of his life.

*T*he rage that Puer Puella felt that evening on his golf course, in his clown costume, ignited by this most unusual of men that he had met merely hours before, was a rage that had been part of him, he realized, for five centuries. And if it had been there for that many hundreds of years, surely it had been there longer than that. In the cosmic scheme of things, he learned, a century didn't last much longer than a jelly bean in the mouth of a starving child.

Puer had no knowledge of his life as Domenico Priami beyond the first ten years, ending that moment in the barn when he re-coiled the whip that was now part of his body. Nor did he glimpse other moments of other lives, before or after that one. But he could feel the quality of the rage within him, how pervasive it was, how familiar it was—just as his desire to love was pervasive and familiar—and so he knew that rage, like love, had been not just present, but growing . . . life after life. Each life had presented him with innumerable choices of love or fear. And each time he chose fear, his rage had grown, a new tendril added to the root of molten iron.

Because in Hyman O'Malley's presence, one's life could open in ways that would otherwise never happen at that moment, given the normal unfolding of karma or destiny, that night Puer Puella exploded like a volcano that had been dormant much longer than was healthy for any living thing in its vicinity. "*Spontaneous combustion*" was his momentary wonder—all of a sudden, with not a second's warning, Whoosh! . . . a person is totally on fire. He didn't care. If he died, he died. If he destroyed everything in his path, it would be nothing. Whatever the price, he would pay it, for he had beheld the deadened heart of 10-year-old Domenico Priami and felt the consequences of a commitment five centuries old. Anything was better than living with rage—and worse, the fear of rage. Meeting it, becoming it, and somehow freeing it, was all that mattered. He willingly leapt into the void of fire that had consumed so much of him birth after birth. All he knew about where it might take him was that it would be somewhere other than where he had been.

He could have fried an egg on the back of his hand he was so hot. He wouldn't have been shocked if he could have swatted an airplane out of the sky by glancing at it. Nor to learn that he was shedding his skin, like a snake. So completely did Puer Puella give himself to this energetic holocaust within, so far beyond management of his everyday self was he, that later he was a little surprised to discover that all of his golf clubs didn't end up wrapped around trees and none of his bones were broken.

So that Puer would not hurt himself, Hyman stayed near him as he bounced and screamed and punched and shook and kicked and leapt across the golf course. Other than that, Hyman was merely present, offering to Puer the strength and acceptance that came from Hyman's own depth of connection to the Earth and to Spirit, from Hyman's passion that Puer free his heart of pain, and from Hyman's total lack of fear of anything Puer could ever be, or do.

Puer was startled to learn the truth about rage. It was not a reaction to any particular circumstances, particular injustices, or particular instances of willful destruction of the human spirit . . . whether caused by him or by anyone else at any time in history. No. Rage was not hatred. Rage was, instead, something much greater. Rage was his heart's response to unfathomable pain: the pain present in the entire universe: the accumulated pain caused by the countless choices made in fear by countless people, including himself, over countless lives since the dawn of existence.

Puer's truest, most honest expression of this reality was a sound that was beyond human in origin, for it lived in what might be called the core of all life. One small part of this sound was the wail of a woman whose baby has been abducted. Another small part was the scream of a dog being roasted alive. Another, the silence of a boy being raped by his father. And another, the moan of every heart that has ever put duty above kindness. These, combined with many other sounds like them, comprised the sound that Puer Puella made over and over long into the night. Every other animal, plant, mineral and molecule of moonlight in the Adirondacks was silent until dawn.

At first light, Puer was lying on his back in the middle of a fairway, Hyman sitting next to him. The perspiration of morning dew was soaking them both. Puer hadn't noticed. Every pore of his body had been weeping, following Hyman's guidance to free the depthless pain that is awakened by rage. For Puer it was the pain of many lives unlived. It was the pain of the choice as young Domenico, and many other choices like it over lifetimes—to trust no one but himself—which really meant to trust no one, not even himself. Or, the absolute heart of the matter, to, above all, not trust himself.

Puer felt the terror of 10 year old Domenico. He felt how that terror had led him to the bullwhip and murder. He felt Bocco's terror that led him to harm everything he touched. He felt Petra's fear, Kradle's fear, and his brother Ottorino's fear—and how their fears had led them to submit or flee. He even felt the fear of his father, Lorenzito, and how that fear caused his father to arrange for Bocco to be their guardian—honoring tradition rather than heed the warnings of his heart. Puer felt the pain of all their choices. And he felt the harm of those choices. He felt something that he'd known only as a thought, a concept, before then: that it was not possible to harm another without harming oneself; indeed, without harming all of humanity, without harming all that lives. Harm was never isolated, never restricted, Puer experienced. The term *"isolated incident,"* as if some act did not have consequences beyond itself, was an impossibility, a fabrication of fear. A man could live alone in a cave from birth to death, and yet his every thought, his every emotion, his every breath would influence the whole of existence.

Puer remembered how afraid he'd been when his beautiful partner and mentor, Clyde Marks, went ape-shit when the two of them were at sea on Clyde's boat, and that it was really Puer's own rage, not Clyde's, that Puer had been afraid of. Now he knew: he'd been afraid that his own rage might consume him, that he might destroy himself, or someone else. That didn't need to be so, he'd now learned with Hyman. Just as he had learned that rage denied, rage unmanaged—rage not felt and released—always harms . . . everyone, everything.

But most welcome to Puer was that, at Hyman's quiet urging, he began to wash the pain of all this from him, giving it to the Earth, letting it ride out of him on his breath . . . breath after breath. Among the strangest of strange experiences that morning for Puer was the feeling that he loved himself for the first time in many, many lifetimes. He couldn't explain it. Later, he would realize that what he was feeling was the beginning of compassion.

Yet this encounter with young Domenico, Puer realized, was but one small slice of one life, not unlike a page from a book, or maybe even just a paragraph, a sentence . . . a mere footnote in the encyclopedia of incarnations.

Imagine all the other choices I've made over all my lives, Puer thought. *Any of those choices made in fear are also calling to be forgiven.*

For the rest of his life, Puer Puella would come to appreciate that among the night's blessings had been the opening of his physical being so that, with continual attention, the fears of lifetimes would have a wide and loving channel of light to ride out into the all-accepting embrace of the Earth.

*T*here are experiences in life that are both so large that they fundamentally clarify one's perceptions, and so simple that they can be expressed in a couple of words. This was the case for Puer Puella. As the carnival of the sun marched in his direction that morning, lighting more and more of the land and sky before it, Puer said aloud to everyone and no one: "Everything matters. Every. Thing. Matters."

In feeling the pain caused by his choice as ten year old Domenico Priami, and sensing how he had allowed the fear of that choice to spread like an epidemic over subsequent lives—even though he was unaware of any specifics—Puer understood how this life had been driven by a kind of terror of being vulnerable.

"It's like all I've ever wanted to do was get revenge," he told Hyman. "Even all this," he said, gesturing to *Extravagant Humility*, "has been little more than me venting my rage at feeling helpless, protecting myself somehow—from Bocco, and all the ways I've been helpless over all my lives. Sure, part of me wants to wake people up, to be a big benevolent clown in the world. That's the part that wants to love. But part of me revels in sticking it to people I think deserve it, which, God help me, means just about everybody—making them look silly . . . forcing them to see themselves in ways they otherwise seldom do. I can feel my jaw get tight just thinking the word. Revenge."

A few moments later Puer spoke again. "You know, part of me would give my heart to a person who needed one. I don't have a big attachment to being alive. I've always known that we live an endless number of lives. Yet, I would want to give my heart in a way that slapped those who destroy so much because they don't know that it is living, not being alive, that matters.

"Man, isn't that crazy?" Puer said. "I am the person I want revenge on."

It was at this point that Hyman tapped Puer lightly on the chest and Puer Puella met that place in his heart where only Spirit resides.

If he had been able to make a sound, the sound would have been laughter. The laughter of knowing how all the plotting and planning and calculating and scheming to be safe over all the lives he either had or would care to dream up were all just so much nonsense. The place in his heart attuned to Spirit wouldn't have cared if he could hit 400, cure cancer, bring about world peace, and raise the apostles from the dead. One's inner heart knows only love. So the idea of not trusting anybody, or of getting revenge, or of protecting oneself from . . . whatever—was ludicrous. It was just his Small Self being afraid. There was nobody to trust or not trust. There was no revenge to get, and no one to get it from. There was nothing to protect, nor anyone or anything to be protected from. The universe was perfect as it is because Spirit, the essence of all, he realized again and again, was love—nothing else. There was no place where he left off and another began. There was only the One.

Sure there was pain. But it wasn't his pain separate from the pain of others; there was no such thing as "Puer Puella's pain;" there was only the pain of the universe, the pain of all. And it was pain that existed, always, within the gentle, compassionate embrace of the One—as everything existed.

Puer remembered something he had heard some religious guy say once: *If you feel distant from God, guess who moved.*

But Puer didn't laugh. At least not at that moment. He laughed later a lot. In fact, he laughed more from this point on in his life than almost anyone else he knew. Even if he wasn't going haw-haw on the outside, inside he was having a party, a party that only got bigger the more he surrendered his fear and everything under it; and if you looked in his eyes you could see the party going on. His only peers in the laugh department would be people like himself: people who had been given the blessing of experiencing what Hyman jokingly referred to as *The Entire Elephant, all at once.*

The reason Puer Puella didn't laugh at that moment, however, was awe. In this case, awe was the feeling that came from appreciating in the most intimate detail how every act, every choice, every horror, every joy, every life, every death, every you-name-it has been an essential, beautiful, glorious step in the journey that brought him to this place of understanding, this moment of possibility, this experience of love—here and now. You thought that life included random events, or accidents, or mistakes, or "bad news," but now you know that's not so. Now you know that, in every face you meet on the street, in every song you write for your Broadway show, in every meal you cook for a family that never says "Yum," in every wave from an unknown child in a passing car, every workout, every purchase, every commute, every prayer, every divorce, every child killed in war—is only Spirit offering another opportunity to awaken, to forgive, to choose love.

Puer's awe also stemmed from other changes felt within. His truest, deepest self was more present, while his personality, the closet full of masks, was almost a distant memory. The earth, and the light of the sky, felt completely different physically—more intimate, an extension of his very own skin, you might say. And his body was now teaching him constantly, as though each nuclei were a radio beacon telling him where to open next, where to free any hold, even the slightest hold. Plus, as he continually cleared his heart, and it grew bigger, weights he had carried on his back for a million miles fell away, one after another. He laughed at the sensation that he had lost a hundred pound beer belly, when what really had happened was the disappearance of a large cramp in his stomach that had been there for so long he hardly knew it had been part of him until it was gone. Another surprise: this new physical self was in continual transformation. His overriding feeling was one of softness—even his bones were soft, like skin—with unlimited energy. And his hearing! What would be the equivalent of having X-Ray vision for hearing? *Clairaudient*, was that a word? Puer not only heard things he never heard before, he was able to truly listen—feeling throughout his body deeper and deeper levels of meaning below what he heard.

Which is why, when he listened closely, he could hear the Great Ones chuckling up their sleeves—celebrating his awakening.

19

The Making of Puer Puella, New-Age Gangster

Puer Puella had been born in Lithuania. He came to America, with his parents and older sister, as an infant, but his parents never became American citizens. Or ever wanted to. They loved America, make no mistake. To Puer's father, nowhere else on earth was there such a feeling that you could do anything. Maybe it was the geography. Compared to America, Lithuania, like almost every other country in Europe, felt small. Its borders were like having to always wear a hat a half-size too tight; it did something to the way you viewed your prospects. Or maybe it was the history. Growing up, Puer's father had worshiped in churches that were built before America was even discovered, at least by Columbus. Such history meant roots, station, place, security. It also meant limitations. Puer Puella's father wanted none of it. His was a passion for possibility. Puer's father wanted more possibility than he could ever take advantage of. He wanted to drown in possibility. He wanted to nurse for all of his life at the ample, sweet breast of possibility. And he wanted his children to have the chance to do the same. His desire was not for achievement. To be great at something. To be well-known. Rich. Famous. Infamous even. No. What Puer Puella's father wanted was quite different. He simply wanted to do what he damn well pleased. And America, so far as he could tell, was the best place on earth to do that.

Maybe Puer Puella's father felt this way because he was so short. He stood a shade under three feet tall. That "shade" being anywhere from a half to three inches, depending on who was doing the measuring, and measured often he was. Why his precise height became a subject of conjecture was that, for one season, Puer Puella's father played for the New York Yankees.

It was a gimmick. Or, rather, he was the gimmick. He couldn't field a lick. He didn't even own a glove. But at three feet minus, he was nearly impossible to pitch to. He walked on almost every at-bat. And if the bases were loaded, and little Tiny Menace pinch-hit, it meant a run, "Gare-on-teed!" as the Yankee's play-by-play man would say. Tiny's orders from his manager were always the same: "Just stand there."

Some Yankee historians claim that the Yankees signed Tiny Menace as much for his name as his size. Back in Lithuania, once kids in his town discovered how small Tiny was destined to be, his family name, Sirmenis, was creatively abbreviated and re-spelled, while his first name, Arunas, was forgotten completely. By the time he came to America, Tiny Menace was the name on his passport. His eldest child, a daughter (who would grow up to be Carmella Puella), was named Lovely. His son's name was Big.

It would be fair to say that Tiny Menace had won as many as a dozen games for the Yankees before the World Series. It was more than enough to justify their investment. Plus, Tiny was a public relations gem. He was funny, articulate, kind, thoughtful, gracious, and clean-living. Oh, and he was as gorgeous to look at as any movie star you might ever think of. Women adored him. Men, because he was so unlike any other man, treated him as though he were a mascot for the entire male species. For his part, Tiny stood there and smiled and bowed and joked and posed for photos with every fan from a circus elephant to the President of France—all the way to the bank, as they say.

For one season.

It might have been more. But Tiny wanted to help his team. He wanted to hit. Maybe not often. Maybe almost never. But if he could hit, or bunt, just once—you know, surprise the pants off of some infield that was taking its usual nap any time Tiny came to bat because they were so darn sure he would never swing—then the Yankees would simply have another weapon in their arsenal . . . to be used in that once-in-a-lifetime situation that—well, granted—might never come up.

Possibilities. That's the way he pitched it to his manager. Possibilities. You can never have too many.

His manager laughed, but then said, "No, let's be fair. Why don't you start taking batting practice."

Tiny was beside himself. He had never been told to take batting practice before. What had been the point? To make sure that he wouldn't embarrass his teammates, or abuse his manager's trust, Tiny paid the team's batting coach to give him extra help when everyone else had left for the day. Tiny also started a program of lifting weights, running and stretching under the paid supervision of a former Olympic decathlon champion. And, he hired a professional nutritionist to teach him what to eat.

His dedication, and results, were more impressive than his manager ever could have hoped. Tiny's physique became like Michelangelo's David. His strength and quickness were compared to that of some of the best boxers of the day. His overall health, and even handsomer good looks, made him more sought after than ever before by the press; by advertisers wanting an endorsement; by the glitterati, whose associations with the *au courant* are chronicled on the society pages; and by the ever-present legions of autograph-hungry children, Tiny's favorites, the only fans whose hair Tiny could even come close to tousling without standing on a chair.

Unfortunately, Tiny couldn't hit worth spit.

Tiny was heartbroken. But not defeated. He was living in America. He was playing for the Yankees. He was rolling in money. He was admired by people from all walks of life. He had a wonderful family. And, most of all, he was doing what he damn well pleased. He was living proof that anything could happen. He could learn to hit, if he never gave up working at it.

As the pennant race wound down, it seemed certain that the Yankees would be in the World Series, and just as certain that Tiny Menace's role, if he had a role at all, would be: *Just stand there.* No matter how long, or how hard, he worked, Tiny still couldn't hit worth spit.

And then came the seventh game of the World Series. Bottom of the ninth. Bases loaded. Two outs. The Yankees trail by a deuce. Tiny Menace is sent up to pinch-hit. His first World Series at bat. What his manager is counting on, or hoping for, is that Tiny will walk, forcing in a run, making it bases loaded, two outs, only one run behind. Another walk, or any fair ball that leaves the infield by the guy up after Tiny, and the Yankees can at least push the game into extra innings. It's the best shot they've got.

Predictably, the count on Tiny quickly goes to three and oh. No one but his twelve year old son, already more than two feet taller than his father, ever knew what happened next inside Tiny Menace, because after he swung at the fourth pitch, and—". . . as if by a miracle," the Yankee play-by-play man would marvel for years—"sliced that ball worse than any golfer who ever lived over the flabbergasted second baseman and into the right field corner for one of the few singles in the history of the World Series to knock in three runs," Tiny Menace died before he could explain himself. All his training, conditioning and nutrition could not protect his heart, so full of possibilities, from being crushed—sandwiched between first base underneath him and a ton or more of jubilant teammates on top.

To the son, Big, who would become famous as Puer Puella, what his father did that day, swinging in a real game, the World Series—on a high three and oh fastball, at that—for the first and only time in his life, was easy to explain: "I could feel his heart, Double M, as if it were my own. He was enraptured . . . overwhelmed by the majesty and beauty of that moment after the ball left the pitcher's hand. In that blink of time, all the possibility of every dream he had ever had was being served up on a silver platter. He couldn't have stopped himself from swinging at that pitch any more than he could have stopped the sun from shining. I wonder sometimes if it wasn't one of the greatest deaths in the history of the world."

*I*t wasn't that Puer Puella's parents chose not to be Americans. They were American in the truest sense of the word. They lived for the magic of possibility. It was just that, while they easily left behind Lithuania's geography and history, embedded in their souls was her metaphysical link to a higher age of human consciousness. This connection they would never give up, for they knew that to be born Lithuanian was to be a direct spiritual descendant of men and women who lived in an Age of Enlightenment, a time long before recorded history as we know it. What proof was there of this age, besides the calling of their hearts? Sanskrit, the most pure and comprehensive language on the face of the earth, and the foundation of the Lithuanian tongue.

More precise than Greek, more copious than Latin, and more refined than either, Sanskrit is not only the world's oldest language, it is also the most perfect—the only language with enough letters in its alphabet to prevent mispronunciation. But that, in itself, would mean little if Sanskrit were not also the progeny of those who understood the relationship between sound and consciousness. The essence of all sound, the *Aum* vibration that reverberates in every particle of existence, expressing *"the word"* or *"voice of many waters"* of the Bible—is Sanskrit in origin.

Puer Puella's parents encouraged their children to revere their true Lithuanian heritage: an eminent culture of sages and saints, existing on the continent of India, and dedicated to the Royal Science of God Realization.

Among the many quotes scissored out of this or that publication and taped to their refrigerator was this: *The reason we like precious jewels so much is they remind us of planes of consciousness we've lived on where those are the pebbles.* Maintaining Lithuanian citizenship was, the parents felt, a symbolic bowing to these ancient spiritual roots.

Later, Puer Puella would also become a citizen of Argentina, one of the few Argentine-Lithuanians in the world. The reasons were not nearly so grand. It made transferring money around and through international banks that much easier, so it was all but impossible for anyone to ascertain just how wealthy he was. But more, Puer like to fantasize that he had been Evita Perón, the dictator's wife, in a previous life. Evita had been an undistinguished radio actress who used her charisma and savvy to strengthen the rights of women, as well as to improve the lives of her nation's lower classes, *the shirtless ones*, as she called them. While winning their adulation, she was such a lightning rod for the fears of the elite that, after her death at the auspicious age of 33, enemies kidnapped her body and shipped it out of the country, where it remained for sixteen years.

"Now, she was a babe," Puer said to himself. "Even her corpse was a great teacher."

*T*iny Menace's boy, Big Menace, named himself Puer Puella after reading Mario Puzo's novel *The Godfather.*

To be sure, Big had a rare intellect. At age 14, coincidentally the year Sylvie Marks died, he designed a solar-powered airplane after observing a tortoise. The design won him immediate admittance to Cal Tech and MIT. It was an honor that Big Menace declined, however, because his "flying tortoise" was the upshot of a whim, a way to explore his own mind, not a passion for aeronautical engineering. Therefore, a few years later, it was no surprise to his mother and sister that, upon making the acquaintance of the fictional Corleone family, Big Menace decided to reinvent the profession of gangster.

The Don's story had saddened him. Big had always been intrigued by a statement he once heard a man attribute to the Old Testament, that *Moses was a good man in his time*. He wondered if it meant that, had Moses lived in another time, he might not have been considered such a good man. And, by extension, whether it meant that anyone's behavior can only be fairly assessed in the context in which it is lived. To Big Menace, the Don was neither hero nor villain. He was merely a man, like any other man, struggling to live with dignity and integrity in a society that, from the Don's perspective, seemed to have very little of either. As far as Big Menace was concerned, that was still the case. But what was particularly painful to Big was the Don's struggle to manage a changing world, a struggle that was even more difficult for his children when they attempted to follow in the Don's shoes. So the question that Big Menace asked himself was: *Suppose a gangster became a master of managing change. How might he do business today?*

Big Menace used the word *gangster* deliberately. Mostly because he liked the ring of it. He liked the way its meaning played on the mind from old Cagney, Paul Muni and Edward G. Robinson movies. Plus, it was a word that was held in such distain that, so far as Big Menace knew, no man had ever used it to refer to himself.

And what do you do for a living?

I'm a gangster. Here's my card.

It was like *charlatan*. No one ever boasted, *I'm a charlatan*.

So the question that Big asked himself was: *What would it take to encourage the American people to reevaluate their prejudices about the word gangster?*

This was not a social cause for Big Menace. He was not out to change the world. Like his "flying tortoise," it was simply a way to learn about himself.

Formal education had always been foreign to Big. He didn't care for its implicit message that the things taught in school were somehow superior to other subjects in the vast wealth of possibility presented by the universe. But he was fascinated by the questions of why these subjects got chosen as most worthy of one's time, and why this or that teacher was someone whose opinion was deserving of special respect? He didn't ask these questions to get on anybody's nerves, though naturally they did. He asked these questions because, to him, they were simply what he wanted to know. His feeling was that his own natural curiosity was a far better guide to his education than a course of study imposed on every kid in town for reasons no one could explain other than to say that school couldn't be tailored to fit the whim of individual students. Big's response was, *No big deal, I'll teach myself what I want to know.* In principle, his teachers admired his independence. In practice, he was a kid they soon began to abhor, since, to Big, there were about ten million intriguing ways you could spend any given minute of your life without ever hurting another person, and he simply refused to do things he didn't care for. The fact that other people might be doing them, or that experts or tradition decreed that these things were essential to being a civilized human, meant nothing to Big. *Why would I want to do something simply because another person says it's the right thing to do, or because all my friends are doing it? Shouldn't there be a better reason than that?* Since no one had an answer, it didn't take long for Big's parents to honor his request to be schooled at home, which basically meant for him to follow in his father's footsteps and do pretty much whatever he pleased. His parents' rules for their two children were three: *Honor your true heritage; do what inspires you; learn from everything.* With those guidelines, Big Menace, long before his father died, became something of a whiz in arithmetic, history, geometry, physics, probability, astronomy, meteorology, the tides, navigation, psychology, piracy, storytelling, and serious bullshitting—to name just a few topics which served him well for years to come by following his fascination, which included shooting pool and playing poker several mornings a week in a local bar with a group of retired Lithuanian sailors.

It went without saying that, for Big Menace, *gangster* could never mean killer, or racketeer, or loan shark, or numbers man, or grifter, or forger, or con artist, or extortionist, and certainly not drug dealer or pimp.

On the other hand, Big loved the idea of giving out hundred dollar tips; making sure little old ladies didn't get bamboozled by their landlords; putting "incurable itch powder" in the sheets of KKK members; sending poor kids to college with a valet (*"Why do scholarships give kids only enough to survive?," he'd say, "It's as if we need to remind them to be grateful? Why not introduce them to the concept of abundance? After all, abundance is the fundamental message of the universe. The world's problems are not about resources; they're about greed."*). To be a man who could open doors for the needy and shut them on the greedy—to bring a little happiness to the world while wearing silk, getting facials and being chauffeured about in a Godfather-era Caddie, all that, while honoring your heritage from a higher age—boy, that seemed to Big Menace like a good way to do a cannonball into Ocean of Possibility.

Besides, this wasn't a lifetime commitment, for crying out loud. It was a lark. He had no career aspirations. He was just trying to learn stuff.

*L*ark or no, like any ambitious undertaking, there were one or two obstacles to overcome. The first was his name. In truth, he loved being a reflection of his father. But the name Big Menace was not a bridge-builder for a New Age Gangster.

Then there was the other problem. How was he going to make money? Oodles!

It turned out that the money was actually easier than the new name. He was, if he said so himself, a computer genius. Self-taught, of course. He'd been reading top-secret government files for years. Not that he was interested in anything the government had to say. He did it simply to keep his skills up. He figured so long as he could hack his way into any government computer system, he could do anything if he put his mind to it. Now that he wanted to be a gangster like no other, his theory would be put to the test.

Many people of genius are remarkably uncomplicated, seeking only the very simplest solution to any problem. Big Menace was such a person, which is why he quickly remembered something he had learned while watching the attendants at the parking garage where he detailed cars one summer: when a lot of money is changing hands regularly, there is a better than average opportunity for a small, infinitesimal sliver of those funds to be diverted from its intended destination with no one the wiser. You just needed the right system. What that meant in plain English, or Sanskrit for that matter, was international banking: banks all over the world buying and selling currency, back and forth, night and day. If Big Menace could just pick the brain of an expert in such affairs, that person's expertise, plus Big Menace's computer skills, might very well make millions.

But before he could look for a colleague, he had to have a new name.

What if the Don had lived another 75 years, and today's newspapers wrote, "Giving the eulogy at Mr. Corleone's funeral was his dear friend and protégé, (*fill in the blank*)"? What should that protégé's name be? It couldn't be Sicilian. Big wasn't Sicilian. In fact, his new name probably shouldn't represent any explicit ethnicity. He wasn't looking to become part of a tribe. Still, it had to be a name that positioned him as a natural extension of the Don's heritage, if not his blood, in contemporary USA. So, something Romanesque, perhaps. Androgynous for sure. Classical. Something sophisticated, yet simple, unpretentious. Easy to remember. Enjoyable to pronounce. And something that would make it a snap for the first name alone to become a household word. At that point, *Puer Puella* dropped out of the sky. The simplest solution. *Puer*, Latin for boy. *Puella*, Latin for girl. And a quick computer search of every phone book from Manhattan to Mandalay revealed hardly a would-be relative in sight.

Bingo!

*T*he next morning, in the time it took Puer to drink a cup of French Roast, his computer told him that among the international monetary brains that stood head and shoulders above the rest, all but one were pretty much spoken for. Rome, Moscow, Washington, Johannesburg, Hong Kong, Tokyo, Buenos Aires, et cetera, had first dibs on anybody considered top rank. The only exception was that fellow who had gone off from Wharton on a sabbatical to Singapore a few years back, and never returned. Press reports said that both his wife and daughter had died tragically on the ocean voyage there. All the data Puer could gather suggested that the man, Clyde Marks, now lived by himself on a boat, sailing the seas.

Hmmm. A fellow who goes wherever he pleases, thought Puer.

Puer's immediate high regard for Clyde Marks went up another notch when Puer discovered that Clyde himself had a very advanced computer system on board his vessel . . . so advanced that Clyde was unreachable by the outside world unless he chose otherwise. *Nice word, unreachable*, Puer mused on July 21st. *Let's see how long it will take me to reach him.*

July 22
Mr. Marks, hello.
My name is Puer Puella. I'm 19 years old. I have not entered your life to cause you any trouble. I can enter any computer on earth,

pretty much, and I haven't ever caused anyone a moment's anxiety. This is different, I realize. And I apologize. I have never actually made contact with anyone whose system I have entered. Usually, I enter only those, like yours, that are very sophisticated. I'm not a vigilante or a troublemaker. I don't steal anything. I don't even pay attention to classified documents. My reason is simply the challenge of mastering cyberspace. I want there to be no system I cannot link to if I wish. That's pretty arrogant, probably. I think of it as being compulsively curious. And just maybe, providing a measure of balance in a world of the compulsively secretive. In your case, however, my motivations are slightly different. I wish to contact you personally. Naturally, I know what the public record says about your life. I presume that business opportunities have no interest for you. But I wonder if you would consider discussing an intellectual challenge. It is one that explores the synergy of leading edge computer thinking and leading edge monetary management— i.e., the buying and selling of currency. My description is a lot drier than the actual opportunity (I hope). By the way, my father was Tiny Menace. Look him up, if you wish. He had a passion for life's possibilities—doing what he damn well pleased. I inherited his passion. I wonder if you, in your way, are a kindred soul. I would be happy to meet you in any port you choose, anytime. Please just give me a couple of days' notice. And should you choose not to respond, you needn't worry. I shan't contact you again.
Yours sincerely, Puer Puella.

July 25
Dear Mr. or Ms. Puella,
Your name is confusing. Both boy and girl. Hard to infer gender. I'd say man, but maybe I'm a sexist old fart. I saw your father get his

hit. Not on tee-vee. In person. I cried for a week. As you know, I've lost people. Too many. But not in so splendid a way. I almost didn't respond. I don't know why I should want to talk to you. I don't give a damn about computers. Or money. I'm not even impressed that you can break into my system. But you ask whether I am a kindred soul. I don't know. But I'm willing to spend an hour finding out. Monaco. La Condamine. One week from today. Being from Philadelphia, I'm partial to Grace Kelly. "*To Catch A Thief*," especially.
Regards, CM

July 26
Dear Mr. Marks,
Good guess. I am a man, three feet taller than my father, but otherwise the spitting image. When we meet, I'll be wearing a purple baseball cap. Hopefully a few other things, as well. But the cap for sure. If I can bring you anything, please ask.
Sincerely, Puer Puella.
P.S., I like your taste in movies, and royalty.

July 27
Dear Puer,
Quit calling me Mr. Marks. My friends call me CM or Clyde. You're either going to be a friend or nothing. Either way, Mr. Marks is out. Please come with fresh scones from Zabar's in Manhattan. 10 am.
Regards, CM

July 28
CM,
If you're not a kindred soul, you old goat, I'm Janis Joplin.
PP.

July 29

PP,

You must be very young. Why do you feel life has to be either/or? Why not, I am a kindred soul *and* you're Janis Joplin? Wouldn't that be much more interesting? No question, I'm an old goat. Ornery. Cantankerous. Opinionated. Short-tempered. I've given up eating with a knife and fork. And I usually stink to high heaven. Are you sure you want to meet me?

CM

July 29

CM,

More than ever.

PP

    And so it began.

    If asked why he wore what he did to his rendezvous with Clyde Marks, an avowed smelly old goat, Puer might have said that he was just trying the follow the maxim *Dress for the job you want, not for the job you have.* So, as promised, Puer wore his purple baseball cap, and with it white linen trousers, a black cotton T-shirt, yellow Italian sandals, and black wraparound sunglasses. Over his shoulder he carried a black leather teardrop bag in which he kept his phone and a few other essentials. In the palm of one hand he carried a medium-sized brown paper grocery sack, in which were a red and white bakery bag of scones and a jar of boysenberry jam, a delicacy of Michigan's Upper Peninsula and one Puer presumed CM's shipboard wasn't overstocked. Puer's wardrobe was nothing special in Monaco's La Condamine harbor, where even the gawkers had money (or dressed like they did), and where yachts approaching the size of Rhode Island docked so that their owners could amuse themselves in casinos where minimum bets can get as flashy as a teabag full of diamonds.

Puer had never been to Monaco before, and obviously he had never met Clyde Marks before, but he knew enough about both so that he didn't expect he'd be surprised by either. "Silly man," Clyde's late daughter Sylvie might have said.

Clyde's boat, though small at about 35 feet, fit right in. Everything about it suggested the hand of an experienced, meticulous sailor for whom cost had not been a factor in the boat's design, construction, or maintenance. It was the sailor himself who was out of place, as if he had just escaped from 20 year's confinement in the Devil's Island Prison for the Criminally Fashionless. Clyde's shirt, Puer would have sworn, was a blue, long-sleeve, cotton oxford-cloth from someplace like Brooks Brothers. Why he couldn't swear to it, however, was that, for the past several years, the shirt had doubled as a mechanic's wipe rag, except on that one day annually when it served as a napkin at the Food Fight Olympics—all without being subjected to the torment of soap and water. From the three new self-made holes in Clyde's World War Two belt cinching up a pair of ratty, oversized chinos, Puer deduced that Clyde had once been a much chunkier man. Clyde's white beard and hair had a definite Methuselah-with-his-finger-in-the-light-socket quality about them. Adding to, or perhaps subtracting from, the man's mystique were his missing two front teeth, their resulting empty space being the perfect fit for Clyde's ever-present lit cigar, the shape, blackness and stench of an arthritic thumb a week after its owner's funeral.

Nonetheless, for reasons that were unclear to Puer at the time . . .

Clyde?

You bring the scones?

I did.

Come aboard then.

Thank you.

I presume you brought jam or something.

Yes, captain. Where are we going?

Somewhere I'm less likely to be viewed as a vagrant trying to heist some prettyboy's toy.

. . . from their very first cup of coffee, and scones, sitting in a couple of canvas chairs on the aft of the *Queen & Sylvie*, moseying into the Mediterranean, gulls hovering like nervous waiters, Puer didn't withhold a thing from Clyde Marks.

Puer explained his genius with computers, his introduction to *The Godfather*, and his dream of being a guardian angel who wore great clothes and was chauffeured around in vintage Cadillacs. He detailed the etymology of his name, and made it clear that he was no criminal. The amount of energy that the world wasted—in the form of time, money, human potential, and other resources—was titanic, to use a suitable adjective. His desire was to detour a small portion of that energy for purposes that were life-affirming. He wasn't a crusader. He was a descendant of men and women of a higher age. He was his father's son. His was a passion for possibility.

All the while Puer spoke, Clyde sat calmly looking into Puer's face; Clyde's gaze never wandering, his cigar frozen in his mouth, its ashes dropping onto his shirtfront. By the time Puer was done talking, tears were rolling down the long, white beard of Clyde Marks, a beard that had been growing without interruption over his increasingly skinny bulldog face since the night Sylvie died five years earlier. From under Clyde's brown Filson long-brim cap (a cap which, Puer would come to appreciate, was symbolic of every one of Clyde's few possessions, regardless of how stinky, for the slogan of the Filson company was at that time '*Might as well have the best*'), his hair, straight and white, also flowed, unbarbered, since Sylvie's death.

And for that matter, Puer noted, so did the old man's eyebrows.

In fact, even though, or perhaps because, Clyde was weeping, Puer felt his own heart turn and his own eyes flood at the sight of Clyde Marks's eyebrows, for they reminded Puer of the first person he loved who wasn't a member of his family: old Mr. Zemyna, the man with the amazing hedges in front of his house.

Old Mr. Zemyna, an across-the-street neighbor growing up, spent every waking hour of his retirement caring for his small yard, and from the spring equinox to Thanksgiving virtually every one of those hours was spent out of doors. Old Mr. Zemyna's vast estate, including his bungalow and his one-car garage, covered possibly a quarter of an acre, yet in that space old Mr. Zemyna created a rose garden, an herb garden, a perennial garden, an all-purpose flower garden in which he seemed to plant every color and size of flower he could find, and this was just for starters. Blue and pink morning glories covered the entire east side of old Mr. Zemyna's brick bungalow, as well as the east side of his brick one-car garage—from the foundations all the way to the roof peaks. As a young boy in Lithuania, old Mr. Zemyna had been a fruit picker, which was why, in his retirement, his yard included ten small but bountiful fruit trees: two of each, "a male and female," he once told Puer—plum, apple, pear, dark cherry, and one fruit Puer couldn't recall. Then there was old Mr. Zemyna's backyard vegetable garden, called *"the Taj Mahal of tiny vegetable gardens"* by the green thumb columnist of the Sunday paper. Puer's mother had clipped the article, which included a photo of a smiling old Mr. Zemyna holding a basketball-size cauliflower, and taped it to their fridge where it remained long after old Mr. Zemyna died. Old Mr. Zemyna's vegetable garden wasn't a vegetable garden in the traditional sense. He didn't have space for that. Instead, it was a wall, made of earth, compost, moss and anything else plants love to grow in. The wall was taller than he was that's for sure, because at least half the time that old Mr. Zemyna tended his vegetable garden, he did so on a step ladder. And boy, from that wall grew everything: tomatoes, beets, kale, cabbage, Brussels sprouts, garlic, parsley, peppers, squash, green beans and a whole array of vegetables unknown to anyone but an aficionado. Old Mr. Zemyna produced so much produce that he gave away just about everything to his neighbors. Because Puer visited old Mr. Zemyna frequently, there were times that, when he arrived, Puer could tell that old Mr. Zemyna, sitting by himself in his yard, had been crying, and Puer sometimes wondered if old Mr. Zemyna cried because his children, who lived in the same town, preferred to buy their fruits and vegetables in a supermarket, "*where you knew what you were getting*," Puer once overheard one of his daughters tell her two kids. Old Mr. Zemyna never commented on his tears, and Puer was too young to be asking. One time, though, old Mr. Zemyna, who liked to joke around, did make a sort of funny comment to Puer's mother. He said, "You know, insanity is contagious. You can catch it from your children." Not surprising, old Mr. Zemyna had zero lawn—"Grass is overrated," he told Puer—but he did have a hedge that ran along the entire front boundary of his property, not counting the brick driveway leading down beside the bungalow to the one-car garage. Actually there were two hedges, one on either side of the brick walkway which led from the front sidewalk to old Mr. Zemyna's front door. Each hedge had been painstakingly sculpted by old Mr. Zemyna into a French curl, each curl, on either side of the brick walkway, the exact mirror image of the other. The gardens of Versailles might have had such ornamentation, though the picture in Puer's memory was of two huge surfer waves, back to back, moving away from one another in opposite directions. Anyway, when old Mr. Zemyna toddled off to heaven to find old Mrs. Zemyna who had moved there before him, his house and yard sat unattended for three years while his children fought over whether to keep the property as a shrine, to which they could charge admission, or sell it—and it didn't take long for old Mr. Zemyna's hedge to become the model for Clyde Marks's eyebrows, with the exception that Clyde Marks's eyebrows, like every other visible hair on his body, were pure, sun-bleached white.

"My daughter would be eighteen," Clyde Marks said, his eyes present and unblinking through his unwiped tears, "You and she would be shaking up the world together."

Then Clyde stood up, turned his back to Puer and, for the fifth time since they'd set sail, peed off the stern, this time flipping his cigar into the sea when he was finished. Sitting back down, Clyde lit another cigar, refreshed their black coffee, and unwound his own story.

He was 57, he began. He had always loved the sea. It kept him anchored, excuse the pun, to the essential rhythm of the universe, and now, as if by some cosmic dispensation, to the spirits of his daughter and wife. Contrary to what others might think, he had long ago surrendered Sylvie and Queenan to whatever higher power there was. He wasn't on the ocean because they had died there. He'd be here no matter where they had died. "I might be ornery," he said, "but I'm not a bitter old man who feels he's a victim of life's vicissitudes." He lived the way he did—in what he considered the utmost simplicity—because he wanted peace. Being as free from social encumbrances as a person can be, while also being intimately connected to the Earth, was, for him, an ideal environment to pursue his goal. Maybe in that way they were kindred souls: he, Puer, and Puer's father. And surely Sylvie. When she was five, she said that all she ever did was "follow thumper," meaning her heart.

Nevertheless, Clyde Marks made it clear that he had no desire to support Puer Puella's "life affirming" ambitions. And his interest in currency trading and computers was even less. His own state-of-the-art system was simply a tool that gave him possibilities, to use Puer's own word, nothing more. As far as Puer being a New Age Gangster, Clyde couldn't care less. "Most of life is theatre anyway," he said. "Be whoever you please. Live with the results."

That didn't mean he wouldn't help Puer. It only meant that his motivations, and Puer's, were different.

"Let me put it this way, Puer," Clyde said, raising his cap just long enough to scratch a dry spot on the top of his tan bald head (cap off, Clyde's head, with its six inch wide part down the middle and long hair to the sides and back reminded Puer of a brown egg wearing a white hula skirt). "If Sylvie were alive and decided to take up Brahma bull riding, I'd be out of this boat in a minute going to rodeos. Do I care about rodeos? I think we both know the answer to that. Maybe I'm just a blubbering fool who was lying to you when he said he'd given his daughter to the universe. Or maybe I'm a man who says yes to whatever feels right, no matter how crazy it is. I don't know, and I don't care. But I feel Sylvie. I felt her in your e-mails, and I felt her again the minute I saw you walking down the dock. So I say, even though I'll probably live to regret it, let's have some fun. Sylvie would be laughing her head off. 'Good for you, daddy,' she'd be saying."

Now it was Puer who was weeping. "I am doing something I never thought was remotely possible since that October day seven years ago . . . talking with my father."

And then they both wept.

Clyde took a fresh scone, broke it in two, and handed half to Puer. Then, each took his half, crumbled it, then tossed the crumbs high over his shoulder to the waiting gulls.

20

Holy Cow

A fraction of a penny on every sale of currency between banks around the world every hour of the day and night, and pretty soon you're talking more than you ever dreamed possible. "Suppose we name our little enterprise *Holy Cow*?" Puer said to CM one day. "It seems that every time I look at our revenues that's what I say."

"*Holy Cow*," Clyde Marks intoned, "delivering the mother's milk of possibility," causing Puer to laugh so abruptly that he blew iced coffee out his nose onto his black tencel shirt, cream leather vest and gray sharkskin trousers.

Soon, their favorite indoor sport was brainstorming what they might actually do with their riches. Casting for possibilities, they played those most enjoyable of no-risk games, "What would it take . . .?" and "What if . . .?"

What would it take to make cross-country transportation—buses, trains, planes—downright enjoyable?

What if you could make sure that virtually every child in America spent their first five years engaged in one of the most important activities in a young child's life—robust, healthy play?

What would it take to make addiction a cause for celebration for all that it is teaching the Family of Man? Perhaps especially the addiction to beliefs, the most pernicious of which is the belief that other people and outside circumstances are responsible for how we feel.

What if eating intelligently were considered as important as reading, writing and arithmetic?

Meanwhile, spurred by the desire to at the very least serve individuals one-to-one, a simple computer program identified countless possible stops for Santa Claus every day. To keep *Holy Cow* invisible for the time being, anonymous donations were made to neighborhood churches, a single string attached. Two-thirds of the gift could be spent at the church's discretion. One third was obliged to be spent on the purchase of a specifically named item for a specifically named recipient. Although the gifts were usually less than a million dollars, the *Holy Cow* partners felt like the reincarnation of John Beresford Tipton from "The Millionaire" TV show of the 1950's.

And then, Clyde Marks went berserk.

*T*hey were twenty miles at sea. The wind unusually calm. On days like this, Clyde loved to just sit and drift, with water all the way to the horizon no matter which way you looked.

All Puer had said was, "You never say much about your son."

CM began in the most reasoned tones, as if explaining to a class of graduate students, as he had no doubt explained to himself a thousand times, "We were just . . . a plain family. We laughed. We ate dinner together. We had a dog. We played cards, went to the movies. We really liked each other. And your daughter, this jewel . . . she makes this decision—to jump overboard. How? How is this possible? She was beautiful. Thirteen. She was the most brilliant, alive, joyful person I ever knew."

Almost inaudibly, Clyde said, "She was as much my teacher . . . ."

And then Clyde's voice clicked up an octave.

"You want to play 'What would it take . . .?' What would it take to make an angel kill herself?"

Then Clyde screamed, "OVERBOARD!" and Puer jumped. Clyde's face, probably because it was deeply tanned, reminded Puer of a large plum.

Clyde screamed again, "I will NEVER believe . . .!" and Puer flinched again.

The words hung in the air for several minutes before Clyde spoke, this time quietly, "No body. No explanation. Nothing. And then Queenan. That I at least understand: her baby. There have been times . . . ." The thought was too intimate to complete. Clyde stared out to sea for a time.

"And now Arjay. Fine boy . . . man. Good man. One of the brightest, kindest people you might ever meet. Art professor at Princeton. But this . . . thing—has made him crazy. Do you know who Charlie Fox is? Young prosecutor? Manhattan? Of course not. Arjay may be as good as dead, too."

Again, Clyde suddenly raised his voice, "Look at me!" he said and Puer jerked.

"WHAT AM I? A bag of bones floating around the world saying he wants peace. I make myself want to puke. Don't you see how much I hate? I don't hate any thing. I hate everything."

And then he began to scream: "EVERYTHING! I just hate." He stood right over Puer, looking directly into Puer's eyes. "DO YOU GET IT?" Clyde screamed. "THAT'S ALL I DO. HATE. THAT'S ALL I AM. HATE."

Now his rage erupted from the very core of him; he was flailing like a man being attacked by bees, bellowing to the heavens.

Puer, by this time, was completely paralyzed. He fantasized diving in and swimming to shore, the whole twenty miles, so badly did he want to escape. He had never been so afraid. To Puer, Clyde was a blind man with a hammer and an uncontrollable desire to destroy.

What Puer didn't know, but would find out a decade later when he met Hyman O'Malley, was the reason for his fear. When Puer looked at Clyde, what he was actually seeing was himself. Puer was afraid of the rage he held locked within his own body.

Clyde ended up sobbing himself into silent oblivion on the deck. Puer eventually covered his partner with a blanket and put a pillow under his head. Clyde lay there until dark, staring at the sea like a dead man whose eyes had yet to be closed.

*B*ecause both men were afraid of their own rage, and the pain under it, and neither had any idea what to do about it, a raw intimacy was born of Clyde's eruption. Open wound touched open wound. Their desire for comfort and predictability had been breeched. Neither was yet able to look upon it as a blessing. Clyde felt shame. Puer felt anger, as though something had been taken from him without his permission. Both responses, they would someday learn, masked fear. It was a testament to their affection for one another that there was never any danger of their friendship falling apart. Somehow, each knew that he would have to grow in order to love the other as fully as he wanted to. Each was willing. So, as best they could, they went out of their way to build new connections of understanding that might compensate for whatever it was that came between them that day. One of those connections was Clyde Marks sharing his feelings about his son's obsession with Charlie Fox.

"See for yourself. It won't take much to hack into his system," Clyde said. "He feels Fox knows more than he's ever said. It's just an instinct Arjay has, and I have to admit, Arjay has very good instincts about people. He says Fox is a three dollar bill. A 'Fugazy' Arjay calls him. Phony. Personally, I think both he and I are a bit nuts when it comes to Sylvie."

"Arjay may be disturbed," Puer said, "but . . . is it also possible that he's right?"

"The one thing I absolutely know he's right about is Sylvie killing herself. There is no way she would do that—not from the desire to destroy herself, anyway. Now, did she jump overboard of her own free will? Fifty witnesses say yes. So there's the rub. The wild card we know of is Fox. He was the only change in her life during those few days before she died, if that counts for anything. They spent quite a bit of time together. He was with her just before it happened. In fact, they were together almost the entire day she died, and the evening before. But did he make her jump? Did he tell her that if she didn't jump, he would murder her family—and she somehow believed him? You can see my imagination has covered a lot of territory. But that kind of stuff seems pretty far-fetched to me, especially knowing Sylvie. She was very wise for her age. A lot like you, but different."

*P*uer decided to do what he could for his friend. He began to review the information Arjay was collecting, without Arjay knowing it. It took nothing to hack into Arjay's computer. Clyde was right. It was a lot of tedious data collected by a man who seemed to have no idea what he was looking for. Given Arjay's scholarly bent, Puer was a little surprised. For example, why had he not interviewed some of the people who had been present when Sylvie jumped? Having their reports was one thing; actually talking to them could be quite another. You'd think a person obsessed would stop at nothing. Maybe that's just it, Puer thought. Maybe, like Clyde, Arjay has simply created an elaborate mourning ritual. Clyde says he and his son are both a little nuts. Who wouldn't be?

More to scratch his own curiosity, Puer commissioned phase one of the neglected research himself, unbeknownst to Clyde. The target was anyone in the immediate vicinity when Sylvie went overboard. The results he got back from the excellent firm he hired were anything but noteworthy, except for one small blip.

Her name was Madeline Ku. She was four years old at the time, sitting on her mother's lap. She had just turned eleven when the interview took place.

She said that Sylvie had been sitting in the deck chair next to hers. In fact, she remembered Sylvie very clearly. They had never met, yet Sylvie had somehow known Madeline's name. She had said, "Your name is Madeline, isn't it? I love the name Madeline. My name is Sylvie. I am so glad to know you." And then Sylvie had given her a piece of ginger rock candy. Madeline remembered wondering if she would ever see Sylvie again because she really wanted to. Sylvie was so happy. So beautiful. Now that she was much older, Madeline knew that she must have imagined it, but what she remembered most about Sylvie was that there were two angels with her. Madeline also remembered that Sylvie was with a friend, a man. A real man, not an angel. He sat in the deck chair on the other side of Sylvie from Madeline. She remembered that Sylvie had given him a present, a pair of socks, which Madeline remembered distinctly because one was gold and one was blue. She also remembered that, for some reason, the man was crying as he was talking to Sylvie. And then she saw Sylvie stand up, tuck a blanket around the man, and whisper in his ear. The next thing Madeline remembered was Sylvie standing on the railing with the angels on either side of her. Madeline again said that she knew that what she had seen couldn't be true. When asked what she had seen, Madeline said, "I saw Sylvie stick out both of her arms—like a scarecrow?—and then she did a backwards summersault off the railing. All the while the angels are at her side, and just as she completes the summersault, while she is still in mid-air, the angels lift Sylvie up under each arm and fly her away up into the night. My mom says I made up that story because the truth was too terrible. I know it was just a child's fantasy, but that's the fantasy I had."

"I owe you," Clyde said to Puer. "This is the first story about Sylvie's death that feels right, although, I must say, it sure doesn't make any rational sense. And you know why I believe it? The socks. She gave me a mismatched pair of socks once. And she asked me to wear them on my birthday every year for the rest of my life. Why I don't know, but that was Sylvie."

"And do you?" Puer asked.

"Never miss," Clyde said.

*H*oly Cow was decorating the nation with anonymous gifts. Charlie Fox, meanwhile, had successfully run for Congress twice and, rumor had it, was about to toss his bow tie in the ring for President. It would be the only election he ever lost.

For Puer, all that remained unfulfilled was his intention to redefine the profession of gangster. It was time to go public. *How* was the question.

"You said something to me when we first met that I've thought a lot about since," Puer said to Clyde one day. "You said, most of life was theater anyway, so I should be whoever I please. Just be prepared to live with the results."

"I'm flattered you remember," Clyde said.

Even if they met on land, they always met at a place that Clyde could get to on the *Queen & Sylvie*. Fortunately, it didn't have to be salt water, which is why one of their most important conversations took place while they were motoring along New York's Barge Canal, somewhere between Syracuse and Rochester.

"So professor," Puer had said the second he stepped on board that morning, "at one point this watery thoroughfare was known as the Erie Canal, today it's called the Barge Canal. Why the difference?"

"See what you get for shooting pool with Lithuanian sailors rather than being bored to death in seventh grade Social Studies?" Clyde said. "You leave it to me to remedy your unwillingness to conform to polite society. Thank God I'm a saint. The Erie Canal began full scale operation in 1825. When the waterway was widened nearly a century later, it was renamed the Barge Canal. I don't know why. End of lesson."

"My day is complete," Puer said.

"That's only because you have standards of academic achievement a snail could hurdle."

Clyde was heading west and Puer was on board just until the following morning. Since the Barge Canal is seldom wider than a hundred yards along its 363 mile length between Albany and Buffalo, winding through some of New York's lushest farmland and all sorts of quaint little burgs, speed is out of the question. Not that this meant anything to Puer and CM. They were never in a hurry in each other's company, which Puer enjoyed all the more since, at least twice a year, Clyde would screech like a drag queen, "These dead ends are driving me crazy," and Puer would get out Clyde's Swiss Army Knife with the built-in scissors and lop a few inches off hair and beard, but never the eyebrows. The result gave Clyde's appearance what Puer called, "a certain 'Santa on holiday' feel."

"More like Santa on acid," Clyde had said.

Puer was wearing khakis, an azure blue polo shirt and a lightweight charcoal gray cashmere sweater.

Clyde, in his ever-present long-brim Filson cap, plus dress shirt and pants that might have come from a store named "Homeless Rejects," was standing behind the tiller, his eye to the water ahead. Puer was lying on the roof of the cabin, on his side, his arm crooked, his head resting in the palm of his hand; he was facing Clyde.

"So why can't I just make up the gangster named Puer Puella? Completely. Out of whole cloth. *Holy Cow* still remaining invisible."

Without removing his cigar, Clyde let out a blast of smoke from the side of his mouth and said, cigar wagging, "Could we have just a teensy bit more information here, so that I might actually participate in this conversation?"

"Lord, you old guys. You're such sticklers for continuity. Thank God I'm magnanimous. Let me start over.

"I want the public Puer Puella to be a guy who is everything: generous, dangerous, kind, unpredictable, trustworthy, yet someone certain members of society will be definitely uneasy around if not absolutely afraid of. Hell, if I'm going to be a New Age Gangster, it seems I need to be outrageous in every way, including the tweaking of schnozzolas."

"Oh, cut the fancy lingo," Clyde said. "You just want to be yourself."

"Precisely, Grumplestiltskin. At least once a week, editors of every conceivable information-dispensing medium on earth will receive from me a story of my latest caper—anything from providing the equivalent of a prep school for prison inmates to embarrassing the snot out of someone who deserves it."

"The prison prep school stuff isn't too far from what we're doing now through *Holy Cow*," said Clyde.

"Except, of course, that nobody's ever heard of *Holy Cow*."

"A minor detail. All that's really new is your adolescent craving to throw a pie in some select faces."

"Since you put it that way I guess I'll have to agree."

Clyde gestured for Puer to keep rolling.

"No, that's about it," Puer said. "I'm hoping the press won't be able to get enough of some colorful, eccentric character who is doing things most people deep down approve of . . . even if some of those things occasionally stretch the bounds of good taste and maybe even legality."

Clyde kept a small bucket of yellow tennis balls within easy reach, in case he met a dog who wanted to play. When Puer finished, Clyde tossed a ball underhand at his partner, who came within an eyelash of catching it between his teeth before the ball bounded into the drink, bobbing off behind them. Puer winked at Clyde.

"Oh, aren't you just the cleverest boy in town," Clyde said, taking his cigar out of his mouth long enough to spit overboard. "But like most clever boys you have let your imagination run a mile ahead of your reason."

"Not a'tall, *mon ami*," said Puer. "My cleverness extends only to having you as my partner, for I know that you will rescue me from any follies of youthful euphoria."

"Stop, please, before I become diabetic," Clyde said.

"A diabetic old goat sailing the old Ear-eye Canal," Puer sing-songed, "Now that's a fun picture."

"Son, if Charlie Fox talked the same nonsense you do, it's no wonder Sylvie jumped overboard. You're going to force me to follow her lead."

Puer pulled himself upright. The two men stared at one another in the silence of the breakthrough. Never before, in the six years they'd known each other, had Clyde Marks ever referred to Sylvie's death in a manner that included humor.

Finally, Puer said, "Well, before you go, my captain, please show me the error of my ways."

"You need to take more responsibility for what you want," Clyde said, carefully taking his cigar out of his mouth and tapping an inch of ash into his shirt pocket. He then held the stogie at eye-level and scrutinized it as if it were a long-stemmed rose, a sign Puer knew meant a soliloquy was on the way.

"Don't expect the media to make you famous, Puer," Clyde said, looking over the top of his smoldering panatela. "Speak directly to the American people. They must look you in the eye and see someone they can trust, and like. Which means that you must open your heart to them, as you have to me. Frankly, you are in a unique position. You're not after votes. You're not asking people to buy anything. There has never been anyone like you. No one has ever gone on TV and said, 'Hi, I'm a gangster. Let me tell you what I'm up to, and how it might benefit you or your town or someone you know.' If you can stand before the camera as you really are, viewers will love you and, I believe, you'll have your puss all over the world in nothing flat."

Clyde raised his cigar a fraction of an inch so that Puer wouldn't interrupt him.

"Now if you can't do that, or choose not to do it, that's fine—you'll still have *Holy Cow*, invisible or not, and you can still do brave and lovely things, but you'll never change the public's mind about gangsters."

"How'd a geezer like you get so smart?" Puer said.

"Clean underwear," CM said. "Plus, you forget, among my many hats has been projecting the value of the world's currency at a given moment in time. And you know what the biggest factor is in the value of just about anything?"

"Elucidate. Please."

"Perception. Do the people running the show know what they're doing? And one more thing, since I'm telling you how to run your life."

"You're doing a better job than I."

"Even you speaking directly to the world on television, the Internet and whatnot isn't enough. What you need is a way to give something inspiring to the world every moment of every day, so that people are always aware of your underlying positive presence. You blabbing about your New Age Gangster shenanigans is but a tiny part of that presence. The least important part, if you ask me."

"Are you saying *Holy Cow TV*?" Puer said. "A resource for the greatest expressions of human dignity and imagination, or something like that?"

"Why not? You want to be outrageous? Make the backdrop for wacko Puer something wonderful. Hell, there's always room at the top. Especially in mass media."

On *Holy Cow TV*, with around-the-clock programming *"offering the mother's milk of possibility,"* Puer delivered a new message every week for the entire six years he was on the air. Some messages were brief. Others long by comparison. Here is the script for number 152:

Hello friends. For those of you who don't know me, I'm Puer Puella, New Age Gangster . . . a major underworld figure, if you will. This week's story is about Isabella Goldfarb of Salt Lake City, Utah. Young Miss Goldfarb, who is 16, has designed an automobile that is intended to reach a speed of one thousand miles per hour and emit not a particle of pollution. Now, of course, Miss Goldfarb's auto is not meant for a quick jaunt to the grocery store or a Sunday drive in the country. It is a test, to help all the world learn what it takes to create a vehicle that is both powerful and clean. I say Miss Goldfarb is sixteen. But she actually completed the initial design of her car three years ago, and for two years after that sent her design to all the world's automobile manufacturers. Every single one of them told Miss Goldfarb that her design is 'imaginative, but impractical.' So, just about a year ago she sent her design to me. She had heard that I can do things that no government or business on earth can do—I can look at something without being motivated by profit, politics, greed or power. And so I had Miss Goldfarb's plans reviewed by an independent team of crackerjack engineers. And they basically said, 'Hey, this looks pretty cool. These ideas should be tested.' So that's what we're going to do. We're manufacturing a prototype car, and very soon we'll be testing it out on the Big Salt Lake test site in Utah, near Miss Goldfarb's home. But that's not the end of the story. Now, it seems, many of the world's auto manufacturers, those folks who didn't care for Miss Goldfarb's ideas, have changed their tune. They have offered millions of dollars to control the test of Miss Goldfarb's car. This is why I am a gangster: to make deals that will help not only Isabella Goldfarb, but also all the other Isabella Goldfarbs of the world. Miss Goldfarb and I have told the auto manufacturers that whatever we learn from testing Miss Goldfarb's car will be free to be used by anyone. Ohhhh my! The auto manufacturers didn't like that. You see, the leaders of these companies, like most leaders, don't really want knowledge; they want power. It's a shame, but that's the way it is. They've each been offering even more and more money if they can have the exclusive rights to what we learn from Miss Goldfarb's car. This is why it's good that I have more wealth than a man can use. Miss Goldfarb and I have said no. The information will be made available to everyone, but there is a price. And the price is this. Each car manufacturer who wishes to share in what we learn must give a healthy sum to a foundation that is being creating to underwrite the dreams of teenage girls like Miss Goldfarb. I was tempted to also have the leaders of these companies show up at the test in bathing suits, then get down on their knees and kiss Miss Goldfarb's hand, while we filmed the event for the world news. But Miss Goldfarb talked me out of it. She has much more compassion for narrow minded nitwits than I do. Thank goodness. Well, that's it for this time. I'm Puer Puella, New Age Gangster.

At the end of each message, a statement appeared on the screen:

Puer Puella
New Age Gangster
Doing brave and lovely things

The general public, well, they weren't quite sure whether all the bulbs in Puer's chandelier were screwed in, but that didn't matter. He was real. And damn, he did some wild things. Who would have thought anyone with all that money and those good looks could be so down to earth?

There was no question he was eccentric: a man with probably too much money, too much time on his hands, and an imagination that would be comfortable if the four authors of the gospels were the Marx brothers. It was a volatile combination. He could be tough. He could embarrass you in public. He could cost you dough. He could even get you put in jail. The question was: *What did the fool want?*

A New York Times editorial asked: Is Mr. Puella a saint, as some suggest? Or is he a man who is very angry about something and simply has the resources to work out his anger in a dramatic way? Or, is he something else altogether?"

*T*he wrangle with Charlie Fox started like most forest fires: completely by accident. Puer had been living in the public's eyes and ears for five years. It was the end of November. Charlie Fox had just been elected President but wouldn't be sworn in until January. On a Sunday morning network interview program, Puer was, as usual, waxing iconoclastic. "As the great German writer, Gunther Grass, said, the first responsibility of any citizen is to keep his or her mouth open. We pay a big price whenever we forget that the President, I don't mean president-elect Fox specifically—any president, any leader—works for the people, us, we don't work for him . . . ."

Quick on the uptake, looking for a spark, the interviewer said, "To put that in gangsterese, Mister Puella, would it be fair to say that you, for one, feel that you own whoever is President—President-elect Fox, say?"

To which Puer smiled and replied, "Now that would be a rather gangsterish way to put it, but metaphorically I think we should all be able to say that. Any leader worth two cents is a servant, although I don't think we've had many Presidents, or many of us citizens, and perhaps most sadly of all many journalists, who really got that."

"Oh, but didn't you once say, Mister Puella, and I quote," said the interviewer, oblivious to Puer's implication, "'You don't become a New Age Gangster without puppets in high places.'"

"Did I say that?" Puer said, feigning astonishment. "Has a nice ring, don't you think? Now, if you're wanting me to say, specifically, that Mister Fox is my toy, that I've got him in my back pocket, that the bum can't tie his shoes without talking with me, that I'm privy to Fox's deepest, darkest secrets—secrets that no one else in the world knows, and things you wouldn't believe, in fact . . . . Hmmm, why not? Consider it said."

And then Puer, imitating the late Mick Jagger, sang the first three words of the Rolling Stones' classic, *Under My Thumb.*

It was a typical, flip, silly, Puer Puella response. He knew exactly what he was doing. Playing. Trying to make a serious point while poking fun at himself and giving others, in this case including the new President, the chance to poke fun at him also. He loved people to think he was ridiculous. It made them scratch their head—thinking all the more—when he did his other magic. And, to be sure, he knew he was offering a morsel of red meat to the tabloids, his personal favorites. He loved to have his picture appear next to the photo of an eighty-year old woman who had just given birth to alien twins, especially if the story was that he, Puer Puella, was the father.

Predictably, Puer's remarks, like others before them, ended up as a headline that sold: *Puer: 'I own Fox.'*

Puer didn't think a thing of it. But for some inexplicable reason, Fox did. From that one statement of Puer's, and Fox's ill-advised replies, news outlets lit up for days.

Fox: "Puella scourge on American values."
Puer: "Fox my toy."

Fox: "Puella role model of evil."

Puer: "Fox under my thumb."

Fox: "Puella to go where the gun don't shine."

Puer: "Fox just another puppet in high places."

It was Clyde Marks who pointed out how funny these headlines would be if Fox were joking. "But it seems President Fox has picked you for an enemy."

"Isn't it ironic that if he really knew how I made money, he would have the enemy he wanted," Puer said.

"Come January he'll have every conceivable government agency looking into you like a mad proctologist," Clyde said. "He'll never discover the source of your wealth, but he'll know just about everything else. Are you up for that?"

"There's not much about me worth knowing," Puer said. "I just don't want you to be hurt. I asked for this. But you didn't."

"Oh, quit being a baby," CM barked. "You think I'm some doddering old fool who doesn't know what he's got himself into? No, don't answer that. But if you start making decisions based on what you're afraid is going to happen to me, I'll take my teddy bear and go home. Don't you get it, you simpleton? I'm having a ball. I love this. I love you. I don't care what Charlie Fox knows about me. He's a child. What's he going to do, ruin my career?"

"Pardon me for caring about you, you old fart," said Puer. "It's just that I find this whole situation surprising. I have no reason to attack Charlie Fox. But I certainly don't intend to let him undermine all we've built.

"Besides, don't you just wonder about a guy who is so insecure that he lets a clown like me get under his skin? That's the message I intend to go public with, if necessary. Unless you have another opinion."

"Not I," said Clyde. "Sounds like a good show."

"The funny thing is," Puer said, "I now have more respect for your son's position that Fox is basically a very strange duck. In your vast experience, oh Solomon of the Seas, would you say that our Mister Fox is hiding something?"

"No doubt," Clyde said. "But not necessarily more than some old boob who spends most of his life on a boat keeping his distance from the world."

"Or his young friend," said Puer, "who makes sure that hardly a soul on earth knows who he really is."

After meeting Domenico Priami on the golf course, it didn't take long for Puer to shut down *Holy Cow*'s original source of revenue.

It wasn't that it was illegal to siphon a drop of every currency transaction among the world's banks. Legal/illegal to Puer Puella was merely a social convention, something that Puer had only nodding respect for, the sort of respect he had for the belief of his grandmother that a wholesome meal was one comprised of three different colors of food. More salient for Puer was that he'd been stealing, an act that contributed harm to life. And while stealing can sometimes be a means of helping others cultivate generosity, or a means to stay alive in a hostile climate, or a means to cripple an unjust enterprise, or a means to awaken the inattentive to the harm of their choices—this wasn't really any of those.

Puer didn't feel remorse or guilt for his years of thievery. His shift in behavior stemmed from nothing more dramatic than his heart's guidance that it was time to change, that any further stealing would be the most serious form of spiritual transgression: acting contrary to his heart's request.

Nor did his guidance tell him to give the money back, perhaps because money is simply a form of energy and he had already transformed whatever he stole into something more nurturing than it had been. Of course all that, he knew, might be nothing more than a fat rationalization. If it was, it was. As best he could, he was simply listening and following, as Hyman put it. Nothing more. He was grateful, however, that his guidance didn't direct him to publicly divulge the story of his wealth. And he was pleased that the fortune he had accumulated over a dozen years, if invested well, could continue to underwrite indefinitely any number of brave and lovely things left undone by the majority of humankind.

Then there was the whole gangster thing. After six years of very public theatrics, he'd more than achieved his goal of having the public reexamine its preconceptions on the subject. Or maybe he hadn't. It didn't matter. He, and many others, had had a good time. What had he learned? That he loved to serve. And that he loved to play. But now there was no longer the compulsion to be special, or to get revenge, or to challenge the beliefs of anybody, or to tweak anybody's schnozzola. If Spirit directed him to continue his broadcasts in any or all of their various forms, he'd be happy to do it. But his reasons would be completely different.

Inner guidance gave Puer no push to take on new endeavors, but he did hear the call to simplify. This set in motion the events that brought about the WOW Foundation, and his own retirement as New Age Gangster. Christie's auctioned his wardrobe. *Extravagant Humility* was sold. The world's most extensive collection of clown clothing was donated to a museum, as were his 108 vintage Cadillacs. The result raised a modestly ostentatious sum for the Tiny Menace Scholarship Fund, the only scholarship in the world serving students under three feet tall, which led it quickly to have more impact on early childhood education than any government program ever. All the rest of Puer's fortune—well, almost all of it—was bestowed upon his sister.

The final month of Puer's on-camera revelations in service of the common good were some of the most watched announcements in the history of television. Only if Elvis and Princess Diana had risen from the grave and announced their impending marriage might viewership have been greater, or more rapt. Puer exited public life—"at least until further notice from the Great Ones"—at the age of 32, the year after he met Hyman, and the year before he met Pearl.

*I*n the ten months from when Fox was elected to when Puer announced his retirement, Puer took a number of good-natured jabs at the President—sometimes going so far as to appear in his New Age Gangster communiques with a finger puppet named Slyly Fox. Puer had no idea that Slyly Fox was the name that Sylvie Marks had called Fox. All Puer knew was that Fox responded to Puer's puppet, and the potential secrets the puppet suggested he was hiding in his wooden head, with uncommon shrillness for a man supposedly so cool.

The fact was, Fox worked like a madman to be nonchalant, magnanimous, gracious, humorous . . . things that normally came rather easily to him. In response to Puer's lampoons, Fox had some of the smartest writers in the nation, led by his sister, pen responses that were actually pretty funny on paper. But since energy doesn't lie, regardless of the words, all that came out of Fox's mouth was the dry ice of anger.

The American public may not have realized that anger is merely fear dressed-up, but what they did grasp was that the Puer Puella they knew and the Puer that President Fox was talking about were two completely different people, and further, that they trusted their judgment about Puer more than Fox's. After all, they'd known Puer rather intimately for more than five years. Yes, he was eccentric—a little meshuga, perhaps. But he was a national treasure, whereas Fox was merely President. And Presidents, while respected, had long ceased being somebody extra special in American society. Fox, therefore, was considered a good guy, even a good President. But he was no Puer Puella.

21

Pearl Listens As God Performs at Gunpoint

"Mister O'Malley, thank you for seeing me on such short notice."

"A privilege, Mister President."

Uncle Charlie sits down at his desk.

"I'll be as quick and direct as possible," he said, sounding as though he were about to reminisce about the time he shut out Harvard. "You did something to me when we met this morning. And I would very much appreciate it if you would explain yourself. Explain what happened, in other words."

Silence.

The creak of a chair. Hyman sitting down.

"Pearl asked me pretty much the same question a short time ago. I'll tell you what I told her. It wasn't actually I who did anything to you, Mister President. Strange as it may appear, the universe seems to use me in a special way. In my presence, some people see things about themselves that can help them, if they choose."

"Help them?"

"People often gain a deeper understanding of what may be driving the choices they make. They might, as you did, revisit an event from this life. Or perhaps relive something from a previous life. Believe me, I have no powers. What people see, or experience, is not up to me. I'm just the mirror."

"Ah, the name on your truck."

Silence.

"What sort of, um, experiences did Pearl have with you today?"

"That's not for me to say, Mister President. Just as I would not reveal to anyone else what you experienced."

"Oh, you wouldn't?"

"No."

Silence.

"Do you know what I experienced this morning?"

"Yes I do . . . in that whatever you experienced, I experienced. In other words, I lived it just as you did, just as if I were you."

"So you know all about Sylvie?"

"I know what you experienced."

"Everything?"

"Everything."

Silence.

"May I ask you a favor?"

"Surely."

Silence.

"I want you to prove to me that this morning wasn't some trick, that you are who you say you are."

Hyman chuckles. "I don't say I'm anybody, really, Mister President. But I'm happy to do whatever I can. What do you have in mind?"

"I want you to give me some other experience, from another time in my life."

"Mister Fox, I have no special . . . ."

"Don't give me that."

Sound of drawer opening.

"Just so you know how sincere I am, Mister O'Malley, I am perfectly capable of shooting you—right here, right now—with this lovely little taser, a stun-gun, if you will. You familiar with these? Police sometimes use them in place of bullets, but the effect, believe me, is quite remarkable. Not unlike being electrocuted."

Hyman chuckles.

"How does that quote go, Mister President? The first person to raise his fist is the first to run out of ideas."

"A nice platitude, Mister O'Malley. But in real life, the amount of time one has circumscribes how many ideas one can entertain. And when it comes to threats to the presidency, time is at a premium. Hear me, Mister O'Malley. You will not be a threat to me, my family, or to this nation. You will please give me what I ask."

Hyman chuckles.

"Mister Fox, I know threats work in your world, but what you say means nothing to me. Think about it. Do you think you could threaten Sylvie Marks? I know you don't believe this, but I'm not negotiating with you. I would help you if I could. I would, and will, do anything in my power to serve you. But you see, what you want doesn't come from me. It is amusing, though, God performing at gunpoint. But I'm sure it's all the same to Him. Why don't we just sit quietly for a while and see what happens. I will just say one thing: you probably won't want to be disturbed . . . ."

Phone being picked up.

Silence.

"Vic. See that I'm not interrupted for the next thirty minutes."

Phone being hung up.

"You have half an hour."

"I have nothing, Mister Fox. Whatever experience you have drawn to yourself has nothing to do with me."

Silence.

Uncle Charlie moaning.

Silence.

Moaning.

"Papa!"

Moaning.

"My love . . . ."

"Why? . . . ."

Silence.

Silence.

Uncle Charlie blowing his nose.

Uncle Charlie breathing heavily through his mouth.

"Leave me."

"Awareness by itself . . . ."

"Leave!"

Hyman getting out of his chair, walking to door, door opening, then closing.

Silence.

Silence.

Uncle Charlie moaning, getting out of his chair, walking to the leather couch, dropping onto the couch. Moaning. Crying.

Silence.

Uncle Charlie rising from the couch, walking around the library. Going to the library's bathroom, washing his face.

Uncle Charlie breathing deeply, moaning, probably staring into the bathroom mirror.

Silence.

Uncle Charlie walking back to his chair at the desk, sitting down.

Silence.

Silence.

Silence.

Silence.

Phone being picked up.

Uncle Charlie clearing his throat. "Vic, ask Shorty to come in here."

Hanging up phone.

Uncle Charlie clearing his throat.

Silence.

Door opens, closes.

Silence.

"Charlie?"

Silence.

Shorty walking, sitting down.

Silence.

"Charlie? Love?"

"We have to act."

Silence.

"Charlie. Why?"

*F*ox would later liken his sudden shift in consciousness in O'Malley's presence to the changing of a TV channel delivered with the surprise of a snakebite. It wasn't so much the speed of the shift—Click, you're someone else—as it was its immensity. One instant you're a young stud driving a stock car at Darlington, the next you're a mother in a primitive Amazon tribe and you've just placed one of your newborn twins on the riverbank for crocodiles because you know that it is evil for anyone to have a double. One instant you're a member of *The Simpsons*, the next you're a German officer in *Schindler's List*. But screw the analogies. The reality was, one instant you're sitting behind the oak desk in the library fingering the taser, not quite listening to O'Malley, the next you are three men: all giants, dressed in white, one standing behind another on the back of an equally gigantic white horse with white wings, a horse that could, if called upon, fly to any spot on the globe.

It was the same sort of hallucination that Fox had had just that morning when he shook O'Malley's hand. And the same that he had had twenty years earlier with Sylvie aflame on the Proteus—which is to say, his every sense told him that this was no hallucination at all.

The horse and riders traveled at the invitation of leaders in conflict the world over. The riders brought understanding, support, wisdom, experience, imagination and hope to some of the most contentious relationships facing humankind. Their mediation often led antagonists to, at the very least, take their fingers off their triggers for a moment, and at most, to explore, if only briefly, what they have in common with their enemy.

The riders were Thomas Jefferson, Vince Lombardi and, believe it or not, Fred Rogers, the host for many years of a national television program for young children. Yet, of course, the three men were, collectively, really one man—well, not really a man, but a mask of a man—a mask of Charlie Fox. His was a large, elaborate mask, as masks often are, since they must be bigger than the fears they attempt to cover.

Jefferson. Lombardi. Rogers.

Breadth. Depth. Grace.

Vision. Passion. Friendship.

Eloquence. Candor. Acceptance.

Jefferson was the smartest, boldest American Fox had ever known of. The Declaration of Independence, of which Jefferson was a significant author, was nothing short of divinely inspired. It was the single most important statement of national common purpose that men of good will had agreed to . . . maybe ever, but certainly in the past three hundred years––despite the fact that it was a lie since it represented the interests solely of those whose skin was white. Plus, Jefferson was a scholar, musician, architect, mastermind of the Louisiana Purchase, and the man responsible for the Lewis and Clark expedition by which America began to grasp the barely fathomable riches that existed from sea to shining sea. Fox was always ready to regale visiting dignitaries with John Kennedy's famous remark about America's third President. Welcoming to the White House a group of Nobel Prize-winners, Kennedy said they were the most distinguished gathering of intellects to ever have dined at the Executive Mansion—*"with the possible exception of when Mr. Jefferson dined here alone."*

Lombardi, the football coach, gave his teams a sense of purpose that his players would follow, through any amount of personal pain. Fox revered the Lombardi mantra, "Winning isn't everything; it's the only thing." To manage such absolutism, overcoming its inevitable challenges to integrity––corners cut, rules broken, truth conditional––took a will both powerful and flexible. He, Charlie Fox, had become President, he was sure, by having such a will, a will that anchored his mission to be a broker of peace among the world's combatants.

And Mister Rogers, a hero Fox had met as a young man by enjoyable coincidence when the two were stuck overnight in a North Dakota blizzard, was the only person other than Sylvie that Fox actually believed when Fred said that he liked people just as they were. Fox aspired to have the world think that he, too, embodied this sentiment.

This mask, The Great Mediator, helped Fox to position himself as one of the more persuasive peacemakers to occupy the Oval Office in years. And therefore, the mask served its other purpose, its primary purpose: to protect Charlie Fox from the need to take too many risks. The mask of *The Great Mediator* allowed Fox to stake out the higher ground from which his fear of vulnerability would be as safe as it could be in a political world.

The theme of the Fox administration was the importance of finding increasing areas of agreement among the world's polyphony of interests. America's world leadership could no longer be defined solely by its military power, its economic vitality, and its enlightened constitution. The simple notion that capitalism and democracy cure all ills was as incomplete as the belief that an adequate bank account and good physical health made a happy person and a harmonious family. Even the most reactionary voices acknowledged that the idea of a world of separate nations with separate interests that were no one else's business, was an anachronism. Charlie Fox argued that the future of the world would be indelibly influenced by how well the United States honored and utilized the strengths inherent in the differences among all her various citizens. Borrowing a term from science, Fox called the U.S. "the beta site for the world's future. No other country contains so much diversity, and the challenge for America is to capitalize on that diversity. The United States must be the leader in helping its own people—and, by its example, all people—to live together more constructively," Fox said.

And now, here he was, staring at O'Malley, feeling the reality of *The Great Mediator*. It had been so well designed. Nearly flawless. His ego was stroked for its service to such a noble ideal. Some people actually used the term courageous about his unwillingness to pander to those who would destroy or ostracize others with differing views. "The initials C.G.F.," a friendly columnist wrote, "stand for more than Charles Greenstreet Fox. In the light of recent events, they also stand for 'Common Ground Fox.'"

And yet . . . it was the child of fear, the belief that the world is a dangerous place and that betrayal is the essential lesson of life. It wasn't that the universe was malicious; it was simply that the universe didn't care: *Smoke or be smoked* was as operative as *Do unto others . . . . Whimsical* was the pretty way to put it; *capricious* the more realistic. Did Fox believe anything more deeply than that? No. And in this moment, denial was impossible. The truth was in his flesh. It wasn't arguable, questionable, deflectable. What drove him, as much as anything else—no, more than anything else—was not bringing the world together; what drove him was making himself invulnerable—safe. Every choice he had ever made served that master, from being an Eagle Scout to his love for Shorty.

And when, seconds after O'Malley spoke and this realization hit, from Fox's mouth came a sound that caused Pearl, listening above, to convulse on the floor in silent heartbreak, her hands on her chest, her teeth bared in agony, yet breath and tears and inner fire carrying her feelings into the earth, so intimately familiar was she with the energy that was consuming Uncle Charlie in that moment: the energy of pain and fear lifetimes old—the pain of life lost, and the fear of feeling it.

And then, seconds later, Pearl heard from her uncle another sound all its own, a sound infused with desolation and grief as he relived an experience from another life—an experience that, because he refused to free it from his being, had fed his choice to hide: his choice to continually build and refine his mask.

Naturally, Pearl couldn't know what former self her uncle met. Or what experiences he relived. She, therefore, had no idea that Uncle Charlie met himself, not just in one previous incarnation, but in two. The first being his most recent life, as a young girl during the second World War. The second, a life five centuries earlier—as Angelo Angelino dying, poisoned by his one true love.

*H*is name had been Claira Lewandowsky.

Eighty years before Claira's birth, the Lewandowsky name had been praised to the rooftops in the person of the renown pianist, the late Leopold Lewandowsky. It was no small source of anguish that, since the glory days of the man everyone in the family called Uncle Leo and the world called The Great Lewandowsky, there had not been born to the Lewandowsky clan a single respectable musician. Each Lewandowsky, male and female, but especially the men with sons, prayed that one of theirs would carry the Uncle Leo spark that would allow the family to once again hold its collective head high in justifiable pride, having proved that God shined upon the Lewandowskys as a family, not merely, as some ignorant people claimed, one member as a fluke.

Boycik Lewandowsky, Claira's papa, was a jeweler according to the sign on his shop's door, though those who turned the door's handle and entered, tripping a small gold bell to make the sound that causes sleeping babies to smile, quickly learned, if they didn't know beforehand, the sign's message was incomplete. An inspired goldsmith with an eye for rare gems and a gift for cutting them, Boycik fashioned exquisite, one-of-a-kind rings. While wealthy clientele were the primary source of his safe's substantial reservoir of cash, Boycik's favorite customers were those he secretly charged a relative pittance so that they might experience the satisfaction of having saved for years in order to purchase a once-in-a-lifetime treasure. But it was Claira's mama, Cora, who wore the piece that Boycik told everyone was the most beautiful he would ever make: her wedding ring. One of Claira's earliest memories was of her mother telling her that someday it would be Claira's wedding ring, as well.

Claira was barely two when her father, sorting gems at the kitchen table and whistling to himself one Sunday afternoon, suddenly realized that Claira was copying on the family piano, with two fingers, the tune he was singing—the last movement of Beethoven's Ninth Symphony. Claira had had no musical training, but from that day forward, she received the best instruction available.

Her parents, but more importantly her tutor, Miss N.V. Snopek, considered Claira a prodigy. Fortunately, Miss Snopek, who specialized in tutoring prodigies up to the age of six, knew precisely how Claira's training should proceed.

"I provide the foundation without which musical genius will never properly flourish," she stated without pretension. The number of previous

charges currently performing in the world's concert halls provided Miss
Snopek all the credibility she needed. Claira's parents, Miss Snopek declared,
must not push Claira to practice more than Miss Snopek required. If Claira
wished to play more on her own, that was fine, but the choice should be
hers. Claira was, after all, first and foremost a child—not an artist—and, in
Miss Snopek's opinion, Claira would never be obliged to serve her family
as the reincarnation of the Great Lewandowsky, unless she wanted to. If
these simple ground rules were agreeable, Miss Snopek said, then she would
consent to assume Claira's training.

Boycik and Cora were actually relieved by Miss Snopek's approach.
As this unbelievable new world opened before them all, Boycik and Cora
thanked God that to be blessed with a prodigy did not require them to lose
the little girl who loved to pound pots and pans with two or three wooden
spoons in each hand.

Claira didn't love the piano more than she loved other forms of play,
but she certainly did enjoy her sessions with Miss Snopek, and was happy to
do all that was asked of her. Her only concern was her mama and papa. More
and more, they were sad and afraid. She saw it in their eyes, and she saw that
they tried to hide it from her. And whether this fear was related to her and
the special place she had in their lives—how much they loved and coddled
her; even more now that Miss Snopek was there—she didn't know. But she
didn't think so. It wasn't just her mama and papa who were afraid. It was every
grownup Claira knew: relatives, neighbors, everyone.

Claira felt the fear around her more acutely than another child
might have. For no doubt many incarnations, the being who was Claira
Lewandowsky had been nurturing a large and limiting belief—that life was
basically untrustworthy. One could never be too careful.

Given this disposition, Claira had chosen her birth family quite
exquisitely. To be "the gift" of an older, supposedly infertile, couple who had
desperately wanted a child gave Claira the sanctuary of being cherished. To

then be the possible resurrection of the family musical legacy after nearly a century only re-doubled the cushion of Claira's life. By age five, Claira had perhaps more worldly security than even her father, the respected artisan.

But of course, our choice of family is determined not entirely by our fears. It is also determined by our soul's desire to free us of all fear—and by a universe whose sole function it is to help us meet and overcome any barriers to love. This is why, often, we draw to us those experiences we fear the most—to give ourselves the opportunity to choose freedom.

The choice of freedom, however, by its very nature, means we may choose instead to hold to fear even more tightly.

It happened quickly yet with overwhelming agony for five year-old Claira. Claira and her mama and papa lived on floor three of their apartment building, so the pounding of fists on doors, the harsh shouting of demands, the shrill of police whistles, people running up and down stairs, and the cries of bewildered and terrified neighbors at five in the morning were heard long before they actually reached the Lewandowsky suite. When the order to open did come, and her father unlatched the door, four soldiers pushed into the living room. Her father was forced to back up to make room for them. Her mother was in the kitchen, as she always was at this time of day, preparing breakfast. Claira, awakened by the commotion and entering the room just as the soldiers did, stood in her nightgown next to her father. Her father put his large hand around her small shoulder and drew her behind him. Claira watched the soldiers from around her father's leg. Her father, speaking in the usual gentle way he greeted customers or anyone else, asked the soldier in charge how he might serve him. The soldier in charge drew his pistol and pointed it at her father. The soldier said something. The soldier then shot her father. Her father flew backwards, knocking Claira down. Claira's nightgown and face were sprayed with her father's blood. Claira crawled out from under her father's leg. She turned and saw that her father's face looked surprised, yet frozen. There was a small hole in his forehead. He made no sound. Her mother ran into the room. Her mother was holding a paring knife. She always sliced oranges for breakfast. The soldier in charge pointed his pistol at Claira's mother and then shot her in the chest. Blood flew out the back of her mother and sprayed the wall. Her mother flew backwards like her father had. None of her blood landed on Claira. Her mother did not move, or make a sound. Her mother, too, looked surprised. Her eyes were open; they did not blink.

All Claira could do was scream. Her screams were screams of incomprehension and fear, the screams of something terrible happening to her mama and papa, the screams that no one was there to protect her. Under these screams were others, screams of rage directed at God for betraying her once again. Could this have been what her parents were so afraid of? One of the soldiers lifted her up and began to carry her toward the door. Claira bit him so severely on the neck that she tasted his blood. The soldier jerked and yelled and threw her down. She landed on the floor, on her back, so hard that she couldn't breathe. She could no longer scream. She fought for air. She looked up. The soldier in charge, the one who had shot her parents, was looking down at her. He pointed his pistol at her. Blessedly, Claira started to breathe again. She looked at the gun's hole, then at the soldier. She closed her eyes. Someone then held her two arms very tightly, and a foul smelling cloth was pressed against her face.

Upon awaking, she was immediately confused, extraordinarily so. Her heart's anguish reverberated through her as though she were living inside a giant French horn that had just sounded the call for the end of the world. Yet, her other senses, as they adjusted to the subdued light, told another story.

Her eyes saw the beauty of a room that she had known before only from her own imagination as her mama read to her stories about a princess who lived in a beautiful castle so tall that when the princess looked out the window of her bedroom she saw the tops of the clouds below her. Claira was lying in a large, soft bed more comfortable than anything she had ever known besides her mama's lap. The room itself was so large that the wall to her left was about as far away as Mister Domagalski's grocery store 20 steps across the street from their apartment. On the wall was a really, really large painting of three dancing bears. She could see it because a light hung over the painting's thick gold frame. In the other direction, down past her feet, way beyond the foot of the bed, were the tallest windows she had ever seen. The tallest drapes she had ever seen stood on either side of each window—four windows in all—and hanging across the front of each window was a white curtain. The four curtains were billowing slowly in the breeze. They made the light enter the room as a mist. To the left of the windows, down the wall a ways, was what could only be a large mirror. It was larger than the entire living room wall of her home. Much larger. Since the room at that point was somewhat dark, she determined that it must be a mirror because reflected in it was a painting very similar to the dancing bears except that this painting was of a bear and a clown hugging. The painting must be on a wall she couldn't see, Claira thought. Looking down over her feet again, in front of the windows, she saw a large round table. On the table was the biggest vase of flowers maybe in the world. Claira was wearing a nightgown that was not her own. It smelled new, which ordinarily would make her happy but now made her sad because it reminded her of her mama and papa and the soldier who had hurt them. Unless, unless it had been a dream, and that she was still dreaming. She heard no sounds except for birds, which she almost never heard at her home. Now she also heard the sound of a river or a waterfall, which she absolutely never heard at home. She lived in a city. The air here at the castle smelled completely different. Not bad. Just different. There was no smoke in it. That was one difference. Also unusual was the perfume of flowers. She turned her head to take in more of the room and was surprised to see many large bouquets, not all of them as big as the one on the round table before the windows, but all quite beyond belief. She had been to the flower man's shop with her mama, and this was the same smell. She was suddenly happy. This must be heaven. Her mama and papa must be in their own room. It must be even more beautiful than this. She must find them. She lifted her head off the pillow and pain struck her in a manner that brought to her mind the cracking sound she once heard when she had purposely stepped on a shiny black beetle. This must be how the beetle felt. She dropped back onto the pillow. She dove as quickly and deeply as she could under the pain to the land of no pain, the land of sleep.

When she awoke the room had changed. The flowers on the large round table were still there, but there was no light coming in from the windows behind them. Instead, surrounding the bouquet was a circle of tall white candles. They were burning. Later she would learn that there were twelve candles in number, and that they would be lit around the bouquet each evening, welcoming her to this, her bedroom, from now on.

So this is heaven at night, Claira thought.

Suddenly she heard a creak from the end of the room where the three bears had danced on the wall. With the exception of a few candles here and there, the room in that direction was now rather dark. Then she heard the swishing sound that women who wear stockings make when they walk in a quiet room. For brief moments, as the swishing sound drew closer, it was replaced by the tick-click of shoes on a wooden floor. Claira remembered from when she first awoke that huge carpets covered the wooden floor. The tick-click was the space between the carpets. It didn't take long for Claira to recognize the limping gait of Miss Snopek.

"Miss Snopek," Claira cried out even while Miss Snopek's body, coming toward her, was still invisible in the darkness. Miss Snopek, limping a little quicker, spoke as she always had, in a tone that left no doubt that Miss Snopek knew what to do, even when horrible things happened. This must not be heaven, Claira thought, because if it were heaven I would be seeing mama and papa. But this must be close to heaven because Miss Snopek is here.

"My child, you are saved," Miss Snopek said from the shadows. And then, when she finally reached Claira's bed, Miss Snopek bent down and put her soft wrinkled hand on Claira's cheek and said again, "You are saved."

Claira cried herself to sleep in Miss Snopek's arms.

When she awoke it was still night. Only a few candles were lit. Miss Snopek sat in a chair next to Claira's bed. "I have to pee," Claira said. Miss Snopek helped Claira to the bathroom through a door just a few steps from the bed. The bathtub had gold feet. The floor was cool to the touch. It was made of marble, same as the steps of Claira's church. As Claira sat on the toilet, her feet snuggled into a small thick white carpet in front of her.

When Claira returned to bed, there was hot chocolate, a jam sandwich and a piece of cake on her night table. Claira ate. Miss Snopek sat with her. Neither spoke until Claira had finished. Then, Miss Snopek lay on the bed with Claira, took her in her arms, and explained. "Your mama and papa are no longer alive, my precious child. But thanks be to God, I was able to save you. Many terrible things are going on in the world. Many good people like your mama and papa are dying. You and I will cry for them and talk to their souls many times. But I have seen to it that you will never be in danger again."

This is what Claira came to know: her parents had been murdered by soldiers who had invaded the Homeland. She, Claira, had been discovered, by Miss Snopek, unconscious next to the bodies of her mama and papa. Miss Snopek had known of a special school for musical prodigies and immediately arranged for Claira to be taken there—here—to live until she was an adult.

The school was actually an orphanage for child prodigies whose parents had been killed in the war, though to call it an orphanage would be like calling Buckingham Palace a home. It was a castle, made as modern and comfortable as technology and a vast fortune would allow to accommodate the needs of some fifty prodigies from the ages of three to eighteen, as well as their tutors, nannies, nurses, and every manner of servant. The purpose was simple: children enjoying the fullest possible life and the fullest indulgence of their genius. Its name: *The School of Angels*.

The horrible circumstances which led a child to *The School of Angels* were not avoided as part of a child's development. The philosophy guiding the institute was that a heart could be either destroyed or strengthened by adversity—and a heart destroyed, for whatever reasons, cannot express its genius. So it was readily acknowledged that Claira's life included the pain of her parent's death—to be sure, of watching her parents' murders. It was also acknowledged that out of that pain Claira was led by God to this new home where she could be loved and appreciated and nurtured as a person, a girl, soon to be a young woman, and as a holder of extraordinary musical gifts.

Miss Snopek remained at the school long enough to make Claira's introduction a comfortable one. When she left, Miss Snopek promised to return from time to time to visit—and to write frequently, both of which she did. Usually, not always, but usually, her visits coincided with the arrival of a new prodigy under her loving wing.

Claira loved the school. Indeed, the worst part of it—the only bad thing, really—was the guilt she felt for loving it so much. As years passed, this guilt was replaced by another, more painful, guilt, one she didn't dare admit to herself: that part of her was glad that, since her parents had to die, they died in such a way that she was given this blessing.

At the age of seventeen, Claira Lewandowsky was being introduced to the world as a pianist of uncommon ability, uncommon even for a prodigy from *The School of Angels*. Not only was she admired for her dexterity and sensitivity in handling the classical repertoire, but Claira was also a surprisingly talented jazz performer. Today, it is a rare musician who can perform from inside the soul of both Mozart and Monk, Bach and Brubeck, Paderewski and Charlie Parker. In Claira's day, it was unheard of. Jazz was in its infancy. Even many years after Claira's inaugural, jazz would be considered primitive, uncivilized, and inferior by many classical critics. At the time, it was beyond imagination that a pianist would debut performing works by Mozart and a relatively unknown Negro from New Orleans, Louisiana, named Louis Armstrong. And in Carnegie Hall, at that.

For the being that was Claira Lewandowsky, the motivation was complex: a love of the music, the pure love of playing—both something highly structured and, by comparison, something almost entirely without structure, something spontaneous from the soul. And then there was the compulsion for security that had been part of her existence for many incarnations. The more outstanding and capable she could be, the broader the range of her talents, the more safety she could weave around herself.

On the afternoon before the morning she was to sail for New York, Claira was invited for tea by the Baron, the school's founder and benefactor. It was a tradition to have tea with the Baron each year on a day as close as possible to one's birthday, as well as on other special occasions such as this, one's professional debut.

They met in the library, so called in name only since there wasn't a book in it. It was a greenhouse modeled after the Crystal Palace, the elaborate architectural centerpiece of the 1851 World Exhibition held outside London. This particular replica was designed to accommodate every sort of plant from the wild strawberry one needed a magnifying glass to spy in the woods of England to a giant palm from America's California. The library was located through a set of French doors off a room in the castle used exclusively for performances of chamber music. This way, the Baron could be serenaded by prodigies while he tended to his affairs. At the very center of the greenhouse was a large ivory desk that, were it a bed, could have easily slept a dozen. Its drawers alone could have held enough gold to purchase several small countries outright. This, the library, was the Baron's office.

Claira and the Baron sat in front of his desk in identical Queen Anne's chairs of white brocade. To the side, a round jade table that would have easily accommodated a New Year's dinner for a family of eight, was covered from edge to edge with tea cakes and crustless little sandwiches, carrot sticks, artichoke hearts, petit fours, marzipan, nougats, vinegar taffy, stuffed dates, ginger covered nuts, tarts of every description, fresh mangoes, strawberries and blueberries, hot chocolate for dipping, hot chocolate for sipping, fizzily cold drinks with Far Eastern syrups, and teas from everywhere tea comes from.

In Claira's honor, the Baron had ordered a candied apple, symbolizing what helpless New York would be like in the hands of the Great Lewandowsky.

Having tea with the Baron was like sitting down at the kitchen table with Santa Claus. Like Santa, the Baron had traveled the world—he would be in the audience at Carnegie Hall—and could, for hours, tell stories that had a way of stealing your breath with anticipation. But what was most remarkable about the Baron was his curiosity. Simply, he listened. It was not possible to come away from tea with the Baron and not feel that your opinions and feelings were sought, accepted and valued.

So Claira was, as always, quite happy to meet with the Baron and didn't mind a bit when shortly after they greeted one another, the Baron was temporarily called away on an unexpected matter. Claira was content strolling the greenhouse. Nor was Claira the least bit disturbed when, Wilfred, the Baron's personal secretary, who had originally interrupted their tea, returned to say that the Baron conveyed his deepest apologies but that he would be delayed another half-hour. If Claira wished to wait, the Baron would be most eager to join her then, but if waiting would in any way pose an inconvenience for Claira and she wished to reschedule, the Baron would gladly do so, if that was Claira's pleasure. And indeed, again, he was most regretful of the interruption. Claira said that she would be happy to wait and enjoy the greenhouse. The Baron should not be concerned on her account.

Alone, Claira started to examine from a discrete distance the items on the Baron's ivory desk. Actually, given its size, the desktop was almost entirely empty. Yes, there were probably more than one hundred framed photos of prodigies. Claira found one of herself. There was a round green blotter in front of the Baron's red leather chair. On the blotter rested a small stack of monarch stationery bearing the Baron's family crest, which Claira knew by heart: a bowl holding the sun held by two hands with wings. Next to the stationery was a gold fountain pen. The only other item, and it was placed on the desk next to the blotter within easy reach for the Baron sitting in his chair, was a blue leather case, a file folder only much more elegant. Claira had never seen one quite like it, so she stood and moved closer to examine its workmanship, which is how she came to notice her name embossed in gold foil on the folder's cover.

The temptation was too great.

Not surprisingly, her entire life at the *The School of Angels* was documented. There were evaluations by her tutors, all of which she had already been made aware. There were few secrets at *The School of Angels*. There was a photo album which documented her entire time at the school, beginning with a photo that was taken before she arrived, since it was of Claira and her mama and papa having a picnic in the park near their home. She had never seen the photo before. The coat she was wearing in the photo was one her mama had bought for her the same day as the picnic, about a week before her parents died. The first photo of her at *The School of Angels* was another she had never seen: of her being carried from an ambulance by stretcher bearers. She, unconscious; Miss Snopek standing next to the ambulance, Claira's coat over Miss Snopek's arm. Many of the other photos were ones she had never seen before either. Most of them were candid shots of her doing everyday things. Nothing special. But it was odd. The photos spanned ten years and yet she couldn't remember a photographer ever pointing a camera in her direction at the time any of these shots were taken. Not that it mattered. The shots were pretty ordinary. Still, someone had been taking snapshots of her over a long period of time without her knowing it. Trying not to intrude, no doubt.

Then came the last folder in the case. It was the thinnest. It contained a small envelope and a single sheet of paper, a letter. She read the letter, and found herself unable to remain standing. It took all her concentration to make it two steps to the Queen Anne's chair. The letter was from Miss Snopek to the Baron, dated possibly the very same day as that last picnic in the park.

In the small envelope was her mother's wedding ring.

Claira held her mother's ring up to her eye, and from one blink to the next the ring became the face of Angelo Angelino's beloved Bella-Viola, staring down at him, tears running off her cheek onto his chest.

"Why are you hiding from me?" he had asked her. Her mouth, her tears, her eyes held no answer.

He wondered, in the moment of life remaining to him, whether he had misjudged his heart. He loved her as the earth loves the sun. And she was ending his life—the life he had placed in her hands more willingly and happily every day since their wedding. Poison. He could feel it numbing him. This was no accident. Yet she loved him as he loved her. She was not trying to destroy him. He knew that much. If anything, she was destroying herself. She was trying to save him . . . from something. Whatever it was, it was so terrible that she could not bring herself to tell him. And this silence betrayed everything he, Angelo Angelino, held sacred. What could be so overpowering that it would outweigh the commitment of their hearts not to hide from one another? What could be so compelling that she would choose to face this adversary alone, not together as one? Some fear had its hands around her throat, its thumbs crushing her life. Why was their vow subordinate to this fear? If she felt it was necessary to kill him, so be it. But to hide from him?

Was this the raw, ugly truth? Was unconditional love a lie? Sooner or later, does every person reach a moment in which he or she betrays the deepest vow a heart can make: loyalty? If Bella-Viola would hide from him, would not anyone hide from anyone? Was the universe, in its moment of truth, untrustable?

*A*fter Charlie Fox met himself in his incarnations as Claira Lewandowsky and Angelo Angelino, this is the conversation he and Hyman O'Malley might have had:

"What am I to do with these experiences?"

"You are a man who longs to love, Mister Fox. Just consider your ability as a mediator. It alone shows how much you wish to bring harmony to your life and to others.

"You are also a man who is terrified of being betrayed, of losing what you love. This makes you addicted to control"

"Addicted?"

"Let me not mince words, Mister Fox. Addiction is the attempt to escape pain. And as such it can be a form of insanity. In your case, it's the insanity of being willing to do anything—anything—to keep from losing control. Today, you have been shown a mask you wear to protect yourself from what you fear.

"You have also been shown two lives—as Claira and as Angelo—that remind you why you are so afraid of betrayal . . . why you believe the world is dangerous more than it is anything else. These lives were merely two dramatic examples. There have been many others. Time and again, you have drawn to yourself situations

that reinforce your belief that life will hurt you if given half a chance. But that is not really what these lives are designed to teach you. You have neglected their more important lessons. They also show you the way out of your fear. And that is, forgiving yourself for any times when you, like Miss Snopek, or the officer who shot your parents, or the Baron, or Bella-Viola, betrayed another. Your fear of betrayal will pass only when you can forgive yourself for being the betrayer that you have been. Today, you have been blessed with meeting yourself as a betrayer in this very incarnation—on the ship to England. I'm sure there have been other times. After all, you're just a human being. If you do not learn to forgive yourself for the times when you have been a betrayer, you will continue to be miserable, more and more each day. It's mathematics. It's how the universe operates."

At that Fox asked, "How does one forgive oneself? I mean, how do you actually do it? It seems like I can't just say 'Abracadabra, I forgive myself.' There must be more to it than that."

"There is," Hyman replied. "But actually the practice is surprisingly direct. Take your designs and actions on the ship, for instance. It is feeling the pain and fear that drove those decisions, and freeing them. Now, that can be very hard for some people. Maybe you. People who are unfamiliar with feeling very much must learn to feel. It means giving up the belief that fear or pain is a thought. It isn't. It is energy you hold within. Perhaps the first thing you'll feel is your fear of feeling fear. That's good. The point is, whatever you are feeling, you feel it and let it go, let it ride your breath into the earth. You just continually go deeper and deeper—feeling and letting go of new levels of fear, pain and unforgiveness."

"That it? That's the process?"

"I call it a practice. And that's half of it. The other half is nurturing yourself, drawing into your body the unconditional love of Spirit. Together—letting go and filling with love—that's the practice of being human."

"Will you help me . . . so I can get the hang of it?"

"My pleasure."

But of course that wasn't the conversation that occurred.

22

Uncle Charlie's Plan
For Getting Rid of O'Malley

Lying on the floor on her stomach, her tear-wet hands a pillow under her chin, Pearl stared minute after minute at a dot of carpet no bigger than a quarter, for it was the universe. Nothing beyond the dark green wool fibers existed. Her body had no more feeling than a lip full of novocaine. What she had overheard was a fantasy. If not for the persistent tingle of her heart, calling her to join her breath, she might have remained immobilized much longer. As it was, in a few minutes she was pissed, slamming her fist into the rug until a small burn on the knuckle of her little finger reminded her that it was her pitching hand. Continuing to breathe—connecting, releasing, filling—she observed her mind attempting to gain control, to understand, to find meaning. Clearing those fears she fell into rationalization: the plan she had overheard her mother and uncle discussing wasn't so dangerous; no, it really wasn't such a big deal. Her breath swept and swept, freeing more fear, taking her deeper, which is when she got to what she had been secretly dreading. In her soundproof closet, the opening in the floor re-covered, Pearl screamed, feeling what a day earlier would have been unfathomable.

It was unworthy to compare her loss to that of a girl her age in a peaceful hamlet suddenly invaded by death squads, but the energy of it passed through Pearl's heart as she felt the betrayal of her every bond with her mother and her uncle. A loss so much more absolute than what she had felt earlier in the day at Carmella's. Now she felt the spastic, cold alabaster fear of her mother and Uncle Charlie, and the mindless destruction being set in motion because of it. Hyman could die, and two of the people she loved most in the world, one of them her own mother, were planning to commit, not just a felony, but the premeditated ruin of another human being, and someone she loved—and that also meant that her mother and uncle were going to lie to her, to her father, to everyone around them, not to mention lie to the entire world. Pearl felt something she had felt that morning as Bella-Viola: *The possibility that a person could die from too much truth*—and she felt herself on the ride home in Hyman's truck: *"Honey, wherever you be let it flow free."*

The blessing she had received that day, even more than meeting her True Self, or maybe it was the result of meeting her True Self, was the awareness that she could make room for anything. Almost unbelievably, she knew she could make room for having her life obliterated; she could join with the earth; she could surrender every wisp of herself to the One; not from wanting it, but from the conscious willingness to act. She washed her heart with breath after breath, freeing again and again, more and more.

She sat up, her coccyx against the closet wall, her feet drawn up, her arms folded over her knees, her head resting on her arms, her tears drying on her black T-shirt; she played with the new reality—How big was it? What would it mean?—before letting even that go and, at least in that moment, accepting, completely, the new, whatever it might be, as is.

Nothing really changed. There was just as much fear as before, just as much loss. In some ways her life was growing only more out of control. But she was bigger. That was it. As long as she kept breathing, joining, feeling, freeing. Bigger. It was a little like taking a closet packed with memorabilia—

memories!—and moving it all into a football stadium. Same memories, more space. A lot easier to manage.

She felt a certain peace, as she had that morning with her body big as the countryside.

Nothing could be more vulnerable than consciously giving everything to Spirit. But nothing was more empowering, either. The past didn't matter. No blame. And the future wasn't something to be managed. There was just now. Bringing all the love she could to here.

And in this present, she felt the call of her heart. Wash your face, it said. Find your uncle, it said. Open your heart to him, it said.

What she would say, or where it would lead, she didn't even wonder.

*C*armella's lavender limo was a quarter of a mile from Pearl's home when Pearl appeared by the road and stuck out her thumb. She was wearing a cream and beige print caftan over dark purple trousers, her hair swept into a chignon. Carmella's driver, Sushiva, who had met Pearl at the *Island of Peace* that morning, braked and called over her shoulder, "Carmella, it appears we have a hitch-hiker."

Carmella, sitting next to Hyman in the limo's rear seat, craned her neck to look ahead through the windshield. "My lord," she said, as if to herself. "I love her so."

Carmella opened the rear door and Pearl got in.

By way of greeting, Pearl said, "Can we go for a little ride?"

"Sushiva," Carmella called. "We're going to postpone our arrival a few minutes. Let's take a drive down by the lake."

As they started up, Pearl immediately knelt in front of Carmella, took Carmella's hand, opened the palm, and kissed it with the tip of her tongue. Then

Pearl removed the string of pearls she was wearing, a gift from Uncle Charlie for Pearl's 16th birthday, and placed the necklace across Carmella's open palm.

"Carmella Puella, this necklace represents my heart," Pearl said, "which I give to you freely and completely, today, and every day, for all our lives to come."

Carmella put her palms together, the necklace dangling through her fingers, and bowed to Pearl.

Pearl then sat across from her two friends, as Carmella immediately put on Pearl's pearls. Against the black leather upholstery Carmella glowed in shades of blue silk. Hyman looked pretty snappy himself: violet T-shirt, fresh pressed khakis, blue blazer, and what Pearl could only imagine were his "Sunday-go-to-meetin'" hiking boots.

"And the message of the evening, my non-guru?" Pearl asked Hyman.

Impersonating Superman, Hyman pulled back the blazer's lapels and stuck out his chest so that Pearl might read the tiny print: *Many demolitions are actually renovations.*

The joy of their three hearts being together was so great that they all just smiled at one another. They each knew something was up, that Uncle Charlie's fear was triggering fireworks of one sort or another, if not that very evening, then soon. But the three friends also enjoyed something rare among members of the human family at that time in history: a certain detachment from the ego's interpretation of events—loosely analogous to what a compassionate parent feels in the face of their four-year-old's trauma at the loss of a toy. Just what *was* worthy of someone's anxiety? The ego of most people could give you an inventory akin to the guest list at a polygamist's family reunion. The three passengers in the lavender limo couldn't have come up with a thing.

"I overheard your time with my uncle," Pearl said to Hyman. "I also overheard his conversation with my mother after you left."

Hyman cocked his head and raised his eyebrows.

"Well, well," he said.

"My bedroom is above the library. Everybody thinks the library is soundproof, but I've rigged up a way to hear what goes on there. I'm a snoop. Of course, I don't really know what happened to Uncle Charlie. Well, I mean I heard your conversation. But as far as what he experienced, I only felt it . . . ."

"Then I'm sure you know plenty," Hyman said.

"After you left," Pearl said, "Uncle Charlie told my mother they had to get you out of the picture. I gathered that they had had a conversation earlier when he told her that this morning, when you and he met, you had threatened him, saying that if he didn't take himself out of the running for re-election by Christmas, Puer would go public and prove that Uncle Charlie had something to do with that girl Sylvie's death twenty years ago. After he told you to leave the library, he called mom in and said you had threatened him again—saying Puer was willing to pay whatever it took to remove Uncle Charlie . . . "

"What do you feel is going on?" Hyman asked.

Pearl's reflex wave of the hand said it was obvious. "Fear," she said. "Whatever part of himself he met because of you has scared him. You're a threat. You know something, some secret. I've never seen him like this. And after I spoke to him, he got worse."

"You spoke to him, love?" Carmella said softly.

Pearl's laugh was empty. "Yeah. I told him the whole story about Bella-Viola."

Hyman puckered his lips but didn't whistle.

"At the end . . .

"Well, I talked about walking around for lifetimes with unforgiveness for killing Angelo. And at the end, I mean, you know, Uncle Charlie's always together, on the outside, but I could tell he felt something like he did this morning after shaking your hand. A little intense . . . for me, I mean."

Pearl gave a soft laugh at a memory.

"About year ago I spilled a glass of milk all over him about a minute before he was to meet with the Prime Minister of Israel," she said. "His only concern was that I shouldn't think a thing of it. And believe me, Charlie Fox likes things just-so. What I'm saying is how much he loves me. Today was the first time in my life I'd ever seen him look at me like there was something he didn't love, or if not that exactly, something he was almost . . . I don't know . . . repulsed by."

Pearl allowed her eyes to drift out the window at the soft glitter of sunset on the waves, but without really seeing anything. They rode in silence for several minutes.

"I need to ask something," Pearl finally said, her gaze not moving from the water.

"I know," Hyman said.

"My uncle is Angelo, isn't he?"

"Lord in heaven," Carmella whispered.

"Yes," Hyman said.

"And today he learned that, as Angelo, he was poisoned by his wife, his beloved, Bella-Viola—me, it turns out—who, in this life, he loves like I was his own daughter?"

Hyman slowly nodded affirmatively. "Now you know at least one reason why you and he are so close," he said.

"God bless him," Carmella said.

"But Pearl," Hyman asked rhetorically, "does it really make a difference what your relationship was?"

Pearl continued looking out at the lake.

"No, I suppose not," she said, then turned back to face her two friends.

"I mean, of course not. And anyway, I can't imagine that he's this afraid only because he knows who he and I were in a previous life. Unless he's losing his mind and has some twisted notion that our relationship today is somehow incestuous because we were lovers five hundred years ago. No, no, there's something about this girl, Sylvie . . ."

"Does it matter?"

"No.

"But remember how Angelo had two mothers? Well, it's like I have two fathers. And right now one of my dads is terrified of something, so afraid that he's planning to do something violent, not to mention illegal, to you. And it isn't the first time. Remember the suicide of Congressman Oscar Valentine? Oh, what am I saying? Of course you wouldn't. He was a big supporter of Uncle Charlie. Unfortunately, he liked boys. It wasn't public. But my uncle found out. My uncle asked him to retire. Mister Valentine refused. A month or so later he hung himself. During that time, Congressman Valentine was video taped engaging in, shall we say, compromising activity with boys at a supposedly very private club. I know this not because it got into the press, because it didn't. I overheard a conversation between my uncle and his friend, Benny Apple, who arranged for the taping, and for all I know made it possible for Mister Valentine to be admitted to the club. It was Benny who played the video for Mister Valentine. I don't believe my uncle wanted Mister Valentine to kill himself, but he did want him to leave public life. I'm telling you this to say that, when Uncle Charlie wants something to happen, it happens."

"I'm sure that's true," Hyman said. "But is that really what concerns you?"

Pearl was quiet a moment before she said, "Somehow, I'm part of what's making Uncle Charlie so afraid. But even if I weren't, I love him. I would still do anything I could to help him. You know, get through . . . whatever he's facing."

*U*nimaginative, yet effective.

As Hyman heard it sketched out by Pearl, those were the words that summed up the general thrust of Charlie Fox's plan. People had been employing it for centuries. The only thing new about it was the name Fox gave it: Aggressive Cancer Treatment—"ACT" for short. When the President had said to his sister, "We've got to act," he was speaking acronymistically, if that were a word, about a program of surgery and intense chemotherapy. Surgery, in this case, meant kidnapping, excising O'Malley from the world for an indefinite period. Then, during his absence, a regimen of chemotherapy in the form of contrived accusations would be employed to destroy O'Malley's credibility—his disappearance itself spun as further evidence of his questionable moral stature. Further, when O'Malley re-surfaced, it would be as a drug addict, a habit conveniently imposed upon him during his enforced sabbatical. Any subsequent meanderings on O'Malley's part that he had been abducted, drugged and falsely accused would be easily positioned as ravings akin to those of individuals claiming to have been waylaid by UFOs on lonely country roads in the middle of the night.

The fact that Hyman O'Malley was basically a nobody made the job that much easier. There was little credibility to destroy. Drug possession, use, soliciting, pornography . . . there were countless ways of creating a trail of legal fact and innuendo that would compromise the man's credibility for life. Sadly, it happened all the time.

Yes, it was a problem, Charlie and Shorty agreed, that O'Malley had two of the most influential friends a person could have in the Puellas. But Benny was resourceful. So long as he knew what he was dealing with, the details might change, but overall success was as close to guaranteed as humanly possible. Benny had handled a lot trickier things than this.

"Yesterday, I would have called it cold-blooded," Pearl said. "And it is. But today I see it more as an example of how fear kills."

Carmella's limousine slowed behind three other limos, each about to turn into the long driveway leading uphill to Pearl's home.

Pearl pressed Hyman, "So if, or when, something happens to you, what are we to do?"

Hyman chuckled. "Do you think this situation is any different than choosing an ice cream cone? Follow your heart, love. And when in doubt, follow your heart some more."

*P*earl had never looked at a party the way she looked at this one. If she had been an artist like her dad or maybe a contemporary Maxwell Parrish, she would have painted a landscape that began with a hilltop on which sprawled a large, white circus tent, its canvas sides rolled up, multicolored pennants waving from its numerous peaks. Downhill beyond the tent would be an immense oak-dotted green lawn, a country road, then a vineyard, a section of lake, hills on the lake's far side, and a setting sun illuminating all through cotton candy gold clouds. Floating above the ground throughout the tent and lawn would be a bevy of larger-than-life three-dimensional balloon masks, each mask with a string that trailed down to the ground. The masks would be colorful and imaginative and witty—all smiling, and each, on the surface, very different from any of the others. They, of course, would represent the preponderance of adult guests. Below the balloon masks, running and frolicking in their entire bodies, would be a number of young children. Some of the kids might be holding a balloon mask in their hands, while others would have no masks at all.

Not too subtle a portrait, Pearl admitted, and a painful one—one she had witnessed, and even participated in, more times than she could count, but never quite so clearly as this.

Shorty greeted Carmella as though she were royalty. Carmella had that effect on people. Probably every single guest made it a point to meet Carmella, even those who had no idea who she was, including the kids. Pearl could only smile. The world in all its faces was drawn to Carmella Puella because Carmella met everyone heart-to-heart. It was no mystery to Pearl why Carmella as Bishnu had called out the name of Krishna at the end of their last incarnation together. Pearl didn't really know what a saint was, but she figured Carmella must be in the ballpark.

Hyman did a most unusual thing. He got up and sang with the band—a song about Shorty and Uncle Charlie. Pearl could tell that her uncle was about to pop out of his skin when Hyman began by saying he wanted to sing a song about the president and his sister. And all during the song, which began . . .

King Ornery the 50th of Ziliac
Awoke with a pain in his iliac,
And like the 49 Ornerys before him
Believed only one remedy would restore him.
"The cure for a Ziliac's iliac," said he,
"Is to gobble up a country smaller than we."

. . . it was clear that Uncle Charlie was waiting anxiously for Hyman to reveal something compromising, or worse. But, naturally, it never happened. At the end of the song, people stood and clapped and whistled. They clapped and whistled for Hyman. And they clapped and whistled for Shorty and Charlie. Hyman's ridiculous lyrics told of the conflicts Charlie Fox was easing because Charlie Fox had a big heart, a rare talent for finding common ground between people, and a remarkable partner in his sister.

Pearl knew exactly what Hyman was doing. He was reminding her uncle that no matter what choices Uncle Charlie made from fear, Hyman, for one, would always know that there was more to Charlie Fox than that.

23
Abducted

ros in the trade called it the Adlai Stevenson, a former United States Senator from Illinois and, at the time of his death, the articulate, witty and principled U.S. ambassador to the United Nations. Rumor had it that Stevenson, considered the smartest man never to be elected President of the United States (losing twice to the war hero Eisenhower in the 50's), did not actually die of a coronary on a London street, as the official story went, but instead had been the target of an assassin who, on a bustling mid-day sidewalk, nudged Stevenson from behind with the tip of an umbrella rigged with an invisible needle delivering a lethal dose of "heart attack." To Stevenson, the prick would have been no more noticeable than a fly landing on his ear as he hurried amidst the throng. Sometime later, however, a minute, an hour, he would put his hand on his heart as if to say the Pledge of Allegiance, then tumble onto the sidewalk, soon to be dead.

In Benny Apple's world, trick umbrellas and the like were a little James Bond of the Sean Connery era—Cold War antiques. But the principle of the "Adlai Stevenson"—administering a pharmaceutical cocktail without the recipient's knowledge, to take effect as desired, from instantly to a few hours later—was as useful as ever.

When Hyman and Carmella returned to the *Island of Peace*, they noticed that all the doors of Hyman's truck were open and the windows rolled down. Hyman investigated, but found nothing to suggest that anyone had taken or left anything. Shortly thereafter, however, Hyman began to feel exhausted, which he simply attributed to the long day. He also had an insatiable desire for fresh air.

"I'm just going to grab an afghan and sleep on the porch tonight, Mel," he said to Carmella.

He awoke in a strange bed in a strange room with a strange man in cut-off jeans, a pink polo shirt and a rubber Donald Duck mask that covered the man's entire head, not just his face. The duck's arms were tan and muscular, but otherwise unremarkable. He wore no watch or rings. No visible tattoos. Since Hyman was flat on his back, he had to turn his head to see the duck, who was sitting next to Hyman, nearly close enough to touch. But the duck wasn't facing Hyman, so Hyman was able to look over the duck's shoulder and see that the duck, wearing surgical gloves, was using a laptop computer to do the New York Times crossword puzzle.

If I'm right, and today is Sunday, Hyman thought, my new friend is either a glutton for punishment or very smart. Sunday, according to Puer, was the killer crossword in the Times.

The very first thing Hyman noticed about his own body was that he had urinated, soaking his pants and the bed. Well, it wasn't exactly a bed, more like a gurney covered in plastic. The second thing he noticed was that smiling had been dramatically curtailed by the duct tape across his mouth.

Itching his nose, he noticed next, was no easier to accomplish. Straps allowed his arms to move less than an inch. He checked his legs. They were similarly secured. So, using what was available to him, Hyman cleared his throat and, when Crossword Duck finally turned from his puzzle, Hyman looked at the little black eye holes in the duck mask and winked.

It seemed they were in a hospital operating room, since it was lit by a large overhead surgical light. Crossword Duck placed his computer, still running, on the small table in front of him. He then turned his straight back metal chair around and straddled it facing Hyman.

"You hear me OK?" the duck inquired.

Hyman shook his head yes, although the duck's voice was a bit muffled behind the mask. Plus he spoke in this raspy whisper. The sound reminded Hyman of a kazoo.

"Good," said Crossword Duck. "As I'm sure you've gathered, this is not your day. They tell me you are a blackmailer. In my book, blackmailers are right up there with attorneys. Parasites, you might say. People without the backbone to do an honest day's work, like knock over Tiffany's. And frankly, I've got shoes that are smarter than any blackmailer I've ever met. But we're not here to talk about my prejudices. In the old days, this is when I would tell you that, if you try to escape, I will kill you. But you see, for reasons that are none of your business, I no longer kill slugs like you. I do, however, collect body parts. I'm not above cutting off your toes or fingers. But I don't think any of that will be necessary. In fact, just to show you what good guy I am, I'm going to do you a big favor. I'm going to make it so you can't even think about escaping. I'm going to take the small pistol I keep here under my shirt and I'm going to shoot you in both legs. Like this . . . ."

Pop! Pop!

The shock was so intense that, within seconds, Hyman passed out. But not before Crossword Duck reached up and ripped off the duct tape over Hyman's mouth so that he wouldn't choke on his own vomit.

*S*ometime in the surreal interlude between being shot and regaining consciousness, Hyman found himself the previous afternoon driving his truck. He and Pearl had just left Carmella's. But that was the thing. There was no Pearl. Hyman was alone. The present stretch of road was as straight as a pool cue, making it possible to see ahead and behind probably the better part of a mile in total. To the front, the road was clear. But in the tall trucker's mirrors off the doors, he spotted behind him what appeared to be a team of fire flies floating just above the horizon, out looking for a party.

In seconds the fire flies were the headlamps of motorcycles. In a minute a family of classic fat-tire Harleys, each a different color.

Through the truck's open windows, the rumble of the approaching engines reminded Hyman of the Tibetan Tantric Choir he'd heard as a four-year-old boy with his parents in Central Park. It was the sound of power, contentment, grace, though the motorcycles added to this combination a sound all their own: swagger—the aural equivalent of the sign in the Yale locker room Uncle Charlie had revisited: *Go Big or Stay Home.*

Hyman pulled onto the shoulder of the road so that he could give his full attention to the bikers as they passed. Each hog was piloted by a man or woman who was surely over 70, maybe 80. All were in white leather, gold helmets and blue goggles—vibrant in the mid-afternoon sunlight of a cloudless sky. As the choir of vintage hogs paraded by, each biker proffered Hyman a casual nod and a thumb's up; their gloves the same blue as their goggles.

Those three colors were Hyman's old friends, part of his interior since childhood when the Swami had introduced him, in deep meditation, to his third eye: the single eye of intuition, the point between the eyebrows, the entryway into the ultimate states of divine consciousness.

Hyman experienced this eye as a ring of golden light surrounding a field of opalescent blue, at its center, a white, five-pointed star. Gold symbolizing creation. Blue the intelligence of Spirit within creation. The star vibrationless Spirit beyond creation.

What wasn't familiar was the sudden blaze of joyful understanding that frankly flabbergasted Hyman with the realization that every one of these bikers had been his intimate in some previous life or other. Which is to say, his mother, his father, his child, his mentor, his enemy, and so forth.

This was like the night as a 10-year-old when his horse Lady died saving his life, and from out of the torrential lightning squall the Swami appeared and held Hyman as he wept himself through heartbreak after heartbreak. Once again, in this night's wild hallucination, the Swami was gathering Hyman in his arms. Not in the flesh, of course, but in an energetic embrace of boundless love that assured Hyman that whatever might occur, however bizarre or dangerous things might shake out, he was secure in the lap of Divine Mother.

When he came to, Hyman wondered for a split-second if maybe he had left his body, so completely different did he feel from any other time he had ever awakened. But since the apparition smiling at him past the bottom of the bed was not the Swami but rather Crossword Duck, Hyman immediately surrendered his disappointment and chose instead to be grateful that he felt no pain.

Actually, he didn't feel much of anything, except that he was very tired. His clothes had been changed. He was now in a hospital gown. He lifted the blanket. His thighs were wrapped in bandages. It took him a moment to guess that he must have had surgery, and that what he was feeling must be the effect of anesthesia. He'd never had surgery before. He was now in a different bed. But this was not a hospital room. It was the master bedroom of an elegant home, he'd guess. A clear solution of some kind was being fed intravenously into his arm. He closed his eyes to rest for just a moment.

When he awoke again, Crossword Duck was gone. A woman, also wearing a Donald Duck mask, as well as surgical gloves and beet red scrubs, was hooking up a fresh plastic pouch of intravenous solution. Nurse or Doctor Duck, Hyman figured. If he wasn't mistaken, he heard the sound of the ocean. No restraints. No duct tape.

No need. He wasn't going anywhere, except to sleep.

The next time he awoke, he was alone. On the rolling hospital table within easy reach was a large plastic bottle of water and a pee bottle. Ah. He used the pee bottle. On the wall straight across from him, up near the ceiling, a surveillance camera pointed at him.

A new woman walked into the room. She was also wearing a Donald Duck mask, along with black skirt, matching tank top and the ever-present surgical gloves.

"I'm your doctor, Mister O'Malley," sounding, through the mask, as though she had a couple of cotton balls in her mouth. "I've dressed your wounds. Everything went well. No broken bones. You're on antibiotics for a few days. We'll have you up walking in the morning. Meanwhile, you see that little device with the button on it next to your right hand? That's for you. The minute you feel any pain or any discomfort coming on, you click that button a time or two and you'll be giving yourself pain killer. Morphine. Use as much as you need. Don't worry, it's regulated; you can't overdose. There's also the call button. Just hit it and the nurse will be right in."

Very cordial, Hyman thought, if not altogether truthful.

Soon after Doctor Duck left, Hyman began to feel the pain of his wounds. He self-administered a couple clicks of medication. Very quickly, it wasn't that the pain was gone, but that it no longer bothered him. He felt like a man who had just discovered he could fly.

Ah yes. So that was why he shot me. Hard to turn someone into a drug addict quickly if the person doesn't have ample motivation to seek it out. Then again, it's hard not to become addicted when there's plenty of desire to eliminate pain. Very clever. If I'm here long enough, I'm going to need a detox regimen of some kind when I get out. I may not be able to overdose, but I can keep myself as far over the moon as I'd ever care to be. And that's exactly what they're banking on, isn't it?

24

Celebrate, Then Deal With Life and Death

There would be no corn pancakes and peaches for Uncle Charlie this morning. The president had returned to the White House the previous evening shortly after the fireworks celebrating her mother's birthday exploded over the lake.

Before dawn, Pearl left her folks a note and jogged the half-mile down to her family's boathouse. She wore red nylon running shorts and a white T-shirt. As morning rose over the water, she sat in meditation on the boathouse roof. For an hour she practiced what Hyman had taught her the previous morning: receiving with each inhale the unending, ever-new love of the Earth Mother, then breathing out all of herself, giving herself completely to Spirit. And with each breath she silently spoke the mantra Hyman said was part of this technique: a Hindu phrase that meant that she and God were one. This, breath after breath after breath. Then she spent time feeling her gratitude for the many blessings of her life—but especially the unimaginable gifts of the past 24 hours.

Then, in the peace of a Sunday morning, the lake beginning to stir from the wind that the sailors in today's regatta were no doubt cheering, Pearl

337

drove her family's ski boat down and across the lake the better part of 20 miles to Carmella's.

"You knew I'd be here?" Pearl called as she cut the boat's engine. Carmella had been standing on her dock when Pearl arrived.

"I had a feeling," Carmella smiled, taking the boat's bow line from Pearl and securing it.

"Hyman's gone, isn't he?" Pearl stated.

"It seems so, my love. He said he was going to sleep on the veranda. But this morning there's been no sign of him, yet his truck is still here. Also, no note, which is unlike him."

"Is he in danger, do you feel?"

"I don't know . . . except to say that fear is always dangerous."

"And we. What do we do?"

By this time, Pearl was standing on the dock. Carmella drew Pearl into her arms and said, "Before we do anything, let us welcome the day and celebrate finding one another again by having our first breakfast together."

Pearl was struck by how calm Carmella was. At best, Hyman was missing. At worst, who knew? Yet, here she was, making time to have a picnic.

Carmella's dock was T-shaped, the top of the T extending into the lake. They sat on the right arm in yellow Adirondack chairs under a large green canvas umbrella. The chairs were so comfortable that you could sit in them all day, it seemed to Pearl, and their arms, shaped like the lid of a baby-grand piano, were roomy enough for a three course meal and a novel. From a small cooler, Carmella produced a container of sliced mangos and blueberries and served them each some on clear cut glass dishes. From a thermos she poured them hot ginger tea. And in a wicker basket from under the folds of a blue flowered tea cloth appeared fresh muffins. Pearl smelled one. "Mmmm. Pumpkin. My fave," she said.

"I'd like to take credit for being a mind reader," Carmella said, "but the truth is I asked your mother last night what your favorite food was and she said 'Pumpkin anything.'"

"Aren't you something," Pearl said. "You know what I told Hyman yesterday? That I wanted to live with you. Like . . . today. Forever. You understand, don't you?"

"Oh my, yes."

"I know. This isn't about my mother and dad. They are my family. You . . . you are my home."

"Hyman's Swami says: 'God gives us our family as tests, but He gives us our friends as gifts.'"

"I like that," Pearl said. "Both are so sacred."

Carmella touched Pearl's wrist. "You choose, sweetheart, when, and if, you live with me. We are already joined in the love of Spirit." Carmella paused, and then said, "On a mundane level, you should know that I will be making arrangements tomorrow for you to be my heir."

"I see," Pearl said. "I get to love you and get rich too."

Carmella laughed. "I knew you'd give it the proper disrespect it deserves."

"I'm sorry," Pearl said, is there something about being your heir I ought to know? You're not about to die, are you?"

"Not so far as I know," Carmella said. "But being my heir is a little more than inheriting wealth. It also includes playing a role in guiding the WOW Foundation, if that's something you choose to do."

"What if I want to be a movie star?"

"Then that's what you shall be, I'm sure."

The lake was big enough so that no matter how busy it became with boats—fishing, sailing, skiing, cruising—it remained peaceful. The light, the air, the landscape of water, hills and sky created an atmosphere that nearly demanded introspection, quiet, rest. The most natural thing was to simply sit in the splendor of the day and do nothing—just be.

After while, Pearl turned to Carmella and said, "I'm just teasing, you know. I will always do whatever you ask, if I am able. I'm willing to learn anything you feel I should. I just want to be with you."

They watched a string of ducks float from out under the dock on a little outing. Carmella said, "Tomorrow I'll provide you keys and so forth for my various residences. I'm also going to establish a bank account for you."

"Why is that? I don't need money."

"It's not the money, my sweet. Consider it training. I will put in your name a billion dollars in assets."

"Good lord! Why, for heaven's sake?"

"So that you may learn to be comfortable with a certain kind of power. The billion is merely a symbol. Someday you may have access to all the money you could ever imagine, much more than a billion dollars, I can assure you. Unlimited wealth means having the potential to influence the world in ways very few people can. And if you are not comfortable with that potential, it will be hard to use it well."

Pearl smiled. "Hyman and I had a conversation about this yesterday . . . how all these blessings I've received: you, him—how everything, really— can be a distraction from the real business of life, if I let them. Do you feel I should tell my folks about this—about being your heir?"

"You know what Hyman would say."

The words, and the reality behind them, brought with them the message that it was time for their conversation to change focus.

"Last night, on our way back from your mother's party," Carmella said, "Hyman made only one comment about the situation with your uncle. He said that, whatever happened to him, you were to decide what action, if any, should be taken."

"Really," Pearl said. "Why is that, do you suppose?"

Carmella poured them more tea.

"Maybe because it's your family," she said. "And anything any friend of Hyman's might do shouldn't compromise your relationship with your family—without your approval. But I'd say there's probably something more to it than that."

Carmella paused. Pearl waited.

"It's his way of telling you that you have all the wisdom you need to address any eventuality. All you have to do is look within. Basically, he's putting his life in your hands, Pearl. And he's saying you are more than ready to manage whatever comes up."

A towheaded boy wearing only green flowered Hawaiian shorts extending to his knees, a kid who'd been in the sun all summer, was standing in a red canoe about 50 yards off shore tossing bits of bread as high as he could into the air, attempting to attract gulls, hoping that one of them would snatch his offering before it hit the water. For a while the few gulls there were would only swoop down and pick up the bread on the water, before it sank, until one, maybe by complete accident, nabbed a piece in mid-air just as it left the boy's hand. The boy screamed, "Did you see that? Did you see that?"— waving so hard that he had to suddenly sit and put his hands on the canoe's gunwales so that he didn't fall out.

Carmella raised her hands over her head and clapped, and then she put her little fingers in her mouth, one in each corner, and whistled a whistle that could have stopped traffic all the way to Katmandu.

The boy looked around, not believing where the sound came from, finally he beamed at the two of them, raised his palm in the air for a high-five and shouted, "Alright lady!"

"Ooooh," Pearl said. "The whistling sister."

Carmella laughed. "Actually, the whistling came long before the sister. A gift from Tiny Menace."

"Who's Tiny Menace?" Pearl said.

"Oh, my love," Carmella said, "we have so much to share," reaching for Pearl's hand.

They watched the boy paddle down the lake, then Carmella said, "How would you feel about talking with Puer?"

"Fine," Pearl said. "But why? I thought you guys kept your distance from one another."

"Oh, that's just for the public, love," Carmella said. "It was Puer's idea . . . so that I could make my own way without the burden of his 'firecracker personality,' as he called it. I've not spent so much of my life in the big, bad world as he has. He wanted me to have time to get my feet on the ground, become comfortable with being a visible person of some influence. And I'm glad he did. It's been very helpful. We're actually very close. The WOW Foundation was actually Puer's idea. I knew it was time for me to leave the convent and learn from the world, but I wasn't sure what I would do. Puer had just met Hyman and was looking to be a much less visible public figure. He said, 'Why don't we establish a foundation?' And that's how it started."

"I don't really know much about Puer," Pearl said. "When Puer was on TV and whatnot I was outdoors, proving to all the boys I knew how tough I was."

Pearl almost said that she had hated girls as a girl. But she realized that that was what she always said, and that it wasn't really true. Now she knew that some fear drove her to compete with boys who were usually bigger and stronger than she was. It was the same fear that drove her to be the best at everything.

"Even by the time Puer and my uncle started feuding, I wouldn't have paid any attention if my mom hadn't gotten so fried about it. I'd hear her on the phone telling people that Puer was nothing but a fancy thug . . . that sort of stuff. So until yesterday when I found out he was a friend of Hyman's, I assumed Puer was pretty rank. That's rather childish, isn't it? Then I met both of you . . . on the same day. You and he are actually very much alike."

Carmella was smiling like she knew some big, enjoyable secret.

"What?" Pearl said.

"A private reverie, my love. That and the realization that Puer and I are very different in at least one important way."

"What's that?"

"If Hyman's really missing, Puer may be the only person we know who can find him."

"Really?"

"You will be amazed at what Puer can do."

What Pearl was first amazed by was how Puer looked when he walked onto Carmella's veranda a few hours later. No bandana. No overalls. No earring. No gold tooth. No eye patch. Only the scar remained. He could have been a banker in his elegant blue suit with the subtle maroon pinstripes. His shirt was as blue as the sky, and his tie of endless magentas, blues and golds was a hand-made silk number that could have been designed by Jackson Pollock, one of her father's idols. As the song goes about the London werewolves, his hair was perfect. His manner, also, was completely unlike yesterday. He was quiet, reserved. Although, like yesterday, his smile and his eyes were the smile and eyes of a man whose heart, if not always at peace, was playful, very much like Carmella's.

Puer and Carmella hugged, tenderly, without speaking.

Puer then turned to Pearl, joined his hands and bowed to her. "Pearl Pearl, we meet again."

Oh yes, the voice. Man, if God had an answering machine, He'd be sucking up to Puer just so He could get him to record heaven's greeting: *"You have reached the number for God. He's having such fun at the moment devising ingenious ways for you to give up your attachment to everything. But please, leave a message. God will get back to you. You can count on it."*

"Mister Puella, you are just one surprise after another."

Pearl told Puer everything she knew about what happened between her uncle and Hyman. She explained their meeting by the lake. She related what she had overheard during their meeting in the library, as well as what she overheard between Uncle Charlie and her mother afterward. She explained who Benny Apple was.

What she did not mention to Puer was anything about Bella-Viola. Her inner guidance simply said this wasn't the time. She also didn't say anything about her former life with Carmella. It would all come out soon enough.

Pearl was grateful when Puer said, "I actually know a bit about the Sylvie Marks story, which I will be happy to share with you later on. Right now I suggest we focus on answering two questions: One, where is Hyman? And two, if he's been abducted, how do we set him free?"

"Do you have suggestions?" popped out of Pearl's mouth.

"I'll be happy to look around a bit, if you like?"

"Look around?"

"See if I can locate him. If I may use your computer, Mel . . .?"

Carmella's hand raised and lowered its index finger.

Whatever was going on between Puer and Carmella was beyond her, Pearl realized.

"Are you saying you can actually find him?" she asked.

Puer smiled. "There's a chance," he said. "If you know what to look for, and you have the right tools, there's a lot of useful information floating around in the ether."

"I'm sure," Pearl said. "But aren't my uncle and Benny Apple rather hacker-resistant."

"You would think," said Puer. "But the government's a bureaucracy. And almost no bureaucracy is stronger than a few, dedicated revolutionaries. I don't mean revolutionary in a military sense. I just mean it in the sense of people whose life goal is not perpetuating a system, but transcending it, as needed."

Puer recognized that he'd just driven off into his own little world.

"I'm sorry," he said. "Allow me to speak English. It may surprise you to learn that, as recently as 1994, some 15 years after personal computers were introduced, the FBI was still using three-by-five cards to catalogue information about criminals. Why? Because many agents and managers were afraid of computer technology. They were committed to not looking foolish, as they perceived it. And these are men, primarily men, who would take a bullet for their country and think of themselves as simply doing their duty, which they are—and yet, they are also willing, implicitly, to undermine the security of the nation just so they don't look stupid in the presence of a computer. Is it any wonder why, as Double M says, managing fear is a most valuable skill? As we now know, this inability to manage fear on the part of the FBI and others has contributed to the nation's difficulty in responding to terrorist threats. Sadly, it is a fear that cannot be changed overnight. You need a few good funerals . . ."

"Funerals?" Pearl exclaimed.

"Some things change only when a new generation is in charge."

"Ah," Pearl said.

"Meanwhile," Puer said, "long before 1994, people like me were hacking into just about every significant computer system on earth. Not to be malicious. Just to do it. So there you have it. On the one hand, a bureaucracy that attempts to move forward against no small measure of institutional resistance. On the other, outlaws, not criminals, but outlaws whose allegiance is to understanding technology and using it responsibly."

Pearl turned to Carmella, "Who *is* this guy?"

Carmella's look said, *I told you so.*

Puer bowed, "Pardon my diatribe. But now you know why finding our friend may be easier than you might think. Of course, if he's been abducted, freeing him is a whole other matter."

25

Hyman & Benny

The next time Hyman opened his eyes, he found Crossword Duck almost close enough to touch. The duck sat cross-legged in a blue leather Morris Chair, its back notched fully upright, his elbows on the oak armrests, his hands in his lap. He looked like a man in meditation if you didn't take into account his mask's perpetual wide-eyed grin. He wore a yellow print Hawaiian shirt over cut-off jeans. His feet were bare.

"Know the time?" Hyman croaked.

"Two in the morning," rasped the duck.

Hyman clicked a hit of morphine.

In front of him on the rolling hospital table was a tall Styrofoam cup, a candy cane straw sticking out of the lid.

"Cranberry juice," Crossword Duck remarked.

Hyman touched the button raising the bed, then reached for the cup. "What is it you want to talk about?" he asked, reading the duck's mind.

The duck adjusted the embroidered pillow in the small of his back and settled himself.

"The other night, when I was carrying you from the veranda, you seemed to awaken for just a split second. You said, 'Ah, there you are.'"

Hyman closed his eyes, his hands around the cup. He was gray with pain.

"What do you know about me?" Hyman asked.

"Nothing, really. Just what I've been told."

"What if what you've been told isn't true?"

"Ah yes, and what if cows could fly?" Crossword Duck volleyed back.

"No, on second thought," he said, "I'll answer your question, just so you *comprende* where I'm coming from." Crossword Duck looked at the ceiling for a second as if asking for a go ahead, then said, "Remember in *The Fugitive* when Harrison Ford tells Tommy Lee Jones he didn't kill his wife?"

Hyman shook his head No, his eyes still closed.

"I'm sorry," Hyman said. "If you're talking about a movie or a TV show, or even a novel, I don't know very much."

"Movie. Harrison Ford?"

Hyman shook his head again.

"Doesn't matter. It's old. Ford plays this doctor who gets convicted of killing his wife. Claims he didn't. Jury doesn't believe him. Gets sentenced to life. On the way to the pen, the prison bus is hit by a train and Ford escapes. Tommy Lee Jones is the U.S. Marshall tracking him down. There's this scene when they first meet face-to-face. Harrison Ford says, 'I didn't kill my wife.' And Tommy Lee Jones says, 'I don't care.'

"You see, O'Malley, at some point we all gotta decide what game we're playing, and then not get distracted by anything that isn't related to that game. For Tommy Lee Jones, guilt or innocence was irrelevant: his game was tracking down people who were wanted by the law. My game is a little different, but the result is the same: I couldn't care less who you are, what you have or haven't done. I must say, the President of the United States says you're a wacko, and that's good enough for me. But hell, you could be Winnie the Pooh. My game is, you're outta commission . . . 'til further notice."

"Then why your interest in the other night?"

"Loose end." Crossword Duck said. "I feel we've met somewhere."

"I'm sure I would have remembered meeting a crossword playing duck."
The duck chuckled, "Yeah, well . . . ."

Then, in the time it takes for two men in a barrel to drop from the rim of Niagara Falls onto the turmoil below—exactly three seconds of exquisite, peaceful suspension—both the being who was Hyman O'Malley and the being who was Crossword Duck (a/k/a Benny Apple) each found himself on an October afternoon some 200 years earlier.

*T*he moment was unprecedented even in Hyman's experience. Never before had he and another person, together, simultaneously, met one another in a previous incarnation.

The two were brothers. Africans. Hyman O'Malley's name was Jamula. Benny Apple's name was Tambo.

For Benny Apple especially, meeting this previous incarnation of himself, Tambo, was freakish because Tambo was dead, freshly killed, lying on the ground, his brother Jamula staring down at him.

Existing outside of its lifeless physical shell, the spirit of Tambo felt only love and gratitude for Jamula, even though Jamula's actions had just led to Tambo's death.

For the spirit of Hyman/Jamula, the moment was one of twisted, grotesque impotence. Jamula had used all of his substantial powers to prevent the harm that had just taken his brother's life, and yet, in the end, was not only completely helpless to prevent it, but in fact had unknowingly contributed to it.

And as if the Great Trickster suddenly decided to pull the rug out from under Hyman and Benny one more time—*ba-doomp-pah!*—the granddaddy of epiphanies emerged like a phantom between them: each had been instrumental in the death of the other in several previous lives.

Their life as Jamula and Tambo was simply the most recent.

*T*hey had been among the youngest surviving children on a slave ship that docked in Roanoke, Virginia.

Whether by chance or providence, the brothers were sold to the same master. Once the auction was completed at the harbor, they never saw either of their parents again.

Tambo grew to be a man who would savage anyone who threatened his security. It was torture enough being a slave, but within that life Tambo would shape his own destiny, or die trying. At the time of his death, he had a reputation as the strongest slave in the South.

Jamula, on the other hand, was more like water. He accepted. And through acceptance, he found joy in the smallest of things. On that first day in America, as they were standing in chains waiting for whatever was going to happen next, a well-dressed white boy about Jamula's age walked up to him, spit something into his own hand, then offered it to Jamula. It was a smooth oval pink stone the size of an almond. The boy motioned for Jamula to put it in his mouth, which Jamula did. The boy then smiled and walked away. Later, Jamula learned that the stone helped him to go that much longer without water. As an adult, Jamula would say that the boy's kindness was proof that horror and beauty were inseparable.

*I*t turned out that the white boy was the master's son. The white boy's name was Badger, Badger McTaggart, named Badger by his father in hopes that he might grow up to emulate the animal's ferocity. The boy did, but not in the way his father had hoped. Badger became the nation's first big star as a female impersonator, a career choice that required as much tenacity as talent. Fortunately, Badger had both in abundance. While Tambo (the future Benny Apple) became a top field hand, Jamula (the future Hyman O'Malley) became Badger's servant, then companion and, eventually, best friend. Indeed, within a year of their meeting, neither one yet 10, Jamula and Badger shared a bed, a practice that continued for the rest of their lives.

It was Badger's father, Anger McTaggart, who imposed the circumstances that left Tambo dead at Jamula's feet.

Because, as adults, Badger and Jamula traveled almost constantly, and when not traveling made their home in Paris or New York City, it was the first time since the two had left the plantation for Badger's theater career at age 16, nearly 10 years earlier, that they were present for the Fall Harvest celebration. They wouldn't have been there even then had not Badger received word that his father was dying and probably wouldn't last till year's end. If this were true, Badger saw no evidence of it upon arrival, save that Anger McTaggart's body was even more the shape of a fiddlehead and that both of his eyeballs and all visible teeth were now completely the color of a stream in a summer flash flood. But that didn't mean Badger's father was going to die. Some men live quite a long time on venom alone.

Fall Harvest was the major social event of the year for the McTaggart clan, much more significant than Christmas, since it was directly connected to the McTaggart wealth. There were days of balls and banquets and hunts and sport—the better the harvest, the more elaborate the occasions. Even the slaves reaped the bounty of leisure and games and feasts.

On the McTaggart plantation, Fall Harvest was also the occasion for what Anger McTaggart had named Nigger Rassling, a half-dozen matches so special that the minimum bet was one hundred dollars.

Anger McTaggart claimed he invented Nigger Rassling, and no one disputed him. It was the world's most elemental contest, he claimed: two buck niggers, related by blood, naked,—"bare-assed and bare handed," as Anger McTaggart put it—linked together by a 10 foot chain attached to the iron collar around each slave's neck, fight to the death, or to the point that each demonstrates to the crowd's satisfaction that he is willing to kill the other.

That was the real point of the contest, as far as Anger McTaggart was concerned: to prove that the Negro was not simply an animal, as many claimed. A dog was an animal. If threatened, it would kill its own with no reservation and no remorse. The Negro had a tiny bit of each, reservation and remorse, making him, in the mind of Anger McTaggart, part-man, part-animal. In the Negro was the God-given drive to survive at all costs, so much so that he was willing to kill his own blood, if need be. This, by Anger McTaggart's peculiar logic, the sort of convoluted insanity that has always been common to racists, made the Negro an animal, since a human, a white man, would never willingly destroy his own blood, unless of course it were tainted. But what the white man and the Negro had in common, what made the Negro *part* human, was the fact that it might pain the Negro to kill his own. Sons had been known to howl for days after killing their fathers in Nigger Rassling.

*S*ince it was common for slave families to be separated, members sold to different masters, Anger McTaggart would frequently have to "horse trade," as he put it, with other slave owners in order to bring together blood relatives—and in some cases, the two combatants wouldn't have seen each other in years.

It was seldom that two top-grade slaves were selected to compete against one another. A good nigger was hard to come by, Anger McTaggart said frequently as if conveying the wisdom of Solomon. Most times, at least one of the participants was being sent a message by his master: Prove yourself or die. Anger McTaggart boasted that he had devised a way for no-account niggers to redeem themselves. Which is why the weaker slave didn't always perish in Nigger Rassling. The participants knew that the goal was demonstrating that they were willing to kill, at which point the crowd would chant, "Feast! Feast! Feast!"—and Master McTaggart would fire his shotgun into the air. Both rasslers were then guests of honor at the Nigger Feast attended by all the slaves.

If the crowd didn't chant and the shotgun wasn't fired, then only the survivor was honored.

Bettors bet on everything they could think of. Would the weak nigger die? Who would be the first to draw blood? Would the match conclude before a cigarette burned down a certain distance?

There was never any warning beforehand as to who the year's rasslers would be. Each couple were announced immediately prior to their match.

At noon on the last day of Fall Harvest, all the slaves in the county were gathered together at the McTaggart plantation. The slaves sat in a large circle, men up front. Behind the slaves, standing, or in wagons, or on horseback, were owners and other bettors, women and children. It was among these that Jamula/Hyman stood, next to Badger. As usual, Jamula was dressed as the valet of a glamorous international artist.

The proceedings began with Anger McTaggart reading from the Bible, then giving a short homily on the dignity of the Negro. Only then did he announce the contestants for the inaugural bout.

When Jamula's slave name, Ray, was the first announced, the sound from the circle of slaves was the combination of shock and relief.

Immediately, bettors started chirping.

Then Badger's dusky alto soared over the crowd: "How dare you, sir?"

Silence.

His father didn't answer, but calmly called out Tambo's slave name: Bob. Bob and Ray would rassle. Only then, as another murmur of understanding became background for the banter of high stakes, did Anger McTaggart turn to his son.

"You know the rules, my boy," Anger McTaggart smiled. "Any male slave on this property at this hour is a candidate for Nigger Rassling. Surely you're not suggesting that Ray is no longer a slave. That would be impossible, wouldn't it? Since nigger Ray belongs to me. Always has. Or had you forgotten?"

"This is despicable," Badger shouted. "Outrageous!"

"Ah, my boy," Anger McTaggart said, "a curious choice of words. Since they are precisely those frequently said behind my back by gentlemen of breeding and station, some of the very gentlemen here today, about the fact that my son prances around the world dressed as a woman, his little kewpie doll nigger in tow.

"But I will give you this, Badger McTaggart," his father said, ending the discussion. "If Ray acquits himself well today, he shall be yours to do with as you please. And should he not, should he die, then, I will gladly roast nigger Ray on the spit, if you like, so that you may have the pleasure of eating him for supper. Either way, not much will change for you, eh?"

"You are an abomination," Badger hissed.

"I may be many things, my boy," Anger McTaggart said, "most of them unflattering, but that particular title, I'm afraid, has already been reserved— by you—in hell."

"*I* will not fight," Jamula (the future Hyman O'Malley) whispered to his brother as they were being stripped and chained together, the wagers of white men flying around them.

"Then you shall die quickly," Tambo said calmly.

Tambo was more than massive. Anger McTaggart once wagered $10,000 that his nigger Bob could whip any other nigger in Virginia. By the time gentlemen stopped taking him up on his bet, Anger McTaggart was $100,000 richer, 10 good niggers had been beaten senseless, and Bob hadn't worked more than a half hour total.

"I may die," Jamula said, "but not at your hands, Tambo. I will not permit you to live with the pain of your having killed me."

"You, a mule, makes no difference to me," Tambo said, but Jamula knew better. Jamula had powers that only Tambo really knew about somewhere inside him. Twenty years earlier, Jamula had kept Tambo alive during the crossing from Africa by feeding him milk from his, Jamula's, own breast, and he was but an eight year old boy at the time. In fact, it was Jamula's milk that had made Tambo so huge and strong. Tambo's heart knew this, Jamula knew, but Tambo denied that his heart even existed other than as something that beat within his chest. This meant that Tambo also denied the memory of the many other miracles his brother performed when they were children. One, for instance, occurred within a few weeks of their arrival on the McTaggart plantation. Young Tambo was whipped severely by an overseer. He would have died if Jamula had not spent the night washing Tambo's wounds and singing. At some point the pain eased and Tambo slept. When Tambo awoke in the morning, he felt as though the whipping had never taken place. Moreover, there was not a scar on his body.

Jamula knew that, should Tambo kill him, someday the pain of it would shrivel Tambo. And there was no need for that to happen, Jamula felt. The only problem was that Jamula might have to reveal some of the power channeled through him. Even Badger wasn't aware of it. Jamula had healed his lover, Badger, of illnesses over the years, but always in such a way that Badger never knew what Jamula was doing. The only conscious evidence Badger had of Jamula's powers was the half-hour each day when Jamula put his hands around Badger's throat.

"I cannot imagine singing as well as I do without your magic hands," Badger had said many times. Little did he know just how true his words were.

*T*ambo (the future Benny Apple) was a black draft horse whose stall had just caught fire. That was the yank he gave to the chain connecting him to Jamula. But instead of snapping Jamula's neck as he intended, Jamula's iron collar broke away and flew directly at Tambo, hitting him right between the eyes, knocking him out cold. Only Jamula saw the burn, in the shape of half a heart, between Tambo's eyebrows.

Anger McTaggart exclaimed. "Lord almighty, throw a bucket on that nigger."

Someone did, and when the water fell onto Jamula's broken collar lying next to Tambo, the collar steamed as though, seconds before the water hit it, it had come out of the blacksmith's forge.

Suddenly everyone stopped talking.

"Let me see that blamed collar," Anger McTaggart barked, and a slave carried it to him on a shovel, it was so hot.

"Piss poor smithing," Anger McTaggart announced. "Quickly now, boys, get us a new collar. Honest folk have money to lose."

*J*amula whispered to Tambo, "You won't be able to kill me, but don't worry. Trust me."

Tambo's dead eyes looked at Jamula as if to say, "Trust left me long ago, fool."

This time Tambo took a length of chain in his hand and started to run as fast as he could, forcing Jamula to follow him. Tambo's intention was to turn as he ran, this way then that, until Jamula lost his balance and fell. Then Tambo would simply drag Jamula around by the neck. Tambo could run all afternoon and not get tired. He'd been in this situation before. Sooner or later Jamula would wear out. They all did.

But Jamula didn't.

He ran three steps behind Tambo like a deer who could anticipate Tambo's every move. Tambo was unable to run or dodge or even somersault without finding Jamula there three paces behind him. And when Tambo whirled and ran straight at Jamula, Jamula also whirled and ran just fast enough to stay three paces in front of Tambo. Then Tambo stopped suddenly and yanked on the chain, expecting that he would jerk Jamula's head off when Jamula didn't also stop.

But Jamula did.

Jamula was like a mirror. Whichever way Tambo moved, Jamula moved also at the same instant, always maintaining the precise three pace distance.

Catching their breath, the two stood looking at one another. Then Tambo started wrapping the chain around his arm, intending to pull Jamula toward him, but Jamula didn't budge. Tambo jerked with all his might, not just once but many times, and for all the effect on Jamula you might have thought the chain was attached to one of the many oaks that shaded Anger McTaggart's lawn.

Tambo charged Jamula, and again Jamula retreated, keeping the three paces between them.

Bettors were becoming restless. There was no blood.

"Fight fair you black sonsabitches," someone shouted. A chorus of derision rang consent.

Tambo, sensing danger, summoned every ounce of rage he had ever known and, with a bellow that sent children racing to their mothers, jerked the chain so viciously that not a soul present doubted that Tambo could have ripped off the head of an ox. But instead of Jamula's head flying off, it was his collar that once again exploded from his neck, and once again hit Tambo between the eyes, and once again knocked him senseless. The wound glowing between Tambo's eyes was a completed heart. Jamula's broken collar lay smoldering in the grass.

Jamula's plan had worked perfectly. Tambo's body wouldn't awake for hours, while his spirit was being awakened in ways it hadn't known since Tambo and Jamula were children. Jamula knew that he had proven himself. Killing an unconscious opponent violated Anger McTaggart's unique sense of fair play. Tambo might suffer the indignity of being whipped by his kewpie-doll brother, but at least he'd be alive without the burden of having killed Jamula.

As Jamula knew would happen, several buckets of water did nothing to revive Tambo.

Reluctantly, amid the jeers and cheers of bettors on either side of the long-shot result, Anger McTaggart strode forward with his shotgun raised in the air. Holding up his other hand for silence, he said, "Friends, this has been a most unusual contest. But fair is fair, and my Bob, the strongest nigger in the land, lies whupped by his own pansy-ass brother."

The right barrel of Anger McTaggart's shotgun roared at heaven.

And then Anger McTaggart said, "May this be a lesson to all of us," and sauntered over to nigger Bob, placed the left barrel of his shotgun on the heart between Tambo's eyes, and blew off Tambo's head from the eyebrows up.

In the silence that followed, Anger McTaggart's eyes found Badger in the crowd. "Have you no shame, sir?" he demanded of his son so that all could hear. "A man's wife, even a nigger wife, even a wife who is man, shouldn't be out in public without any clothes on."

*B*enny Apple removed his rubber mask and dropped it into in his lap. He had the look of a man who'd just stepped out of a sauna.

He pulled a monogrammed handkerchief from his back pocket, wiped his face and blew his nose. His eyes he wiped a second time with the back of his hand.

Hyman's eyes remained closed. Tears flowed freely.

The night was quiet except for the slight ever-present sea breeze.

The two sat in the silence.

Finally, Benny said, "So this is why Charlie Fox is apoplectic about you."

Hyman opened his eyes and blinked a few times, nodding. He took a sip of cranberry juice then placed the container back on the table.

Benny sniffed a small laugh.

"I had a fellow take a bullet out of me once simply by pointing his finger at the wound," he said.

Hyman nodded in understanding.

Benny said, "This cat and I are all alone in some mountain cave 600 miles from noplace, and after he heals me I ask him if he's got any way to heat water, some tea would taste good. He pours water from a jug into a cup, then sticks his finger in the cup for about two seconds, then pops in a few leaves, and man, that brew was near scalding."

Hyman nodded.

"Guess we know why I felt we'd met," Benny said.

Hyman softly cleared his throat. "And here we are again."

"Yo," Benny echoed. "Here we are again."

The words hung in the air as you would imagine a smoke ring might in an air-tight room.

Then, as if speaking to himself but allowing Hyman to overhear, Benny said to the night, "You know . . . I understand Charlie Fox better than most people . . . ."

The sound of his own voice seemed to awaken Benny. "He made this whole thing up about you, didn't he?" Benny said, touching Hyman's hand.

"Yep."

"You and he met and he had some sort of experience—like you and I just had—and he freaked. Am I right?"

"You are right."

"Well," Benny said, placing his mask carefully next to the Styrofoam cup and wiping his eyes again. "I guess you and I are just going to have to put our heads together and figure out where we go from here."

Benny then leaned closer to Hyman and put up his right hand, fingers pointing to the sky. Hyman put his right hand squarely on Benny's. It was the most gentle, loving high-five in the entire world that day.

"I'm sorry," Benny said.

Hyman nodded.

Their eyes were brilliant with tears.

Benny could see that Hyman was whipped.

"Let's talk again after you've had some rest," Benny said. "After breakfast maybe. Give me time to make something up. I don't know what we'll do, but we'll have some fun."

A small grin appeared on Hyman's face as he closed his eyes to sleep.

"I'm sure we will, brother," he said.

As Hyman surrendered his consciousness to the One in sleep, something that had been ruffling the edges of his awareness suddenly became perfectly, unmistakably present: the realization that his former friend and lover, Badger McTaggart, the female impersonator, was, in this incarnation, none other than Puer Puella.

Not that it made any difference, he joked to himself.

Except for the fact that no one knew about it, when Hollywood made the film about the life of Puer Puella, they could have done a lot worse than open with the story of Hyman O'Malley's rescue that morning. Unfortunately, it occurred before Benny and Hyman could work out a plan of their own.

The setting: a rather posh seaside bungalow in the Hamptons. The kind with servants' quarters. Inside, a man sleeps in a hospital bed, his thighs bandaged, tubes, monitors and other typical medical paraphernalia support him. Four other people are about the home: two men, two women. The two women are a doctor and a nurse. The two men have pistols concealed under their Hawaiian shirts. This is not a family reunion.

Their cover is they are old college friends leasing the place for a season of Big Chill, a common occurrence out there where lots of unfamiliar faces spend the summer.

It is sunrise. Birds chirping. Paper boy throwing strikes from his bike. Yachts setting off. And six obvious transvestites prancing through the morning dew in cocktail dresses and spikes.

They knock on the bungalow front door—rap, rap, rap—and when Benny, the head Chiller, answers, they say that they are on their way home from an all night gala *"you wouldn't believe!"* and could they please, please cut through the yard *"quick as a bunny to the beach"*—it would make the hike to their own bungalow so much shorter, although, truth be told, it would be hell on their pedicures. Benny isn't terribly surprised since "girls" of this persuasion are not unheard of in the Hamptons in season. He laughs and says, "Be my guest," just as one of the ladies does the tiniest bow-legged hitching up of her panty hose and draws from her lovely behind a small pistol which is in Benny's mouth before he can say *La Trockadero*.

Next, as we see a large lavender helicopter descending on the beach, the only sound we hear is a beautiful Gregorian chant sung by a children's choir. What follows is a fast-paced montage of rescue activity, some of it violent but not lethal, interspersed with a slow-motion aerial: looking straight down on what half-seems to be the blossom of a large flower floating over white sand. It is our patient wrapped in a navy blue blanket, six colorful transvestite commandos, three on each side of him, expertly transporting their prize to the chopper that whisks them all away toward Manhattan.

The ladies, natch, don't break a nail.

Meanwhile, another, even bigger, helicopter, blue, has landed in the backyard, and a team in sequined jumpsuits quickly loads, on stretchers, the unconscious bodies of the four Chillers.

Next, an airplane view of what we assume is the Alaskan wilderness—no sign of human life as far as the eye can see.

Cut to the inside of a cabin somewhere in the middle of that wilderness. The Chillers, having awakened from their Adlai Stevensons, are reading a typewritten note.

It says:

Dear Kidnappers:

The nearest town is 150 miles. Your nearest neighbor is 50 miles. You have food for a year. Winter will set in any day. Spring comes eight months later. You have all the clothes you will need. You have no firearms, nor any form of communication with the outside world. You have neither maps, nor compass, nor any clues that will tell you specifically where you are. Pilots never fly near here in winter, and seldom during other times of the year. No one will know where you are until you emerge to tell them. If you are to survive, you will need to be more attuned to your heart than you were in your most recent assignment . . . .

Dissolve to a shot of a computer screen where the letter is being written. Camera pulls back to reveal the handsome, scarred countenance of the writer, our hero, Puer Puella, in shirt and tie. The camera moves away from Puer, revealing the beautiful study where he's sitting, then it moves out the window, and up into the sky so that we see the *Island of Peace* compound and then up even further so that we see the patchwork panorama of New York's Finger Lakes in late summer.

The Gregorian choir comes to heavenly resolution as the film's title appears:

Puer Puella, New Age Gangster:
Doing Brave and Lovely Things

"*P*lease don't hurt anyone," Hyman had said over and over to Meryl Streep. At least, that's what he remembered. Everything happened so fast, and he was pretty groggy.

"Mister O'Malley?"

He had been awakened by the whisper of a man who looked like the actor's twin sister.

"Do you understand me?" Meryl said. He put his hand on Hyman's.

"Yes."

"Good. You are safe. Your kidnappers have been neutralized. My colleagues and I are here to rescue you. We're taking you by helicopter to a private hospital in Manhattan. Mister Puella will meet you there. To make your travel painless, I am going to sedate you. Don't worry. We may be glamorous, but we are all highly trained professionals. We rescue people for a living. Just relax and enjoy the ride."

"Listen to me," Hyman remembered saying, as Meryl went about his business. "This is very important. Please don't hurt anyone."

And he thought Meryl had said, "I understand. Believe me, everyone is alive and well—most importantly, you."

"What's your name?" Hyman thought he asked at some point.

And he thought the answer he heard was, "Why, I'm Meryl, Mister O'Malley. Meryl Streep."

*L*unch at the Dame Edna, Manhattan's most exclusive private hospital, was among Hyman's favorite meals: Russian cabbage pie and strawberry rhubarb cobbler—the orders of Puer, no doubt.

It was now mid-afternoon, and Hyman had awakened from his post-lunch nap and had just returned from walking down the hall and back, assisted by two of the most lovely transvestite nurses you could imagine: Marilyn Monroe and Ella Fitzgerald they said their names were.

He sat in a chair and looked out over Central Park. Mahogany, marble, lemon-sandalwood furniture polish, fresh flowers, Persian carpets. It was like a tiny, elegant hotel. Could a Plaza suite be more comfy? He doubted it.

Hyman had never been a hospital patient before, so he had nothing to compare this experience to, but he was quite sure this was unique. If nothing else, he felt supremely confident that the doctors and nurses he had met so far knew just how to handle someone who had been through the trauma of being kidnapped. Plus, it took no time at all for them to figure out what was going on with him physically—his wounds and his morphine intake. And they did it all in such a deeply caring yet lighthearted and unselfconscious manner that you could feel your body healing in their presence.

When Puer walked in with Pearl, Puer dressed in a New York Yankees uniform with Tiny Menace's number 05, Pearl wearing all white, her black hair, unbraided, flowing below her shoulder blades, Hyman burst out laughing.

"What?" Puer squeaked, a wave at the surroundings, "You expected General Hospital?"

The friends hugged.

Hyman held the face of each in his two hands, first one then the other.

"Thank you," he said. "Thank you."

Puer had brought with him a pink nylon suitcase, which he now unzipped and placed for easy reach on a footstool next to his friend. "T-shirts," Puer said, "from Mel."

"Wonderful, thank you!" Hyman said. "I'd like to pick one now, if you don't mind."

The three sat in silence, meditating briefly.

Then Hyman, eyes closed, felt around in the pile of shirts and pulled one out.

Some smiles are all in the eyes, just a flash, a spark, all that's needed to convey the ocean of shared understanding below the surface. These were the smiles Puer and Pearl offered Hyman when he held up the pale yellow shirt with the message: *Never spit in a man's face unless his mustache is on fire.*

Hyman had been wearing fuzzy sky-blue slippers shaped like poodles with socks that definitely weren't a pair: one red with blue polka dots; one orange and green striped; also a plain white T-shirt and baggy flannel madras shorts in crosshatches of lavender, lime green, hot pink and white—wardrobe compliments of the Dame Edna. The change of shirt from white to yellow, even with the inspirational message, didn't change the overall sartorial statement all that much as far as Puer was concerned.

"You still look like the blind shoplifter from Neiman Marcus," he said.

"Those socks, by the way, remind me of my partner Clyde's daughter, Sylvie," Puer looked at Pearl. "On the day she died she evidently gave a pair of mismatched socks to your uncle—one gold, one blue."

"Well, well," Hyman said.

"Whoa," Pearl said. "Well, well, is right. My uncle wears those socks, or ones just like them, every year on my mom's birthday."

"The plot thickens," Puer said.

Hyman grinned. "This is your creation? Dame Edna?"

"A little project I started before I retired, actually," Puer said. "It began with the transvestite commandos. Clyde and I created them as part of *Holy Cow*—simply because they are so effective. Nothing beats the surprise of 20 transvestites in sequin gowns and flawless makeup parachuting behind enemy lines, so to speak—especially when the ladies can kick your butt like Jackie Chan. Remember when the British Prime Minister's son was abducted? The Brits got the credit for the rescue, but it was my girls, as they like me to call them, who did the job."

"How did the Dame Edna start?" Hyman asked.

"I don't know, really. Something just clicked. Or many things clicked. You can never have too many good places where kidnap and torture victims can recuperate. Then there is the healing power of humor, or just not taking yourself seriously—and, to me, there is something inherently funny about having a very high-powered clinic, serving people with emotional and physical pain, where all the professionals are transvestites. I don't know, I just thought it might work. And it has. Another thing is, there are no settings that I know of where a gifted professional, if he also happens to be a transvestite, can be himself. Transvestites aren't clowns, you know. And they're not men who wish they were women. They're men who know they're men and prefer to dress like a woman. But to our patients, most of whom are just regular folks, being cared for by a sensitive, understanding and skilled man who just happens to be a transvestite is, strangely perhaps, very comforting. Our patients often think of *themselves* as freaks, since they've had experiences that separate them from the mainstream. Since a transvestite is a freak in our society as well, a kind of bonding takes place here that you might not find in other settings. I know it sounds crazy, but it seems to work. The key of course is having great people. Wearing a dress and killer makeup, by itself, wouldn't mean much."

"I can see why you keep it quiet," Pearl said.

"How do you mean?"

"Well, this is completely different from Puer, New Age Gangster. That was just you. And Mister Marks, who was a willing participant. This involves the staff of the Dame Edna—all transvestites, for that matter—and your patients."

Puer looked at Pearl as if he had just learned that she had been reading his mind for the past ten years.

Hyman asked about the kidnappers, and when he was told where they had been taken, he got very quiet, and then said, "Puer, this must not happen. You must free them. You must bring them out."

"Alright, Double M, if you say so," Puer said hesitantly. "But they aren't in any danger, you know. Their leader . . ."

"I know who their leader is, my friend," Hyman said.

And the way he said it brought a whole new vibration to the conversation.

"Then you know he's one of the world's most skilled cold-weather survivalists," Puer said, wanting to get at what prompted this unprecedented intensity from his friend. "This is child's play for Benny Apple. He's spent lots of time in Alaska."

"I believe you," Hyman said. "I am not questioning your judgment, your motives, or Benny's skills. It's me. I must do all I can to insure that he is safe. Can you understand that?"

"Well, what I understand, Double M, is what you want, and I'll make that happen." Puer took his satellite phone out of his pocket. "What I'm less clear on is what is behind your request."

But before Puer could hit the speed dial, Hyman said, "Benny is my brother."

After dropping the Chillers into the wilderness, the commando team landed in Anchorage for refueling. It was there that Puer reached them and changed their orders. Since the day was waning, the commandos said they preferred to wait until dawn to return to the wilderness, so they would have unlimited light. Puer said of course.

Then he said, "Tomorrow, when you arrive in New York, please take the other three back to their bungalow, but deliver Mister Apple to the Dame Edna. Tell him his brother is waiting for him."

At four a.m., Puer's phone rang. He was sleeping in his usual room in Carmella's apartment. Pearl was down the hall in Carmella's bed. No one but his sister, Clyde and Double M called this number unless it was urgent. Which reminded him. He'd give Pearl the number in the morning.

"Joe's bar and grill, where the elite meet to eat."

"Bad news, P," said Jodie Foster, the lead commando. "Ice storm. Siberian Sidewinder, they call it here. Comes out of no place. Nothing moves 'til further notice. Hope to know more in a couple of hours. Keep you posted. Sleep tight."

"Thank you for caring and sharing," Puer said as the line clicked dead.

Two hours later, the news was worse. Two hours after that, worse still. Two hours after that, a disaster had been officially declared. It would be several days before they could fly in.

It turned out that the Sidewinder's whole damn family invaded Alaska: brothers and sisters, aunts and uncles, cousins, in-laws, dogs and cats—each one as mean and nasty as the next. So surly and ill-tempered that, in some parts, 10 feet of snow fell that first week. Another 10 feet the following week. Even in Anchorage, everything shut down. The commandos ran out of panty hose.

"P," said Jodie Foster, "we'd take a dog sled out there if we were sure we'd make it. Don't worry. At the earliest opportunity, we'll get them. It's not like they're going anywhere."

A few days at the Dame Edna and the patient was well enough to travel to *The Island of Peace*. And there, nearly three weeks after Hyman's rescue, Puer received the call from Jodie Foster: the commandos had reached the Chiller's cabin, finding the door open, three people dead, Benny Apple missing. Of the three dead, the man, sitting at the kitchen table eating oatmeal, had been struck in the head repeatedly with a piece of firewood. The two women died of exposure, in each other's arms, in the outhouse, fifty feet behind the cabin, dressed as if they were about to set off on a long overland journey, the dead man's blood on their hands and clothes.

*T*he blizzard hadn't been more than a few days old when Benny admitted to himself that his doctor and nurse were not cut out for an intimate relationship with Mother Nature. It wasn't that surprising. He'd worked with the two on other occasions. They carried their weight. But the thrill of the clandestine wore thin as soon as it strayed very far from the familiar. A bungalow in the Hamptons was their speed. This had nothing to do with them being women. It was more that they were infatuated with their education and the prestige of their profession. And other than a few soldiers, mountain climbers, deep sea divers and a monk or two, Benny had never met anyone whose professional credentials helped them enjoy the only moments in life that are really worth anything: when every decision, if it's a bad one, can be your last. *When is one ever more alive?* Benny had watched some of the sanest, most mild-mannered people in the world go absolutely Bellevue with cabin fever—but usually only after a week or more of isolation. Doctor and Nurse duck, as Hyman would no doubt call them, were approaching warp-speed mind loss virtually overnight.

If his buddy, Abdul Robb, a/k/a Mister Mellow, Benny's fellow Green Beret, could keep a lid on things at the cabin for a week to 10 days, Benny could find help. On snowshoes, Benny could make 150 miles in four days—if he had snowshoes, knew which direction to travel, and the blizzard let up.

But those were merely bumps in the road. He could improvise snowshoes. And even without the sun or a starry night, his own inner guidance system was seldom more than a few degrees off in Alaska. All he really had to do is find a familiar landmark. If you knew what to look for, sooner or later there'd be signs. The blizzard was the blizzard. Dangerous, yes. He'd just have to deal with it. The issue wasn't survival; his chances were as good as they get. The question was could he make it to civilization then back to the cabin by snowmobile or dog sled before the two medical fruitcakes decided to run off naked into the sunset screaming for fried clams.

He'd been humping at a good clip for three days. Because the snow was perpetual, he followed a river. At night the visibility was zero, so he had to stop. But he built the biggest fire he could and set out traps he'd contrived back at the cabin and by each dawn caught at least one snowshoe rabbit, which was rather remarkable in a blizzard. The second night out he'd made himself a stew that was one of the best meals he'd ever eaten. Too bad he had to be someplace. He could do this forever. He'd love to wander the wilderness with Hyman. That would be a terrific way for them to get acquainted. He could take care of Hyman. It was a funny thing to be as old as he was and meet a man whom, very quickly, he cared about as much as anyone he'd ever known. A brother. Quite something for an only child.

When possible, he made camp under a large fir, rigging a tarp—just enough to keep the snow from piling up directly on him, and plenty cozy for a night's rest. The one thing about a blizzard is, if you know what you're doing, you'll never be cold. As soon as there was even a scratch of morning light, he'd be off again.

Then, there was the very best part. The wolves. Every night, they howled at him. And he howled back. He was home.

He took the name Moon Dog when he was in Special Forces. At the time, it was a name that sounded cool more than anything else—spooky and dangerous: a good guy who could also rip your throat out sort of thing. A radical shift from Oxford, which was as much his intention as any other. But then, he bunked next to Bat Man, an Apache, who would be Benny's best friend until Bat Man took a spear through the eye in Cambodia. It was Bat Man who told Benny that Benny hadn't chosen Moon Dog at all, the name had chosen him.

"At least that's what my grandma would tell you," Bat Man said. "She says we come into this world at a certain time and a certain place because we have certain lessons we need to learn. That's why we choose our tribe, our parents, our brothers, sisters, friends . . . all our surroundings. And when we're born, we arrive with a name given to us by the Great Spirit, only we don't know what the name is—we must discover it. Or, as my grandma says, we must be open so that the name will reveal itself. Our name is our teacher for this life, helping us to become who we really are. Moon Dog is your name. Now you must learn what it means."

"What's Bat Man all about?" Benny had asked.

"Rebirth," Bat Man said.

"Meaning?"

"When you're ready, white devil," was all the Apache said, smiling a small smile.

It wasn't until Benny had saved Bat Man's life that the Apache actually answered Benny.

"Most men join the Berets because they are scared to death of death, Moon Dog. They want to face what they are afraid of—losing themselves.

Now, most of them don't know this. They think they have no fear. That's why they run around snarling how tough they are, flashing their teeth. I don't do that, as you know. But what you don't know is why I don't. You see, I have already died. You might say I am death."

"You're running me in circles, you heathen savage," Benny told his friend. "Don't forget. I'm a Rhodes Scholar. You Apaches gotta make things simple for me."

"Moon Dog, man, I've been through a ceremony that would send most Green Berets crying to mama," Bat Man said. "Don't ask me about it. I can't reveal much. But I've been brought as close to death as you can get and still survive. I've been humiliated, demeaned, tortured, starved, forced to dig my own grave and been buried alive. I've had to give up every notion of personal identity. And when I did, I was reborn. What I experienced was no different than if I had died and come back a brand new baby. I just did it all in this body. I'm my grandma's grandson. Part Mayan. I'm a shaman. All shamans are reborn. That's why they know things. That's why I know that when you die, wolves will serenade your passage. It is a great blessing."

Wolves had been serenading Benny for years. It was one reason why the Alaskan wilderness was home. He'd known a pack to surround him in the night, coming just close enough that all you saw were three dozen eyes glowing in the firelight. At times they would hardly make a sound. Other times they'd howl for hours. He'd howl back. More than once he'd awakened in the night to find a wolf standing over to him, or sniffing his face, growling some sort of message. For whatever reasons, he had never known a moment's fear around them. He was sure that's why they didn't kill him. Somehow, he was one of them.

But he was still working on the meaning of his name.

Wolf has an enormous sense of family within their pack.

Benny had no family to speak of. He was an only child and both his parents had been assassinated by the same political group that had kidnapped him when he was five.

Wolf takes one mate for life and is loyal like Dog.

Benny'd never had a mate. A few girlfriends, a couple that might have gone someplace if things were different, if he were different. But calling to say, "Honey, hold dinner for six months, will you? I gotta run off and impersonate (or kill) two gentleman of Verona" was not a marriage, and he hadn't yet met the woman he would happily give that up for.

But loyalty. That he had in spades. "Till death do us part." Amen. Not that loyalty was free from complications. He really was like a dog. He'd served Charlie Fox long after he should have quit, or at least started asking better questions. Why hadn't he sniffed out the fiction Charlie was peddling about Hyman? Loyalty? The thrill of the game? Or was it that he, Moon Dog, had given up taking responsibility for some of the choices he was making? Sure, he didn't kill people anymore . . . if he could help it. But maybe that was just a lot of air itself. He may have crippled Hyman for life. For what? Because he listened to Charlie Fox rather than his own wolf medicine?

Wolf's senses are keen because Wolf lives within the vibration of the moon—the unconscious that holds the secrets of knowledge and wisdom.

Baying at the moon, Bat Man said, is an indication of Wolf's desire to connect with new ideas which are just below the surface of consciousness. Benny lived this desire. Yet, too often he ignored it.

Wolf is the pathfinder, the forerunner of new ideas who returns to the clan to teach.

Where he was right then, finding his way in the wilderness, was a metaphor for his life—for himself as Wolf. But where was *his* clan? Who did *he* return to? Who would *he* teach? What family would *he* strengthen?

The night fire was dying and the wolves had moved off when an explosion caused Benny to spring up to a seated position, and just as he began to grasp where the sound had come from, the ponderosa pine he was under, its stem at least three feet in diameter, dropped under the weight of a century of blizzards onto both of Benny's legs, crushing them, and pinning Benny for the three remaining days of his life.

Dear Hyman,

I promise to stop beating myself up for shooting you if you promise to stop feeling responsible for my untimely demise. I want you to burn this letter, and when you do I want you to burn any guilt with it.

I've always hoped I'd die alone, but I didn't know why until now—and now, the truth is, I've never been less alone.

I was kidnapped and held for six weeks when I was five. My parents were assassinated before I was 20. I've killed more people than I've made love to. My whole life I've wondered who my family was. Then I met you.

If I'm this connected to you, who am I not connected to—who is not my family? Charlie Fox? This bozo Puer Puella? (Tell him nice job, by the way.) The pope? My kidnappers? The assassins of my mother and father, and all those I've murdered and mutilated? All are me. As are the wolves who keep vigil as I die. I hope they eat me.

Some poet I read once said that wildness is the state of complete awareness. That's why we need it. My life, in all its turns, has been the search for that awareness. Yet, I've always wondered. Who do I give to? Who do I teach? What family do I nurture? How do I give myself away?

Now, here, with the wolves, the land, the winter, I know. I give myself to the earth—all I am to All That Is. There is no better place for me than right here, right now.

I do regret not sharing the wilderness with you . . . well, in this life.

It's a nice feeling to know we'll meet again.
Until then, I remain,
Your brother,
Benny

26

Pearl, Shorty, Charlie & Sex

earl had never before flown in a lavender, 50 passenger jet with (among other things) elk-skin Barcaloungers, a gigantic movie screen, and an "out-of-order" sauna full of stuffed animals—Carmella's personal taxi to destinations worldwide.

It surprised Pearl, at first, that Carmella would travel in such luxury, until she remembered what Carmella had said about the billion dollars she was giving Pearl. Wealth can be a distraction, if we let it. But then Pink, the pilot, a woman whose jumpsuit and Mohawk hair told you everything you needed to know about how she got her name, explained that the jet had been a gift that Carmella had wheedled out of an Arab sheik.

"Well, wheedled might be a bit strong," Pink said. "The sheik had flown in to where we're presently headed—that tiny airport overlooking the lake—to ask Carmella's help in something. They'd never met before. Carmella was there in her lavender limo to greet the sheik. And when Carmella sees his jet, the exact same shade as her limo, the very first thing she says to Omar the Oilman is, 'You must give me your plane,' and darned if the guy doesn't say, 'It's yours, sweet lady.' I thought Carmella was joking, but it turns out she'd had a vision: a lavender airplane rescuing abandoned orphans around the world.

"And for the most part," Pink said, "that's all this baby is used for."

Today was obviously an exception, since Pearl was the only passenger, traveling to her home from Manhattan. Though, come to think of it, after today, she might be an orphan herself . . . in her way. In fact, she really already was, regardless of whatever happened when she got off the plane.

It was Thursday, two days after the reunion with Hyman at the Dame Edna, and exactly seven days after first meeting him.

That meeting had taken place the previous Friday afternoon, when Hyman, walking along the road in front of Pearl's house, had stopped to watch her pitch. Their experience by the lake happened Saturday morning. Her mom's party was Saturday night. Hyman had been abducted shortly after midnight on Sunday morning. He was rescued early Tuesday. By noon Tuesday, Pearl and Puer were on their way to New York. Yesterday, Wednesday, her mom called to ask if Pearl could come home to meet with Uncle Charlie, who had ordered an investigation into Hyman's disappearance. At that news, Pearl had felt the air leave her body.

Puer had said just the right thing: "Breathe."

And then he said, "Try not to project. Don't plan. Just be present. Open your heart. Let it happen."

On the plane, a Vermont teddy bear in her lap along with her bottle of water, that was easy advice to follow, since the focus of seemingly every square centimeter of Pearl's body was sex.

Pearl had had a few sexual adventures, or "explorations" as she thought of them, but none had included traditional intercourse. Not that the boys she had been with complained. And it wasn't that she'd been especially wary of AIDS or other disease. She'd exchanged bodily fluids, as they say. But then, each of her two sexual partners had been her friend since childhood. Playing ball, jumping off cliffs, the school play, she'd even been sky-diving—there had always been a certain "I'll show you mine if you show me yours" quality to whatever they did. It had simply evolved into sex. It was exciting. And comforting, really, experimenting with guys you liked. There was a special tenderness she felt toward them, and expected to always feel. But there was, Pearl knew, a whole other Mt. Everest of intimacy awaiting her: giving herself completely to the love of her life, should she be so lucky to meet the man.

Her mother would tell her that she was about as naive as a young woman could be. Pearl couldn't deny it. To Pearl, the most sexually exciting union imaginable was for her and her beloved to commit their lives to one another and, through their marriage, to Spirit. She wasn't quite sure all the reasons why, but her technical virginity was a part of that commitment, as was trusting to Spirit whether their love-making created a child. This had nothing to do with beliefs about birth control. That should be a choice available to anyone. This was a matter of spiritual surrender. Granted, she might have second thoughts if she were pregnant 10 years running and didn't have a nickel to her name, and she sure wouldn't advocate her choice for anyone else, but for now, for her, it was right. Commitment-wise, it was the *Full Monty*. Even more so given what she'd experienced since meeting Hyman O'Malley.

Also naive, perhaps, was her sense that she would recognize "Soul Man" the second he walked in the door. Oh, hi. You're it. Given that she'd rather pump iron in a room full of jocks than go on a date, she also had been pretty sure that he wouldn't show until after college.

Had been.

But now here was the retired New Age Gangster himself, about whom she knew almost nothing except what she was terrified to admit.

They'd met what—five days ago?—and her mind was now off the charts gaba-gaba: Whoa. Slow down, girl. It's just hormones. What did you expect, he's beautiful, scar and all. But he's what, twice your age? For all you know he's got a girlfriend, maybe even a wife. Can you say "in-fat-u-ation"? He used to be your father, for God's sake. Wait till he finds out you murdered him. Get out your vibrator, then see how you feel . . . .

Right. Yes. Of course.

Except. There was last night.

It was their second night in separate bedrooms in Carmella's apartment. Pearl had nearly walked down the hall, shucked her T-shirt, climbed into his bed and said, "We're going to spend the rest of our lives together."

And the crazy thing was, she knew as well as she knew her own phone number that he would have replied with a tremor in that Stradivarius voice, "I know. I love you so much my bones hurt."

And in the morning they would finger-paint each other's faces with her blood and his semen, wondering whether, during the night, a soul looking for a wild and loving home had chosen them to be its next set of parents.

And when they (sheepishly) shared their news with Carmella, she would smile and say what Hyman would say, "If you're trying to surprise me, you're going to have to work harder."

"How's our Mister O'Malley?" Uncle Charlie asked.

They had just sat down around the kitchen table, an oval of oak, the place where most family business got discussed. On bitter winter mornings, the rose terra-cotta floor felt luxurious on Pearl's bare feet, thanks to the radiant heating system under the tiles. Forming a semi-circle around the table were a dozen large windows—spanning east, south and west: beginning with the hills to the east across the lake and the lake itself, a mile wide below them, then their own vineyards sweeping up from the lake to the county road in front of the house; and finally, on this side of the road, their large shady lawn rising past the house to the grassy plateau above, where Shorty's party had been. Pearl loved this room. You felt as though you were in nature, not hiding from it. A half-dozen large, well-tended ferns, each at the end of a thick green rope, hung from the vaulted oak ceiling. The table was plump enough for a dozen people, which meant that when there were only three of you, you could maintain a considerable physical distance from one another, if you wished. Her mom sat at 10 o'clock. Uncle Charlie at 1. Pearl at 5, the windows facing southeast to her back. Each person had a tall glass of water. There was nothing else on the table except for the Lazy Susan in the center, on which was a white starfish the size of Pearl's hand when she was 12.

Breathe.

"His spirits are fine," Pearl said, "but he could be walking with a cane for the rest of his life. It's a bit early to tell."

"What hospital is he in?" Shorty asked.

The fact that Pearl chose not to answer her mother went unnoticed as Uncle Charlie jumped in, "When your mother told me he'd been abducted right after her party, I thought it only right that we try to help . . . ."

"—Find out, you know, who and why," Shorty said. "Do you know who found him?"

Pearl's gaze was locked on the starfish.

"I must make a confession," she said.

Her mother and uncle glanced at one another. Neither said anything.

Pearl looked up. "I do know who rescued him," she said. "And I do know where he is. And I also know what happened to the people who kidnapped him. But I'm not prepared to tell you."

The only sound, drifting in through the open windows from a distance, was her dad mowing the ball field.

As if asking for the time, Uncle Charlie inquired, "Pearl, what are you talking about?"

"What is it you feel you know?" her mother added, a little more direct.

Pearl got up and turned to face the south, the late afternoon sun clearing her face. Her mom and Uncle Charlie had probably wanted her to sit between them. In important meetings, Shorty and Charlie calculated everything. Without even thinking about it, Pearl had finessed them. Now, as they spoke to her, the sun was in their eyes. It was more difficult for them to read her, whereas the light revealed to her every nuance of thought and emotion that crossed their faces. Not that she needed to see them to feel what they were feeling. In her uncle's world, where advantage was always a consideration, she had the power position at the table. This was crazy, she knew. The only so-called power she had over them was something that they wouldn't consider power at all: the peace of mind of speaking from her heart—of not calculating.

But in fact, she felt powerless.

What she was about to say would crush these two people she loved. To love so much, and to have everything out of your hands . . . .

Open your heart.

Pearl turned and sat back down. She turned and sat back down at the table where so much of her life had taken place. She turned and sat back down where she had played poker with princes and lobbed popcorn into the mouths of movie stars. She turned and sat back down at this place where she had eaten most of her meals since infancy—and without intending to, or even suspecting that it might happen, she opened a black hole that would become her mother's permanent retreat, and she ended her uncle's career as President of the United States.

"It breaks my heart to say this . . . ."

Breathe.

"I need to tell you both a number of things, so if you would, please don't interrupt me until I finish."

"Of course, sweetheart," assured Shorty.

Pearl took a sip of water.

"Uncle Charlie, I overheard the meeting you had with Hyman O'Malley last Saturday afternoon in the library. When you threatened to shoot him. And when you demanded that he give you another experience like the one you had earlier in the day with him.

"Right after that, I also overheard the conversation you had with mom about how Hyman was blackmailing you and you had to get him out of the picture. I heard your plans.

"And not only did I overhear those conversations, I tape recorded them. I didn't tape them in order to hurt you. I've been taping conversations for some time. In fact, I intend to give you all my tapes."

Pearl took a sip of water.

By the look on Uncle Charlie's face, you'd have thought she was talking about a no-hitter she'd just pitched. He was alert, interested, smiling.

"Last Saturday, Uncle Charlie, after your conversations with Hyman and with mom, I decided to tell you about my experience that morning with Hyman, about meeting myself in a former life as Bella-Viola Priami, and about poisoning my husband in that life, a man named Angelo Angelino. As you may recall, your reaction, when I told you this story, was soooo . . . I don't know what: fearful is the only word that comes close—you have never looked at me that way. It scared me. So I asked Hyman directly if you had been Angelo in that life. Normally, he would never reveal such a confidence, but because it was obvious that you were extremely afraid of Hyman for some reason, and were planning to hurt him, and now you were afraid of me, Hyman broke his rule and said yes—you and I, Uncle Charlie, were married in a life we shared 500 years ago. We were more than married, we were very much in love. That may explain a bit about why we're so close in this life."

"You know all this how?"

"Please, mom, don't interrupt. I know this sounds preposterous to you. But right now, you need to take your own advice. Facts are friendly. Wait until everything is out on the table before you start saying what is and isn't true.

"Thank you."

Breathe. Just let it happen.

Pearl took a sip of water.

"Please believe me when I say I don't want anything from you. I'm not trying to convince you of anything. I'm not trying to force you to do anything. I'm just sharing with you what my heart guides me to say.

"Uncle Charlie, I have no idea what else you may have experienced with Hyman O'Malley in the library. I just heard sounds. And I don't know what happened when you first met Hyman, either, over by the lake. What I do know is that on both occasions, you became more disturbed than I have ever seen you. And, obviously, whatever you experienced was big enough so that you made up the story about Hyman and Puer Puella blackmailing you. I was there when the two of you met at the lake. And I overheard your entire conversation in the library. On neither occasion did Hyman O'Malley threaten you in any way.

"I do know, however, from your conversation in the library, that a long time ago you had a relationship with a girl named Sylvie Marks—who she is, and what your relationship was, I have no idea, except that it seems very important to you, and I have come to learn that she once gave you a pair of socks that are either the ones you wear every year on mom's birthday, or are very much like them. Whether Sylvie Marks has anything to do with your attempt to hurt Hyman, I also don't know. And I don't need to know.

"I can't promise that I will never share what I've said here with another person, but I can say that I will never share it with anyone who would harm you. Whether you believe me or not is out of my hands.

"I love you both very much. You have always encouraged me to be true to myself. And now, because I love you, I cannot participate in any lies about Hyman O'Malley, Puer Puella or anyone else."

Pearl took another sip of water.

"That's all I have to say."

Her mother, in her turquoise T-shirt, was sitting up straight in her chair, her hands folded together on the table, her face unreadable to anyone but Pearl. She was in shock. It was the look she had on September 11, 2001.

And it was the look she had when the ambassador told her that his wife was having an affair with Pearl's father, Tommy.

Uncle Charlie, in his white shirt with the stars and stripes cufflinks and one of his "farmer bow ties"—green with white polka dot hay bales—got up, emptied his near full glass of water in the sink then refilled the glass from a bottle in the fridge.

Pearl's dad, by the sound of it, was weed whacking in the ditch by the road.

Pearl didn't recall what she had just said. Not exactly. But she felt that she had spoken with love as best she could. And now, she felt, directed at her in a form that she wouldn't have recognized a week ago, was a firestorm of fear under a mask of parental concern.

"Well," Uncle Charlie said, softly, smiling. "That's quite a story. It grieves me that you have been in such anguish. I don't know exactly what has happened to you in the past few days—since you met Mister O'Malley—but it certainly seems that something has changed the Pearl I know. I hope we can help you. I can't imagine a psychiatrist in the land who wouldn't find your tale a little peculiar. You tell me this long, convoluted story about us being married 500 years ago and you poisoning me, as well as killing your father and several of your brothers in that life, and then you think it's strange that I look at you in astonishment? It seems to me that it is you who are acting in a way that is totally out of character."

Uncle Charlie glanced at his sister to see if there was something she wanted to add. The fact that she didn't look at him, and was gazing out the window, told him to continue.

"I must say, Pearl, that you did make one comment that I thought was especially mature. And that is that you intend to hand over the tapes you made illegally. As you must realize, any private taping of the President of the United States is a matter of national security, and that any unauthorized taping is a violation of federal law with some pretty severe penalties. And just because you're my niece doesn't make you immune. Now, I have no doubt that you intended nothing malicious by your taping, but that is beside the point, as I'm sure you know. The fact that you willingly, deliberately did it demonstrates not only unfortunate judgment on your part, but also, inadvertently perhaps, makes me, your mother and father, you yourself—and the entire nation, for that matter—vulnerable.

Uncle Charlie removed from his shirt pocket his black Mont Blanc fountain pen and a white 3 X 5 card. He took the top off the pen and scratched a few words. He then put the top back on and laid the pen on top of the card on the table—squarely in front of him.

Looking at the card, Uncle Charlie said, "Pearl, you know that we live in the age when the eyes and ears of all sorts of people looking to further their ambitions are riveted on our family. It would take so little for someone to learn of these tapes."

He looked at her over his tortoise shell half-glasses. "Let me ask you, is there anyone at all, other than the three of us, who knows you have taped conversations of the President?"

Silently Pearl let out a long breath.

"No," she lied.

"Are you sure?"

"I'm sure."

"And yet . . . . You say that you might very well share with someone else the story you have just told your mother and me."

Uncle Charlie expected a response, Pearl knew. But she received no guidance to say anything, so said nothing.

Uncle Charlie was a master at what Vicky Ski called "unbloody interrogation." He never raised his voice. He never directly threatened. He didn't make things personal. He would always say that he knew your motives were honorable, but that circumstances beyond his control—national security, credibility, the good of the party, et cetera—obliged him to make certain choices. Sometimes those choices beyond his control included cutting your head off.

Uncle Charlie continued: "I appreciate that you would never reveal anything to anyone who would harm me. I'm sure you mean that. But you are also very smart. You know that someone's intentions do not guarantee security. If you were positive that your mother and Tommy would be murdered unless you handed over your tapes, your good intentions might be severely challenged, wouldn't you say?—as anyone's might. History is full of examples to prove that the greater the number of people who share a confidence, no matter who those people are, the greater the chance that that confidence will eventually be revealed. It doesn't matter what's on those tapes. All that matters is that they were made."

Uncle Charlie picked up his pen and held it between the fingertips of both hands, staring at it.

"The question here, Pearl, isn't whether you will be prosecuted, because of course you won't."

Carefully, precisely, he put the pen back on the card, then looked at her. A flash of insight, not unlike meeting Carmella as Bishnu: Pearl saw her uncle, as a young man, practicing these moves in front of a mirror.

"The question is actually a much bigger one," Uncle Charlie said. "How do we, as a family, move forward? What do we do, now that you have demonstrated a willingness to make choices that put us all, as well as the nation, in jeopardy?"

He said it so informally, with such apparent warmth. Yet, underneath, was the quick razor across the heart: he was telling her that she was responsible for her family's happiness and security.

Again, he was inviting her response, and again she had none.

"He's so cool he doesn't have to bludgeon you," Vicki Ski had said during one of their sisterly gabs. "Once he draws blood, just a drop—oh, you're letting down the nation, and because of that you're disappointing me—he'll all of a sudden move on to something that appears to be almost an afterthought, something of only passing interest. It's smoke," said Vicky Ski. "That seemingly frivolous question he asks after he's intimated what a shit you are is what he really wants to know."

"How did you manage to tape these conversations?" Uncle Charlie spoke casually as though he were asking where she'd put the day's newspaper.

And so she explained. The vent. Curiosity. Learning. She went through the entire list of conversations overheard and conversations recorded. She didn't leave out a thing.

This was, she observed in Uncle Charlie's face, the worst possible news—much worse than finding out that he and she had been sweethearts in a former life. That he could dismiss. But knowing that so much of his life had been revealed to another person, even Pearl, without his knowledge—and not only revealed, but taped, so that denial was all but impossible—caused Uncle Charlie's pallor to resemble . . . O man, what was the matter with her? She couldn't help a small smile—A seasick crocodile.

She'd seen "How the Grinch Stole Christmas" four million times.

"Pearl!" her mother almost shouted, as if Pearl were about to eat a live rat. "What are you doing?"

Pearl looked at her mother. "Mother . . ."

She started to say more, but realized she would have been arguing, reacting, so she said nothing and opened to the fear and let it move through her.

Her mother spoke instead.

Her mother hadn't listened. Couldn't listen.

"Mister O'Malley has threatened your uncle in the name of Puer Puella, who, as you know, is a crackpot with a history of trying to destroy the President. I say threatened, but it is much more than that. Puella and O'Malley are, for some sick reason, attempting to blackmail your uncle: either he resigns by Christmas or they will make public something your uncle is supposed to have done 20 years ago. Honey, these are not the ravings of some schizophrenic off his medicine. Puer Puella is one of the most influential people in the U.S. In fact, he might be the only person in the nation who can make up fanciful stories about anything he pleases and be believed by a good number of people. A person like him, who admits he's a fool, and admits he makes up things, still has credibility because allegedly—no, not allegedly; he really has done right by a lot of people. There's no telling the kind of damage he can do. And what he wants is for your uncle to take the story of Puella's threat public: perhaps to have Puella arrested and charged with threatening the President. That would give Puella just the platform he wants.

"Yes, you're right. You did hear us talking about removing Mister O'Malley from the picture. But I'm sure you will recall, we did not speak about hurting Mister O'Malley in any way. We had no idea he was going to be shot. Our goal was simply to put a little pressure on Puella to reconsider, to let him know that the President of the United States is the wrong person to threaten. I personally have nothing against Mister O'Malley. My feeling is he's being used by Puella. We know that he and Puella are friends. I'm sure O'Malley believes whatever Puella tells him.

"Now, let me say one further thing so that you have the full picture here. We know for a fact that Puer Puella staged the rescue of his friend, O'Malley. I'm sorry we lied to you, and in a way asked you to come home under false pretenses. I just didn't want to involve you in this sordid mess. But now, we know, Puella has broken the law by kidnapping the people who were holding Mister O'Malley in a safe house. We must free those people."

Uncle Charlie has lied to my mother. Whatever Hyman means to Uncle Charlie, it is so terrifying that he willing to lie to the only person in the world who is unquestionably loyal to him.

"I know that you think highly of Mister O'Malley," Shorty continued. "And I know that you have just become friends with Puella's sister. But what is going on here is something much bigger than your infatuation with a couple of nice people."

At this, Uncle Charlie leaned forward. "What we need to know from you, sweetheart, is anything you can tell us that will help us ensure the safety of Benny Apple and his colleagues."

Except for when she found her father naked with a model in his studio, the model and her dad too consumed to be aware of her discovery, Pearl had never felt so sad. And, in truth, by comparison, that was nothing to what she felt now at the kitchen table, the setting sun illuminating the scene in front of her with a honey gel: key lighting the masks of these two people she loved so dearly and now knew so differently.

Was it merely serendipity that this encounter should take place today? Exactly one week earlier was the last full day of their old life, the day before Hyman walked on the scene.

Since then, she had died, and a new Pearl had been born, or was being born. She looked the same. But inside, her family might never know of her real change, although they were sure getting a glimpse of it today. She could never have spoken to her mother and uncle in this way a week earlier.

Her mother, Pearl was quite sure, would hope that Pearl was going through some teenage insanity—so uncharacteristic of Pearl but probably inevitable.

"Every teen has got to crash and burn at least once," her mother might say. Would it be so strange for Pearl to be momentarily seduced by a Svengali, or to become a Carmella groupie?

"The girl's in college, what do you expect?" her mother might say, crossing her fingers like most parents that it wasn't more than that.

Pearl couldn't even imagine how her family would react if Puer were her lover. Except her father. She'd once overheard him say to a friend (out of her mother's hearing) that Puer Puella was one of the great performance artists of the 21st century. "Of course," her father had joked, "the century is reasonably young."

They were both lying, her mother and her uncle. Her mother lied about not knowing that Hyman would be shot. She may not have known it technically, but she knew the plan included turning Hyman into a drug addict. Other than that, Pearl knew that her mother was speaking the truth as she understood it.

Her uncle, however, was lying in every direction . . . to the point, most drastically, of lying to his sister.

Feel the pain and unforgiveness you still carry for when you have betrayed. Feel how you and Uncle Charlie are one. Feel how you and your mother are one. Join. Let go. Forgive.

Vicky Ski called them the Siamese Twins, and so did most of Washington. When it came to politics, talking to one was the same as talking to the other. That was their strength. They shared everything with each other. He was President because they were a team. And now, Uncle Charlie had used his sister's unwavering belief that he would always tell her the truth to gain her unwitting collusion on this one matter, the one thing about which, for whatever reasons, he felt he could not come clean. He had probably used Benny Apple in the same way.

What is it that could be so frightening? And just as fast as that thought appeared, Pearl heard the voice of Hyman, "If you knew, would it bring love more alive in your heart?"

Obviously not.

Breathe.

Whatever it was, the bond between her mother and her uncle was now breeched. Her mom might not learn the facts, but somewhere in her she already knew the truth.

Energy doesn't lie.

Another truth: Shorty and Charlie had deliberately attempted to destroy Hyman. Not murder, maybe, but that was a technicality. Pearl had always been proud of the fact that she pitched the way her mom played politics. No prisoners. Pearl had humiliated the best hitter in the nation last spring. Four consecutive strikeouts. Secretly, it was the highlight of Pearl's season. But this was different: her mother and uncle were doing something unethical, illegal. Could it be that this wasn't new—that it was only new to her, that they had always done whatever it took to win—that they had always lied to her when necessary?

Join. Let go. Forgive.

Uncle Charlie was right. How *did* they move forward as a family? Everything was different.

Her commitment was to love. Nothing else. Pearl would do all she could to protect Hyman, Puer and Carmella from the craziness of Uncle Charlie. But she would also do all she could to protect her mother and uncle from self-destruction. Not that she was responsible for protecting anybody. She didn't feel that. But what do you do? Here were two people on fire. Any desire she may have had about bringing the "true facts" into the light disappeared. All she wanted to do, or knew to do, was love these people.

"What I can tell you is this," Pearl finally said. "The people who abducted Hyman were themselves abducted and taken to a safe house. How I know this, or who was involved in Hyman's rescue, or where Hyman is at this time, I will not say. It simply doesn't matter. All that matters is that Hyman is free and the kidnappers have not been harmed; and soon they will be free, as well."

Pearl let out a long breath.

"Uncle Charlie, I hope that you will accept the tapes as a symbol that I would never intentionally put you at risk."

The President took a long time to answer. "I want to believe you, Pearl," he said, "but, sweetheart, how can I?"

The answer was, of course, "You probably can't," which Pearl said. But as her lips came together to also explain why, Pearl was inspired to keep them pursed until the urge to speak left her. For what she was about to say was, "People who don't trust themselves can never trust anyone else."

Instead, she said, "I think I'd like to stay at Carmella's until I go back to school."

Initially, Pearl stayed away because her presence, she felt, would remind her mom and uncle of the lie between them. Her love, therefore, might best be offered in the form of distance. But then, very quickly, life just happened. When she wasn't at college she was with Puer or Carmella, or both. Pearl didn't sleep at her parents' home ever again.

27

Hyman's Journal:
The Making of St. Porcine

*A man does not have to be an angel
in order to be a saint.* —Albert Schweitzer

It is fitting that my name in that life was Abraham. It has a rather kingly ring, and I was nothing if not regal. I was the abbot. I ran a monastery. My wavy hair was bleached and trained to resemble rays of the sun haloing my face. I was the benevolent shepherd, God's perfection my only desire. Perfect beauty. Perfect humility. Perfect harmony. And because righteousness was my middle name, I was not above murder to achieve my ends.

I've seen only a handful of movies. One of them, "Saving Private Ryan," contains a scene where a German soldier and an American soldier are fighting to the death, hand-to-hand. They're in a small room, a bedroom maybe, on an upper floor of a mostly bombed-out apartment building. The German has a knife and, after a protracted clash of men doing everything they know how to stay alive, the German (a few more incarnations as a warrior under his belt) is able to insert the tip of his knife at the American's solar plexus and slowly, against the American's great resistance of the impending reality, push the blade upward into the American's heart. In that final struggle, the German lay atop the American like a lover, their breaths entwined as well as their bodies. That sense of intimacy, tenderness even, yet ultimate dominance

395

by the more seasoned man, was one of the threads of my relationship with the monks I led.

My right hand in that life was a young monk I shall name Brother Moon, since I shaped him to be a reflection of me, or at least the reflection that suited my ends. He took over as abbot upon my death, permitting me to rule from the grave.

How unremarkable this story is—fear preferred to love.

Certain spiritual practices result in a greater than everyday ability to manipulate the physical universe. My best trick was offering you a bowl of fruit that, no matter how much of it you ate, always remained full. My faculties, exhibited judiciously, inspired awe far beyond our cloister walls. Many considered me a saint, or something close. They failed to realize that flashy powers and knowing God are two completely different things.

It is comical in hindsight. I worked for years developing the ability to create fruit at will, ignoring the fact that, thanks to the heavenly grocer, it would have taken a lot less energy to simply go to the market.

A young boy came to our abbey. Let's call him William, as in conqueror. He might have been 10, at most 13. He knew God. I should have been touching his feet, so pure in spirit was even the way he wiped his nose.

A quivering dog in a lightning storm, that was me in the face of all I would need to relinquish in order to know the Divine as William did. And much worse, my disciples would realize just how un-saintly I was.

Ah, but still, I was Abraham. I would never toss a supplicant into the street. Instead, I created the circumstances in which William would choose to leave on his own or (like many before him, though none so innocent) be destroyed.

It was neither difficult nor obvious. In my monastery there was a right way to do everything. Rules were clear, enforcement strict. William couldn't be bothered. He didn't dismiss rules; he just never considered them. It was like teaching a chicken to bake a cake. Maybe harder. But there were no exceptions to my commandments, and so William was in a state of continual reprimand, each one a little more fierce than the last.

He didn't mind. He was a boy who, if you told him he was so useless that it would take him a million years to know God, would dance with joy that, tomorrow, he would be one day closer.

William wasn't the first to be banished to the outdoors in winter, but he was the first who chose to live on his knees at the ocean's edge. He died an ice sculpture. A praying angel.

On the day he was buried, William's spirit appeared to me, thanking me for giving him so many opportunities to surrender himself to God. Without me, he said, he might not have experienced the sacred presence in this lifetime, and that I, therefore, was a great soul. He said that he would do whatever he could to inflame hearts everywhere to seek God through me.

I whimpered, silently.

That night, lit by stars on snow, my protégé Brother Moon and I dug up William's casket, hacked his corpse into small pieces, and fed the morsels to our pigs: an Inquisitional ritual of ultimate revilement—casting a soul into a thousand year wasteland devoid of contact with beings in any form. My spin to Brother Moon was that William had always been possessed, and that I had kept him with us in the prayer that God's grace would work a miracle. But alas . . . . That was why William was unable to follow even the simplest direction. And why the devil had been able to seduce William into believing that winter was summer.

How easy it is to lie when one lives with internal panic and the awe of those around him.

But William's spirit transcended ceremony. Again he appeared, prostrate, thanking me over and over, saying how I had helped him give up his last remaining attachment to himself as a physical being. And again he said I was a great soul, and again he said that seekers for generations to come would be drawn to God through me.

I shared none of this with Brother Moon, to be sure.

I had a nightmare. My monks ate the pigs. The spirit of William entered them. Infused with the Divine, not one revered me anymore. So I ordered the pigs sold to an itinerant butcher whose route wouldn't bring him within a league of my monastery for many months.

The visits from William stopped. We bought new piglets. Life returned to normal.

Until, that is, a breeze started to blow that miracles were occurring throughout the land. Blindness, palsy, hunchback, infertility . . . . Cured.

Such things happened on occasion. Always they were investigated, and almost always were found to be the work of the devil. Anything the church couldn't take credit for, it condemned. Execution by fire was the most painless penalty. As expected, Lord Poobah (we'll call him), master of the realm, ordered an inquiry and, also as expected, enlisted the most revered person in the land to supervise it: moi.

Naturally, each miracle recipient had eaten bacon or chops, hocks or a pickled foot procured from one itinerant butcher.

"But Abbot, what will you tell Lord Poobah?" Brother Moon asked, fearing what might be revealed about the diet of these miraculous porkers.

Foolish boy.

"I shall tell him the truth, my son. Those pigs came from our cloister. Everything else is irrelevant."

And so, by murdering and defiling the saintliest person I had ever met, and lying about it, I became even more venerated, just as William had predicted. And the more venerated I became, and the more the number of postulants joining our brotherhood grew, the more I quivered in my private moments. My fear wasn't that the truth about William would be revealed. It was that the truth about me would be revealed—my addiction to being thought of as holy.

My powers allowed me to contract pneumonia the following winter, and after I died my monks and other believers pestered Rome for my beatification as the saint who used the common pig to work miracles—as I, of course, knew they would.

It is amusing and painful to imagine myself as St. Porcine. For centuries butchers and pig farmers praying to me, yet here I am still forgiving myself for the devastation I created in fear all those lifetimes ago. I have a lot of empathy for tyrants, from turf-hording bureaucrats, to wife beaters, to genocidal maniacs bent on destroying an entire people. I've been given the questionable gift of appreciating in ways that span incarnations that, when we live in fear, all bets are off—harm is the only sure thing.

William visits from time to time. Still supporting me how many incarnations later.

Usually we simply embrace in the sanctuary of the unconditional, but there are occasions when I might be taking myself a tad too seriously, at which he is not above bringing me to my senses by asking, "Care for a ham sandwich, Abe?"

One time he tisk'd: "Oh, you poor boy. You have nobody to kill this time around but yourself."

I knew his meaning: dying to life through forgiveness.

28

Kisses

Dear Benny,

Viewed from an airplane over the Alaskan winter, there are times when a pack of wolves camping around a fallen fir stands out almost as much as a pair of plaid boxer shorts the size Dodger Stadium.

Sorry to report, the wolves didn't eat you. They had a more pressing agenda: standing sentinel over their departed brother. I envied them.

You ask a lot when you ask that I give up feeling responsible, even obliquely, for your sudden departure. But you ask no more than the Great Ones do every minute: Forgiveness. And not forgiveness of someone else, but forgiveness of ourselves—myself. I have friends who say that forgiveness is the essence of love, for only with forgiveness do we grow in our ability to live from our sacred center, our inner heart, that place where we experience the One Of All That Is.

But forgiveness, as you know by now I'm sure, isn't an idea, a concept. It requires feeling the fear and pain associated with our choices that harmed, whether from this life or some other—choices for which we still hold ourselves accountable.

So your request, whether you knew it or not, goes to the very nub of the many times we have harmed one another. The pain of it you are well aware of, if for no other reason than it is comparable to the pain of not seeing one another again in this life—of not being able to celebrate on this physical plane the sacred teacher we have been for each other for incarnations.

I am grateful for the reminder to free anything that might lead me to harm you—us—again.

Your will requests that your ashes be scattered in the farthest reaches of the Alaskan wilderness. I hadn't known you considered it your home. I'm glad you got to die there.

You'll appreciate this: I've "appropriated" (as in stole) a bit of your cremated remains, and, when the time comes, I intend to have them mixed with some of my own ashes, as well as the ashes of your note to me and this one to you, and have us sprinkled over your home together.

May we forever help one another step ever deeper into the wilderness of Spirit.

Your brother,

Hyman

*T*hree weeks after Pearl's meeting with her mother and Uncle Charlie, mid-September, Hyman lay in a hammock on Carmella's veranda, sleeping the sleep of the dead under a down comforter, his journal held to his chest. His T-shirt was baby blue and read: *We can never meet the same person twice.* The day before, he had received Benny's letter, less than 24 hours after Benny's body had been found by the transvestite commandos. The commandos had video recorded everything, so Hyman had seen for himself the circle of wolves honoring his friend, his brother. Hyman had spent the entire previous night on the dock, alone, crutches at his side, occasionally howling at the waning moon. Now exhausted, he napped in the breath of the Earth Mother: an almost imperceptible breeze that had dried the tears of a million mourners on its way to consoling him.

*P*earl had postponed returning to Stanford until the search for Benny Apple was resolved. She would now be leaving in the morning.

She and Puer sat at the end of the dock, their feet in the water. The day, which started cool, had warmed up. Pearl wore white shorts and a plain white T-shirt, a white rose snugged into her hair at the top of her spine where her braid began, complements of Carmella, who brushed Pearl's hair every day.

Until Benny was found, Pearl had chosen not to open the door of past lives with Puer. For most of this day, however, the two had been sharing with one another all they knew about their former selves as Bella-Viola and Domenico Priami, and where Charlie Fox, the former Angelo Angelino, fit in.

Pearl experienced fresh dimensions of pain. She felt ever more deeply Bella-Viola's losses—and now, to be sure, her own losses as Pearl in this life, particularly of her mother and uncle. And beyond that was the pain of her connection to the deaths of Benny and his colleagues, the pain of her connection to Hyman's losses at the death of his former brother, and the pain of feeling Puer's anguish at his participation in the deaths of the Chillers.

Her dad, slightly drunk, had said, "Your mom told me the story, Pearl. I'm sure there's your version. Tell me if you want. Just remember, I love you no matter what the hell is going on." It was rather comforting, actually. She had asked her dad to take her to the airport tomorrow.

For Puer, the pain of his role in the deaths of the Chillers, and the pain of his friend Hyman, was similar to looking at his face for the first time after he'd accidentally run into the grappling hook and slashed himself from lip to ear. The scar, less than a year old, was still raw. Puer also wept as he felt in new and deeper ways the consequences of the choice he had made 500 years earlier as 10-year-old Domenico Priami.

"Guess that's what Hyman's T-shirt today reminds us," he said to Pearl. "We're always new, always changing, so we forever feel our experiences, our former lives, differently, more completely I suppose, if we're lucky."

"With more compassion, maybe," Pearl said. "It's strange, but there's a lightness I've never known before—from feeling and letting go of sorrow for events of lifetimes ago."

It was not uncommon for the lake to be glass in mid-September, even in the afternoon. The myth was that once the summer residents departed, the lake gave itself back to the natives.

"I appreciate why Double M says don't get infatuated with your past," Puer said, his bare feet swishing the water, his forest green hiking pants rolled up to his knees, his yellow T-shirt untucked. "Can you imagine meeting, not only yourself in a whole bunch of other incarnations, but then also knowing how everyone you know in this life was connected to you previously—not just in one life, but in several . . . many . . . maybe lots?"

Pearl smiled. She was remembering the movie "Home for the Holidays" and thinking of all the stories she had heard from friends about family gatherings. "Imagine the soap opera of Thanksgiving dinner," she laughed.

"The 600 faces of Me," Puer said, "and the 600 faces of all my lovely crackpot relatives."

"What a novel," Pearl smiled.

"Yeah," Puer said, "but saints, I'll bet, see right through a person's incarnation wardrobe."

"Mmmm," said Pearl. "That's what you and I are trying to do, isn't it?" She glanced at Puer, who was already looking at her. "I mean, I don't think of you as Domenico, which helps me to not think of you as Puer, either. I see you pretty much as a soul. And my desire is to experience you completely as a soul."

Pearl made a fist and touched the end of Puer's chin with it. "Of course, you make it easy to see you as just a soul, mister. Who can keep track of all your worldly personalities? One minute you're GQ Joe, next you're Bozo the Clown."

At that, Puer put his arm around Pearl's shoulder and said, "May I entertain you all the days of my life," then leaned over and kissed her, for the very first time, gently on the cheek.

Pearl brought up her hand and held Puer's head to her cheek. They sat like that, cheek to cheek, for a long while, their eyes closed—the first time in well over five centuries, and maybe, really, ever, that Bella-Viola and her father had embraced. It was an embrace of gratitude, an embrace of acceptance, an embrace of forgiveness . . . an embrace of farewell.

Pearl lowered her hand. She and Puer looked at one another. Pearl then placed her hand on his scar and kissed Puer, not Domenico, a whisper on the lips, a butterfly alighting, resting in the warmth, then ever so slowly taking flight again.

Again they looked into one another's eyes, then touched their foreheads together, after which Pearl took Puer's hand, drew it to her mouth, and kissed it ever so briefly with the tip of her tongue. Pearl got up. Puer brought his feet out of the water and rose as well. For several minutes they stood together, holding hands, facing the lake, facing west, the direction of surrender, rooted as if their feet sunk miles into the earth. Then they turned to walk back down the dock toward shore. But before they had taken a step Pearl lifted Puer's hand to her cheek, then, in a move that raised the heart rates of Olympic judges not even born yet, executed a perfect slow-motion backflip into the lake, pulling the love of her life in on top of her.

When they came up for air, laughing, Puer sputtered, "Do you know the story of Sylvie Marks?"

"Not really," said Pearl. "You know Hyman. Why? Do you know the story?"

They were treading water.

"I don't know what went on with her and your uncle other than the socks. But I do know that she apparently died after doing a back flip off the stern of a ship. And I know she was dressed all in white, and had a white rose in her hair."

"No lie," Pearl squealed. "That was three years before I was born!"

They reached the dock's ladder, which they held onto while remaining submerged from the neck down.

Pearl shot a stream of water through her two front teeth, washing Puer's face. "What are you saying?" she sputtered, "that I'm Sylvie Marks?"

"I'm not saying anything," Puer said, spraying a mouthful of lake into the sky so that it rained on Pearl's head. "I'm just talking. Maybe you're Sylvie. Maybe her spirit is having fun with you. Maybe life is just full of beautiful coincidences. Beats me. I know one of these days I'd like to introduce you to Sylvie's dad. Other than that, I don't know nuthin'."

"You know we're going to spend the rest of our lives together," Pearl said.

Puer was very quiet, looking at her intently.

Pearl had to breathe. She heard him saying that this wasn't possible, that he was nearly old enough to be her father, that he had a girlfriend, that he was gay, that he had no intention of ever being married, that Carmella was in love with Pearl and that he would never do anything to hurt Carmella, that Pearl was too young to make such a commitment . . .

But this was just fear, and Pearl let it wash into the lake.

"I know," Puer said. "I love you so much my bones hurt."

29

Epilogue:
Ten Years Later

Earth to Hyman:

Do you remember saying to me "Pearl, 10 years from now, would you write me a letter and tell me what you've learned?" Well, today's the day, Mr. O'M. So grab a chair. Get comfy. And no whining when you start wishing you had asked for a postcard.

(But before we begin, there is the teensy matter of your promise. You swore and hoped to die that, when you received this letter, you would come from wherever you are to wherever I am so that we might hang. How considerate of Divine Mother way back then to tell me to twist your arm in that direction. Your global gallivanting has kept us apart far too much. I love our phone chats, and our occasional rendezvous in foreign ports (particularly the exotic ones like Fargo and Ashtabula), but what I want, really, is extended face time. So with this epistle finally in your hand, I shall anticipate that you'll be making immediate travel arrangements to the *Island of Peace*. Certainly so you'll be here for the birth of our babies.)

I'm sure I could ramble here for days, and probably will, and a lot of it you've heard before (and anyway, you're the guy who told me news doesn't mean new), but I can give you the brush of what I've learned in the past decade—easy.

Having an "illuminating" experience may transform a person's life on one level, but it sure doesn't mean that all her habits, addictions, preferences, beliefs, et cetera, et cetera, suddenly disappear. It's not like she's been zapped by a magic twanger, froggy, that makes pain and fear vanish. To me, enlightenment is less of a destination and more of a practice. Kind of like great hitting, I suppose. The so-called "enlightened person" is merely someone whose on-base percentage is in the All-Star range and growing when it comes to the practice of living in conscious attunement with the One.

Next, I've learned that changing myself is not the goal; loving myself is—completely, as is. Throwing a party whenever fear drops by is up there on my "A" list.

And finally (because who can remember more than three things), I've learned that, when we really feel/experience/understand/get/realize who we all are—beings of endless, ever-new love (or as your Swami says, ". . . a tiny bubble of laughter in the Sea of Mirth . . .")—dealing with Zorba's "full catastrophe" is not necessarily a piece-o-cake, but it does begin to include a generous dusting of grace. I see "whatever" for what it is: something that needs attention in order for me to grow in love. Along the way, all the heretofore nasty beasts, while they're still alive and growling, become more and more my friends.

Re-reading these paragraphs I appreciate how empty they remain. How could you possibly infer from them those events and revelations during the past decade—heck, during the past few hours—that have brought me to my knees? For example:

- The discovery that Uncle Charlie is actually my biological father.
- Being the target of certain political/religious groups who have sworn to kill me.
- Knowing that each of the three babies in my belly left their previous life on September 11, 2001 in the terrorist destruction of the World Trade Center.

- Puer's devastation at the death of Clyde Marks.

And these are just four.

You'll recall I never did meet Clyde. As you also know, Clyde had prostate cancer. But what you may not be aware of is the last email he wrote to Puer.

Here's a portion:

I had it before we met, evidently. (I'm sure you recall how often I peed.) By the time I got it looked at, it had spread. I wasn't willing to get off the boat, and besides all the possible treatments were gruesome and couldn't even begin to guarantee results. And as you know, in my book, longevity is overrated.

Then, after Arjay's depression got the best of him and he hung himself, I just wanted to be close to Sylvie and Queenan. And now I will. Minutes after I send this to you, the Queen & Sylvie will be scuttled, me behind the wheel, a Monte Cristo clinched between my remaining teeth; the hatches have been open long enough for the sea to be lapping my belt buckle as I type these words. I know you'll be heartsick. I am heartsick leaving you. You may even write me snotty letters and toss them in the drink, figuring somehow they'll get delivered. Fine. May it be so. But I also know you'll understand. I'm not depressed. I'm dying. All the medical whiz kids in the world couldn't keep me alive another three months.

Before we met, you asked if you, your sweet dad, and I were kindred souls—people with a passion for life's possibilities—doing what we damn well pleased. I think we have answered that question, you and I. I love you in ways I never dreamed were possible. I can't imagine your dad would mind if I call you my son. Never have I been happier than when you look at me as both your father and your friend. So I know you will understand why my last grand adventure must be to feel as deeply as I can the level of surrender and trust that Sylvie felt as she leapt into the sea.

Of course Puer understood. But he loved Clyde Marks in ways even I cannot imagine, and Puer loves me like a sailor loves the wind. To have his friend just disappear, boat and all, while fitting, has been a tremendous loss for P. He's never said so, but I know he wishes that when he looks out over the lake at the *Island of Peace,* he could see Clyde's boat moored at a buoy off the dock. Puer likes mementos. To have no reminder of his friend, not even his ratty clothes or his Filson cap, is a very big loss for P; in a way, even bigger than the loss of Clyde himself. Puer once asked me to give him the lipstick I was wearing the first time we kissed. You know, the tube? I've seen him open it from time to time and smell it. I've also watched him paint my breasts with it on the anniversary of that kiss . . . but that, as you might say, is another story.

I needn't say much about the Charlie situation since you're intimately aware of my journey with it, but I will say one thing. I am actually rather glad that neither my mother nor uncle knows of my discovery, and possibly never will. For one thing, we have enough stuff keeping us apart. Me presenting this to them wouldn't make their lives, or mine, more whole. For another, daddy doesn't know, and, as far as I'm concerned, should never know. But beyond that, the truth of it is mine to deal with. My feeling of betrayal, connecting me to times when I have betrayed. My feeling of being a tainted child of incest, connecting me to my beliefs about what's pure and what's not. The mirrors of how I have deceived to satisfy my small self.

And at the same time I feel their love, mom's and Charlie's, a love that transcends their fear of intimacy with anyone but one another. Man, I'd like to be a fly on the wall of their past lives together. I'm sure it would be just as juicy as Puer and me. I know, I know. It doesn't matter. But you gotta admit, it would probably make a heck of a movie.

The pain of my loss of Charlie is particularly fresh since, this morning, unannounced, I popped in to surprise my mom and wish her Happy Birthday (I'm writing you from the *Island of Peace* where Mel and I are recuperating after putting the finishing touches on her latest book, which Puer wanted to title *What If The Hokey-Pokey Is What It's All About?*) and there playing the piano in his blue and gold socks was my uncle. It was the first time I'd seen him since I learned of our biological relationship two years ago.

In fact, it was only our third meeting since the day after your rescue. The first, you may recall, was Benny Apple's memorial. (I was sorry you weren't well enough to get up and say a few words, did I tell you that?—*The Love Story of Mirror Man & Mr. Apple*) The next time was nearly eight years later, which would make it two years ago at mom's 50th birthday party (the day after which, in the attic, exploring an old trunk full of Charlie's memorabilia, I accidentally discovered the plain #10 envelope with *Charlie* written on the front in my mother's handwriting. Inside was the lab report, on which Mom had written, "Charlie, we have our child. Pearl is not Tommy's. All my love, S."). The party was a surprise thrown by daddy. Mom would have probably skipped the country if she had known it was coming . . . so has she changed since the birthday party you were part of. I grew up a lot that night. Hugging Charlie this morning was like hugging a telephone pole. He has convinced himself that I betrayed him. I get that. I also get that him being my father, and the secret he carries about it, must make this whole business with me unbearably Kafkaesque. Is that the right term?

You know of course that, until my alleged betrayal, Charlie and I talked regularly. He'd been known to interrupted Cabinet meetings long enough to say he loved me. And I'd travel with him a few times a year and attend occasional shindigs at the White House or the Kennedy Center or wherever. I was the closest thing to "children" that a bachelor President could have . . . until his scheme to destroy you blew up in his face. Now, you know, we don't ever talk. So you can be sure he wouldn't have been there this morning if he'd known I might drop in. The only contact he initiates is sending me a present each birthday. Last year, it was a ten foot brass Buddha from Thailand that now sits in its own gazebo on Carmella's dock. These gestures are ways he denies the distance between us. They are also how he expresses his love—a love that is beyond anything he can ever reveal. Crazy as it sounds, I'm quite sure that one major reason Charlie chose not to run for reelection was so he could stop including me (and my mom, really) in his life without it looking too obvious. You understand, don't you? To Charlie, I am the symbol of all he is trying to deny. I am a link to you, to Sylvie Marks, to Puer, to himself as Angelo, to his betrayal of my mother, and of course his betrayal of me, really, by being my secret biological father. I am a symbol of many choices he has made in fear, not the least of them resulting in the death of his friend, Benny—the second death of a loved one he played a role in (in this incarnation), the first being Sylvie's, though what exactly his role was in her death only you and he know for sure.

[I'm cooked. They say in that famous book, *How to Write a Letter*, that when your tears fill a water glass, it's time to say "mañana."]

Next Day: The anniversary of your abduction:

I beg your pardon if it seems like I'm covering some old ground, but I've not put much of this in writing before.

Even if Benny and his pals had come home without a scratch, my uncle's political life was irrevocably altered—not because he had broken the law, or that you and Benny had discovered your bond over many lives, but because he had betrayed his sister, his closest friend and confidant, and the person with whom he shared what is indeed his biggest secret. I sometimes wonder if, for my mom, finding out the origin of the socks wasn't the equivalent of discovering that your one true love has had a mistress for the past 20 years.

After that meeting between Shorty, Charlie and me, it was inevitable that, sooner or later, mom would realize the truth, and for each of them it would mean a breech in their relationship that might never be put right, since neither is yet able to acknowledge what they are really feeling. The path of least resistance for my uncle, therefore, would have been to create an artificial distance between him and my mother—as he has with me. I'm not convinced that resigning was always the only solution he considered, but once the bodies of Benny and his cohorts were found, you could feel Charlie's fear go through the roof. And I'm sure things turned even more surreal for him when it became apparent that Puer and I were together. Even today, I shake my head at how fast things happened, including Charlie's announcement not to seek reelection. The fact that it occurred before Christmas was just too eerily ironic, since you'll recall that was the deadline he told Shorty you had threatened him with.

As if anyone needed proof that the world can be weirder than we can ever imagine, the word on the street is that, eventually, Charlie and Carmella may both be contenders for the Nobel Peace Prize one of these years.

There is a part of me that would love to see Charlie win it. Carmella would be more excited by a World Series game if her beloved Bombers were playing. Oh, she'd use the recognition to serve humankind, blah-blah-blah, but you can say that about any event in her life. It's all the same to her. She knows who's in charge and, as she says, "Thank heavens it's not me." Things might be a bit dicier for C. G. Fox. He'd be strongly tempted to allow the award to reinforce the walls he's built around his heart. My hope for him is that he'd be reminded of who he really is (a being passionate to love, not passionate to "do good deeds" and be recognized as St. Charlie). I don't expect that would be the outcome, but I know that Divine Mother is sneakier than anything I can imagine.

Charlie helps me to examine how I shape reality to accommodate my fears. When he announced that he wouldn't seek reelection, he said it was because his commitment to America was not so much to be President, but to be active in helping America be a role model to the world in finding common ground among people of diverse interests, cultures and beliefs. He felt he could serve that goal better as a private *Ambassador of Understanding* than as President of the United States. Considering that he was a virtual shoo-in for reelection, the pundits had little choice but to believe him, despite their incredulity.

Really, it's unfair of me to speculate on the ghosts that haunt my uncle. What I do know is that he is one of my most important teachers, and has been over many lives. It's actually very gratifying to say that, as I become more whole, I love the being he is now much more than I ever loved the old one, the man I called Uncle Charlie, the man with whom I was, quote, close.

My folks, too, although my mother has been as much a stranger to me as I must be to her. A big part of her died 10 years ago. Betrayal, I believe, sucked the life out of her. I wonder if it is a version of what many people experience in the wake of a catastrophe. Post Traumatic Stress Disorder. Isn't that the term? She hardly speaks. Her hair is completely white. The skin of her face, which used to be a cover girl's fantasy, is now more the texture of a well-used catcher's mitt—the result of her incessant tanning bed and oil treatments. She's given up her career. ("When your uncle retired from politics, I retired, as well," she once told me.) She runs marathons—about one every other month, a punishing schedule—and says she's writing a memoir to be published "someday": all solitary endeavors. She talks to me if I ask her things, and she always puts on a smile when I call, but she's not home, really. The old her would have licked her chops at the prospect of three grandchildren to dote on. She is the best teacher I've ever had when it comes to loving someone unconditionally—without expectations, perhaps even without hope. Giving up hope . . . that is the ultimate surrender for me. The most terrifying. The pain of losing my mother while she is still in her body is like no other pain I've known. There is hardly a day when waves of it don't move through me.

I once attempted to explain to mom my relationship with Carmella, and mom asked me if I'd considered seeing a psychiatrist. In her denial, she's convinced herself that something bad happened to me when I met you. Well, maybe not convinced. Maybe it's more that she has no space for anything other than the easiest explanation. My story about Charlie and me being lovers in another life has always been beyond the pale for her, as well, and now I understand that it isn't just because the idea of knowing one's former lives is foreign to her. (My former sweetheart, now my father.) So you can appreciate why I haven't told her about Puer as Domenico. (My former father, now my sweetheart.) And then there's the odd fact that, at 21, I was all of a sudden one of the nation's wealthiest women.

But you know, it's funny how things evolve. It has taken having my life threatened for mom to "mother" me, if just a little. There is now a flicker of life between us. But I can't tell you about that without also telling you about daddy.

When dad took me to the airport the day I returned to Stanford 10 years ago, I told him how much it grieved me that he was killing himself with his addictions. It was the first time I had spoken to him directly about it. The fact that I wasn't angry I'm sure made it a lot easier for him to hear. I told him I would love him no matter what he did, but that his choice to bury himself in alcohol, women and his art was very painful because it denied his beautiful heart. He didn't have much to say, but surprise, surprise—soon after that, he wrote me a letter thanking me and saying that he was in a treatment program.

Daddy has been sober for nine years now. And besides the joy of seeing him come alive, he has motivated me in ways that, while welcome, are curiously linked to me becoming a target of religious/political "extremists" who, so far, have only made a lot of noise about their commitment to kill me.

[I'm sorry, I've got to stop. If you hadn't shown me how to join the Earth, the pain I meet would shrivel me—as it has my mother and Charlie, it grieves me to say. I guess this is another thing I've learned. Anyway, break time again. When you're eating for four, and at least three of those four are making a ruckus that it's chow time, waiting is not an option.]

Next day:

For the first three years of his sobriety, daddy didn't create a single piece of art, at least not in the traditional sense of the word. He didn't even make me a birthday card; he bought one, which, for Tommy McGonagle, is like the White House chef bringing home take-out from McDonalds for Christmas dinner. It was his way of shaking loose everything about his former life. Instead, he purchased an old, run-down cottage, a "handyman special," and fixed it up when he wasn't going to AA meetings or hanging out with other guys in recovery. Plumbing, electric, masonry, roofing, cabinets, floors, the whole bit—he'd never done any of it before. And that was the point. But you should have seen it when he was done. The man's got a gift. *Architectural Digest* took pictures, and not entirely because the editor was dad's college roommate and daddy's this famous dude.

All our neighbors and friends were invited to the grand unveiling of The Tom Mahal, as one of his AA buddies called it. When I arrived, it was good to see a couple of Sheriff's cruisers and a fire engine outside. Since dad used to be a volunteer fire fighter himself, I figured it meant that some of his pals had stopped by on their way home from a call.

We were all inside, oohing and aahing. Someone had made a model of the cottage out of cake. The cake must have been three feet tall and more than that long, but with all the people who came to woo-woo dad on his masterpiece (a lot of checkbooks were within easy reach in case the place were for sale), the cake was soon reduced to a memory. Then, just as it was getting dark, dad asked everyone to gather outside in the field next door, that he had something important he wanted to tell them.

Here's what he said:

I've asked you here, because you are my friends and neighbors, to witness a celebration of sorts—a ceremony to symbolize a big step in my life.

I started working on this cottage merely as something to occupy my mind and my body as I was coming out of the fog of alcohol addiction. Plus I felt I needed to do something I'd never done before.

Soon, however, the cottage started to become an addiction in itself. I wanted it to be fabulous. I wanted you all to say, 'Oh that Tom, isn't he a talented fellow. What a constructive thing to do for a guy who's trying to dig his life out of a hole. He must be the poster boy for AA.'

They say in AA that you have to change everything about your life, most of all the way you think. So I knew that the more I fell in love with building this cottage, the more I was simply thinking in my old alcoholic ways—the ways I had to change. My daughter is always telling me that the heart is the most important guide in life. Well, my heart tells me to put my whole body and soul into everything I do, but also surrender whatever I do to a power greater than myself.

In honor of this commitment, I hope you will join me in giving away this beautiful cottage.

Dad then signaled to one of the fire fighters, and whoosh!—within seconds the cottage was ablaze.

You're the guy who says energy doesn't lie, so you can believe that everyone there felt the seismic "Holy Shit!" thunder through the crowd like a herd of buffalos stampeding across a kettle drum the size of Grand Central Terminal. At the same time, perhaps only I consciously experienced the thoughts and feelings of every person there. It's a faculty that just seems to have come my way since I met you; more and more over the years, I might add.

I don't have to tell you that my dad's art has always included a strong element of surprise. So while torching the cottage was a personal statement for my father, not an artistic performance, for him to incorporate the unexpected was as natural as the Big Bad Wolf knocking on the doors of the three little pigs. He didn't mean for the fire to offend or hurt anyone. Dad was just trying to open his heart. Personally, I feel he showed a lot of courage, especially when what he assumed would be a celebration turned out to be a lot more.

A woman, Kate, had a seizure. She had grown up in an abusive home where her father destroyed precious possessions in moments of rage—and my dad's action had triggered a cellular memory. No one but I knew that part of the story; everyone else presumed it was an event unconnected to the fire. Despite the presence of several doctors and other medical emergency pros, who dispatched her to the hospital as quickly as possible, Kate died of a cerebral hemorrhage early the next morning.

Dad's fire also assaulted a lot of beliefs, particularly the belief in the value of tangible assets. I can't tell you how many people were really steamed that the place "had gone to waste."

He was a jerk drunk; now he's a jerk sober, was about as polite as some feelings got.

But not all. A boy of 10 stood transfixed until only coals were left. He had always been afraid of big fires, and now he wasn't afraid anymore. And, taking my dad's lead, a man and his wife used the fire to burn their fears of letting go of their children, who would soon be off on their own in the world.

I had never shared my "mind reading" talents with my folks. I don't share them with anybody, really, other than Puer and Carmella, who find them no more remarkable than my ability to chew. But I was instructed to tell my dad what had actually happened in response to his fire. Basically, I went through the entire guest list and explained how each person had reacted.

"My God, Pea," he said. "Kate died because of me."

"No, dad, she didn't," I said. "Kate died because she was filled with fear that she had been holding onto for years, maybe lifetimes, choosing not to release it. Same as the reverend who thinks you're self-indulgent. Or your buddies who are angry underneath their chummy exteriors because they lost a chance to buy a choice piece of real estate for reasons that seem crazy to them. You were only a mirror showing them themselves. Their reactions are entirely their own."

"Yeah but, still," dad said, "if I hadn't done something so big and unexpected—I mean I could have warned people what was about to happen—maybe Kate would have had a chance to deal with her fear in, I don't know, some other way."

"Daddy, as Hyman says," says I, "'Why don't you leave something for God to do?' Who are you to say that this death wasn't the most rewarding experience of Kate's life because it taught her in a way nothing else had the price we pay for holding on to fear? And maybe now that she's learned that lesson she will be able to make healthier choices in her next life. I don't know. All I know is that anytime we start managing anyone's life but our own, we have no idea what we're doing."

"Still," daddy says, "this really does change things . . . I mean, how I surprise people."

"Ah," I say, "That's a whole other story. You are now more aware of the potential consequences of your choices. Don't beat yourself up with that awareness. Use it. Bring it into your heart, make it part of your heart's love. You did all a person can do in a given moment. You opened your heart as best you could. Learn from the outcome, but don't chastise yourself for it."

(Sound familiar? Good lord!)

This spring, the memory of dad's cottage fire returned to guide me as I was about to speak in public for the first time in a very high profile way—giving the commencement address at Stanford, not a decade after my own graduation. When I went within and asked what I was to say, the only answer I received was, "Just be naked."

At first, as I reviewed the story of my life since I met you, I laughed imagining the possible tabloid headlines as a result of my talk:

"WOW Foundation Exec Murdered Father In Former Life;
Married Him In This One"
"Fox's Niece Says: 'My Uncle Was My Husband 500 Years Ago'"
"Nobel Candidate, Carmella Puella,
Hires Little Brother From Previous Life"

But of course, the universe wasn't asking for ego melodrama. Just honesty. My dad and his fire reminded me of what it takes to be naked, as well as the power of communicating with an unforgettable symbol. Guidance said, "Put the two together, but remember . . . some people, in reaction, will choose to hate you."

I did, and they did, and all of a sudden I'm on the cover of every major publication this side of Popular Mechanics, and my life, as they say, will never be the same again.

[Sometimes a single sentence will surface with such pain that all I can do is lie on the ground and sink into the earth.]

Next day: anniversary of your rescue:

The venom shot in my direction has been tremendous. I understand what it must feel like for a leader to know that there are people out there who would like to see you dead, and still others who would like to pull the trigger. I am sad not to have Charlie's counsel, but thank goodness I have Mel and P, who have helped me to find the mirror of myself as a person so threatened by another's views that I would destroy that person. Among other things, I have met myself in a previous life as a man of learning, a so-called scholar, who used intimidation, money, blackmail and sexual favors as a means of intellectual persuasion. Oh, the many faces of fear. I was a spiritual leader: the abbot of a cloister, the hand-picket successor to a man who many thought to be a saint. (Could that man have been you?)

I must say, it has been very "purifying" to be the recipient of threats so grotesque that you find yourself marveling at the fertile minds behind them even while you feel the chill of their reality. I have meditated on Gandhi, who lived knowing that "today" might be his last. I have asked him for guidance. "Die regularly," I hear. I read somewhere: *The person who keeps death before his eyes will always overcome his cowardice.* My goal is to live as Gandhiji did, in such a way that, no matter the circumstances of my last moment, the name of God will be on my lips.

All I did was offer to pay to any graduating Stanford senior an amount of money equal to their tuition for the past four years if he or she would promise not to attempt to make the world a better place to live.

Are you wetting your pants?

I can just hear you, "Well, you sure know how to get somebody's attention."

Evidently.

Here's the slash and burn version of what I said:

What do you suppose it really means to be the change we wish to bring about in others?

I feel it means that we can never bring alive in the world any more love than we have in our own heart. To the extent that we are unwilling to open our heart—basically, to give up our addiction to fear—to the extent that we hate, to the extent that we judge, to the extent that we blame, to the extent that we feel we are unworthy— that is the extent to which we will be unable to influence the world in a positive way, because that is the extent to which we are unable to love.

All of you have exceptional courage. Some of you have the courage to climb Mt. Everest, some the courage to become a great scholar, some the courage to go to war for your country (even if the war is misguided), some the courage to hock everything you own and start a business, and some of you even have the courage to raise children.

But allow me to ask you: Do you have the courage to love yourself as you are?

Please permit me to challenge you to be pioneers in the most exciting and rewarding adventure a human being can undertake—putting all your courage and all your passion to work in service of being a person of kindness, and love, and generosity, and possibility.

I'm sure it comes as a surprise to many of you that I represent a foundation that invests tremendously in uplifting the lives of children around the globe, and yet I am standing here suggesting to you that if your commitment is to improve the world, you very well may be kidding yourself.

We draw to our foundation some fabulous associates, young men and woman just like yourselves. But do you know what the most difficult part of my work is, and why some colleagues don't remain with us as long as they wanted to initially? When they really, really, really get it that there is no helping another person, there is only loving ourselves—it's too big a request.

Some colleagues would willingly walk through gunfire to bring a starving child a cup of milk, but when asked to look at their motivations—when asked to feel that perhaps they are walking through that gunfire because they hate themselves, that their belief that they can "never do enough" comes not from love, but from an unwillingness to forgive themselves for times when they chose fear—they run.

My colleagues and I remind each other every day that we are not giving children food, or medicine, or safety, or influence; we're giving only one thing: the love of our hearts. If you come to our foundation to serve others, you won't last, and you cannot really help. But if you come to love yourself—and the pain of the world is the laboratory in which your love grows—then, whether your time with us is long or short, you will serve not just those who are recipients of our largess today, but everyone who will ever live. The food and all the rest—these are merely ways that our love expresses itself. It is only the love within our own heart that makes the world a healthier place.

Don't misunderstand me. I hope you do cure cancer, eradicate hunger, raise compassionate children, build beautiful cities and write music that stirs every living soul. And when you die, I hope that your example will inspire generations of men and women to do brave and lovely things left undone by the majority of humankind. But whatever you do, whether you run the United Nations or walk the dogs of movie stars, the only difference you can ever make in the world is the difference you make to yourself— whether you learn to choose love in more moments.

And that, in my experience, is the most heroic undertaking on earth.

My mom hit it on the head when she said, "Honey, your message may not have been that far out of the box, but your proposition surely was."

And because this is where my mother has lived, helping people appreciate the impact of their public utterances, she opened my eyes to what was what.

"If you thought you were going to make an offer worth a few hundred million dollars and not get attacked by some very vocal and influential people who would be threatened by the boldness of your approach, or would view it as self-indulgent grandstanding by some privileged, holier-than-thou Mother Teresa wannabe who has probably never washed a dish in her life, then it just proves their point—that you are naïve."

Mom wasn't being harsh. Just the opposite. She was absolutely right. Even more, it was a magic moment because it meant that she was "momming" me once again . . . if only in this limited, momentary way.

As you know, there is a bounty on me. One of those groups that so many of our leaders have quaintly called "the evildoers" has proclaimed that my offer to the Stanford grads represents the epitome of American moral decadence. And there are many Americans who agree with them. I am a symbol. My assassination, they trust, will also be a symbol: the world's rejection of a Godless people. Lordy, how many people have I killed in the name of God and goodness? I can just feel Divine Mother smiling at the perfection that one of the little beings in my belly was a terrorist in his last life. He died on a plane that hit the World Trade Center in '01. (The other two died as a result of that plane crash.) I remember you saying once that God has an impeccable sense of irony.

I don't know a tremendous amount about my children on the way, but I have been privileged to receive a flash or two about their most recent deaths.

[But before we head off in that direction, I need to wait for tomorrow. Meanwhile, I shall meditate, take a hot bath, then maybe eat a hot dog with grape jelly. You laugh. Just wait 'til you're pregnant in your next life, mister.]

Next day: the anniversary of the day Puer and I first visited you at the Dame Edna:

One of my babies was an 89 year old woman.

She had traveled all the way from Harlem to lower Manhattan that morning to meet her great-granddaughter, who worked in an office pretty high up. This was a first for the old woman. In her entire life she had never left Harlem except once, when she was first married more than 70 years earlier, traveling by train to South Carolina with her husband to visit his family. She knew no whites; didn't want to; never had any reason to. She didn't hate them, but common sense said they were unpredictable. That morning, before she left her apartment, the woman had remarked to her sister that what she was about to do took even more courage than marrying Mr. Waddington, her late husband. She'd been 14, he'd been 25. Mr. Waddington had been dead now nearly 40 years. That morning, September 11th, 2001, for what would be the only time in her life, she traveled into the heart of white America, eight miles, a hundred-plus blocks, and an entire world away from the address she'd lived at since her wedding day.

The visit was to be a gift to her great-granddaughter: to see with her own eyes the child's beautiful office with the breathtaking view, to meet the child's "associates," as her great-granddaughter called them. The old woman would do things for this child that she had never done for anyone else. The child was bent on teaching her Great Na not to be afraid of a thing just because it was new or different. Why didn't Great Na come and see her in her office? And since Great Na only went out mornings, why didn't she come this Tuesday first thing, the child would clear her schedule, they would go to the top floor and have tea on a linen tablecloth and look out over the city and pretend they were the richest people in the world. Her great-granddaughter had sent a car and driver to chauffeur her Great Na. As the car pulled up in front of the World Trade Center, the driver handed Great Na the telephone and said that her great-granddaughter was on the line. Her great-granddaughter said that she would be right down to meet Great Na and the two of them would ride up the elevator together. Great Na said absolutely not, that she wouldn't be treated like an invalid; she could very well find her great-granddaughter's floor. Her great-granddaughter had laughed and said that she would be there to meet Great Na when Great Na got off the elevator. The plane, flown by terrorists, struck the building while the elevator was on its way up.

It simply slowed and stopped. The lights went out. A battery powered emergency light went on. A fire alarm began to ring somewhere outside the elevator.

The only other passenger was a bicycle messenger, a white boy, a carrot-top with cornrows, face full of freckles, entire left arm from his wrist to up under his dark green T-shirt was covered in stars of many different sizes—blue tattoos.

They had stood in the silence for many minutes before the messenger said, "They call me Starman." The boy had a gap between his two big front teeth. Great Na was relieved when, just as she could no longer avoid giving her name, Mrs. Percy Waddington (she always used her husband's name in unfamiliar settings), Starman said, "Ma'am, I spend a good bit of my life in elevators, and I've been stuck more than once, so I know we can't necessarily count on someone rescuing us anytime soon. Would it be okay with you if I open this door and see what's what?"

Evidentially taking her silence as consent, from his backpack the boy pulled out a number of strange looking gadgets and gizmos along with what reminded Great Na of the crowbar her husband kept in the trunk of their one and only automobile, a Studebaker, long since turned to junk. "The magic tool," Starman winked at Great Na. Then, his arms and head awhirl like Jazzy the short-order cook in her favorite diner who could whip up a dozen completely different orders at the same time, Starman somehow got the elevator door to open.

"Ma'am," he said, "you are good luck."

From the floor of the stopped elevator to the floor of the foyer it opened onto was a drop of about three feet.

"Ma'am, I have a suggestion. See how this feels to you. While I hold the door, if you don't mind getting your dress a little dirty, you could sit right here in the elevator doorway, dangle your feet and gently step down——that might be easiest. You'll be fine. Take my hand if it helps."

Even then it was difficult for Great Na; she was using muscles she hadn't used in years. Her blue flowered Sunday dress was going to be a mess. She was very slow, she knew. She expected the boy to get frustrated, that he had a lot of places to go. She almost told him to go on without her, that she could make it on her own, but she knew that was ridiculous. Without him the door might shut. Without him she might have already fallen, maybe broken her hip again. But the young man acted as if it were the most natural thing in the world for a white boy to be tending to needs of an elderly black woman he had just met, even if that woman had yet to say a single word to him. He didn't mind. He just went right on as though her silence were fascinating. He seemed happy to keep up both sides of the conversation. He wasn't in a hurry. He wasn't afraid.

That was the biggest thing. He was not afraid.

And so, miraculously, she wasn't afraid. If he said they'd be okay, they'd be okay. This was his world, the white world. She was the stranger. She trusted him; she didn't know why.

Once they were out, she headed straight for the ladies' room. After she had washed her hands and straightened her dress and hair, and found the boy looking out a window in a big unoccupied office with pillowy leather chairs facing a windowsill on which rested a large pair of binoculars, she noticed they hadn't seen another living soul.

The boy said they were on the 13th floor and that the only way out was to walk down the stairwell but that she was not to worry he would help her; heck, he'd carry her if he had to; in case she hadn't noticed, he was very strong, he laughed: opening all those elevator doors, you know. They heard occasional shouts in the distance for anyone still on the floor to immediately get out, but still they saw no one else. With the exception of the fire alarm, the floor was all but silent.

It wasn't that Great Na knew that she was going to die. She was simply prepared to accept whatever fate God had in store for her because she knew for certain that she could never walk down 13 flights of stairs. And being carried was out of the question. It was undignified. She wouldn't tolerate it. And if her back ever went out, the brace she was supposed to wear whenever that happened was at home. It was time to give her life to her Lord. If He wanted her to come home to Him, that was fine with her. And if He wanted her to live another day, He could certainly see to that. She was just going to get herself a drink of water, sit in one of these comfortable chairs by the window, spruce up her lipstick, enjoy the view . . . and wait. She would thank the kind white boy and send him on his way. He could run down those stairs in two shakes. But when she told the boy of her intentions, he said, "OK, whatever you like," and plopped down in the plush leather chair next to her. They were facing north side by side.

What was it about white people?

"Young man," she said, "I'm sorry if I didn't make myself clear. You must go. I want you to leave. Now. Please."

He was smiling at her.

"You have been very kind to me," she said. "Thank you. But you must leave now." And then it just came out of her. "I don't know what I would do if you got hurt because of me." Suddenly the fire alarm stopped. They both looked around. There was nothing but silence.

"Why are you here?" the boy asked.

"I came to visit my great-granddaughter."

"Have you ever been here before?"

"No."

"What does your great-granddaughter call you?"

"Great Na."

"The way you say that, she must love you very much."

The statement was a little impertinent, but Great Na nodded.

"OK, Great Na, here's what we're going to do," Starman said. "I'm sure your great-granddaughter is worried to death about you. So it will be my honor to stand in for her. Whatever she would do for you, I shall do."

"Why would you do this, you're white?"

The boy laughed as though she had told a good joke.

"Yes I am, but only for the past 24 years, so far as I know. I'm sure we've both been every color under the sun many times over in all our lives before this one, and maybe in our next life I'll be the Black woman and you'll be Starman."

Great Na couldn't keep herself from chuckling at this strange boy. Her church didn't hold with reincarnation. But there was something about this boy: he didn't look at her as though she were invisible as most white folk did. Quite the opposite. When he looked at her, she felt the same way she did around her sister—they'd known each other so long that secrets were impossible. She knew that arguing with him was futile. For the first time in her life she knew someone who wasn't Black. For the first time in her life, she wasn't Black, though exactly who she was she wasn't quite sure.

Neither of them spoke again.

He took a fresh bottle of water from his backpack, loosened the top and handed the bottle to her. After sipping, she handed the bottle back with a nod, then got out her lipstick. They sat watching the view. Her great-granddaughter was a lucky girl to have this to look at every day. Great Na had never known silence like this in Harlem. Eventually, the boy put out his hand. Great Na took it, the hand that led to the stars, and held it until the building, and the two of them, disintegrated.

Great Na left her body a very different being than she had been for all but those last few moments of her 89 years. She had known joy before, but not quite like this. This was the joy of surrendering to the Light. And then it was something even beyond that: it was a joy that came from sitting with the boy, freeing the fear that had kept her in Harlem.

It was funny, too. I'd have lived in Harlem anyway, she thought. But before I met the boy, I felt I had no choice. Fear had been the boundary, not Central Park, Morningside Heights and the Harlem River.

Great Na felt the meaning of the words "amazing grace." How many times had she sung that hymn? And now, for the first time, she felt what could only be grace amazing: the truth that you can change yourself in a flash. All you had to do was let go of fear. She also felt the pain from years of choosing to see herself as different, separate, other than, less than . . . . From this grace, from this pain, her heart's passion to love—to free itself of all fear—began to lead her, in harmony with universal law, to experience in her own way the unconditional love and splendid synchronicity of life: she had drawn to herself, and would always draw to herself, precisely what she needed on her journey Home to her Beloved Lord, her journey to Oneness, including, of course, the circumstances of her next birth somewhere down the road.

*D*ouble M, I relish the prospect of discovering why the former Great Na has chosen me as her mom, and why I have chosen her—or, more accurately, him, since in this incarnation the being who was Great Na has chosen to be a Lithuanian-Scot of the male persuasion. May the Great Ones grant us many years to find out.

The other little man scheming inside of me, negotiating for at least one of my breasts to be chocolate milk, was one of many people that September day in '01 who knew, before it happened, that this was to be their last day on earth.

I've been visited by the images: countless special moments that people had in the hours or minutes prior to leaving their bodies. Many "angels" were busy behind the scenes arranging last contacts that would, amidst the enormous pain, give the abrupt rupture about to occur a measure of completion, and thus of harmony—over time, at least. A few people knew consciously of the impending transition. No surprise. As you taught me, there are old souls amongst us who see the future as easily as the rest of us tell if our fingernails need cleaning. But most of the people I'm speaking of did not know consciously that this was to be their last day. Only as their souls left their bodies was a somewhat stunned and grateful "Ohhhhhhhhh!" part of their exit. Such was the case for my new son, the former Italian firefighter, who spent many hours in the early morning before sunrise that day lying next to his little girl as she slept, praying that he could find a way to ease the torment with his wife over how their daughter should be . . . what was the word? His wife called it *raised*. He called it *loved*. He was seriously considering the biggest step of his life: taking his daughter and moving to another state, far away from Brooklyn, where he had lived all his life, 29 years, and within a one-hour drive of every living member of his family, and his wife's family. Divorce was almost unheard of in their families. Moving away, worse than suicide. "At least with suicide you have a grave you can talk to," he once heard his mother say.

It was the first night, a few years earlier, that his wife forbade— forbade!—him to go to their crying daughter in her crib that the firefighter's heart felt what must be, he was sure, the greatest devastation a person can feel—even greater than having your child die. Your child calls to you and you do not respond. It's not that you can't respond; that would be painful enough. It's that you choose not to respond. The firefighter knew that his daughter was not in physical pain, or hungry, or anything like that. A poopy diaper. That was not the cry. This was the most elemental of cries, the one that says, "Daddy, come show me you're still here."

From the moment she was born, the firefighter's daughter inhabited his body as well as her own. He knew when she wanted him—sometimes to hold her, other times to just be close enough by so that she could see him, or feel him in the same room. He knew these things, just as he knew when she was hungry or perplexed—jeez, just as he knew when *he* was hungry or perplexed. He had no idea before their daughter was born that this would be what it meant to be a parent, this merging of hearts or whatever it was. And for sure his experience was not common to all parents. His wife, for one, didn't know their child in the way he did. His wife and their daughter did not share that special something that would allow his wife to feel their daughter when their daughter's blood spoke, or when her heart felt those goose bumps that follow in the wake of a passing ghost, or when her throwing of food onto the floor from her highchair said, "I don't like this" versus when it said, "I love you to pay attention to me" versus when it said, "I see an angel in the corner who looks hungry." To his wife, their daughter was, genetics aside, a separate person. The firefighter knew that his wife would give her life for their daughter, but not because his wife and their daughter lived in one another's skins, but because, to his wife, that's what a mother did, and his wife was committed to being a good mother. That's why she read all the books. And her books told her that a child needs structure, a child needs predictability, a child needs to develop autonomy—her own sense of self, independent of her parents. There was no reason, his wife said, why a normal, healthy child cannot learn that part of the bedtime ritual of stories and stuffed animals and a drink of juice also includes the time when mommy and daddy leave her by herself to go to sleep, and that cries for attention will be ignored. And if, later, the child wakes up in the night and isn't ill or terrorized by a nightmare, there was no reason why she should expect that crying out will bring a parent running. It was all part of providing boundaries that the child can count on. "Besides," the firefighter's wife told him, "are you saying you know more than the experts? Read a book. Then talk to your own mother. A child needs a schedule, a program. And if our child doesn't need one, I do. You can't just rush to her every time your imagination tells you she's calling you. You're being selfish. You're undermining our need to have time for ourselves. Did you ever think of that?"

The firefighter had so little to say. He hadn't read the books. He didn't even use words like *undermining*. His mother, he knew, agreed with his wife. His brother's wife agreed with his wife. Hell, before his daughter was born, he would have agreed with all of them, if he'd thought about it. His job was not raising the kids, or so he believed before his daughter's birth. He was the provider. In ten more years, he could retire, and he wouldn't even be 40. Yeah, his wife worked, but he was the main breadwinner; she was the main parent. His new feelings, therefore, were completely foreign, completely out of character, to who he had been before he became a dad. Plus, he was firing blanks when it came to expressing his feelings in words. If he'd been Shakespeare, he wouldn't be fighting fires. He'd tried it a few times with his wife. "The thing is, I can feel what she's feeling. It's like we're in the same body." His wife said it was the kind of thing you'd expect a child molester to say; it was creepy; where did he get these ideas? The firefighter felt like one of those handicapped kids who everybody thinks is an idiot because he can't talk normal, but once somebody hooks the kid up to a computer, they find out he's just as smart as anybody else, he just needed a way to communicate. Meanwhile, the child is just full of frustration, anger, humiliation, shame; boy the list went on and on. There was so much the firefighter wanted to say, but didn't know how. This was hell enough. But no pain compared to that of feeling his little girl's heart call to him—*Daddy, let me see you're still here*—and he was prevented from going to her by "the rules," and by his own inadequacy, a word he'd learned from his wife.

If he took his daughter and left, everyone in his family would write him off—if he told them the truth. They'd think he was insane, really. An unfit parent. His wife might have him arrested for kidnapping and the rest of his family would say it served him right. He thought about lying, saying that he had found out that his wife was having an affair. There was no question that it would destroy both their families. But his brothers would believe him. His mom and dad would give him, the Eagle Scout, the benefit of the doubt. They all knew he loved his wife. He did. And they knew he loved having a family. They would believe that it would take something like an affair for him to suddenly give up his flesh and blood, not to mention the only job he had ever wanted, and move cross-country. They would understand that the betrayal of his wife must have been so painful that all he could do was get out . . . that maybe he'd gone a little off his rocker. Well, at least that part would be true. "You want counseling? You get counseling," his wife had said. "There is nothing wrong with the way I'm raising our daughter, O Great Mind-Reading Fireman."

His daughter had called out to him that last night in her soft, almost inaudible whimper that only he could hear. Knowing there would be hell to pay in the morning, the firefighter had taken his pillow and an afghan into his daughter's room and lay down on the floor next to her bed. Whenever he did this, after they talked or he made up a brief story, he and his daughter would eventually sleep and find themselves together in their dreams. In the dream they shared just before he awoke, he was lying on her bedroom floor in his fire suit, he even had his oxygen mask on, and his daughter, in her nightgown, was lying on his chest with her ear pressed to his heart. The room was on fire, but he was not concerned.

At 5AM, when he got up off the floor to make coffee and get dressed, the firefighter's daughter surprised him by whispering, "Daddy? Bring me back a present." He almost said, 'But I'm not going anywhere, sweetheart,' but he didn't because he saw that she had been talking in her sleep. Five hours later, after his body had been obliterated, never to be found in any recognizable form, he realized what his daughter had known in her heart: that he was going away, and that she was asking him to come back and visit her, before he left for good, so that she could feel what he would be feeling when he no longer had a body.

When the firefighter's daughter was told by her mother that her daddy had died in an accident, the girl was very quiet, as if deciding something, and then she said, "I know." Her mother was too distracted by her own grief to ask, or even wonder very deeply, what her daughter had meant. But in the years that followed, the firefighter's widow came to wonder whether the connection between her husband and her daughter had been as imaginary as she had once thought. The girl was beautiful, and well-behaved—a mother's dream. She was kind and generous and smart. But the girl would say things every once in a while that would send shivers down her mother's back. "The terrorists were not responsible for daddy's death." "Daddy's body didn't suffer at all when he died, but his heart was a little bruised." These were not the pronouncements of a child. The mother would sometimes ask her daughter how she came to one of her conclusions, and the daughter would say, simply, "Daddy." At first, the firefighter's widow thought her daughter might be emotionally disturbed, living in fantasy. And maybe that was true. But the thing was, her daughter was the most peaceful child the mother had ever known; much more content and happy than the mother herself had ever been. Besides, the experts said the girl was just compensating. It would pass.

The firefighter did bring his daughter a gift as she requested. It happened within minutes of his death. By that time, he had realized that seeing the world through your own eyes, and assuming that what you see is pretty much all there is, is very much like driving your car in the garage and assuming that you are traveling the world.

The building crushing him to death was mildly surprising, but not in the least painful. One moment he was a body (or believed he was), and the next he was spirit. "Ohhhh," he said to himself. Now he knew that he had never been a body, really. He had always been spirit. His body had been just a place his spirit lived for a while—no more permanent than his firefighter's suit.

He saw the lives of both his wife and daughter unfold from this day forward based upon the impact of his love for them. He was deeply moved by the power of love, even a little bit of love, for its power extended far over the horizon of anything a normal human might call "the future." Generations not even born yet would feel his love for his wife and child.

He felt the clarity of truth that his wife and daughter had been his teachers.

His wife's actions reminded him of the pain he had caused when he, like her, had used structure as a shield or a weapon. The only reason his wife was so fiercely attached to structure was fear, the fear of losing control, the fear of being judged a lousy parent, the fear that she really was a lousy parent. He learned that all of his agony over his daughter had nothing to do with his wife, or his daughter, but only his own fear.

His daughter, so little, yet she had shown him that he was much more than his mind had ever imagined. Indeed, in the peace beyond understanding that occurs as our physical body drops away, the firefighter became aware that humans are never as small as their minds makes them out to be.

He saw the probable future of the three of them if he had lived and had continued to be a man of fear. Everyone's fear would escalate. He and his wife would be divorced, the first in their immediate families. Their daughter would be a rag doll they fought over. Their daughter's inner voice would disappear, obscured by apprehension and maybe cynicism. And even if she did call to him in the middle of the night, "Daddy, come show me you're still here," his heart would no longer be able to hear hers.

Then he saw the probable future if he had lived and did live from his heart. He saw their daughter starting school, blooming as a teen, a college student, a lover, a wife and mom of her own. Looking out, he saw their daughter's children, and their children, and all the other members of his family, and his wife's family, generations into the future.

And so, with this awareness, shortly after his death, he met his daughter in her heart and stayed with her for long enough that his vibration would remain visceral within her after the initial trauma of his physical passing had waned. It would remain there her whole life, if she chose, the mantra of a heartbeat: *Only love. Only love. Only love. Only love.* If he had had all the time in the world, his message wouldn't have been any more than those two words.

Hyman, the story I make up about why the firefighter has chosen this family is a simple one. In addition to whatever other desires he is here to address, there is the call of his heart to love big. Given that Puer, Carmella and I reside together, and that you, Uncle Hyman, will be expected to engage in some heavy-duty spoiling for at least the first forty years of his life, I'd say my boy chose a good womb. The only problem I've detected so far is that he died with 15 chocolate bars in his dinner pail. And it wasn't like he was selling them to raise money for the parish poor. They were lunch whenever he was fighting a fire. So you see I wasn't hyperbolizing when I said he's been negotiating for chocolate milk to be on the menu from day one. By the time they are born, he'll probably have the other two organized into a union and will pop out with a list of demands in his chubby little hand, you-know-what right at the top. Those firefighters, they're relentless. Puer says maybe you could ask one of your avatar pals for a hand. Jesus perhaps. Anybody who can turn water into wine shouldn't be fazed by "choco-lactation."

*S*peaking of which, it's that time again. Tomorrow: her highness.

Next day:

#3, The Queen, is the only one we have a name for so far: O'Malley Mella Gandhi Puella. We hope you approve. Puer and I want our children's names to be a source of inspiration—"role models of joy and irreverence to aspire to," as P puts it. Has it dawned on you that these kids are the children of the man who created Extravagant Humility and the Dame Edna? Forget Halloween. Have you thought about what they might choose to wear to school? Or to visit King Hoopie of Baloopie in his Palace of Stuffed Shirts?

Man, imagine being able to follow your heart when you are the child of Puer Puella, one of the great children of all time.

She, O'Malley Mel, was the terrorist. It is ironic perhaps, since all I really know of these souls is a sliver about their most recent deaths, but I feel closest to O. It's the passion for annihilation—to give up everything for God—that joins us, I'm sure. Well, that and the rage.

You were there, speaking of *Extravagant Humility*. You recall Big's mask as Puer Super Angel, creator of the Great Moment of Truth, when terrorists discover in the afterlife that killing yourself and every infidel you can take with you doesn't get you to the land of the 72 dark-eyed virgins, as advertised, and that your rage in response to pain does not end when you destroy others. That particular ammonia capsule under the nose is the awakening of O's spirit in the wash of the World Trade Center brutality that I have had the privilege of experiencing. And it has been, as you would surely know, both harrowing and enlightening.

I call O "her," but she was a man, as all the terrorists were that day, you'll recall. I am quite sure that most people would be surprised to learn that what our former terrorist experienced first upon leaving his body is simply what we all experience as we transition: the pain of personal unforgiveness nestled in enormous peace and acceptance—the unconditional love of the Mother that stems from total understanding. His ego, had it not already been rendered superfluous, would have been surprised and confused that the Presence was not one of judgment. Our terrorist's belief that God was wrathful, and who clearly distinguished the good guys from the bad, was suddenly without substance. There was certainly no heavenly celebration for destroying the enemies of Allah; there *were* no enemies of Allah; and he, the terrorist, was not condemned as a murderer. Besides his own unforgiveness, there was only love.

The blessing of being able to experience what my terrorist experienced in the initial moments of his afterlife reminds me how little difference there is between a terrorist and the rest of us—me, to be specific. The passion for God is within us all. And when that passion is filtered through fear in any of its myriad forms, the craziness we humans can perpetrate knows no bounds. How many games did I pitch from rage? Virtually every one before I met you. How many times, in how many lives, have I felt justified in crushing or wounding others in the name of God or righteousness or humanity? I'm sure it's many. In that monastic life I mentioned, I would tell my charges that if they ever left the cloister it meant that God had abandoned them and they were doomed to hell. What drivel! Those of us who feel that terrorists are evil and "we" are not, live in denial that is perhaps equal to that of the terrorists themselves. Funny how there's always that tricky symmetry to things.

Of course, I know first-hand that experiencing after death the harm of our earthly choices does not guarantee that we'll make different choices in our next life. If it did, man, we'd all change pretty dramatically from one life to the next. It took me five centuries, who knows how many incarnations (not to mention meeting you) to even become aware of the unforgiveness I was carrying around from my life as Bella-Viola. And that represented just one brief chapter of my soul's journey, a journey that ain't over by a long shot. So I know that my terrorist will face the same fears all over again, since life is a matter of continually meeting our fears until we free them.

My daughter has chosen a large and demanding life for herself—as have we who have drawn her to us. I'm sure the queen will be well served that she is named after you, Gandhiji, and my sweet Carmella.

(Then again, stretched out on the floor next to me is our dog, Einstein, and he can barely do simple algebra. So, you know, names can count for only so much.)

[That's about all I can handle for today, Double M. Einstein and I are going out to smell the world. "Finally," he just barked, "something worthy of my intellectual engagement." Who knew?]

Next day, early-early, the lake glass—just as it was . . .

Of all the ways my life has changed in the past 10 years, the most important change (dare I say the only real change) occurred in those few brief minutes that first morning by the lake when, in addition to meeting my samurai mask and Bella-Viola, I experienced my True Self. Everything else––even Bella-Viola, you, Puer, Carmella, my kiddies on the way, and all the earthly dramas of this incarnation and any former ones I'm privy to––is small potatoes by comparison.

Even should my mind go crackers as an old lady (or maybe not so old, considering I'm about to have triplets), I'm sure I shall still feel in my bones and blood my True Self: the light and fire of unconditional love and unconditional acceptance that is the essence of all that is. You see, I don't live with just the memory of that morning's precious awakening; my cells are alive with the conscious, palpable vibration of it.

Gone was my identity.

Silent was the perpetual chatter of my mind.

Absent was the drive to be anything.

Evaporated was the need to do anything.

And vanished was the quest for amassing knowledge.

Empty of every familiar born of fear, I experienced what could only be called my heart's desire. Understanding. Not the mind's acquisitiveness, its grasping, its need to build, to know, to hoard, to leverage, but the soul's openness without aspiration, its attunement without conditions or preconceptions, and thus its recognition that every conceivable question has already been answered, and that life has nothing to do with creation and everything to do with discovery.

And what I discovered within me that day—and thus what has become more and more awake in me every day since—is that a butterfly's flutter in Africa can indeed contribute to an Oklahoma tornado. There is no incidental corner, or being, or feeling, or action, or thought. Separation is an illusion.

Differences are an illusion. A smile of the heart in any backyard kisses babies who won't be born for a million years. Every choice ever made reverberates throughout the web of creation for all time. And so, no matter what sound I ever hear . . . or what image I ever see . . . or what object or being I ever touch . . . or emotion I ever feel . . . or food I ever taste . . . all I will ever be experiencing—truly—is the call of the universe to love. And it is a call expressed, among other ways, by the most powerful word in any language, more powerful even than the word love itself, for this word represents the choice that sets into motion all of one's life that leads to joy, a word that I feel and hear and touch and taste in every atom of creation, for it is the word my heart speaks unendingly . . . with passion.

"Yess!"

The End
(Except for what follows)

About the Author

Steve Roberts champions
the most fear-provoking point of view
the world has ever known:
Everything is a gift,
and the business of life is discovering how come.
He's also a fellow explorer
of life's two most important questions:
What's going on,
and what's the healthiest action I can take in this moment?

He speaks, consults, draws
builds stone sculptures and writes essays.

OneMansDance.com

(And finally...)

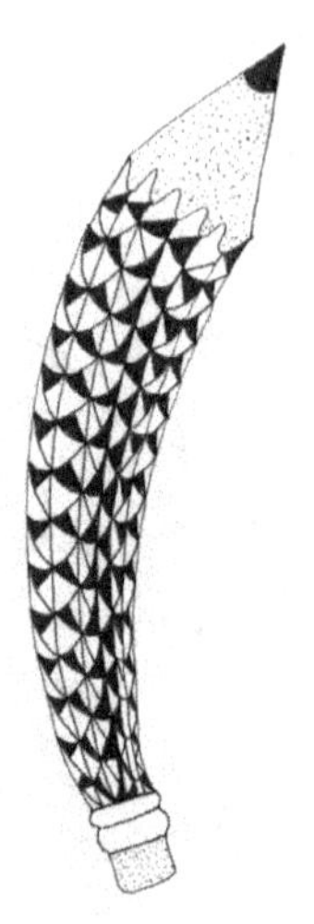

Your Turn

Sharing your experience of Mirror Man
may very well deepen its meaning for other readers.

Starting with the guy who wrote it.

OneMansDance.com/MM